PRAISE FOR *SUN*

C000220520

A Finalist for the 2019 Whis
Fiction, sponsored by the Wri

"This is a compelling and beautifully told tale of endurance and faith. Mothers everywhere will be drawn to Lukia Mazurets, a no-nonsense Ukrainian woman who in 1915 must protect and save her family when her husband goes to war. Lukia's arduous journey with her children is a true story of the little-known Ukrainian diaspora. Gripping, illuminating, and personal, this story is a must-read."

—*Martha Conway, author of The Underground River*

"This is material ripe for literary exploitation, and Stevan carries it off with real panache, seamlessly braiding together the familiar stories that her mother passed on to her in Canada with the meticulous research required to fill it all in. And, while back stories of emigrants from Galicia and Austro-Hungary have been told, the events of Sunflowers Under Fire take place in a part of the Russian Empire, Volhynia, we hear very little about.

Incident after incident, character after character, I was carried into worlds - from hardscrabble village life to wartime detention camps to ancient peasant rituals, not to mention intimacies of family life - that opened up in this page-turner of a novel."

—*Myrna Kostash, author of All of Baba's Children,*
working on The Ghost Notebooks

"A skilled storyteller, with an eye for detail and the ability to draw readers in with compelling characters and page-turning plots."

—*Lorraine Devon Wilke, author of The Alchemy of Noise*

"Sunflowers Under Fire is a remarkable story of a remarkable woman who was a survivor at a very dark and difficult time in history. It is a book about courage, resilience and love. I can highly recommend it."

—*Julia Wilson, Book Blogger, Christian Bookaholic*

SUNFLOWERS
UNDER
FIRE

ALSO BY DIANA STEVAN

A Cry From The Deep
The Rubber Fence

SUNFLOWERS UNDER FIRE

A NOVEL

DIANA STEVAN

ISLAND HOUSE PUBLISHING

Library and Archives Canada Cataloguing in Publication

Island House Publishing
ISBN: 978-1-988180-04-5 (paperback)
ISBN: 978-1-988180-05-2 (Mobi)
ISBN: 978-1-988180-06-9 (Epub)
ISBN: 978-1-988180-07-6 (PDF)

Cover design by Ares Jun
Formatting and layout by Polgarus Studio

Printed and bound in the United States

For my mother,
Eudokia Klewchuk (nee Mazurec)
a natural-born storyteller.

"As a flower strains toward the light, so a man strains with thoughts, words and deeds toward the motherland. For the sunflower, the sun is the only guide; for the man, the motherland is the one and only treasure."

Ukrainian Folk Saying

DUTY CALLS

A UGUST 5, 1915, started out like any other day. The sounds of war echoed in the distance, but on the farmlands surrounding the village of Kivertsi in Volhynia, life went on as usual. That comforted Lukia Mazurets, who asked nothing of life except the means to feed and shelter her growing family. She looked out her farmhouse window at the field of grain swaying in the wind, a scene so gentle it was hard to believe that if the war moved any closer, men's blood would be spilled on the soil.

She then peered down the dirt road leading to the main artery. No sign of Gregory. She'd hoped her husband would give up his foolishness and return from Lutsk, but the only movement was the dust swirling above the road.

A sharp labour pain forced her to grab hold of the windowsill. She gritted her teeth and breathed deeply until the agony in her lower abdomen had passed. The pains were coming more quickly. Lukia realized she could wait no longer.

She rolled up the sleeves of her housedress and twisted her long hair into a topknot before putting the kettle on the hot cast-iron plate. Then she spread a half dozen burlap bags on the floor of the *komorra*, where she kept cucumbers, sauerkraut, potatoes, and carrots. The smell of the fermenting cabbage soothed her, but not enough to combat the sharp aches or quash her anger.

Why in hell had Gregory chosen this time to go to the city? It was a half hour ride away by horse. He knew she could deliver at any moment. Groaning, she pushed her frustration aside and placed a goose-feather pillow at the head of the burlap row, and beside it, a sterilized knife on a tea towel and an old sheet. Satisfied with her arrangement, she crossed herself three times, each time saying, "In the name of the Father, the Son, and the Holy Ghost." She clasped her hands. "Please God, make this one strong." Her first baby had died shortly after childbirth. Her last one had managed to live only six months. The five they had now were strong, but if this one died she would insist on no more pregnancies. Her heart wouldn't be able to take it. Besides, she was forty, not an age to keep having children. Nor an age to birth them by herself.

Yet here she was alone. Hania, her eldest at thirteen, had gone with her two younger brothers to a nearby farm to sell eggs. The older boys, Egnat and Ivan, were in the fields with neighbours, who'd offered to help cut their barley, wheat, and oats. She couldn't even call on her mother or her sisters. Her mother lived with Lukia's brother Pavlo in the Carpathian Mountains and was probably out on the road in that district, curing the sick with her herbs.

Panashka, the one sister that lived close by, had her own troubles with an alcoholic husband who spoke with his fists. Lukia didn't think he'd be too happy to have his wife leave their home to help her sister. Not if it meant he wouldn't have supper waiting for him when he came into the house after working all day in the fields. Besides, even if Panashka could help, it would take Egnat too long to deliver a message that his mother was in labour. His aunt lived on a farm near Kovel, about three and a half hours away by horse.

The more Lukia thought about the possible risk to herself and the baby, the more she realized she should've asked Hania to stay home, at least until her father got back. But she'd been too upset with Gregory to think straight. Well, there was nothing she could do about it now but pray for the best.

The next pain radiated around to her back, reminding her she'd forgotten one last thing. She went to the kitchen cupboard and got a clean rag and a bottle of *horilka*. She poured a little of the homebrew into a saucer then soaked one end of the cloth in the alcohol. Clutching the rag, she made her way back to the komorra, lifted up her skirt and lay down on the burlap bags. The sharp taste of the vodka-soaked cloth dulled the pain as she pushed in concert with the baby's momentum.

She lost track of how long she lay there, hollering with each push, praying the baby would slide out easily. This one was larger than the others, but thankfully her hips had widened through birthing seven. She put her hand between her legs and, after a few more thrusts, felt the moist crown of her infant's head. "Almost here," she mumbled.

She braced herself and yelled with one final push. Her baby slid out, slippery and shiny with streaks of blood and white fluid. Lukia looked between her infant's legs and laughed. "I expected a boy." Then, holding her daughter with one hand, she used the other to cut the umbilical cord. Shortly after, her baby howled. When her greyish skin turned pink with the first cry, relief surged through Lukia like water rushing through a broken dam.

The horrific labour pains were soon forgotten as she watched her baby suck greedily. Even her anger at her husband seeped away. Shivering, Lukia reached for the sheet to cover herself. She gazed at her daughter's face and whispered, "Eudokia," a name she'd always loved.

After a nap with Eudokia, Lukia placed another clean cloth between her legs to stem the bleeding and went to the kitchen to prepare supper. She was stirring cabbage with tomatoes on the stove when she heard the front door creak. She turned to see Gregory standing in the doorway wearing a soldier's uniform.

Her worst fears had come true.

Lukia choked back tears and showed her back, but not before she saw Gregory's eyes widen with the discovery that she was no longer with child. Her legs felt rooted in cement while she waited for an apology. None came. He stood for a few minutes, as if he too was waiting for some word, and then went into their bedroom, where Eudokia lay sleeping.

Gnashing her teeth, Lukia stirred the vegetables with force. She tried to calm herself to avoid spilling any precious food. Not long after, Gregory returned to the main room. As if nothing out of the ordinary had happened, he came up behind her and fondled her breasts. She whirled around and pushed him so hard he stumbled on the uneven clay floor.

"What?" he said, grabbing the top of the spindle chair to keep from falling. "You have a beautiful girl and you're angry?"

"What's this?" She poked his khaki shirt.

He stretched out his arms and twirled around, showing off his new uniform. "I look handsome, yes?"

For a moment, she admired his fine figure in a tunic, breeches and leather boots, but once she saw the peaked cap in his hand, her fury rose like smoke from a dying fire. The badge on his cap displayed the Romanov colours of black, white, and orange.

He grinned. "They also gave me a greatcoat, a knapsack, and a rifle."

"What's it to me?"

"Don't say that. The Germans and Austrians are already advancing on Warsaw. Lutsk could be next."

"That's what I'm afraid of."

"Frown all you like, but I promised the Tsar and Tsarina I'd help fight these devils."

She spat. "The hell with the Tsar and Tsarina! You promised me first."

"What are you saying?"

When we got married," she said, arching her eyebrows, "the priest said we were one flesh, and now you want to tear us apart? We may have to leave at any moment. We'll be forced to run."

"If we win this battle, you won't have to leave."

"How do you know? Our army, biggest in the world they say, has been fighting for a year and where has it got us? Nowhere. From what I've heard, you'll be lucky to be fed." She shook her head.

He tightened his lips. "Stop shaking your head. You only make matters worse."

"And what are you going to do, speak Russian?"

"The Tsar isn't stopping us from speaking Ukrainian anymore."

"Oh, he's had a change of heart, has he?" She waved her fork at him. "It's probably because he needs Ukrainians to do his dirty work. Well, I spit on the Tsar. We're nothing to him."

"Lukia—"

"And what if you get killed?" She put her left hand on her chest to ease the pounding.

Gregory's brow furrowed. "I'll be safe. You'll be safe, too. The government is organizing shelter and food for refugees."

"Ha. As if they could organize anything." She checked the cabbage, found it tender, and took the pot off the stove.

"Don't worry. You'll be sent somewhere with the children."

"Somewhere," she said, glaring. "How will you find us?"

"I'll find you. Don't worry."

"Oy, you have an answer for everything. Are you forgetting I just had a baby? You may as well drown me with the family—then you'll know where to find us."

"Enough already!" he said, stamping his foot. "I have to pack. They're sending me to the front."

"Go then!"

"You want me to leave like that?" His warm brown eyes searched hers, begging her to understand. "I will need your prayers."

At that, she softened. With a lump in her throat, she said, "I will pray for you and the others."

"You're a good woman."

"If I was so good, you wouldn't be leaving me."

"Don't say." His eyes glistened with a sadness she hadn't expected. For a moment, she thought he might change his mind, but then he turned and went into their bedroom to bundle up his things.

She stood in the doorway and watched him pack: tobacco, endpapers, a comb, a mirror, wool socks, and underwear. She wanted to give him reminders of home—of his wife and family—but she had nothing to give. No photos, no keepsakes.

She followed him outside, where he called Egnat and Ivan, who left their implements in the field and came running. When Gregory saw Hania and their two youngest sons coming up the road, returning from selling eggs, he dropped his knapsack on the ground and hugged his children, one by one, telling them to take care of the farm and their mother. Lukia teared up, wondering if this was the last time they'd be together.

While Egnat went to hitch a horse to the wagon, Gregory took Lukia in his arms. She inhaled his sweat and tobacco smell, trying to cement it in her memory so he'd be beside her, no matter what lay ahead.

He stepped back and held her shoulders. "Look at our land. Our rich black earth. This is what we fight for, this is what lasts. We do it for our children and the children that will follow."

Unharvested stocks stood tall in their half-shorn golden fields, seemingly defying the nearby war threatening their bounty. A black stork glided over the grain as it headed for the woods beyond. The land was what kept their hopes up day after day. There were many times she had picked up a handful of dirt to smell the rich loam and relish its feel as it slipped through her fingers. Gregory was right. They couldn't afford to lose it.

As if he could read her mind, he said, "Our German settlers were sent to Siberia. Their property was taken away."

"Of course," she said. "They're now the enemy."

"The Tsar is promising those lands to veterans when they return home."

"Oy. You can't believe what the Tsar says."

"Listen, I also heard that those who don't fight for our country could lose their farms. What would we do if that happened?"

"And what would I do if I lost you?"

"I'll be careful."

She shook her head. How careful could he be, with Germans dropping bombs from the sky? Where could he run if a grenade was thrown?

Her eyes watered again. "Be safe. Go with God."

He kissed her deeply, his dark moustache bruising her lips one more time. When he let go, her impulse was to grab his jacket and keep him at home. Instead, she stroked his cheek. His eyes fastened on her briefly as if looking longer might keep him from going. Then he picked up his knapsack, climbed into the wagon beside Egnat, and left for Lutsk.

A BASKET OF FOOD

L UKIA AWOKE WHEN it was still pitch-black outside. She glanced at the cradle in the corner. Eudokia was still sleeping. Lukia then felt for Gregory and touched a cold empty bed instead of his warm skin. She imagined him standing around awaiting orders in Lutsk with hundreds of others, relying on officers to take care of them. Did they have any idea of what they were getting into, of the sacrifice the Tsar expected them to make?

The more she ruminated, the more panicked she became. When would she see her husband again? She had to see him one more time. She decided to make him lunch—he probably wouldn't be fed properly before he left for the front. The notion of surprising him gave her the spark she needed to prepare the food.

She went to the main room, where Hania slept with her brothers. Lukia gently shook her shoulder. "Hania, wake up. I need your help." Next, she prodded Havrylo and Ivan, who were asleep on the ledge above the clay *pich*, no longer warm from yesterday's cooking. They muttered when she sent them to sleep in her bedroom.

After Hania had gone to help Egnat milk the cows, Lukia tied on her apron and began to make the dough for *piroshky*. She also cooked the cabbage filling and put the chicken—that Egnat had killed and plucked the night before—into the pich to roast.

By the time Hania returned, the dough had risen. Lukia and Hania worked together, rolling chunks of dough into flat rounds and scooping the cabbage filling into the centre of each circle. Though they made the piroshky quietly, Gregory's departure occupied their minds.

After they'd prepared a dozen or so, a frown fell on Hania's face. "I'm worried about Tato. I don't want him to go to war."

"I'm worried, too, but what can we do? He's a stubborn man. All we can do is pray."

"I have been, Mama." Hania pinched the edges of one circle around the filling. "War is insane. When I dropped the eggs off at Panye Striluchky's, I heard her tell her husband that brothers are fighting brothers. How could that be?"

"A terrible thing. I heard this, too." Lukia stopped rolling the dough and looked up. "Depends on where they live, what they believe in. One brother in the Austrian army fights against his brother in the Tsar's army. Poor parents. How they must be suffering."

Lukia loosened her aching shoulders and began to roll again, one circle after the other. By the time they'd finished making the buns, the sun was up and Eudokia was howling for another feeding.

After Lukia had finished nursing, she expressed some breast milk into a small tin container and placed it in the cool komorra. Hania would need it to feed her baby sister during her mother's visit to the city.

Though wishing she could sit down for a spell, Lukia got dressed, picked up the basket of food and four litres of fresh cow's milk and set out for the two-and-a-half-hour walk to Lutsk.

Lukia trudged down the dirt road and stopped periodically to massage her hands, sore from carrying the heavy basket and milk. As she made her way to Lutsk she mulled over how her life had turned. She'd lost her wedding band two years ago, and since then she'd had a string of bad luck. Her baby, Fedor, had died; the war had started and her husband had joined the army. If only she hadn't lost her ring. She'd been taking water from the well when it slipped off her finger and fell in. Immediately, she'd searched for something to pull it out with. She found a long stick, but even with that she couldn't retrieve it. She interpreted the loss as a sign her life with Gregory wouldn't go well.

She couldn't fathom her husband's reasoning. How could he leave the surety of his land and the comfort of his family? He seemed bent on risking his life for a tsar who had never shown any compassion for his people. But then again, with war nothing was ever sure.

In Lutsk, she manoeuvred her way through the hordes of civilians clogging the main roads. They had fled the war zone in Poland on foot and in wagons—women, children, and aging parents, as well as men who looked too weak to fight. Their gaunt faces and dusty clothes revealed the hardship they'd undergone to get this far.

She walked with the refugees, being careful not to step in any horse manure or twist her ankle in the ruts made by wagon wheels. Further down, a sea of brown uniforms filled the ditches. Hundreds of Russian soldiers sat with rifles by their sides. They chewed hemp seeds, spit tobacco, joked and shared stories as if there were no battles to be fought. Passing them, she glanced at each face, searching for her husband's. Beads of sweat pooled on the young men's foreheads—a result of the midday sun's beating on them and the fear of what lay ahead.

One youth—not much older than Egnat—sat apart. He stared

at something beyond the men around him, his eyes glazed over. Had he been pushed to enlist or had it been pure recklessness on his part? Did he know that war was no ordinary game? That it wasn't like the ones he'd played as a child? She asked these questions but she knew that once a young man had made up his mind, there was no stopping him. But wait, she thought. Wait until those first shots are fired and he's running to save his life, more scared than a rabbit.

She took her eyes off him and pushed ahead. She was thankful none of her sons were old enough to go.

She found her husband at the end of the line, talking with a few soldiers.

"What did you bring?" he asked, his face lighting up at the sight of her. He took the basket, lifted the hand-embroidered cloth covering the food and began to distribute the cabbage-filled buns to his fellow soldiers. "My Lukia makes the best piroshky in all of Volhynia."

She grabbed his hand. "Gregory, what are you doing?"

"Let go," he said, yanking his hand away. "You don't understand." He passed more buns around then took a big bite of a piroshka, smacked his lips and turned to the bear of a soldier beside him. "Very tasty. My wife baked us a chicken, too."

Gregory's husky companion smiled sheepishly as he bit into a bun.

Her brow wrinkled in frustration. Gregory broke the chicken into small pieces and handed them to the soldiers near him.

"You crazy fool!" she said in a low voice. "I didn't sleep all night. I'm still leaking from our baby's birth and now look what you've done. You don't have enough left for yourself."

"Don't worry," he said. "Maybe one of these men will save my life because I gave them something to eat."

Her scowl remained. "I hope you're right."

"I'll be home sooner than you think."

"Ha." She kissed him then, savouring his strong arms around her and his familiar smell. She wanted to plead with him to stay, tell him going to war was insanity but she'd already tried that. She held his gaze. "Take care of yourself."

Only a Matter of Time

WHILE STANDING AT her husband's side, Lukia had noticed a soldier on the road watching them as if his mission was to ensure they weren't doing anything illegal. He had a stern face, a ruddy complexion, and a bulbous nose. The rank insignia on his shoulder strap indicated he had a commanding position.

As she began walking home, he approached her and said in a deep voice, "I beg your pardon. I saw you talking to Gregory Mazurets. Are you his wife?"

"Yes. Why do you ask?"

"I'm Sergeant Kozlov, in charge of this unit. When your husband first signed up, I admired his shirt and he told me you'd sewn it. You're a fine seamstress."

"Thank you," she said, smiling with pride. Though used to getting praise for the garments she'd stitched, she never tired of hearing compliments on her work.

"We need someone to sew our uniforms. The fabric pieces have already been cut. You'll be paid handsomely if you do this for your country."

She raised her eyebrows. "It's wonderful how you think. My country takes my man away so I won't have his help on the farm, and now you expect me to have time to sew uniforms."

"Panye Mazurets, I know. You are saying what's true, but our country's at war. We need help from all our people."

"And what if we have to leave at a moment's notice? I'd have to leave everything."

"That I know, too." This time, he wasn't smiling.

She studied his face. He seemed genuine enough and respectful—he'd addressed her as a married woman. And he was right. Each subject had a duty to the cause. She cleared her throat. "Maybe I can find some time after supper."

They negotiated a price, and then she followed him further up the road to where a temporary shelter had been set up. Under its roof, he gave her a bundle of wool fabric pieces, buttons, and thread. Although she'd struck a good deal, as soon as she left the sergeant's side she regretted her decision to take the work. The package was heavier than the food she'd carried to her husband.

Lukia lumbered back along the row of soldiers, some restless to get going, others lost in thought but all showing the bravado of young men who had never fought before. Just ahead stood an Orthodox priest with long, flowing hair and a grey beard. Dressed in a black cassock with a narrow brocade scarf stretching down to his ankles, he led a group of soldiers, bowed in prayer. After she walked by, she looked back to see them line up to kiss the ornate wooden cross the priest held. Sadness enveloped her as she thought of their mothers crying at home. She brooded about the devil these young men would soon face and crossed herself. She prayed they would have God on their side.

With the hefty load and the afternoon sun beating down on her, she had to stop often to catch her breath. Frustrated with her inability to walk faster, she gritted her teeth and hoped Eudokia wasn't giving Hania any trouble. She'd only managed a short distance from Lutsk, when the soreness between her legs intensified, a painful reminder of what she'd gone through the day before. She began to believe she'd been very foolish—

especially since Gregory had given most of her hard work away. Hearing horses' hooves behind her, she stepped off the road. But instead of passing her, the wagon slowed to a stop beside her. She looked over and recognized her neighbour, Ihor Striluchky.

"Lukia, may I give you a ride?"

She could've wept with joy. "May God bless you, Ihor."

He climbed down and heaved the cloth bundle onto his wagon. "What are you doing carrying such a heavy parcel?"

"Ach, you know. I don't like to pass up a chance to make some money."

"Not always a good idea." He took her arm and helped her climb onto the worn wooden seat. "A little bird told me you had a baby."

"Could this little bird be my screams you heard?"

He laughed as he whipped his horse forward. "Your voice is usually so beautiful but yes, I heard you yelp the other day when I walked by your property. You scared my cows."

"I'm sorry. I hope it didn't turn their milk.

"No, they're used to my wife and me barking at each other."

Lukia chortled. "You're a good man." They settled into silence as they passed one farm after the other. She gazed at the golden fields of grain lapping up the sun's rays. Each homestead looked like a postcard promising serenity and security, a place she wanted to preserve for her children's future. She thought back to the young soldiers she'd seen. In battle, they would care little about the land they trampled when survival and victory were at stake.

The wagon wheels scraped along the bumpy road, making the ride uncomfortable. Lukia squirmed to change the position of her bottom, which ached in several spots.

Ihor turned to her. "I'm sorry I don't have a wagon with springs, but I see you are well. How's the little one?"

"She's fine, thank God. How's your son? I heard he enlisted."

"Yes. Nina cried when he told her."

"Naturally. He's just a boy."

"I don't know what's to become of all of us."

Lukia clucked her tongue. "Only God knows."

Up ahead, a young boy popped out of the forest that lined one side of the road, and then quickly disappeared back into the woods.

She turned to Ihor. "Did you see that?"

"That young fellow? Yes, it's sad. He and his family have been hiding in the forest with the others. Tens of thousands of refugees from Galicia, Ukrainians like us, running from the war. They're under Austrian rule, so they can't get work permits. The local police are afraid they could be the enemy."

"How do they survive?"

"Looting abandoned properties. Foraging in the forest. Relying on the kindness of strangers."

"How do you know this?"

"I caught one of them trying to steal one of my chickens."

"What did you do?"

"I gave him the chicken but told him I'd shoot next time.

"I hope he appreciated your generosity." Lukia couldn't imagine shooting anybody. She hoped it wouldn't come to that. Hungry people were desperate. She wouldn't mind sharing what she had as long as her own family didn't starve.

Suddenly, Ihor ran over a deep rut in the road. She winced with the jolt, adjusting her bum once more.

"It still hurts?" he asked.

"Of course. It can't be helped." They rode the rest of the way without talking. The rough ride seemed to speak for them. Life wasn't smooth. Bumps and holes were not only unavoidable, they were expected.

When Ihor turned his wagon down the narrow road to her farm, Lukia scanned the land—nearly five *deshyatin*, most of them seeded with grain. Not much for a growing family and to make matters worse, it was broken up into parcels here and there. Even the cow's pasture was down by the creek. With the farm divided over a large area, it was hard to keep track of what needed to be done. To get to some parts, they had to skirt a neighbour's farm, making for disputes over boundaries or wild life found on one's property. She had hoped their situation would improve in time, but with the enemy on the horizon, their future couldn't have looked bleaker.

She turned to Ihor. "We may have to leave our farms sooner than we think."

"I've been told."

"We lived twelve years with Gregory's parents. It worked out in the beginning, but after we had a few children, we had to move out on our own. It took us four years to build this farm. Four years!" Her voice cracked when she considered how quickly they could lose all they'd worked for.

"What can we do?" said Ihor. "It's not in our hands."

She groaned. "Oy, misery." The idea of leaving turned her stomach. She wished there was some family she could go to, but in wartime no one was secure. She shut her eyes to keep from crying and only opened them again when the wagon stopped near her front door.

Their two-room house—as good as any around—had been built from a forest of oak, ash, maple, and elm trees. Resembling a boxcar in shape, it served them well, as did their livestock. Lukia glanced across the yard. Their rooster was chasing chickens and their two pigs were rolling in a mud enclosure.

"Are you and Nina ready to leave if you have to?" she asked.

"Who's ever ready?" He looked at her garden by the house. She and Hania had planted sunflowers, potatoes, onions, garlic, beets, cabbage, cucumbers, and corn. "It's a shame," he said, sighing. "We work so hard to get so little and then this beast comes along. You wonder what God is thinking."

"That we're all fools."

"It's true what you're saying."

She turned to him. "Thank you for the ride. I'm making *borscht* for supper. Would you like some?"

"That would be lovely."

"I'll send a jar with one of the boys later." She could hear Eudokia wailing from behind the door. "My child is hollering. Give my best to Nina," she said, stepping down from the wagon.

At the sound of gunshots, they both looked to the west. The battle seemed closer now. Ihor doffed his cap. "Until we see each other again." He then urged his horses forward.

She dusted off her skirt and entered the cottage to the screams of her baby, who was in Hania's arms.

"I'm sorry, Mama," said Hania. "She didn't want to take the milk."

"Maybe the heat spoiled it." Lukia laid her package by the door and quickly took off her *babushka*. She had one breast out before she even reached her baby. Half-gagging, Eudokia greedily sucked. It was always the same. Nothing could replace a mother's breast.

The following evening, Lukia and Hania gathered the children around the pich. The boys, sensing a serious matter, sat for once without poking one another, their eyes watching their mother.

The last to sit down, Lukia took her time to think about what she wanted to say. She patted her apron, wiping away the creases, and then looked at her two eldest offspring: Hania, barely in her teens, and Egnat, at ten, still a few years from growing hair on his face.

She cleared her throat. "Nu, we have to be strong together. You all know your tato joined the army. Egnat, you're the oldest boy. You're now man of the house." She groaned inwardly. If it weren't for countries led by crazy fools, mothers wouldn't be asking their young to take on a grown man's role.

But Egnat seemed pleased. He stretched his short frame and grinned at Hania and his brothers. Ivan, nine and almost as tall as Egnat, reached around Michalko and patted his oldest brother on the back.

Michalko's eyes widened. "When can I go and fight? I want to fight like Tato."

Egnat swatted him. "You're just a squirt."

"Ow," said Michalko, rubbing his arm.

"Six years old and the squirt wants to fight."

Lukia glared at Egnat. "That's not nice! Leave your brother alone." She beckoned Michalko to her side and put her arm around him. She bent her head. "When you can chop wood and kill a rabbit, then I'll think about you joining the army."

The others giggled, but Michalko gave Egnat a self-satisfied look.

She sighed heavily. "I don't know if we'll have to leave, but you've heard the gunshots in the distance. War can move very fast so I want you to stay close by in case we have to leave suddenly."

"I won't go," said Egnat, puffing out his chest. "They can't make me."

"Oh yes, the government can." She then reassured her children with the words she needed to hear. "I don't want you to worry because nothing is happening yet. As long as we're together, we'll get through this. Tato wouldn't have left us if he didn't believe we could manage."

Her children nodded, their actions contradicting the strain painted on their faces.

"Egnat," said Lukia, changing the subject. "Have you and Ivan milked the cows?"

"Yes, Mama."

"Good. Ivan, go and make sure the door to the chicken coop is closed. The last thing we need is to lose some to the foxes." Ivan rushed out the door before she finished her sentence.

With Hania helping to settle two-year-old Havrylo in bed, Lukia went into her room to stitch a few soldiers' tunics. Her spirits rose when she picked up the fabric. She loved seeing a garment take shape. She had a flair for fashioning garments and could create anything she saw on the streets of Lutsk without a pattern. Because of that, her family—though poor—dressed in the latest style.

As she basted the brown wool sleeve seams together, she wished once again that she had a Singer sewing machine like Anna, her brother Petro's wife. It would make her life so much easier. She'd talked to Gregory about it, and though he saw the wisdom of buying one, they hadn't been able to figure out where they'd get the money. And with the war escalating, the likelihood of improving their lot was no longer imaginable.

Faraway gunfire jarred her as she pulled the needle through the cloth. She couldn't help but think the wool serge was too thin to protect her husband from bullets or keep him warm. He'd mentioned the army had given him a greatcoat but that would hardly be enough during the winter months, especially on an open battlefield without shelter. She envisioned him walking through a blizzard, his head down, his moustache coated with ice, his frozen fingers gripping his bayonet. Her lower lip trembled. Pushing her troubled thoughts away, she sewed until she could no longer keep her eyes open.

Unwelcome Visitors

L IFE WENT ON without Gregory. With harvesting underway, Lukia had no time to recover from her trip to the city. Soon after Eudokia's birth, the neighbours who'd been helping with the farm work had to return to their own fields. That meant her three oldest sons were out on the land, cutting the wheat, oat, and barley stalks. The swish, swish of the scythes and sickles made a kind of music, that drifted through the house's open windows as Lukia and Hania cooked and did their chores.

By nightfall, the boys complained of sore muscles. Their hands cramped even using a knife and fork. It bothered Lukia to see them suffer, but nothing came without pain. Again, she was forced to choke back her anger at Gregory for leaving them with so much work. However, she understood that the land they loved could be under siege at any moment, and without patriots like her husband, everything could be lost.

After the grain was cut, Lukia and her children gathered the stalks into piles, the piles into sheaves, the sheaves into bunches set to stand with their heads pointing to the sky. Lukia and Hania took turns checking on Eudokia, who slept outdoors in a basket by the shady side of their cottage. Lukia felt fortunate that her brother had harvested early. Once their grain dried, they would use his thresher to load the stooks.

While the family toiled, Havrylo played an imaginary game, his chubby legs kicking up dirt. Lukia admonished him when he ran past where they were working. Outside of that interruption, there were only a few breaks. Every day meant back-breaking work until sundown, not made any easier with the hammering of warfare in the near distance. With each rat-a-tat-tat breaking the silence, Lukia and her children would look to the west. They all knew that somewhere on the horizon, young men were falling, never to get up again.

With war around the corner, Lukia had Eudokia baptized in Kivertsi's Ukrainian Orthodox church. Normally, baptism took place forty days after a child's birth, but these weren't normal times. There was also no time for a celebration. Her sister Panashka acted as godmother and Gregory's brother-in-law Dmitro, godfather. If her daughter should die prematurely, at least she'd be allowed into heaven.

Lukia hadn't been home long from church and was about to make lunch, when Ivan came running in out of breath. "Mama, some soldiers are here to see you."

Shivers ran up her back. "Where's Egnat?"

"He's in the forest with Michalko. He found a fallen tree and they're dragging it home."

"Good. You better go help them."

While Ivan ran off, she wiped her hands on her apron and went outside. The soldiers—one raven-haired and handsome, the other much older, portly and seemingly bald under his cap—sat on their horses and were looking around the farm.

"Madam, is your husband home?" asked the older one. Greying whiskers framed his lips. The dark circles under his eyes suggested a lack of sleep or deep worry.

"No, he's out fighting the Germans."

"That's good to hear. Are you alone on the farm?"

"I live here with six children."

"Six?" He turned to his companion and laughed. "These peasants don't waste any time."

She ignored the insult. "What brings you here?"

"You and your family have to evacuate. You have to be out of here by tomorrow."

"What?" Stunned, not knowing how to escape what was happening, Lukia felt like running in all directions, like a chicken with its head cut off. Her knees buckled. "I can't leave yet. It's harvesting time."

The handsome one glanced at the fields as if they were nothing. "The Germans could arrive any moment. It's for your protection as well as ours. We don't want them or the Austrians taking you prisoner, forcing you to work for them." The officer stared beyond Lukia, causing her to turn. Hania stood in the open doorway for a few moments before disappearing back in the house. "Or worse yet," he added, "raping you or your daughter."

"Oy," Lukia said, placing a hand on her heart.

"We'll be burning all the homes in the district so they won't have anywhere to hide. You can burn your crops yourself, if you like."

She felt bile rise in her throat. "Nobody said anything about burning. You can't do that."

"Those are our orders. Each refugee will get six rubles a month."

"Six rubles? Will each of my children get six as well?"

"You must be joking," said the older one, barely concealing his surliness.

"That's scarcely enough to feed me."

"You're lucky to get that. Find the rest of your family." He turned his horse around. "We'll be back in the morning. Make sure you're ready to go. Just take what you need."

Panic joined the bile in her throat. She swallowed before saying, "Where will we go?"

"Siberia. We have trains at the station to take you."

Her stomach sank. "Siberia? Winter is coming. It's too cold there. We don't have the right clothing."

"I'm sorry," said the handsome one. Before she could complain further, the soldiers kicked their horses with their spurs and galloped away, dust rising behind them.

Lukia stood immobilized, as if she'd been frozen stiff by the iciness of his words. She watched the soldiers disappear behind the bushes on the crossroad. She'd heard enough about Siberia's brutal landscape to know that life there would mean hardship she couldn't fathom. It was a place where many had perished. She wanted to scream, blame those who'd started this crazy war, but what good would that do? She had to pack and be ready to leave tomorrow. But first, she had to tell her children.

May God Help Us All

LUKIA'S HEART POUNDED as she stood in the doorway watching Ivan hurry out of the forest, followed by Egnat and Michalko. She dreaded having to tell them about the soldiers' visit.

When Hania—with Havrylo clinging to her legs—joined her at the door, Lukia said, "They're returning without a tree."

"Ivan must've told them there was no point chopping more wood."

"What?"

Hania frowned. "Ivan heard you and the soldiers talking before he ran back to the woods."

"Oy. I wanted to tell the boys myself."

"Is it true? Do we have to leave?"

Lukia nodded. "May God help us."

Hania put her arm around her mother just as Egnat arrived breathless, holding on to his side. Winded as well, Ivan sat down on the bench by the door and stretched out his skinny legs. Michalko ran up to him, his face pale and drawn.

Egnat planted his feet squarely in front of his mother. "We can stay and fight."

"With what?"

"We have a rifle. We can get more." His unwavering stance and serious eyes reminded her of Gregory. One day, her eldest son would be no man to trifle with.

"I can help," said Michalko. This time, Egnat didn't mock him.

"I'm sure you can," said Lukia, ruffling Michalko's hair, "but there'll be too many."

Egnat clenched his fists. "Mama—"

"Don't say it," Lukia said sharply.

"We can't leave," said Egnat, his voice rising. "Who will take care of the farm, the cows, our horse?"

How could she tell him she didn't know? Likely the animals would starve or be requisitioned by the army for food and transport—if the looters didn't grab them first. "Son, we have no time to argue."

Egnat kicked the ground and walked away.

"Where are you going?" she shouted. "I need you here."

Sullen, he turned back but avoided his mother's eyes. She understood his frustration. It coursed through her veins as well.

"I hate them all," said Ivan.

"I know," said Lukia, as she sat down beside him, "but we have no choice." She put her arm around his shoulders. "We have to do what they tell us."

"If we go, how will Tato find us?" Ivan whimpered.

"Don't worry. Somehow Tato will find us, or we'll find him. But now we have to get to work. We have much to do."

Lukia had reassured her son, but his question underlined her own doubts. It was bad enough in peaceful times: typically, one village didn't know what was happening in the next. You only found out if someone visited the other place and brought the news back. With the country at war and its citizens fleeing, Lukia had little faith in the government's communication services. How would her husband learn their destination? How would she find out where he went?

These matters weighed on her mind as she prepared to leave.

While Hania baked bread and two chickens to take with them, Lukia sent the boys out to gather eggs, milk the cows and pick whatever vegetables were ready. Once Eudokia was settled, Lukia started packing. She tried to keep her children's grim faces off her mind. Egnat's especially. Whenever she saw him stroke the horse and whisper in his ear, she recognized the animal meant more to Egnat than even his own brothers. He'd spent hours grooming him to show off in the village and now he had to leave him behind.

With a heavy heart, Lukia stuffed several clean flour bags with the family's clothing. She put a large pot, a frying pan, dishes, cups, spoons, a rolling pin, a large canvas cloth, and matches into a burlap bag. In another, she piled potatoes, onions, garlic, and a cheesecloth bundle of spices. Then she got a wooden crate from the komorra and filled it with a sealer of pork fat and canisters of flour, sugar, and salt: the staples for varenyky—or perogies as her Polish neighbors called them.

Every step she took was like walking through a swamp in a heavy fog. Her children's sad faces drifted in and out of her vision. Nothing seemed real. And yet everything being packed had to be considered carefully. They could take only what they could carry onto a train. In Lutsk, she'd seen Polish refugees lugging all they could in their carts and on their backs. She'd even seen one wagon with a sewing machine and a live chicken. No one knew how long this war would last.

Once the kitchen was stripped of what they needed for the road, she took a moment to rest. Glancing at her sewing goods in the corner of the room, she felt pleased that at least she'd finished the uniforms and Egnat had collected the money from the sergeant. Perhaps the army would need more of her services in Siberia.

She was sorry the children wouldn't get a chance to say goodbye to their friends. Neither would she to hers. But then again, maybe they were already gone. She recalled once more the lined faces of those escaping, trading one misery for another. She and her family were about to join them on roads that took them far from home, away from everything familiar.

She breathed in the smell of the bread Hania was taking out of the pich. It might be a long time before they had freshly baked bread again. "You've done a good job," she said, tears pooling in her eyes.

"Is there anything else you want me to do?"

"We'll need water. Lots of water."

It was still the middle of summer, and they'd be travelling on dusty roads with no shade. Together, Lukia and Hania filled a large tin container and a couple of glass jars with clean water from the well. Lukia also had to keep her milk going, if nothing else.

That evening, Lukia made sure the children ate well, which meant she had to coax her two oldest sons. Ivan picked at his food; Egnat pushed his plate away.

"Egnat, we don't know when we'll be able to eat like this again," Lukia said.

"How can I eat if I'm not hungry?"

"I need you strong. I need you healthy." She held his gaze until he pulled his plate closer and started eating.

Havrylo wanted Egnat and Michalko to sing the folk songs he liked to hear after supper, but no one felt like singing. Instead, the family took a bath in the creek, not far from their cottage. The clear cool water revived the spirits of Havrylo and Michalko, who laughed and splashed each other as if there were nothing to fear on the horizon. But Lukia, Hania, and the older boys washed in silence, occupied with thoughts of what lay ahead in the black hole of an uncertain future.

Afterwards, when the kerosene lamps had been extinguished and the children were asleep, Lukia knelt by her bed. She gazed at the two icons hanging over the headboard—the Last Supper and the Virgin Mary with Child. On the outside of each frame was draped a *rushnyk,* a white linen towel she'd decorated with red and black cross-stitched flowers in the tradition of her *oblast.* She would pack these items last. With hands clasped tightly, she prayed for Gregory's safety, her new baby's health and a safe journey to that godforsaken place, Siberia.

A PROMISSORY NOTE

U P BEFORE DAWN, Lukia found packing a challenge with Eudokia crying to be fed every two hours. Thankfully her other children helped. While the younger ones gathered eggs and fed the animals and the few chickens that were left, Lukia, Egnat, and Hania carried all the bags and crates out to the wagon. They also packed a spade, an axe, and a saw.

Lukia had just finished feeding Eudokia when she spotted the returning soldiers through her bedroom window. She quickly laid her infant on the bed, buttoned her housedress and went outside.

"Good day, Panye," said the older, portly soldier. Though he seemed better mannered today and had addressed her as a married woman, she was too upset to be polite in reply.

"What's good about it?" said Lukia, snarling. Her attention turned to Ivan and Egnat, who were straining to lift their trunk, filled with their bedding, on the wagon. The soldiers got off their horses and helped to heave it in place. Her demeanour softened a little—at least they had the decency to give a hand.

The portly one glanced at the other goods by the wheel and shook his head. "We told you to take only what you needed."

"There are seven of us," she said. "We need it all."

He made a face and mumbled something to his partner. She pointed to the sacks of grain stacked against the south wall of the cottage. "What am I going to do with all my grain? I'm not leaving it here for someone to steal."

The soldier clenched his teeth as if about to argue with her but then seemingly changed his mind. His jaw relaxed and he asked, "What kind of grain?"

"Oats, wheat, barley. We're only halfway through harvesting. If I could stay, I'd have twice as many bushels. I'm being forced to leave it all behind."

He grunted. "You're lucky I've been a farmer longer than I've been a soldier. Show me what you have. Maybe I can help." After he'd examined her grain and estimated the weight, he wrote the date, the amount, and the name Farazsheev Krylow on a piece of paper he'd taken out of his pocket. He signed the note and handed it to her. "On your way to the camp, ask to speak to this man. He's a captain in the Tsar's army. He'll pay you."

She looked at the scribbled note with some irritation. She'd never been to school, so reading was a challenge. However, she had learned—through her children—to make out most words in a simple message. "What kind of help is this?" she demanded, waving it in front of his face. "How do I know he'll pay me?"

"I'm telling you he will. I wrote it down."

She folded her arms. "You better not be lying."

"I'm not lying," he said with a faint smile.

She looked at the paper again. "Farazsheev Krylow. That's a funny name. Fairy wings. What kind of name is this?"

He shrugged. "That's his name."

"You said I can find him on the way to camp. Where exactly?"

"He's well-known. Just ask any soldier at the station. He'll point you in the right direction."

"And my animals?"

He searched her face as if she could help him with the answer. "I don't know. The army may take them somewhere safe. They'll be tagged as belonging to you."

"But who will feed them when we leave?"

"That I can't tell you either, but such good animals, we won't let them starve."

She exhaled sharply. "This is crazy. You know it's crazy."

He looked sympathetic but said nothing, only shrugged again.

She glanced at Egnat. Luckily, he was too busy loading the wagon to pay attention to the argument. He would be further distressed knowing there was no clear plan when it came to their livestock. She hoped the soldier wasn't lying about not letting the animals go hungry, but she'd learned long ago that people in authority couldn't always be trusted to tell the truth.

Swearing under her breath, she returned to the cottage, where she took a small rag out of her apron pocket. She tore off a strip and wrapped her promissory note in it. She then undid the top button of her housedress and tucked the small fabric packet into the front of her brassiere.

Satisfied that the note was safe, she made a final visit to their cows, pigs, and chickens. They seemed more restless than usual. The cows shuffled, the pigs stomped, and the few chickens clucked as if a fox were on the loose. Although she'd never thought twice about slaughtering a chicken for supper, she was sad to say goodbye to the fowl that had served her family well.

While the children climbed into the packed wagon—the younger ones sitting on the older ones' laps—she went through the two rooms of her cottage to make sure they hadn't forgotten anything. The furniture was all that was left. No personal articles remained and there was nothing on the shelves or in the cupboard except for some empty bottles and tins. It was as if a mighty wind had blown through their home and whisked any traces of the Mazurets family away.

Lingering in the doorway, she swept the farm with her eyes. On the harvested section, some fallen straw remained to be gathered for feed or thatching. That didn't bother her as much as the golden stalks of barley left uncut. They swayed gently in the breeze, a picture of calm that sharply contrasted the churning in her stomach.

"It's time to go," the handsome soldier said to Lukia. "You'll miss the train."

The portly one cut in. "Give her a moment."

She took one more look inside, put her hand on the latch and pulled the door shut. The noise of it unsettled her further. It sounded like the lid of a coffin going down for the last time. She swallowed hard before walking to the wagon. Egnat was already perched on the driver's seat; his brothers and sisters were in the back.

She sat down beside her eldest son. The family gaped at their home as if their eyes were cameras and could take a lasting image. Their eyes widened further when the soldiers lit torches and flung them onto the thatched straw roof of their house. It didn't take long for the fire to catch and the flames to engulf their dwelling. The sunflowers by the side of the house shrivelled in the blaze spreading beyond the walls and into the yard. The boys averted their faces when bits of embers flew in their direction. Havrylo blinked, looked as though he was trying not to cry. As the smell of smoke filled Lukia's nostrils, she coughed and turned her face away.

"My God," she said. "It's all going and for what?"

"We can't leave any refuge for the Germans," barked the portly soldier. "We'll burn the crops later. Let's go.

Egnat snapped the reins and clucked his tongue to get the horse moving.

Lukia said softly, "Lord, give us the strength to get through this." Hearing Eudokia cry, she turned to take her baby from Hania.

As Egnat followed the soldiers down their farm road, Hania and Ivan sobbed. Lukia said to them, "When the war is over, we'll come back and build another house."

"Don't cry," Michalko said to Ivan. "We're going on a train ride."

"Choo, choo, choo," said Havrylo, too young to understand the magnitude of what was happening.

For fear of bawling herself, Lukia didn't look back at the farm. She crossed herself three times. The rest of the family followed suit as they rattled down their road, muddy from the previous night's rain. They hadn't gone far before they found themselves stuck in one of the ruts with one wheel buried deep. No matter how hard Egnat whipped the horse, the animal's hooves kept slipping.

"Enough!" said Lukia. "Don't be stupid. If you keep hitting the horse, we won't be going anywhere. Help me down."

Shamed, Egnat jumped off the wagon and rushed to his mother's side. After passing the baby to Michalko, who carefully cradled his sister on his lap, Lukia took Egnat's hand and stepped onto the rutted road.

"You drive," Lukia said to Egnat. "Ivan, Hania and I will push the wagon." The sheer madness of what she was about to do, so soon after giving birth, wasn't lost on her. She could tear the scar between her legs. She glared at the soldiers for not helping then stood with two of her children behind the wheels.

They were about to push when the handsome soldier hollered, "Wait!" He gave the reins of his horse to his partner and came to the family's aid. Lukia gave the soldier a grateful nod but moments later returned to blaming him and his partner for the predicament her family found themselves in. With all hands pushing, it didn't take long for the horse to work its way out of the muck.

Once the wagon got rolling again, Lukia's thoughts jumped ahead to where they were going and how long they'd be there. Siberia was as close to the end of the world as she could imagine.

"Lukia!"

The voice sounded dim and far away.

"Lukia!"

She felt someone tugging her arm. "Mama, Mama, wake up," said Hania. "Tato is calling you."

Lukia half-opened her eyes. "Hania, I'm tired. Leave me alone."

Hania tugged her again. "Tato's here.

"Lukia! It's Gregory!"

Startled, she awoke and sat up groggily, noticing they were on the main road in Lutsk. Their wagon was making little progress on a road clogged with soldiers and hundreds of other refugees, walking and riding in carts to the train station. It took a few moments for her to register that her husband was walking alongside the wagon.

Hania and her brothers shouted, their voices overlapping. "Tato, they burned our house!" "They're sending us to Siberia!" "Can't you come with us?" "When will we see you again?"

"Children," said Lukia, "how can he answer you? Tato doesn't know." She turned to Gregory. "What are you doing here? I thought you'd gone to the front."

"We're waiting for more armaments. Also, food."

She didn't want to hear he was hungry. Didn't he know what pain that caused her? "I told you that you shouldn't have given that chicken away."

"Lukia, don't. . ." His eyes pleaded for her to stop criticizing. She was tempted to toss him some food, but she had only enough to feed her children for a few days. Surely the army would supply him with something to eat soon.

The road ahead was cleared of a stall, and a soldier yelled at them to keep moving. "Listen," Gregory said, "when you get to the train station, ask the officer there to send you to the Caucasus. Tell them your husband's in the army. The Caucasus is warmer than Siberia." He looked back and saw his unit beginning to move in the other direction. "I have to go." As the wagon rolled on without him, he cried, "Be strong!"

"Gregory. . .!" she shouted at his back. She was going to say more but stopped when she realized he wouldn't hear her over the sounds of horses' hooves, other soldiers barking instructions, and wagon wheels grinding on the road. She'd forgotten to tell him about the note for the grain. He'd be proud of her for getting at least something for their efforts. Bobbing up and down, she strained to get one last look at him through the throngs on the road, but he'd disappeared from view.

A MOVING PRISON

AT THE TRAIN station, Lukia got a pittance for her
wagon even though it had a strong wood shaft and was
better built than most. Hardly enough rubles to buy a
few chickens. Same for her sturdy draft horse. One of the refugees
told her the army was requisitioning horses, using them for the
war effort. Even the livestock. It wasn't fair. But who could she
complain to? All the farmers were in the same boat.

Lukia and her children stepped onto the train platform and
jostled their way through the teeming crowd. The sharp smells of
unwashed bodies, garlic, and fried onions on clothing assaulted
their noses as they pushed forward past soldiers herding hundreds
of peasants—mostly mothers and their young families looking
lost as they dragged and carried their possessions in crates, trunks,
and canvas bags.

Lukia left Egnat in charge of his brothers and sisters near one
of the platform poles and stood in line behind a half dozen other
women waiting to speak to a tall blond officer, who looked as if
he were barely off his mother's breast. When her turn came, she
asked him if she and her family could go to the Caucasus.

He hesitated. "Panye, why do you even mention this? If you
were told Siberia, then that's where you have to go."

"Listen," she said, raising her voice to be heard over someone shouting nearby. "I just had a baby. We don't have the right clothing. Tell me, would you send your mother there?"

"Panye, I understand. This is hard for everybody."

"What do you know what's hard?" Her throat tightened. "I'm alone to take care of six children because my husband left to fight for the Tsar. Our house was torched. We watched our home go up in flames."

His gaze softened. "You say your husband volunteered?"

"Yes, and he told me to ask to be sent to the Caucasus. Others are going. Why can't we?"

"Panye, let me see," he said with a sympathetic nod. He then looked down the row of freight cars, waved at someone down the track, and put seven fingers in the air. Lukia glanced in that direction and saw an older man in uniform give the beckoning sign. The young officer turned back to her and smiled. "It will be alright. You can go there."

"Thank you." She shook his hand in gratitude.

Lukia and her family jostled their way through the crowd to a boxcar that held at least ten others, huddled near the open door. They moved over to allow Lukia and her children to climb aboard. The interior of the boxcar was filthy. Old straw littered the floor and the urine and manure smell confirmed that the dark substance on the wood planks was more than just soil dragged in on someone's shoes.

"This is shameful!" she said to a stout man, who was standing near the door. "We're being moved like animals."

"Look," he said, pointing to a small sign on the wall. "These freight cars are for forty men or six horses. I think they're planning on squeezing forty of us in here."

Staring at the sign, she shook her head and said to Egnat, "Get the empty burlap bags from the trunk and lay them on the floor. At least, we can sit on something clean."

Crouched in a dark corner was an elderly couple with a teenager, who appeared to be their grandson. They were talking to one another in Russian. Lukia exchanged pleasantries with them and learned they had arrived from Kovel, the village where she'd been born. Their conversation quickly petered out when it was determined the old couple knew none of the people she had mentioned.

After organizing their belongings in the cramped quarters, her children grew quiet. Lukia assumed they were as shocked as she was to have landed in this dingy space. She gazed at her daughter, who was resting in her arms. How was she going to survive this trip? How would they all? She moaned and said a silent prayer. They soon joined the others by the open door to get some fresh air and watch the soldiers fill the boxcars with refugees.

When Lukia saw an official walking by, she suddenly remembered her promissory note. She quickly handed Eudokia to Hania and, with help from a stranger, jumped down on the platform. "Please wait!" she bellowed at the official, who was now a car-length away and couldn't hear her because of all the station noise. She pushed her way through the throng until she caught up with him. "Please, wait a moment," she said as she tapped him on the back. He turned around looking surprised. She pulled out the note buried under her housedress and showed it to him. "Where can I find Farazsheev Krylow?"

He read the note, rubbing one end of his long handlebar moustache. "What's this?"

"This is a promise that I'll be paid for my grain."

"Good luck," he said, his eyes crinkling in amusement.

"What do you mean, good luck?" Her throat went dry and her fists tightened. "I want to speak to someone higher up."

He shook his head but said, "Come with me." They walked down the row of boxcars until he found a superior, an immense man with bulging eyes in his round face.

He scrutinized her note, then said, "If he'd given you a bigger paper, you could've at least wiped your ass with it." The two men laughed and poked each other in the ribs.

The official with the moustache waved his arms to simulate a bird flying and said with a smirk, "He flew away."

She glared at the men. Mocking smiles plastered on their faces. They were making fun of the name, fairy wings, but they were also laughing at her as if she'd been duped. "That's how you talk to me! Your mother would be ashamed of you. Both of you." Pointing to the name on her note, she said, "When you finish laughing, tell me where I can find the captain."

The superior, looking admonished, said, "Ask when you get to the Caucasus."

"Is he there?"

"Maybe." There was a loud whistle down the tracks. "You'd better get back on board."

Frustrated, she rushed back to their boxcar with the soldiers' jeering tone and laughter ringing in her ears. Her heartbeat quickened and she gulped to catch her breath. What if she couldn't find this captain? What would they do if they ran out of money? She'd brought some savings, but that wouldn't last long.

When she climbed back into the car, a few families were already eating their midday meal. She crossed herself, signalling to her children huddled on the perina that it was time to pray.

After the Lord's Prayer, she added, "Thank you, God, for sparing us a Siberian winter." Following a chorus of "Amen," she unwrapped the cloth covering the basket and took out a plate of roast chicken. She broke the chicken apart and handed one piece to each family member. Hania then passed a loaf of bread around. Next came the bowl of boiled eggs and a clean tea towel full of vegetables—radishes, tomatoes, carrots, and cucumbers—picked from their garden. As two sealers of fresh milk were circulated, she reminded her children to enjoy their lunch. It would be a long time before they'd have such a tasty meal again.

As the train clattered over the tracks, Lukia stared out at the misery beyond the open boxcar door. Villages and farmhouses burned and smouldered. The land was layered in soot. Fields of grain had been left to go to seed or set on fire. Everywhere she looked, she saw only scorched earth or families fleeing. In her oblast of Volhynia, the German settlers had been forced to vacate first. Next were the Jews, and now the Ukrainians. But there were others: Lithuanians, Armenians, Poles, Latvians, and of course, Russians.

It was the Russians who concerned her the most. They regarded her people as inferior. The only saving grace Ukrainians had was their religion. Because they were mainly Orthodox like the Russians, they weren't treated as badly as the others. For that reason, Lukia kept her Orthodox cross visible above the neckline of her housedress. She didn't want to be mistaken for one of the Jews, who the Russians suspected were collaborating with the enemy. She hadn't seen it herself, but she'd heard stories about Jews being beaten for no reason. Someone had told her it was because their Yiddish was often mistaken for German. At least, she knew one language from the other and could manage a few common expressions. It also helped that she spoke Polish and Russian.

When the train slowed down, she saw a young woman with a small child standing near the tracks, two measly bags of belongings by her feet. The sorrow etched on the mother's face grew deeper as the train passed. Maybe she'd hoped it would stop for her. For a second or two, their eyes had connected and Lukia wished she could've done something to ease the young woman's plight.

Tired from standing, Lukia joined her children on the perina. Again, she worried about where they were going and how long they would have to stay before they could return to pick up their lives—if Russia won the war. The government had promised all their homes would be restored after the fighting was over. But could anyone trust government? For some reason, Gregory did. What a cruel joke played on him! On all of them. The Tsar had always taken advantage of those who had little. Nothing had changed. Why couldn't Gregory see that?

Lukia's life had been hard; she'd paid a price for love. She could've married Stefan, a young man from Dubno, where she grew up. When he was courting her, he'd bought her a parasol and a beautiful scarf. It must've cost him a lot of money. If she hadn't seen his temper, she would've become his wife.

She 'd been twenty-one when Stefan first saw her in the village. Smitten, he'd spread the word he wanted to meet her in order to propose. Not long after, an elderly neighbour took Lukia to visit Stefan, who invited them into his kitchen. They sat down and listened to his appeal. He kept repeating that he loved her and would take care of her and her mother. Lukia found him charming at first, but when she hesitated, not knowing if she could come to love him in return, his demeanour soured. As well, the neighbour was jittery, as he'd left much work to do at home and the sun was already setting. He told Lukia to hurry up. When Stefan heard the old man's order, his eyes darkened. "Sit and be quiet!" he yelled, spit flying out of his mouth. Witnessing such an angry reaction, such disrespect for an elder, she became so frightened she rejected Stefan.

Years later, after she'd married Gregory and had a few children, she saw Stefan again. She was walking to town barefoot and he drove by with a woman beside him in a phaeton—a fancy hooded wagon with springs that didn't jiggle. Feeling ashamed because she was dressed so poorly, Lukia averted her face, hoping he hadn't seen her.

She shook her head at the memory. What was the good of that kind of thinking? She couldn't go back in time. Anyway, she didn't love him. Never had.

She wondered if Stefan had joined the Tsar's army. As soon as she thought of that, she brooded about the danger Gregory was in. Would she ever see him again? The Caucasus was a huge territory on the southeastern edge of Russia, thousands of kilometers from home. If Gregory knew where they were going, he could write her some letters. Egnat could read them and assure her that his father was still alive and unhurt.

She regarded her six children. She couldn't imagine raising them without a father, and yet all around her, on the train and in the countryside, there were thousands of families like hers, headed by women traveling to places far from home and far from the men they loved. What was to become of them all?

Lukia woke up disoriented. She'd dreamt of Gregory fighting one German after another as they ran toward him with their bayonets extended. Though the reality of the boxcar was terrible, she was glad to have escaped the nightmare. She was also thankful to find her children slumbering with their faces calm and their bodies pressed against one another.

Now that they'd settled for a long ride, Lukia worried there would be no place to bathe Eudokia, whose belly button had become infected. The skin around it was dry and scaly. Lukia had cleaned it with a little of their drinking water and applied a salve, but so far there had been little improvement. Her fears mounted. She'd lost one infant to a fever, another to a flu. Back then, she'd had help from the village doctor and her mother—who had healed many with herbs—and still her babies hadn't survived. What hope did she have on a train with no outside help in sight?

Lukia and her children had been travelling for days. Along the way, their train stopped at various stations to pick up food and supplies that were becoming increasingly scarce. There was enough water to quench their thirst, but not enough to bathe properly.

At one stop, a young woman with four children, all seemingly younger than six, climbed into Lukia's boxcar. The woman said "Good day" in Ukrainian and stood there glancing around, unsure of where to settle. The freight car was already at capacity.

"Please, come over here," Lukia said. "We'll make room for you and your children. Egnat, Hania, help move our things." Egnat and Hania sprang into action and piled their belongings on the trunk. The elderly couple with a teenager squeezed together as well to make room.

"Thank you," said the young woman. She patted her two youngest—fair-haired twins, each clutching one of her legs.

My God, thought Lukia, at least I have older ones to help me out.

Now the boxcar was more cramped than ever. Lukia's boys—who were used to running through the fields and woods—squirmed from sitting too long in one place and poked one another in irritation. Thankfully, the train stopped frequently. At stops where they were sure the train wasn't going to move any time soon, Lukia and her children got off to breathe fresh air and stretch their limbs. The break was also an opportunity to dump their pail and relieve themselves, either at the station's facilities or in the tall grass or bush, which was what they used if the line-ups were too long.

Most of these stops were short, but some lasted hours—or more than a day when their boxcars were diverted onto another track to allow the military trains to go through. Lukia welcomed such stops, a relief from the stench of the congested boxcar, even though these delays made the trip even longer. Outdoors, she talked with women from other cars who shared her concerns about their journey, destination, and future.

It was all worrisome, not knowing how much further they had to travel and how they would feed themselves if the food ran out before they got there. The government said they would assist along the way and not let anyone starve, but she doubted their promises, even though, at some stations, officials handed out loaves of bread. These humble offerings were appreciated, but they were hardly enough to squelch anyone's hunger pangs. She recalled how the higher-ups had treated their own soldiers before they were sent to the front. If the soldiers weren't fed properly, what hope did the refugees have? They were only civilians, dispensable in war. Would the Tsar and his family ride in a boxcar if they had to run away? No, they would be taken to some luxurious retreat, where they would dine on pheasant and caviar. It was always like this. In the end, the only person you could depend on was yourself.

During the long breaks, Lukia made sure her family stayed close together. There'd already been word that at one of these diversions some cars had been decoupled without warning and a few families had become separated, causing unimaginable distress.

It was hard for Lukia to keep track of her sons when they had a chance to roam outside, where Egnat, Ivan, Michalko, and Havrylo liked to amuse themselves by imitating soldiers. Egnat played the captain while they crouched behind bushes and mimed the shooting of invisible enemies.

Hania would stroll by herself through the brush that lined the railway tracks. Already developing some curves, she attracted admiring glances from soldiers, both young and old. And who could blame them? She was beautiful with her long, braided brown hair, sparkly dark eyes, and sunny disposition. Who wouldn't fall in love with a girl whose face lit up whenever she encountered a child at play or a young mother suckling her infant? Soon Lukia would have to sit down with her daughter and advise her on how to protect her virginity.

As for her baby daughter, her infected belly button showed no change. At three weeks old, Eudokia still wasn't gaining weight. This wasn't surprising given how little milk Lukia was producing.

But how could she produce more when there was a shortage of fluids to drink? The cow's milk she'd brought was long gone, and their water had to be rationed. Soldiers had told them that the army had depleted most of the wells along the train tracks and the water that remained was contaminated. Terrified of coming down with dysentery or typhoid, Lukia refused to take any of the water offered at stops along the way and warned her children not to drink any.

Lukia also feared catching a disease from fellow refugees. She and her children wore scarves over their mouths. In every boxcar, someone was sick or dying from cholera, dysentery, or pneumonia. In some freight cars, the living would sit alongside a dead and decaying body for days, its stench unbearable, until they reached a place where they could deposit their loved ones. Young and old bodies were dragged and carried off the trains. Mothers tried to shield their children's eyes from the horror. If there was time, there'd be a proper funeral, which accounted for the many white crosses they saw along the tracks, but most refugees were buried with little ceremony without a priest or a plot. The uncontrollable sobbing that followed each quick burial was accompanied by the *clickety-clack* of the train and ceased only when those grieving dropped off to sleep. Lukia fretted about how much longer they'd have to suffer the putrid smell of death and the horror of watching people lose those they loved. Tears would rise in her throat and sit there like a lump of food hard to swallow.

She gazed at Eudokia's sweet face. How much longer before she fell truly ill? To fortify her children and herself, she added minced garlic to their food. She wasn't the only mother thinking this way. Most of the boxcars reeked of garlic and onions, both known to have medicinal properties. These smells combated the odour of rotting flesh.

Mothers also comforted their young through folk songs. Ballads about young girls going to dances and young men waiting to take them home floated out of boxcar doors, sometimes accompanied by an accordion or a tsymbaly, a bittersweet reminder of better times at home. Lukia and her children often sang a song about white snow on mountaintops and a girl walking through the meadows. While they sang, Lukia assured herself that at least her baby didn't have a raging fever. At least it wasn't cholera.

And so it went, day after day, in their moving prison.

THE TSAR'S DAUGHTER

WITH THEIR DESTINATION still days away, Eudokia took a turn for the worse. She ran a fever, her belly button leaked pus and the skin surrounding it became red and chapped. She'd lost so much weight the bones in her frail body were visible. Her crying bouts seemed endless as Lukia waited for the next stop to alert the authorities she needed help.

She peered out the small opening at the top of the freight car door. No station in sight. The never-ending sound of the train clanking on the tracks competed with her baby's incessant cries. If she'd been on a passenger train, she could've walked from one car to the other seeking help, but here, she was stuck. Her anxiety intensified. Her heart raced and she had trouble breathing, leading her to panic. What if she had a heart attack? What would her children do? Hania would have to manage her four brothers and a baby. How could she do that, when she was little more than a child herself?

Lukia closed her eyes and forced herself to breathe slowly. Then, to calm her baby and give the others in the boxcar some peace, she dipped a clean piece of rag in whisky and stuck it between her baby's lips. The alcoholic soother succeeded in bringing Eudokia's crying down to a whimper, giving everyone around a much-needed break.

At the next stop, Lukia heard that some nurses from the Red Cross had joined the boxcar convoy to the Caucasus. Their plan was to move from car to car to see who needed assistance, but Lukia wasn't taking any chances. She called out to a station attendant standing near the tracks reading some form. "Please, I need a nurse right away. Please tell someone my baby is seriously ill."

The attendant looked over his spectacles, nodded, and left his post. She strained at the door to see where he'd gone. She tried to look down the tracks, but with so many crowding around the opening, she had difficulty seeing anything. Groaning, she rocked Eudokia and waited and waited. Lukia's eyes were heavy from lack of sleep and her body ached from holding a sick child for so long. When the train began to move, her spirits sank further.

Hours later, they were still on the move. Eudokia's bawling increased once again in length and volume. A few of the refugees, exhausted themselves, gave Lukia looks of annoyance, while an old man, delirious and bone-thin himself, barked at her in Russian. "Can't you shut her up?"

"She's sick," Lukia said, even though it was obvious.

The old man continued to scowl at Lukia, but eventually pulled his jacket over his head and tried to sleep.

The train seemed to move even more slowly. Seconds seemed like minutes, minutes like a quarter of an hour. Finally, they came to a stop and were told they could stretch their legs and use the temporary outhouses set up near the tracks.

After disembarking, Lukia handed Eudokia to Hania and ran to a soldier further down the line. "Please! I beg you," she said, tugging his sleeve. "My baby won't stop crying. She's very sick. Please get me a nurse!"

Patting her on the shoulder, he hollered at a group of military personnel gathered on the platform, "Where is a nurse? We need one right away!"

A pleasant-looking woman, with her hair tucked under a nurse's hat resembling a nun's veil, stuck her head out of a boxcar door a little way down the track. When she saw Lukia waving at her, she shouted, "I'll be there soon."

Though Lukia had managed to get a nurse's attention, she couldn't breathe easily. She kept her eyes fastened on the boxcar holding the Red Cross worker. It might've been only five minutes but it seemed like an eternity before the woman jumped down on the railway platform then turned to grab a black satchel from someone inside the car.

At Lukia's boxcar, the nurse looked with sympathy at Eudokia crying in Hania's arms, her face red and her arms and legs striking out in protest. As the nurse unwrapped the thin blanket covering Eudokia, Lukia shook with emotion. "My child's stomach is rotting. You can see her guts. Please help her."

"I'll see what I can do," the nurse said in a soft voice. "Do you have something we can lay her on?"

Egnat immediately climbed back into the boxcar and within moments threw out a perina, which Lukia caught and spread out on the grass beside the tracks. Embarrassed that the bed covering was soiled, she bent down to wipe off what dirt she could with her hand.

"Don't worry about that," said the nurse, taking her stethoscope out of her satchel. "Not much you can do about these filthy conditions."

Hania laid her sister down on the bedcovering. Eudokia screamed and kicked as if she were being pierced with needles as the nurse examined the infant's chest and abdomen.

"Oy, oy, oy," said Lukia. Her other children huddled around, all anxious about their sister.

The nurse took a vial of liquid from her bag.

"What's that?" asked Lukia.

"Carbolic acid. It will clean the sore."

"Will she be okay? I can't lose another."

The nurse's brow creased as she cleaned Eudokia's belly button with gauze soaked in the medicinal acid. "I can't promise. I've seen this before. Some recover, some don't. I'll get her some milk and we'll have to wait and see."

Lukia bit her lip. "I don't know how to thank you."

The nurse shook her head. "There's nothing to thank me for yet." She then applied some powder over the area she'd cleaned. "Keep it dry."

"What's your name?" Lukia asked.

"Olga Nikolaevna."

Lukia wondered if she'd heard right. "What?" Olga Nikolaevna was one of the Tsar's daughters. What was she doing working for the Red Cross? Lukia studied her. She recognized the face from the pictures she'd seen of the royal family on the newsstand in Lutsk.

"Olga Nikolaevna," she said again, smiling. "But just call me Sister. I don't advertise my name. You know, not everyone is happy with us."

Speechless, Lukia and her family exchanged looks of disbelief. They had never come close to the Tsar or anyone from his family before. Given the political climate, Lukia was surprised the nurse had given her name. The Tsar's daughter was vulnerable working on the trains; she wasn't with her own people but among troubled and diseased peasants. The Romanovs had enemies inside Russia—enemies who wanted nothing more than to wipe out the entire royal family. Lukia's husband had said that those opposed to the Tsar were followers of Lenin and Trotsky who believed in a workers' revolution, but Lukia didn't know anyone who belonged to their movement.

Without thinking, she took Olga's hand. "May God bless you for what you're doing."

Olga patted Lukia's hand in return. She then folded her stethoscope and placed it, along with the vial and powder, back in her satchel. "I think your baby will be fine, but if she isn't, let one of the soldiers know. There are several Sisters of Mercy travelling on the train with you."

Not long after the nurse left, Eudokia settled into a deep and peaceful sleep. Lukia didn't know if her baby was exhausted from crying or whether she was on the mend. Either way, Eudokia at rest meant Lukia could rest as well. Still, it was hard to calm down after the nurse's visit. She wasn't just relieved that her baby had received some aid—she was also excited, like her other children, that Eudokia had been attended to by royalty. Egnat strutted, as if he'd been the one to get help from such an extraordinary nurse, and Lukia wasted no time telling her travelling companions her baby had been treated by the Tsar's daughter. They were as stunned as she was. The teenager with the elderly couple from Kovel said teasingly, "Next stop, the palace."

Lukia chortled. It was a relief to joke now that there was hope again. She wished she could tell Gregory about Olga Nikolaevna, but he'd probably gloat about it. She could almost hear him say, "See. Isn't it good I joined to help the Tsar?"

In the morning, Lukia checked Eudokia's belly button. The oozing had stopped and the redness around it had lessened. With the fresh milk the nurse had provided, Lukia was able to nurse and Eudokia's appetite returned. The painful crying also ceased, bringing smiles to the others in the boxcar.

A few days later, they arrived in the Caucasus, a land populated by people foreign to Lukia. She was told these deeply tanned and bearded men and their women, who were covered from head to toe, weren't Christians. They were mostly Muslim, a religion Lukia knew nothing about. She was also surprised to find that even though the Caucasus was in the south of Russia, its climate wasn't warmer than the one she'd left behind. Lukia shivered as she gazed at the lofty firs and the snow-covered peaks in the distance. This mountainous region promised to be wet and cold in the coming months.

A MEAGRE SHELTER

IN THE CAMP, shelters were laid out as far as the eye could see. A soldier led Lukia and her children to a makeshift army tent in a field of other tents staked close to one another. The canvas refuge, though meagre and musty smelling, was sturdy and well-sealed. A good protection in case of rain, severe winds or chilly nights. A cold winter in this miserable place would be another matter. Dismissing her worries about freezing for the time being, Lukia found the icon of the Virgin Mary in their belongings and hung it on the metal ring of a tent pole.

The families around her were mostly Russian. Whenever she heard anyone speak Ukrainian or Polish, she looked over but so far there was no one she recognized.

After Lukia and her children had unpacked, they stood in a long line that snaked through the campsite. It took an hour to get a few slices of bread and a large tin bowl of soup with *kasha* from the Red Cross. They then huddled in a circle on the open ground and took turns dipping their spoons. Though the thin broth was basic and bland, Lukia welcomed the relief agency's paltry offering. It would do for now. Soon, she'd have to figure out how to supplement these meals with preparations of her own.

The good news was that Eudokia's belly button had healed. And with clean water from the well near the camp, Lukia's milk flowed freely once again. Eudokia sucked happily, which stimulated even more milk production. Lukia was reminded of how her son, Fedor, had been too weak with fever and couldn't suck. He had died well before he was a year old. She had become pregnant with Eudokia soon after, so she'd barely had time to grieve. God took, but He also gave.

The government had given some thought to their situation, as there was a market less than a kilometer from camp. But money was required to buy food. Each family was given six rubles a month, hardly enough to feed one person, let alone seven. And with the end of the war nowhere in sight, Lukia doubted the funds she'd brought would be enough.

Wasting no time, she went looking for the captain who was supposed to reimburse her for the grain she'd left behind. Lukia approached two young soldiers who were helping the displaced get settled. This time when she mentioned Farazsheev Krylow, the name on the promissory note, there was no mocking laughter. The soldiers recognized the name and pointed to a series of military tents on the hill behind the camp. She could hardly believe her luck. What if she'd gone to Siberia? However, she curtailed her glee, reminding herself she hadn't yet seen this captain, nor had she been paid.

She dragged herself past the tired families, soldiers, and Red Cross volunteers to the army barracks at the top of the hill. There, she was directed to the largest tent. When she entered, Captain Krylow raised his bald head from the reports on his table and gawked at her as if he'd never seen a woman before. "What do you want?"

She unfolded the worn piece of paper and showed him what was written on it.

He scrutinized it for a few moments and then leaned back. "For grain?"

"Yes," she said firmly.

"Good." The captain passed the note to a sergeant seated nearby at a table with a battered metal box on it. "Pay this woman."

The sergeant glanced at the paper and opened his box. After counting out the promised rubles and handing them to her, he said, "Count them again. I don't want any dispute later."

Finding the amount correct, Lukia smiled. "Thank you." She started to go but then turned and said, "Have you heard how the soldiers around Lutsk are doing? My husband was stationed there. The last time I saw him he was marching to the front."

The sergeant furrowed his brow. "We heard yesterday—Lutsk has fallen."

"What? But my husband . . .?" She couldn't continue. The inside of the tent swam before her eyes.

He shook his head. "There were casualties. The army retreated to the east. We can only hope your husband was with them."

Lukia took a step away from the sergeant.

"Are you all right?" he asked.

"Yes, thank you. Just a shock. I'll be fine." After accepting a drink of water, she left the tent and walked slowly down the hillside path. The sergeant's words echoed in her head— "We can only hope your husband was with them."

Near the bottom of the path, she stopped when she noticed she was still clutching the money the sergeant had given her. She opened the two top buttons of her housedress and tucked the rubles inside her brassiere. She wished Gregory could see how well she was managing on her own. Aagh! What was the use? He obviously didn't worry about how she managed. If he did, he wouldn't have joined the army. She immediately felt bad for thinking ill of him when he could be injured or dead on a battlefield. "Come back to me, darling," she said, under her breath.

As she headed to her tent, she remembered how taken she'd been with Gregory. The way he walked, his steps determined, as if he knew where he was going in life and there was no holding him back. And his warm brown eyes, how they shone and creased when he said something comical or when he teased her. She couldn't stay mad at him for long. He knew that. He'd taken advantage of her good nature, she was sure of it. Why else would he have left her to care for their children on her own? He probably expected Hania would help, but that wasn't fair. A young girl shouldn't be tied down taking care of children. That would come soon enough.

When she reached the tent, she had to put further thought aside. Eudokia was crying to eat again.

Word of the Russian army's disaster at Lutsk spread. The Tsar had taken charge of the military and the losses were mounting.

As time went on, grumblings about the army's failure increased. Complaints could be heard throughout the camp.

"What does he know about combat? He's led a pampered life."

"They're being sent to battle without a proper meal."

"They don't have enough guns, can you imagine? What kind of army is that?"

"The right hand doesn't know what the left hand is doing."

All the complaining did nothing to ease Lukia's mind. Knowing Lutsk had fallen, she couldn't stop imagining Gregory lying in a ditch, wounded. But she'd remind herself that he'd shared the food she'd made for him with his fellow soldiers. Surely his generosity would give him an advantage should anything go wrong. If he was injured, his brothers-in-arms would take care of him. It was small comfort in the hole of despair created through gossip.

With no idea of when or if she'd see her husband again, Lukia tried to put all her focus on her children. She'd accumulated enough money to keep them fed at least until spring—if they were here that long. Mercifully, the fruits and vegetables at the local market were plentiful and cheap. As well, there were chickens to cook over a fire and pork hocks for hearty soups. And in the woods were wild pistachios ready for picking. Despite the available food, Lukia was still afraid of getting sick. Living in such close quarters meant that if a disease were to spread, there would be no hope.

It was all too much to bear, and yet Lukia couldn't let her children know her fearful thoughts. It would scare them further. At nights, she tossed and turned, dreaming the world was on fire. Everyone ran, pushing their way through the crowd, even stepping on each other's heels to get ahead. No one was safe from the explosions lighting up the sky. She saw her children running ahead, and then they disappeared through a door standing by itself on a high hill. She yelled but the door shut before she could get their attention. She tried to run toward them but each step took effort, as if she were walking through deep wet sand. One night, awakened by the horror of it, she found her body drenched in sweat.

"Mama," Hania whispered, "Mama, what's the matter?"

"Nothing," said Lukia, breathing fast. "Just a bad dream."

She reminded herself that bad dreams meant the opposite would happen. It was what she'd been told as a child, and it was what she told her children whenever they had a nightmare. But now she had doubts. She couldn't shake her sense of foreboding.

On one of her visits to the marketplace with Egnat and Ivan, Lukia found a farmer—a swarthy-looking bearded man dressed in a striped caftan—with a wagon-full of ripe watermelons. His crop was fresh and ripe, but he was charging so much that the men going to work at a nearby factory walked by without stopping. Even his two teenage sons were unable to convince anyone to buy. Lukia continued to watch from a few stalls over but nothing changed. She was surprised by how much he had left after the crowd had dispersed. Surely on such a hot day, he could've sold a few. As she continued to watch, a solution to her problems formed in her mind.

Lukia approached him. "Excuse me, sir. How much would you like for your watermelons?"

His face brightened. "How many would you like?"

"All that you have in your wagon."

"All? You want all of them?" He turned to his sons incredulously. The older one shrugged, indicating he was just as perplexed.

"Yes, all."

"You want to eat them?"

"No. I want to sell them."

The farmer's dark eyes widened at first and then softened. "You have only half the day left. What good will it do you if you can't sell them? And with thieves everywhere, they'll be gone before the sun rises."

She thrust her chin in the air. "Don't worry. I'll manage somehow. And please sir, since you expect me to be robbed, give me a fair price."

They didn't haggle long. In the end, Lukia bought the lot for half of what he could've got if he'd sold them one by one. It was still a gamble, though. She pushed the niggling thought away and promised the farmer that once his watermelons were gone, she would return the wagon. She saw him smile as he walked away, probably thinking she was a fool.

Once the farmer and his sons were gone, she said to Ivan and Egnat, "Take the bags of food home. Egnat, you stay in camp and cut some wood. Ivan, I want you to bring me back a sharp knife and a big plate. And hurry."

After Ivan had returned, she sliced a watermelon and arranged the pieces on a plate to put on the open wagon bed. The vivid red fruit looked appetizing in the late-afternoon sun. When the workers began streaming past on their way home from the factory, she pointed to the watermelon and hollered, "Boys! Cheap! Juicy!" Each piece was offered at a fraction of what an entire watermelon cost, but if each piece sold, the total would amount to more than the price of a whole watermelon.

The odd worker stopped and bought a slice. "Very tasty," a few remarked. "Sweet." Before long, others stopped to buy. Lukia was tickled her plan was working so well, but she realized she needed to keep her excitement in check. Her neighbouring sellers were giving her curious looks and she didn't want to annoy them, as they might object to a stranger doing so well in their midst. By the end of the day, she had sold all the watermelons, except for the best one, which she'd kept for her family.

Sure enough, the jealousy of the other sellers showed itself on the next market day in the sneers they gave her when she passed by. Lukia was afraid that one of them might be tempted to steal her fruit if she tried selling watermelons again. It didn't matter that "Thou Shalt not Steal" was a commandment they all followed and that men in these parts could have their hands cut off if they were found guilty of theft. Not wanting to push her luck, she stopped selling any more watermelons. Though lamenting she'd lost a way to make more money, she now had enough rubles to tide her family past spring. Maybe by then, they'd be on their way home.

Lukia's resourcefulness hadn't been overlooked in the camp. Soon after her success in the marketplace, a young woman—who wore her long auburn hair in a single braid down her back—approached her while she was rolling up the canvas window flaps of her tent one morning. Lukia had seen the woman before. At times she congregated with other Russian women not far from her tent.

"Good morning," said the young woman in Russian. "My name is Natasha."

"Pleased to meet you," said Lukia, replying in Russian as well. "I'm Lukia Mazurets."

"I heard you're a good businesswoman."

Lukia laughed. "I just did what I had to."

"Your skills would be good in the party. The Bolsheviks are looking for people with talents like yours to wrest control from the Tsar and his people."

"You're a Bolshevik?" Lukia regarded Natasha with more interest, as she'd never met one before. She considered them a godless bunch that wanted to overthrow the Tsar.

"Yes," said Natasha, standing up straighter. "Lenin says we never should've gone to war. We have more important matters to fight about at home."

Lukia nodded. "I agree with you. This war has given us nothing. It's only taken away the men we love. Is your father fighting for the Tsar?"

"No. He's supporting Lenin," Natasha said pointedly. "We farmers and workers have to stick together. Lenin believes we should all share in the motherland. He wants to redistribute large properties, so we all benefit, not just those born into rich households. The glory belongs to all of us."

Lukia wasn't sure how to respond. She was surprised the young woman was talking so openly about a party that was considered to be an enemy of the government. Though Lukia believed in more land for all—she and Gregory could certainly use more—she didn't believe in taking what wasn't hers. She also didn't want to get into a political argument with someone she didn't know, so she said diplomatically, "I know the Tsar has made a mess of things, but he has a firm grip on power."

"Not for long," said Natasha. "There's a growing movement. Lenin hopes we won't need a revolution, but if it keeps going this way . . ." She trailed off and looked back at the group gathered near her tent. Her mother, a heavyset woman with a cane, was beckoning her. "I'd better go, but think about what I said."

Natasha's words were unsettling. Lukia couldn't trust anyone who didn't believe in God. It was enough her country had been turned upside down with this war against the Germans and Austrians. Now this young woman was suggesting there was more trouble to come within their borders, from their own people. Feeling suddenly old, Lukia slumped down on a nearby stump. Oy Gregory, she thought. What will become of all of us?

The days blurred. Lukia spent them shopping, preparing meals, and washing clothes in the mountain stream nearby. Even so, her family's survival was always on her mind. A few weeks after her day at the market selling watermelons, she approached an officer and told him she'd sewn soldier uniforms prior to coming to the Caucasus and would be willing to sew more. He was glad to oblige and wasted no time bringing her several bolts of brown wool serge.

The mundane tasks did little to help her forget the desperate times they were living in. Others were of the same mind. To blot out their misfortune, for even a little while, families got together around a fire after supper to sing folk songs of love and remembered landscapes. At times, their songs would be accompanied by the banduras, violins, accordions, or tsymbaly. None of the Mazurets family had an instrument, but they had finely tuned voices—except for Ivan and Havrylo, who sang despite their off-key notes. When one of the musicians played a kolomayka, the children would be the first ones to dance. The boys attempted Cossack jumps, splits and turns, while the girls daintily spun around them. Michalko tried to coax his mother to join the circle, but Lukia was often too tired to get up from the crate she sat on.

No matter how much the music lightened Lukia's spirits during these evenings, her nightmares continued. In the daylight, she would console herself by interpreting her dreams as before. Anything negative had the opposite meaning. Someone crying in a dream meant joy was on its way. She had accepted this interpretation without question.

That was before there was war. Back then, war had been as far away as the moon.

THE DREADED SCOURGE

ON THE FIRST warm spring day, Lukia shook the perinas, one by one, outside the tent. Somehow, she and her children had survived the winter. Bits of dust and dried mud flew through the air, clouding her view for a few moments. She'd tried to keep their bedding clean but it was impossible in their crowded living arrangement. She considered washing the goose-feather-stuffed coverings in the river but realized that drying them would take too long in the damp weather.

Other women were also shaking out their bedding while their children ran around playing hide-and-seek or tag. The women's eyes looked deadened, work and worry taking its toll. Outside of the small group of soldiers who oversaw the campsite, there were few men around to help, or to provide comfort of any kind. Even the women who were willing to cheat on their men had few options, as the soldiers were young and more interested in girls who had recently reached puberty. The older women might as well have been living in a nunnery.

Besides loneliness, the unending days in camp also brought dread. Typhus was spreading. Already, two families had lost children, and one mother was lying in bed with chills and a fever. The government had resorted to taking away the deathly ill in wagons. Lukia had heard through rumours in the camp that the infected ones were thrown, still alive, into a pit to be buried. Their families never saw them again. She couldn't imagine having a child taken away, never mind one that was still breathing. She tried to banish the horrific thought by closing her eyes. When she opened them, she saw the tall cedars bordering the campsite. Their magnificence soothed her, but not enough to calm her fears.

Lukia knew the dreaded scourge came with dirt and poor ventilation. With that in mind, even though the morning was still chilly, she opened the outside tent flaps to let the fresh air in.

Hania approached and put her arm around her mother's waist. "Eudokia's asleep."

"Good. She likes when you sing to her."

"I'm going for a walk. I'll see if Oksana can come with me."

Lukia smiled. At least her children had found some companionship in the camp. "Go but watch out for those soldiers. I've seen how they look at you."

Hania laughed. "Mama, you have such an imagination."

Lukia's eyebrows drew together. "I'm not imagining. I can see what's going on. You forget I was young once, too. I know how men think."

"Don't worry so much," said Hania before walking off, her long brown braids glistening in the early light. Lukia's stomach twisted as she watched her daughter. At fourteen, she already had ample breasts on her slender body, and her swaying hips were those of a young woman. An innocent, she didn't know men got excited when they saw beauty like hers. Lukia didn't want to scare her about men's intentions, but she also wanted to keep her safe. When she was her daughter's age, she had also laughed at her mother's warnings. Fortunately, she'd found a good man.

While Eudokia slept under an icon of the Virgin Mary, Lukia made up the beds. Once she'd straightened the perinas, she looked at the beautiful icon and thought about home. It was the middle of the Great Lent with its seven weeks of fasting. In Kivertsi, she and her family would be asking one another for forgiveness before confession. And on Palm Sunday, they would receive willow branches at the end of the church service. She smiled when she remembered how her family would gently beat one another with the willows and chant, *I'm not hitting, the willow is hitting, in a week's time, it'll be Easter.*

She could almost smell the sweet saffron fragrance of the Easter bread. She would make four or five round and tall loaves of *paska* from soft dough, and then ask Hania to wash her face in the water used to rinse the bowls to make her skin beautiful—a practice and belief that had been passed down through the generations.

Following the Easter mass, the parishioners would form a circle in the churchyard with their covered baskets at their feet, and when the priest came around to bless the food with his censer, they would fold back their embroidered cloths to expose a golden loaf of paska decorated with birds, crosses or curlicues. There were also *pysanky*—raw blown eggs dyed and decorated with traditional patterns and colours—*kybassa* with its powerful garlic smell, a large square of butter with a cross on top made of whole cloves, a dish of horseradish, and boiled eggs coloured by beet and other vegetable dyes.

Afterwards, the family would gather around the table, say the Lord's Prayer, and take a piece of a blessed peeled egg that had been cut in as many pieces as family members. And after they'd clinked their glasses of vodka and supped at a table laden with all Lukia could afford to make, they'd pass around the coloured boiled eggs.

She smiled when she remembered how Egnat always made sure he got the strongest egg. He would take one from the bowl and test its shell with his teeth. When he was satisfied, he would hit his tato's egg with his egg and say, "Christ is risen." Gregory would reply, "Indeed He is risen." Others around the table would follow suit, cracking eggs with each other. Somehow Egnat had a knack for picking one that would survive all the abuse. At the end of the family's egg cracking, he'd hold up his unbroken egg and gloat.

These memories fuelled her, gave her hope she'd celebrate this joyous time again with her family. Putting aside her dread of what was to come, she stacked their sheepskin coats and felt-lined boots in the corner of the tent. She was thankful she'd brought them, even though Gregory had been right about the Caucasus. It was warmer than Siberia, but there had been weeks when the temperature dipped below the freezing point. Their breath had come out in wispy strands of soft white, painting the air. The dampness had chilled their bones, and they'd gone to bed with fur hats on their heads, their bodies fully clothed under their perinas.

Though the weather had improved, the camp conditions had not. With the spring thaw, there were now more people at death's doorstep. The mother who'd been lying ill with typhus had died. Lukia had seen two soldiers, with cloth masks over their mouths, go into her tent and carry out her body. Her small children cried on an elderly woman's shoulder. Would the old woman be next? And then what would happen to her grandchildren? The horror of such a scene couldn't be shaken, not with daily news of someone else being struck down.

A few days later—as if Lukia's thoughts had been a premonition—Egnat went out to get a pail of water and returned pale and trembling. Ivan was by his side carrying the empty pail in one hand and supporting his brother with the other.

"Mama," said Ivan, "Egnat's sick."

Lukia felt Egnat's forehead. Just as she'd feared, it was hot.

"Oy, son," she said, her voice cracking. "You're shaking."

He looked as if he might fall any moment. She put her arm around him and took a quick look outside the tent to see if anyone was watching. She hoped no one had noticed Egnat's weakened condition. If they had, they might alert the death wagons. Her chest tightened. There was no way anyone was going to take her boy.

"I'll get him into bed," she said to Ivan. "You take the pail and get some cold water from the river. And get Hania. She took Eudokia for a walk around camp."

With fright on his face, Ivan left without saying a word. Lukia helped Egnat lie down. "Does anything hurt?" she asked.

"My head." Egnat coughed into the pillow—a deep, rattling cough. Shivering, he whimpered, "It feels like needles going in and out."

"My poor son. Let me take off your clothes. I need to boil them. I want to make sure whatever has stuck to you will have an easier time leaving." She feared he had typhus, the ghetto's disease, but there was no one to ask. No one she could trust. After undressing Egnat, she took the perina off of him.

"Mama, I'm cold."

"I know," she said in a measured tone, hiding her dread. She pulled a nightgown from the trunk. "This is clean. It will have to do." Once Egnat was dressed, she poured a cup of water from a pitcher and put some to his lips. "Take a little at a time. This will help bring your fever down."

She looked out the opening and saw Hania running to their tent with Eudokia bouncing in her arms.

"Ivan told me," said Hania. "I came as fast as I could."

"Good girl." With her daughter's help, Lukia changed their sleeping arrangements. They made a bed for Egnat on one side of their cramped quarters, to keep his bedding from touching that of his brothers and sisters. The terror of getting what Egnat had filled Lukia's mind. She could see the same terror on her daughter's face.

When Ivan returned from the river and learned he'd be lying next to Havrylo, he wasn't happy. "He kicks at night."

"Never mind," said Lukia. "Better a few bruises than a sickness like Egnat's." She then told the children to keep quiet about their brother if they didn't want him carried off.

"I won't let anyone take Egnat," Michalko whimpered. "I'll punch whoever comes."

"No one is taking him," said Lukia sternly. "We just have to be quiet and not tell anyone he's sick, understand?"

Michalko nodded as the other children looked gravely at their listless brother, who was usually the strong one.

Seeking solace, Lukia got down on her knees in front of the Virgin Mary icon. "Blessed are you among women and blessed is the fruit of your womb, for you have given birth to the Saviour of our souls. Reject not our prayer in our trouble but deliver us from harm. Amen."

Lukia's mother had brought the icon back from a pilgrimage to the cathedral and monastery at Pochaev. It was the place where, centuries before, a couple of monks had seen the Mother of God standing on a stone encircled by flames. Thereafter, a few miracles were recorded. The Mazurets family could use one now.

Several days went by with no relief. Egnat continued to suffer from a fever and chills. Lukia kept the door open for fresh air but closed it whenever she saw the oxen-drawn death wagons approaching. Her palms sweated and her heart pounded until they'd passed. Every day, the carts were heaped higher with both the dead and the nearly dead. The sound of metal wheels hitting the loose stones on the road sent shivers up her back. She feared not only for her son, but also for the other children, especially Eudokia. She was eight months old and healthy, but her belly button infection had taken its toll. Lukia didn't think her baby was strong enough yet to weather an illness as bad as typhus.

A day later, the dreaded thing happened. A death wagon stopped at their tent. When Lukia opened the canvas flap, being careful not to open it too wide, she saw at least fifteen to twenty people crowded in the wagon. Some were dead, others were scarcely clinging to life. The driver, a grim-looking man in a long overcoat and worn cap, stepped down from his seat and approached Lukia, who stood in the entrance with her legs apart and her arms folded, ready for a fight.

He took off his cap. "Good day, Madam."

Lukia tried to keep her lips from trembling as she said, "Why are you stopping? What business do you have here?"

"One of your neighbours said you have a child infected with typhus."

"The neighbour's mistaken," said Lukia. "It's true I have a sick child, but it's just a bad cold. He also ate something bad and it has to work through his system. He'll be all right in a day or two."

The man narrowed his eyes. "You know you're taking a risk. If he has typhus, you could all get sick."

"I tell you. My son's sickness is nothing to worry about."

"Let me see."

Lukia moved her body to fill as much of the entrance as possible. "Do you have some document that says I have to let you in?"

The driver looked back at his assistant, who was seated at the front of the wagon. The assistant shrugged. The driver turned back to her and said, "No, I have none, but I hope you're right for your sake and your family's."

Once the wagon had moved on, Lukia fell apart. She shook violently. Her legs and arms refused to stay still. She couldn't get the picture of all the sick and the dead out of her mind. Had she made a mistake? To protect her son, had she put them all in danger?

Michalko, who was seven and had been playing nearby, came running up to his mother. "Mama, did that man want to take Egnat away?"

She took a deep breath to calm herself before answering, "Yes, Michalko. He did, but I wouldn't let him." She hugged him. "Egnat will get better. Go and play with Havrylo. I'll call you when supper is ready."

After Michalko had run off, she went back into the dimly-lit tent. She wanted to scream to heaven, Haven't we had enough? What more do you want from us? But she didn't want to distress Egnat, who was half-awake. Lukia bit her lip to keep from crying. This was no time for tears.

Lukia spent the early evening laying cool damp cloths on Egnat's forehead, trying to bring the fever down. He tossed in obvious discomfort and spoke gibberish.

She lay beside him and stroked his hair. "It's okay, son. You're dreaming. Mama's here." While soothing him, she thought of how much she'd come to rely on him for support. He'd never let her down, even though he was only eleven.

Egnat's hollow eyes opened and he looked intently at his mother. "I saw Jesus. He called me. He was standing by a cherry tree with his arms wide open. I don't know what he was saying."

She swallowed. "He was probably saying, You'll be all right."

Comforted, Egnat nodded off.

Just outside the tent, Hania cried out. "Mama!" Lukia braced herself. Why was her daughter being so loud?

The tent flap—closed to keep the neighbours from spying—was suddenly pushed open.

"Hania! What are you doing?" said Lukia sharply. How could that girl be so insensitive? What if someone saw the sickness inside?

"Why are you yelling, woman?" asked someone gruffly.

It took a moment for Gregory's voice to register. Lukia stared, wide-eyed, at her husband as he entered the tent. With dark circles under his eyes, he looked both tired and older. He was dressed in a khaki wool coat and held his sheepskin hat in his hand. Her hand flew to her chest. "Is that you, husband? Am I dreaming?"

"Who else were you expecting?" he said with a grin.

"Gregory." Lukia almost stumbled as she stood up. He put his arms around her. She inhaled his familiar smell, now mixed with dirt and what she assumed was the odour of embedded fear. She stepped back and held his hands—rough and dirty from his time in the trenches—revelling in the fact he was standing in front of her. "I can't believe it. You're alive. Thanks be to God. Your guardian angel has been at your side. How come you're here?"

"We're stationed not far from your camp. We've been fighting the Turks."

"Oy, the Germans weren't enough?"

"I go where I'm sent."

She shook her head and sighed. "You don't know what trouble we've had." She directed his gaze to Egnat, lying in the corner. Gregory took one look at his eldest son and his face blanched.

"To see you all like this . . ." He choked on his words as he glanced at their cramped quarters. He then knelt by his son and stroked his forehead. "How long has he been like this?"

"About four days," said Lukia. She placed her hand on her husband's back. She was grateful he was here to share the burden, if only for a short time.

He lifted up his son's nightdress, exposing the rash covering his arms and chest. Gregory moaned at the sight.

Egnat opened his eyes, but it wasn't clear whether he recognized who was leaning over him.

"I've seen lots like this," said Gregory, in a low voice. "We've lost many to this disease. Can't help it. Rats and lice. It's these damn conditions. We have to take him to the river. It will cool him even more. Maybe the fresh water will clean him better than we can in this filthy place."

Lukia gripped her husband's arm. "We can't let him be seen. The neighbours told the officials Egnat was sick and they've already come by with a rack to take him away. I stopped them, but the next time I might not be able to."

Gregory's brow creased. "In that case, we'll have to cover him up and wait until sundown."

"Yes, after everyone's turned in for the night."

He gazed into her eyes. "Wife, you've aged."

"And you haven't?" she said, teasingly. She caressed the wrinkles on his deeply tanned face, the lines on it dark, as if etched with dirt.

His jaw stiffened. "It's this goddamn war."

"I know. Are you here to stay?"

He shook his head. "Just for the night. When I asked one of the soldiers if you were here, he pointed out your home."

"Home? Ha."

Gregory's face softened. "We are all suffering."

In the late evening, after the camp had grown quiet, Lukia and Gregory dressed Egnat in women's clothing and put a babushka on his head. His face was barely visible and if sighted, could be mistaken for a woman's. Then Gregory peered out the tent opening. Satisfied there was no one around, he and Lukia left Hania with the other children and half-carried Egnat to the water's edge.

While they were bathing him in the cool, clear water, they were startled by two women from a nearby village. They'd come to the river to wash some sheets. Lukia and Gregory were further surprised when the older villager, with hair as black as coal and wearing a brightly coloured skirt, came over to them and said in Ukrainian, "Your son has the ghetto's disease, doesn't he?"

At first Lukia didn't know what to say, but since the woman spoke kindly and seemed unafraid she said, "Yes. We're trying to bring his temperature down."

"Bend him over and let him get rid of the poison."

The woman spoke with authority, so Lukia and Gregory did as she suggested. The villager even helped them get Egnat down on his knees. She then pushed his head gently down so that he began gagging. It wasn't long before Egnat threw up all over himself and the stranger.

"Good," said the woman, rinsing her skirt in the lake. She wrung the fabric out as best she could. "Now take him home and give him *romyanyk* and a jigger of vodka."

Lukia knew about the chamomile herb with the yellow flower and its medicinal properties but had never heard it was a help with typhus. She wondered if her mother would've recommended it had she been here. "We're from the camp. I have no vodka and as for romyanyk, I don't know where to find it."

"Wait here. I don't live far. I'll get you what you need." Picking up her skirts, the villager ran off; her friend stayed behind.

Lukia and Gregory washed their son with a clean cloth which they had to keep rinsing and wringing. When the older woman returned, she handed Lukia a clean rag with the chamomile herb wrapped in it and a small sealer partly filled with vodka. "Make some tea with it, and don't forget to also give him a jigger of vodka. Keep him covered and check his face in the middle of the night. If he has red cheeks, a red nose, and a red chin, he's your son. If not, bid him farewell."

Lukia choked back tears before thanking the woman for her trouble. Clutching the cloth with the romyanyk, she helped Gregory support Egnat on his walk back to their tent. Once he was settled, they covered him with a light perina. Lukia kept vigil through the night. For the first few hours, Egnat lay listless, but then he asked his mother for another sip of the chamomile tea and alcohol.

As they waited for some sign of recovery, Lukia and Gregory talked about their time away from each other. They spoke quietly so as to not disturb their other children. Lukia knew she and her husband should've been resting as well, but the time they had together was so precious and so little.

She was horrified to hear how badly the Russian troops had fared—they'd lost tens of thousands of men to the enemy. And Gregory was delighted to hear of the Romanov daughter's tending to his baby. "You see, Lukia, they're not all bad."

"Ha. One good deed doesn't make up for all the years they collected gold and jewels while their countrymen starved."

Gregory groaned. She knew this was one matter they'd never agree on, so she left the subject of the Tsar and his family and talked instead of her life in the camp. The hours went by, and she fought to keep her eyes open.

"Go to sleep," said Gregory. "I'll watch him for you."

"You're tired, too. Anyhow, how can I sleep with how things are?"

"Go. I insist. I slept a little already."

She frowned. "When?"

"You don't think I'm capable of watching our child?'

She was too exhausted to argue, and soon fell into a deep sleep. When she awoke, it was daybreak. She looked over and saw Gregory grinning. She rushed over to Egnat and pushed aside the perina to see his face. His cheeks were red and so were his chin and nose.

"Mama," said Egnat, his eyes open and bright. "I'm hungry."

Tears of joy caught in her throat. "My son," she said, fondling his hair. "You are my son." Then she looked outside at the cloudless blue sky, crossed herself and said, "Thank you for your mercy. Thank you for sparing Egnat."

"Don't thank God," said Gregory. "Thank the old woman."

"When did you become such a heathen?" said Lukia sharply. "Who will protect you in battle?"

"I'll protect myself or my fellow soldiers will protect me."

She frowned and was about to snap back when Egnat said, "Mama, I want something to eat."

"Of course you do," she said and turned to Ivan, who was waking up. "I need you to go to the market and get some hollow buns."

"What?" said Gregory. "You have nothing to feed him?"

"He hasn't eaten for so long I'm afraid what I have will make him constipated. I don't want to take a chance."

"Why can't Hania go?" asked Ivan, stretching.

"I want Hania to wash all these clothes and bedding in the river before it infects the rest of us."

In short order, Ivan was back with several buns. Lukia gave one to Egnat along with a glass of milk. When he asked for more, she said, "You have to eat slowly."

"Tato," said Egnat, "I thought I had dreamt you."

"No, son, I'm here but I'm afraid I have to go now."

Egnat made a face. "Will you come back soon?"

"I hope so." Gregory gave Egnat a hug. He kissed Eudokia lightly as she slept and then kissed Lukia, who clung to him longer than usual.

"When will I see you again?" she asked.

"Pray to your god. Maybe he has the answer."

She pursed her lips. "Gregory. Don't be like that."

"Stay well, my darling."

Her heart lurched as she watched him walk away then stop and kiss his other children: the younger boys, who were playing around the campsite, and Hania, who was on her way back to their tent, her hands full of wet washing. At least, she thought, he's seen all of us one more time.

Gregory was scarcely out of sight when the driver of the death wagon—loaded with dozens of the dead and dying—came around again. This time, Lukia smiled and said, "My son is eating already. See how mistaken you were."

The driver raised his eyebrows. "Good to hear." He tipped his cap as he drove away.

After the wagon with all the cursed had left, she looked into the distance, in the direction her husband had gone. She couldn't believe he'd just been with them. He had come and gone like some apparition. Her body ached for him. He'd reached for her in the middle of the night, but she'd been too tired to respond. And now he was gone. Would she see him again? Oy, Gregory, what madness is this?

News from Home

A PRIL'S SUNSHINE BROUGHT renewed hope. After the soggy ground had dried, Lukia and Hania aired their bedding on a boulder that hadn't been claimed by others. Eudokia slept, wrapped in a perina, near a blossoming cherry-plum tree. Lukia knew the tree's pink star-like flowers fluttering in the breeze would keep her baby amused if she awoke.

The boys had escaped their chores and run off to play. Back on the farm, Lukia would've kept better track. There, with few distractions, temptations rarely got in the way of their helping. But here, there were other children frolicking, soldiers with guns to admire, and the odd musician sitting out in the open fiddling or striking the tsymbaly.

It lifted her heart to know her sons were having fun in such dismal circumstances but she fretted about their schooling. It had been almost a year since the oldest three were in class. Egnat had turned eleven before Christmas, Ivan was going to be ten in another month and Michalko was now seven. Michalko should have started school the previous fall, but with the war he never got a chance. She wasn't as concerned about Hania. School wasn't as necessary for her. She'd get married someday, have children to raise and a husband and home to manage.

When Lukia and Hania had finished tidying up, they sat on the boulder and watched others at work or chatting about the latest rumours. Though Lukia had little time for friends in camp, she worried about Hania. Her one friend, Oksana, was already chasing young soldiers. It wouldn't be long before Hania was pursued by some suitor. Although still a girl, she'd been receiving her monthly since she was twelve, making her vulnerable.

As if fate was already bent on teasing her, Lukia noticed a young man—tall and reed-thin with fair hair—walk by and look at Hania with interest. By his demeanour and stature, he appeared to be older than Hania by a couple of years. Thinking of his age reminded Lukia that Hania's birthday had come and gone with little ceremony, when Egnat was sick. She felt bad about that, but she knew her daughter, being the forgiving type, wouldn't hold it against her. The young man turned and gave Hania a second look. Her daughter didn't see, as her eyes were closed, her head tilted toward the sun.

She was glad her daughter hadn't seen the tall stranger eyeing her. There would be time enough for flirtations down the road. She shuddered when she saw how Hania's breasts pushed against her thin cotton shirt. Her daughter was bound to be big-breasted just like her, another asset that would attract men like flies. Soon, she'd have to have a talk with Hania about men and how to handle them. She'd have to tell her how to defend herself. Especially the ones who might brush up against her as if by accident.

She would also have to sew Hania some new clothes, with room for growth. Lukia had packed a few meters of red-white-and-black-checked traditional cloth to make her daughter a beautiful skirt—red for the sun, white for the light, and black for the night—as well as some plain white linen for a new shirt. With no farming to do and the soldiers' uniforms finished, maybe she'd even have time to sew something new for herself.

Lukia stared once more at the young man, who'd stopped to talk to a soldier just beyond the cherry-plum tree.

Hania opened her eyes and looked in the direction of the tree, where Eudokia lay sleeping. "She's never slept so long."

"It's all this fresh air." Lukia then noticed Hania and the young man exchange a glance. "Hania, do you know that young man over there? He keeps looking this way."

"Oh, that's Bohdan Pilutik. You know his parents."

Lukia blinked in surprise. "They're here? When did they get here?"

"This week. I thought you knew."

"I didn't know. Where are they staying?"

Hania pointed to an area across from them. "They're on the other side."

"We'll have to call on them." Lukia looked over at Bohdan again. "He's grown. I remember a little *smarkach*."

Hania's mouth fell open. "Mama, how can you call him that? He's hardly a snot-nosed kid. He's seventeen."

"How do you know?"

Hania shrugged. "I think I heard it."

"The way he's looking at you . . . Is he a nice boy?"

"I don't know," Hania said, sounding irritated. "He's all right."

"Why are you upset?"

"I'm not," Hania said tersely.

Lukia moaned quietly and wondered what her daughter was keeping to herself.

With no church in the vicinity, Lukia had taken to praying in their tent before she left for the market on Sunday. Back home, no one would even consider going to a market on the Lord's day of rest—of course, none would be open—but here, amid non-Christians, she had to put aside her feelings and go, as this was the best day to attend.

There was the usual hustle at the bazaar with Christians, Muslims, and Jews haggling over the cost of food and other household goods. Beside their makeshift stands, adults watched over their produce and wares while younger family members held on to their goats, which were for sale as well. The sellers were mostly Muslim, young and old men with beards dressed in colourfully-striped caftans or shirts with pants. They all wore some fashion of head covering—peaked newsboy caps, wide-brimmed felt hats, white scarves wrapped low on their foreheads, tall sheepskin Cossack hats, or embroidered black headgear that hugged their skulls.

Though the sellers were aggressive, the offerings were poor compared to what they'd been when Lukia had first arrived in the region. Of course, it'd been late summer then; fruits and vegetables were in abundance. After buying some cabbage and potatoes, she stopped at a shop that sold staples. She asked for sugar, but the vendor, an elderly man with a long white beard, said that none was available

"When do you expect to get some?" asked Lukia. Her children would be disappointed if she couldn't make fruit compote or rice pudding. The shortage could also mean that the Red Cross wouldn't be handing out sweet biscuits to the refugees, a treat that made camp life more bearable.

"Not soon," he said, chewing tobacco. "It's so bad the people in Bogorodsk rioted."

"Where is that?"

He spat out his tobacco. "It's in the bush country, north of Moscow." Dark brown remnants clung to the few blackened teeth he still had in his mouth.

"Who told you?"

"A soldier. He heard the news through the wireless. Several thousand people were involved. Some of the crowd threw stones, broke shop windows and then went into the shops and stole the goods."

"Terrible."

"The police had to call the Cossacks to get the people under control. Two men were killed and three more were seriously injured."

Her brow tightened. "Oy. Isn't it enough that our soldiers are fighting?"

"Yes. While they're away fighting, the peasant kulaks who avoided conscription took over their land and raised the prices on their crops. Greed, that's what it is."

"What you say is true, but what can we do?"

He shrugged. "Come back next week. Maybe then I'll have sugar.

Sugar she could live without; there was still honey. But if bread-making ingredients became scarce, what then?

After unloading her market purchases in the tent, Lukia tramped up the hill to the military tents overlooking the refugees' site. She peeked into Captain Krylow's tent and was pleased to see his familiar face.

He looked up from his papers. "Can I help you?"

"Captain Krylow, I'm Panye Mazurets. I came to see you in September about my promissory note."

He grinned. "Ah, yes. You don't have another one, do you?"

She shook her head and smiled. He was a handsome one with his neat moustache, but she'd never been attracted to a man other than Gregory. Even now, after having been on her own for so long. "I hear the war still isn't going well. Is there any more news from Lutsk?"

He leaned back. "Archduke Josef Ferdinand of Austria has made the city his military headquarters."

"I had hoped . . ." She felt a sudden sharp pain in her forehead.

"I know. We had hoped too."

She took a few deep breaths. "Our village is near Lutsk, what's left of it. If it's been taken by the enemy what chance do we have of going home? What will happen to our farm?"

"We're doing the best we can. Right now, it's hard to say."

"We have a deed. Surely that would be honoured."

"That could help, but in war there are no guarantees."

The words "no guarantees" echoed in her mind. What did anyone in command care about the farmers, whose fields were being shelled and run over by tanks and heavy army boots? Farms could be lost forever. Young men, fighting to keep the land, were being sacrificed on bloody fields as if they were only pawns in a chess game. Would their deaths amount to nothing?

Lukia wrung her hands. "I'm also worried about my mother. She lives in Galicia, in the Carpathian Mountains. Is she safe there?"

"Is she on the side of the Austrians?" he asked, with a scowl.

"She's eighty-one, hardly a threat. She can't help where she lives." She didn't tell the captain her mother lived with her brother, for fear of the questions that might raise. She didn't want her brother to be named an enemy of Russia. She hadn't seen Pavlo since the war started. Who knew where his loyalties lay.

The captain hesitated. He seemed to be weighing his answer. "The Austrians have recaptured Galicia. It's quiet there now."

"Thank you," she said in a voice just above a whisper. She didn't know whether to be relieved or not.

As she walked back to her family's campsite, she felt as though a great weight had descended on her. Her husband, mother, and brothers were somewhere far away, caught in the fight. Would she and her children ever leave this godforsaken place? Would any of them come out of this war alive? Would Gregory, her love? With Lutsk damaged and under enemy control, she suspected her village was also occupied by the Germans or Austrians. She couldn't lose her beloved farm. It was all she had to keep her family from starvation. She suppressed a sob when she saw a mother, just ahead, scolding a little girl for playing in the mud. Where else was the girl supposed to play?

A Surprise Christening

A FTER ANOTHER RESTLESS night, Lukia woke up lamenting she had no adult to lean on for support. She'd hoped to befriend her sister-in-law Katerina Mazurets, who had arrived with her baby a few months after Egnat recovered from typhus. They were from the same village. Katerina had married Fedor, Gregory's younger brother and even though the two women hadn't formed a close bond prior to the war, Lukia hoped they'd get along better now that their husbands were both in the Tsar's army.

However, she hadn't counted on Katerina's melancholia, which had emerged after she gave birth and showed no signs of letting up. In the beginning, Lukia had taken food to her sister-in-law—beet borscht or cabbage soup—but no matter how many overtures she made, Katerina kept to herself. It didn't help that the soldiers had put her in a tent at the other end of camp; days went by without them seeing each other.

It therefore came as a shock when Lukia walked out of her tent that August morning to find Katerina standing by the door. She was wearing a wrinkled housedress and lace-up black boots; her brown hair was uncombed and the sweater over her dress improperly buttoned.

"Good morning, Katerina. I'm surprised to see you. Where's Stepan?"

"My neighbour is watching him." Katerina held her hand to her chest and took a few deep breaths.

Lukia's brow furrowed. "What's happened?"

"One of the soldiers told me an Orthodox priest is coming to visit today. Maybe he could baptize Stepan. What do you think?"

"Why not? It's time your son was baptized." Lukia was relieved. Her sister-in-law might be depressed, but she had enough wits to consider her son's soul. "It's wonderful the priest is making the rounds," said Lukia. "Maybe I'll also get a chance to confess my sins."

Katerina looked around. "Is Hania here?"

"She's picking blueberries. Why?"

"I'd like her to be Stepan's godmother."

"It would be an honour."

Katerina smiled. "Good. I'm going to ask Bohdan's mother if her son can be godfather. Please tell Hania to get ready."

As Katerina hurried back to her tent, Lukia grabbed a shawl and, seeing that Havrylo and Eudokia hadn't woken yet, left quietly. She found Egnat nearby, talking to one of the soldiers. He was holding the soldier's pistol and waving it around. Lukia shivered involuntarily as she witnessed her son's pleasure at holding a firearm. Why did boys and young men glamorize warfare? It wasn't a game and yet she knew that one day, if there was another war, she would be powerless to stop Egnat from enlisting, just as she'd been unable to stop Gregory.

"Egnat," yelled Lukia. "Go get Hania. She's down by the river, in the blueberry patch with Ivan. Tell her to come home and get dressed. Auntie Katerina wants Stepan baptized today, and she wants your sister to be godmother. The priest is on his way and she has to be ready when he gets here."

Egnat handed the soldier back his gun. "Maybe I can try it later."

Shaking her head, she said, "Yes, maybe, so you can shoot yourself in the leg."

"I'm not crazy," said Egnat, laughing. "I won't shoot myself." He smiled at the soldier as though he were a friend. "My mother always worries."

"Only when you do stupid things," said Lukia. As if she didn't have enough on her mind. Now she had a son who was fascinated by guns.

The christening took place near the cherry-plum tree by Lukia's tent. Besides Katerina, her baby, the godparents, and Lukia and the rest of her children, there were a few others—Bohdan's mother, an elderly man, and several older women.

The ceremony was rudimentary, as there was no font of holy water. The priest— a robust man with a neatly trimmed beard— had brought a flask of water blessed during the Feast of Jordan.

The priest turned to Katerina, who was holding Stepan. "Please give the child to the godmother."

Trembling, Katerina handed Stepan to Hania, who struggled to keep the child's muslin slip from riding up his plump legs. Hania leaned the baby's head back while the priest anointed his forehead with oil in the shape of a cross and sprinkled blessed water over his hair. Fortunately for both Hania and Bohdan, the infant was quiet and seemed to revel in the attention.

During the ceremony, Lukia was startled to see Hania and Bohdan exchange an amorous look. She hoped it was nothing but puppy love, which rarely amounted to anything. Everyone knew it was bad luck for godparents to fall in love with one another, and to marry was a sin.

When the christening was over, about thirty people lined up in front of the priest to seek forgiveness for their sins. The priest sat on a chair a soldier had brought down from the officers' tent. One by one, the penitents knelt on the hemp rug in front of the priest. He covered their heads with his long gold brocade scarf, bent under the fabric to hear their confessions and then, with his hand on their crowns, asked God to forgive their sins.

The annual confessions never took long, and for that, Lukia was grateful. She'd heard Catholics had to mention every sin they'd committed—if they forgot any, back they went. She was sure that would take all day.

When it was Lukia's turn, the priest bent under the cloth and said in a low voice, "What is your name?"

"Lukia Mazurets."

"When was the last time you were in confession?"

She had to think. It seemed so long ago. "Before the war, in Kivertsi."

"And have you sinned since the last time you asked for forgiveness from Our Lord?"

"Yes, Father, I've sinned."

"Are you sorry for your sins?"

"Yes, Father, I am sorry."

Then he asked God to forgive her and made a sign of the cross over her head.

Lukia wondered if the priest would've said more if he'd known what she was truly guilty of. There'd been many times since she left Kivertsi when she wished her countrymen would kill enough Germans and Austrians so she could go home. She didn't care how many, as long as she could have her husband back. Was wanting someone dead during wartime as big a sin as wanting them dead during peacetime? After some deliberation, she concluded it was probably a sin either way.

UNDER SIEGE

O NE AFTERNOON WHEN Lukia was at the well by the camp, she heard gunfire in the distance. Her sister-in-law, Katerina, who'd also arrived with her pail, looked in the direction of the shots.

"Oy," said Katerina, visibly shaken. "I thought we'd escaped all that."

"No one expected the war would last this long. We've been here two years already." Lukia lowered the bucket into the well. "I can't imagine having to move again."

"It's the Tsar's fault," said Katerina, her voice rising. "A neighbour told me one million of our soldiers have died, more than from any other country."

"One million?" Lukia remembered all the soldiers she'd seen in Lutsk, eager to fight. Were they dead now, lying bloodied and mangled far from their mothers? Was her Gregory among them? A lump formed in her throat and she gasped. She tried to push the terrifying images from her mind.

"He also said the men are short of rifles and bullets. He said hundreds of thousands of soldiers have defected."

"No! It can't be," Lukia said vehemently. "Our soldiers wouldn't run away." She thought again of her love and how willingly he'd thrown himself into the army.

"I tell you. They're running. Who can blame them. They don't have enough to eat. The railway is breaking down. The whole country's a mess."

Lukia pulled a bucket of water from the well. "Thank God our sons aren't old enough to fight."

"Yes. Thank God," said Katerina, crossing herself.

On her way back to her tent, Lukia passed two soldiers standing by the side of the path. Overhearing them talking about the Tsar, she stopped and pretended to tie her shoes.

"The Bolsheviks forced him to abdicate. Lenin is behind this. They're keeping the Tsar and his family in Alexander Palace."

For a moment, Lukia was immobilized. Then, worried that the soldiers would notice her eavesdropping, she hurried away.

The royal family was under house arrest. What could this mean for Gregory and the soldiers in the Tsar's army?

The news of the Romanov family under siege was disturbing. Ever since the Tsar's daughter nursed Eudokia back to health, Lukia had come to look upon the royals in a more positive light. Still, who could blame Russian workers for thinking otherwise? Young Russian men—sons, husbands, fathers, brothers—were sacrificing their lives and for what? Lenin said they were fighting an imperialist war. One royal family against another, just because the heir to the Austrian throne had been shot by some Serb. The Tsar had anticipated that siding with his Serbian ally would lead to an easy victory but he hadn't considered the enemy's modern machine guns. With breadlines in the news and no sign of the war ending, the citizens had revolted against him. Lukia wondered whose side Gregory was on now.

She hadn't seen her husband for over a year. If he had escaped death, was he lying somewhere in a hospital somewhere or had he been captured? It was bad enough living in these rootless primitive conditions, but to not know when the day-to-day nightmare would end was agony.

Putting aside her worries, Lukia set about cleaning the floor of the tent. The children had dragged in mud again. She grabbed the worn straw broom and swept what floor wasn't taken up with their bedding and belongings. Her thoughts turned back to Olga Nikolaevna and how she'd served admirably as a nurse on the trains. The royal had seen and heard the effects of war—the broken limbs, the seared minds, and the screams of pain. She'd been a help to many, yet knowing the Bolsheviks, who had nothing but scorn for the royals, Lukia doubted they'd be merciful.

With stories about the Tsar's family spreading around the camp like wildfire, Lukia decided to visit Bohdan's mother, Marusha Pilutik, a woman who made it her business to know what was going on. How she did, Lukia could only guess. Maybe she was intimate with the officers. In war, people acted in surprising ways. Lukia had never been disloyal to her husband, but then she had a good man. Hania had told her that Bohdan's father was the opposite, a quarrelsome man, who became violent when he drank.

Carrying a basketful of laundry, Lukia found Marusha at a river bend not far from camp. She was bent over scrubbing some towels, her blonde hair partly covered by a flowered babushka. With her girlish curves, she looked like a much younger woman—someone the soldiers would admire.

"Good day, Marusha. It's a good day for washing."

Marusha looked over her shoulder. "Ah, Lukia. I haven't seen much of you lately. You've been busy with that brood of yours."

"Yes, but not too busy to worry." Lukia took a few of her sons' shirts from her basket and dropped them in the shallows of the river. "Have you heard the news?"

"About our Tsar and Tsarina?"

"Yes," Lukia said, taking the soap out of her apron pocket. "Is it true? They're being held prisoner?"

Marusha nodded and swished her towels in the water. "What's to become of them? I thought once Rasputin was murdered—"

Lukia dropped the soap. "What? I hadn't heard this. What happened?"

"A noble shot him in the back. Prince Yusopov. The nobles were fed up with the way Rasputin conducted himself. He acted too much like a royal. Even though he was the Tsar and Tsarina's advisor, he wasn't for the war and talked against the Tsar behind his back. What's more, he had the Tsarina's ear, which many complained about."

"I know he was a problem," Lukia said, picking up the soap. She began scrubbing a shirt then stopped. "Is it true he raped a nun?"

"Yes. They say his sexual appetite was huge. You know what I would've done with him?" Marusha laughed as she twisted one of her towels into a rope.

Lukia chortled as well. "That would be too good for him."

"And he was supposed to be some kind of holy man, a mystic." Marusha clucked her lips. "He also drank like there was no tomorrow. He took bribes and got many of his friends elected to high government office. With the Tsar away leading the troops, he convinced the Tsarina to use her power."

"How sneaky of him." Lukia rinsed the soapy shirt in the river. "Still, I heard she couldn't thank him enough for saving her son's life. Poor boy, a hemophiliac, bleeding to death. But Rasputin cured him. It was a miracle."

"I know," said Marusha, arching her back. "A miracle."

Lukia looked up from her washing. "You know the Tsar's daughter saved Eudokia's life."

"Katerina told me. God bless Olga Nikolaevna."

Lukia gazed at a branch flowing downstream. "It's frightening. Their lives changed forever. What will the Tsar and Tsarina do now?"

"What can they do?" Marusha frowned. "She has only herself to blame. No one trusted her even before she got involved with

Rasputin. You know, she's German. And to take up with that mad man, what was she thinking? He was sucking at the teat of the rich, milking it for all he could get, and she couldn't see it. Not even the Tsar could control her."

Lukia harrumphed, "Some leader. He can't manage his home or his country." She watched Marusha gather her wrung-out laundry. "Have you heard any news about our men?"

"No, nothing. We must pray."

"Yes, we must."

Marusha stretched her arms in the air, took a deep breath and picked up her basket. Facing Lukia, she said, "I must tell you, your Hania is becoming quite a beautiful woman. A good catch for some young man. My Bohdan is obviously interested."

Lukia couldn't help but frown. "You know they're godparents for Stepan, so marriage is out of the question."

Marusha looked startled for a moment, then said, "What a shame. True love is not easy to find."

"I know, but what can we do?" Lukia groaned. "This war has been hard on our children. I hope this war is over before Bohdan is asked to face any of these horrors."

"Yes," said Marusha, sighing. "We have to hope." She then turned and lumbered up the grassy incline as if carrying a load twice its weight.

Upon returning to the tent, Lukia found Eudokia outside, picking pebbles off the ground; Egnat was sitting on a stump, whittling a stick.

"Are you watching she doesn't put them in her mouth?"

"Yes, Mama."

"Where's Hania? She should've been back from the market by now."

"I haven't seen her."

"Come, child," Lukia said to Eudokia, who needed no prompting.

In the tent, Lukia propped herself up against the pillows by the wall, took Eudokia in her arms, and pulled out her right breast. Her children's sucking over the years had taken its toll. Once large and firm, her breasts now sagged. She wondered if Gregory would still find her attractive when he returned from war. She hoped he would. If he didn't, she'd remind him that breasts were meant for feeding children.

As she watched Eudokia suck greedily, Lukia felt a surge of gratitude that this one had survived. Her boys were strong, too. She hoped they'd wouldn't become soldiers like their father, but Ukraine always seemed to be under some other country's thumb. Their land with its good earth was the envy of the countries bordering it. It had been like that when she was growing up, it was like that now, and the way it was going, it would be like that for generations to come. Over the centuries, it had been invaded by many.

How could Gregory support such an extravagant regime while he and his fellow farmers worried about survival? Foolish, foolish men. She clucked her tongue and told herself to stop dwelling on what she couldn't change.

Just then Hania burst into their tent, sobbing. She flung herself down on the perina beside her mother.

"What happened?"

Eudokia took a break from her mother's nipple and looked at Hania.

"I was so scared ... the Tatars ... said Hania, through her sobs. "They tried to take me."

Lukia's hand flew to her chest and she gasped. "Oy, child." She had been afraid of this. She'd seen the Tatars ride by the camp on their horses—swarthy young men yelling and laughing as if they were above the law. She put Eudokia down on the perina and buttoned up her shirt. "Where was this?"

Hania wiped her tears on her sleeve. "I was walking home from the market. I was by the woods, out in the open, and they came galloping behind me. One of them swooped down and tried to grab me. I dodged him and jumped into the ditch." She gulped. "I'm sorry, Mama, I dropped the eggs and milk."

"Eggs and milk we can buy anytime. But you, we can't." Lukia took Hania in her arms. "Shhh, don't cry. Next time, Egnat or I will go with you. We'll take a big stick."

"I hope I never see them again."

"You know what to do if one of them grabs you? A good strong kick to his apples and he'll let go, remember that. And yell like someone is killing you."

Hania smiled. "You know me, Mama. I have good lungs. I can scream with the best."

Lukia laughed. "Thank God for that."

With so many in camp, who would've thought the Tatars would be so bold? She'd heard of them kidnapping young women for brides. They were a nomadic tribe and known to have more than one wife. Her stomach churned with anger and regret. How could she have been so foolish to let Hania go alone? Her daughter would also have to be wary of the soldiers in camp. Though they were occupied with matters of war, they were still men with men's desires. It was up to each family to guard their own.

Given the Tatars' bold moves, Lukia decided there was no time to waste in telling her daughter about what was at stake. One bright spring afternoon, when her sons were fishing in the river and Eudokia was napping, Lukia sat down with Hania on a couple of crates outside their tent. A basket of clothes to be mended was between them.

"There seems no end to this mending," said Lukia, taking a pair of pants from the basket. She examined a leg seam. "Look at this. I don't know how Ivan keeps tearing his clothes. Good thing it's by the seam." She threaded some dark brown thread through the eye of her needle. "I don't know what I'd do without you. It won't be long before I'll have to get a broom to chase the boys away."

Hania snorted as she darned a sock. "You have nothing to worry about."

Lukia raised her eyebrows. "I'm not so sure. Look at the way Bohdan's been looking at you. And those Tatars! When I think—"

"I got away," said Hania, interrupting. "I'll be more careful next time."

"Good. You have to be. You have to hold on to your virginity. People can be cruel."

Hania bit her lip.

Lukia sensed her daughter's discomfort but the conversation was a necessary one. "Listen," she said, meeting her daughter's gaze to ensure she had her attention, "when I married your tato, it was a nice wedding. I wore myrtle in my hair. It meant I hadn't slept with my husband before I got married. Lots of villagers came and the night after the wedding party, they waited outside the house until we were finished. You know what I'm saying."

"Mama, I know what men and women do."

"I know you know but wait, I'm not finished. After your tato and I had sex, he had to take my white underskirt with the blood on it and hang it on the chimney. That way, the wedding guests could see he married a virgin."

Hania's face turned crimson. "How awful."

"Yes. But it's awful, too, if a man breaks a woman's hymen before marriage or he marries a woman who's been with another man. He wouldn't be able to look another man in the face. It's a shame on the whole family."

"Were you worried there'd be no blood?"

"Sure, I was worried. Sometimes the hymen gets torn through riding a horse or some other heavy activity, but I was fine."

"That was good."

"Hmm. Some friends didn't think so. They came from another village. When they saw my blood-stained skirt, they were afraid. They didn't know our tradition. They didn't come to the after-wedding lunch."

"What did they think, that Tato had stabbed you?"

Lukia chortled. "Maybe." She finished mending the seam and took the thread between her teeth to cut it.

"Will I have to go through this, too?"

Lukia put the pants down on her lap. "I know how people talk. If they find out a girl has slept with a boy before she marries him, they'll call her a whore."

"What about the boys?"

Lukia threw her hands up. "They have their own rules. Listen, boys will say anything to have sex. They'll even say they love you to get between your legs."

"Mama," said Hania. "Not every boy."

"Never you mind. Boys are boys. You have to be careful, not go off somewhere alone with a boy. Boys respect a girl who waits until she's married to have sex."

Hania didn't say anything, just stared into the distance. Lukia hoped her counsel had registered. It wasn't fair how it was, but that was life.

BULLETS FLY

ANOTHER WINTER PASSED and still there was no sign of peace on the horizon. The refugees heard only a constant rumble of dissatisfaction with the Tsar. In January there had been a fierce battle between Bolshevik fighters and Ukrainian troops in Lutsk. Up until that point, it had seemed as if they'd all been on the same side, fighting on behalf of the White Army.

Months later, on a July morning in 1918, another shock reverberated through the camp. It wasn't the rooster's crow that woke Lukia but the shouts of her neighbours. Half-asleep, she heard soldiers talking as they walked by.

"It's true. They shot them in cold blood. Lined them up and then . . . paff, paff, paff."

"The children, too?"

"Yes. The Bolsheviks showed no mercy."

Lukia's heart stuttered. Who were they talking about? The soldiers' voices faded. She quickly got dressed and went outside. A group of women stood near the iron grates where families often cooked their meals.

Marusha was already there with a sweater over her nightdress. She turned when she saw Lukia approach. "You've heard they've killed the Tsar and his family." Her tear-stained face showed her grief.

"What are you saying? All of them?"

"Yes, even young Alexei."

Lukia sucked in a breath. "My God! Why?"

"A soldier told me Lenin was afraid. With all the unrest in the country, he worried the Tsar would get too much sympathy and regain power. The Bolsheviks decided to not only kill the Tsar, but his whole family."

Lukia crossed herself. She found it hard to believe Olga Nikolaevna had perished as well. She was so kind, the way she'd treated Eudokia and reassured Lukia. Maybe she'd been spared; maybe the Tsar's daughter was still working on the trains.

Marusha's father, a bent-over man with a wrinkled face and grey moustache, hobbled over. "Look at that," he said. "Lenin was against the war and yet he used bullets to get his way."

"They even killed the Tsar's servants and doctor," said Marusha.

Lukia shook her head. "The Bolsheviks are supposed to be on the side of the workers."

"Maybe they panicked," Marusha's father said. "Men do crazy things when they're afraid. This is only the beginning. Lenin's not a fan of our people."

Out of the corner of her eye, Lukia spotted Natasha, the young Russian woman who'd asked her to join the Bolshevik party. She was standing on the other side of the fire pit with a few Russian women and a teenage boy. They seemed to be rejoicing—their talk was punctuated with laughter.

Lukia couldn't help but think that the Tsar had brought all this on himself. He didn't deserve to die, but he had sent the army into battle without proper arms and gas masks. The poison gas the Germans used was lethal.

Overwhelmed by the news, she dwelled on her husband's troubles. Gregory, as a member of the White Army, would now be targeted in the Bolsheviks' revolt against the Tsar and his followers. The killing of the Romanovs underscored the fact that no one was safe.

Each day, the rumblings grew louder. A treaty had been signed—Russia was out of the Great War, but still no word about when the refugees could return home. And there was no word about how much of the country Russia still controlled. The Great War might have ended, but a civil one had taken its place. The rumour was that different factions were trying to take power now that the Tsar was dead. The White Army—who had supported the murdered Tsar—was fighting against the Red Army, the godless Bolsheviks. The Whites had even managed to get the Cossacks to join their fight, but even with these fierce warriors by their side, there was no assurance of victory.

Those in camp were divided. You were either for the Tsar or for Lenin or for the Poles. As if that weren't enough, the Allies, the Polish forces, and the Ukrainian underground armies were also trying to stake out territory. Most shocking was the report from one of the soldiers that Ukraine had declared independence months before. Since the truth was unavailable, all anyone could do was entertain rumours and hope for the best.

With word spreading that the Bolsheviks had moved one of their fronts to the Caucasus, Lukia was afraid to venture far from camp, but the family had to eat and that meant she had to take her biweekly trip to the bazaar. The less-than-a-kilometer walk to the market wasn't long in normal times, but now that the enemy had shifted and the Bolsheviks were in the neighbourhood, the trek seemed endless. It was also arduous walking with a five-year-old and a three-year-old, who wanted to stop and pick up stones or watch butterflies land on wildflowers. She wished she could've left them behind, but the older ones had chores they couldn't do with the little ones underfoot.

As she trudged down the railway tracks with Havrylo on one side and Eudokia on the other, she stayed alert. Every dozen or so steps, she glanced to her right and then to her left. On each side of the tracks, the ditches were covered in long brush. Beyond was the forest. Good hiding places for men wanting to do harm. She also looked over her shoulder whenever she heard a sound she couldn't identify, imagining it as evidence the enemy was close.

They weren't even halfway to the market when gunfire exploded all around them.

It was as if all hell broke loose. Bullets and shouts pierced the air. She pushed her son and daughter to the ground and fell down beside them. Havrylo whimpered. Eudokia screamed. Lukia quickly put her hand over her daughter's mouth. "Be quiet!" she whispered in her ear. When she removed her hand, Eudokia sniffled and bit her lip to keep from crying out loud.

Lukia took off her large babushka and covered her children with it. Lying between them, she cuddled one under each arm. A pig came running seemingly out of nowhere and tried to get under the scarf. She sensed he was as terrified as she was but nudged him away. He refused to leave and stood close by, unsheltered.

Raising her head from under her babushka, Lukia tried to see where the shots were coming from. Half-hidden in the trees were the Bolsheviks on one side of the tracks firing at the White Army on the other. She recognized the fighters from the clothes they wore. The rebels were dressed like common workers—a mishmash of pants, shirts, and caps—whereas the Cossacks were decked out in worn khaki uniforms and white caps with a blue band around the crown.

When a flurry of bullets ricocheted off the trees, Lukia ducked back under her babushka. She hid just in time. The bullets skimmed over them, lifting her scarf. She could feel her children's hearts pounding through their shirts as they pressed against her body. She gasped several times, fear making it hard to breathe. She kept her head and her children's down, waiting for the shelling to stop. It was then that the pig farted in her face. She suppressed a laugh and wondered if God was playing a joke on her.

"He stinks!" said Havrylo quietly.

Eudokia held her nose. "Foo, pig."

"Shhh."

After what seemed like an eternity, an eerie silence enveloped them. It was as if all the animals and birds had taken flight, leaving behind only the trees, plants, and stones. Eudokia squirmed beneath Lukia's arm. Havrylo's leg twitched. Not entirely convinced that the soldiers had moved on, Lukia kept the children down with her arms while she raised her head slightly and scanned the tracks and the forest around them. There was no one. She breathed a sigh of relief. It took a few moments for her pulse to slow down and her body to stop shaking. They, along with the pig, had survived.

Lukia crossed herself. "They've gone. You can stand up now."

Havrylo and Eudokia disentangled themselves from their mother. Eudokia started crying and put her hands up. Lukia picked up her sobbing daughter. "It's nothing," she said, stroking her back. "Don't cry." The pig shook its head a few times, then wobbled away.

His face flushed and his chin puckered, Havrylo kicked at the stones by the tracks. He turned his back and Lukia could tell he was trying to be brave. "Havrylo, the worst is over."

She picked up her babushka and her eyes widened. She stifled a cry. Several bullet holes had pierced the flowers and leaves. They'd come so close to being shot. How much longer, God, she prayed silently. How much longer?

Still shaken, Lukia and her children arrived at the bazaar midday, when the crowds were at their peak. Various groups huddled at the edge of the marketplace talking loudly and with great emotion. She couldn't make out their language, but from the direction they pointed, she understood that they were reacting to the battle that had just taken place.

Lukia ventured on toward the sellers of household goods, handicrafts, animals, poultry, and produce. Their stalls were organized in rows on the rutted stony field. Horse-drawn carts jockeyed for position with cows and sheep brought in for sale. The farm-sized area was an ideal setting for a marketplace as the land wasn't much good for anything else. In comparison to other visits she'd made with the children, she found this one easier. Having been frightened, they stayed close to her for a change. It was a good thing, as she was so rattled she might've resorted to spanking if they'd strayed.

After walking past a number of stalls, they stopped by two men standing by a pen of chickens. While she figured out which chicken to buy, Havrylo and Eudokia petted a malnourished white horse attached to a wooden cart. Lukia paid for a hen and the older man cut off its head on a chopping block. While she waited for the headless chicken to finish running, she bought some eggs.

The seller knew a little Russian, so Lukia attempted a conversation. He was hard to understand, as he threw in the odd Turkish word. "Have you had any trouble today?" she asked.

"No, but I heard about the *dövüs* up the road."

Assuming he was referring to the fighting she'd witnessed, she nodded. "Yes, I was afraid for my children."

He said nothing more as they waited for the chicken to succumb. Close by, Havrylo and Eudokia watched a skinny dog chew a meaty bone. Once the chicken had stopped moving, the seller put it in a burlap bag, tied a string around the bag's opening and handed it to Lukia.

She glanced back at her children and saw that Eudokia was now at a pig's trough, one stall over. She was scooping up slops with her hands and was about to put them in her mouth.

"Eudokia! Stop! Put that down. No, bad! Bad! That's for pigs." A few of the female shoppers looked over disapprovingly. Lukia flushed. "She's little," she said to the women. "She doesn't know." She wanted to add, You'd do the same if you were hungry. Instead, she rushed over to her daughter and, taking a handkerchief from her sleeve, wiped her hands. "Mama will get you something to eat."

Lukia bought a hearty grain loaf and asked the children to spit in their hands to clean them. Then she tore off a hunk for each child. Her stomach grumbled. She was tempted to tear off a bit for herself, but knowing there was just enough bread left for the rest of her family, she put the loaf back in the bag. Then she checked the rubles in her pocket. There weren't many left. She didn't know how they'd make it through another winter.

Back at the camp, Lukia heard plans were underway to move the refugees back home. Now—with the civil war raging—the worry was transporting them there safely. But what would they go back to? Their two-room farmhouse in Volhynia had been torched. Was there even a farm left, or had it fallen into enemy hands? She looked around the camp. Rows of dirty tents were filled with destitute families, many of them ailing. The threat of disease and certain death was only a few steps away. Home had to be better than this, no matter what was left of it.

Lukia was reminded of this when she took her next trip to the market, this time with Ivan and Egnat. They weren't far from camp when they came across a Cossack digging his own grave. Three Bolsheviks were standing around him, rifles in their hands, watching him dig. Tensing, she averted her eyes. Egnat hesitated. He appeared to be mesmerized by the horrific scene. With a cross look, she motioned him to keep going for fear the Bolsheviks would take notice of his curiosity and stop them.

The young man, who was digging, turned to one of the
Bolsheviks. 'Victor," he said, "you're my brother. Let me at least
say a prayer, ask God for forgiveness." The man called Victor
asked the other two for mercy and they agreed to let the young
Cossack pray. After the man said an Our Father, his brother shot
him three times. Her heart pounded so hard she thought it would
leap from her chest. She held her sons' hands tightly and walked
away quickly. Even though she'd quickened her step, she felt as
though she were escaping in slow motion. Thankfully, both boys
were either wise enough to remain quiet or too scared to speak.

She couldn't believe what she'd seen. She had four sons; they
were brothers. To think that one of them could turn against the
other made her shudder. As if Egnat could read her mind, he said,
"Mama, I would never kill my brother, even if I had a gun to my
head."

"I pray to God you never find yourself in that position."

Ivan put his arm around his older brother and they walked like
this until they got to the market. Once there, Ivan clung to his
mother's side like a toddler. Egnat stayed silent, brooding over
what they'd witnessed. Like his father, he kept his emotions
hidden.

Later that day, Lukia learned they wouldn't be leaving anytime
soon. With over two million refugees clamouring to return home,
the government was unable to cope with all the transportation
needs. Besides, the authorities were wrapped up in thwarting
rebellions.

Although anxious to return to Volhynia, she wondered if
she'd be trading one hell for another. She'd learned from the Red
Cross nurses, who'd been making the rounds, that fighting had
continued in her region despite the fact that the Austrians and
Germans were gone and Ukraine had won independence, a

victory that should've been celebrated. It had been a hard-fought battle, but now the Ukrainians had to fight both the Poles and the Bolsheviks to maintain control over Lutsk. The nurses also announced that another typhus outbreak was travelling fast throughout Volhynia.

Realizing they might have to stay put until spring, she got down on her knees and beseeched God to give her the strength to carry on.

PACKING UP

NOW THAT THEIR days in camp were nearing the end, Lukia and her children enjoyed the evenings around the campfire with others from her region. The familiar smell of burning wood, along with the singing of old folk songs and the playing of banduras, accordions, and violins, lightened the emotional load they carried. Lukia sang with gusto, pleasing Eudokia, who clapped and twirled in front of her mother. During one of the rousing tunes, Michalko attempted a Cossack leap into the air, fell, and immediately did a somersault, as if his attempt at leaping had been only a joke. Lukia laughed along with the others at her son's cleverness; he'd turned a failure into a gag that everyone could enjoy.

The next time Lukia attended an evening circle, she noticed once more the amorous glances between Hania and Bohdan. Lukia had to admit the young man was attractive with his muscular body, pleasant face, and unruly blond hair. He turned many girls' heads. He'd be a good son-in-law for some mother, but unfortunately, because of the church's rules, not for Lukia. After a few dances, he and Hania slipped away from the crowd and walked hand in hand toward the river.

Anxious her daughter was about to commit a grave sin, Lukia asked Egnat to watch over his sister and young brothers and left the campfire to follow Hania and Bohdan. With no light to guide her, she had to step carefully through the brush on the uneven ground. Straining in the darkness, she saw the young couple slip into the woods that bordered the water.

"Hania," yelled Lukia. "Where are you going?" There was no answer. She hollered again, her voice echoing through the starless night. "Hania, where are you? Answer me!"

Within moments, her daughter's sweet voice rang back. "Mama?" Encouraged, Lukia continued to walk toward the forest. Her daughter soon emerged, looking sheepish, with Bohdan right behind her. "What is it? Bohdan and I were just going for a walk."

"That's nice," said Lukia, "but I need your help. Tomorrow's another big day and I have to get the children to bed."

The young couple turned to one another, looking disappointed, and then reluctantly followed Lukia back to camp.

Later, when the young ones were asleep, Lukia reminded Hania of what boys wanted. She also reminded her of the church's teachings. It was a sin for godparents to marry one another, and that whatever was between them had to die once they returned home.

When her daughter pouted, Lukia said, "You're young. You have lots of time to find a good husband."

"I'm seventeen. I'm old enough.

"Shhh. You'll wake your sister and brothers." Though Lukia thought she'd been reasonable with her advice, Hania didn't say good night. She went to sleep with her back to her mother.

On her final trip to the marketplace, Lukia went alone. She'd left Hania to watch the two youngest, who were still sleeping after a late night of dancing. She bought eggs, cheese, and bread and then hurried back. As the road was rocky in spots, she walked with her head down to avoid tripping on stones. She'd gone only a third of the way when she bumped her head on something hanging from a tree. Looking up, she saw the legs of a young man dangling. His skin was ashen and his mouth agape. She almost dropped her eggs in fright. He couldn't have been much older than Egnat. He was either a Cossack or a Bolshevik—she couldn't tell. Another son lost and for what? What barbarian had taken such a young life? Her stomach lurched as she thought about the young man's mother, back home praying for her son's safety, unaware of the horror he'd faced, unaware she'd never hold him in her arms again.

She looked up and down the road but there was no one around to help bury him, and to linger was to invite trouble. She made a sign of the cross over his body, mumbled a prayer, and then walked on as if she had lead in her shoes.

Lukia returned to camp to find Hania sitting in the sun cleaning the mud off her shoes and Eudokia and Havrylo playing hide-and-seek with two other children. The pleasant scene did nothing to settle her nerves.

She decided to pay a visit to Marusha.

With her mind occupied with the image of the hanging young man, she almost ran into Captain Krylow, who was walking toward her.

"Panye Mazurets," he said.

"Captain Krylow, I'm sorry. I wasn't paying attention."

"You look pale," he said kindly. "Is anything the matter?"

Her tale of what she'd just seen rushed out of her like a roaring river. She hardly stopped to take a breath as she also told him of the time she'd been shot at and of the young man she'd seen digging his own grave. She held her stomach. "War is man's folly."

He cocked his head. "Is it folly to rid yourself of those who would shoot you in the back?"

"But brothers killing brothers?" she said, her forehead creasing. "They're barely adults. What do they know?"

"Even the young are capable of evil." The captain glanced at a soldier walking by, carrying some papers. "Tell the others, I'll be there shortly," he said to him. He turned back to Lukia and smiled. "Listen, you're going home soon. It will be better again."

She shook her head. "I wish I could believe that. What are we going home to?"

His eyes glazed over. "Panye Mazurets, I pray your husband comes back."

"Thank you," said Lukia, swallowing hard.

He squeezed her hand and walked away.

Having shared her frightening experience with the captain, Lukia no longer felt the need to see Marusha. She stood for a few moments and admired the snow-capped mountains beyond the camp. For all their beauty and stillness, they'd also been witness to man's blunders.

GOING HOME

THE TRAIN RIDE back to Lutsk was a solemn one. So much had changed in the three years since she and her children had left. Watching villagers flee and their homes burn had been tragic but returning to an even more ravaged land was hard to bear. Fields, that had once been neatly planted with rows of golden wheat, lay empty and torn up from war's bombardments. Farms that had once echoed with children's laughter, cattle's braying, and turkeys' gobbling were silent, as if they too were in mourning. Lukia noticed that the Tsar's portrait had been removed from the train stations and civic centres and that the militia had replaced the police. Fear hadn't left. It had only changed colours.

She looked at her children, huddled together in the cramped boxcar. Eudokia had fallen asleep with the rocking motion of the train. Havrylo sat cross-legged watching his older brothers throw a potato back and forth. For a while, it was harmless play but when the potato hit the wall and ricocheted off, hitting Havrylo in the shoulder, Lukia scolded them. "What are you doing? No more!" She put her hand out. "Give it to me." She looked around at the other refugees crouched in the boxcar and shrugged. "Children. What can you do with them?"

Havrylo picked up the potato from the floor and handed it to his mother. Egnat and Ivan looked elsewhere, avoiding their mother's angry face.

Ignoring her brothers' antics, Hania sat beside her mother, embroidering a shirt for herself. Her fingers flew, as she pulled the needle with red thread in and out of the white cloth, producing one tidy cross stitch after the other. Lukia wished she knew what her daughter was thinking. Hania had spent her last hours in camp with Bohdan, despite her mother's warnings. Lukia was thankful the boy lived in a village several kilometers away from Kivertsi. Both families needed to rebuild their homes—there would be little time for the young couple to fan the flames they'd ignited.

She glanced at her sons again, their faces downcast. Perhaps she shouldn't have stopped their fooling around with the potato. They had found some pleasure where there was little. Every second boxcar carried someone afflicted with typhus. At stops for the toilet, water, and scanty food rations, Lukia saw several refugees holding their heads or walking in delirium. Those who'd been struck with the illness while in camp struggled to stay alive in the unsanitary surroundings. The weakest ones died quickly, and for them, graves were dug at stops by the sides of the tracks. Prayers were said hastily by anyone well enough to attend these funerals. No one wanted to linger, not with typhus in the air. Egnat had weathered the devil's illness, but could they count on this beast to leave the rest of them alone?

At the Lutsk train station, Lukia needed help disembarking. She felt weak and attributed her state to the long journey. She had to lean on Egnat to get down to the platform. Ivan jumped from the boxcar to assist with the unloading. Hania and Michalko passed their belongings to the older boys, who piled their goods at their mother's feet.

They were almost finished gathering their belongings when Lukia heard a familiar voice. "Lukia!" She turned to see Gregory's sister Irina striding toward her. Overjoyed, Lukia almost collapsed in her sister-in-law's arms. "Oy, what we went through."

Irina kissed her. "I thought I'd never lay eyes on you and the children again."

"I thought so, too," said Lukia, her throat tight. "How have you been?"

Irina's lips pressed into a thin line. "Nothing is the way it was. What's more, the hellish illness is taking our people faster than we can properly bury them. But what can we do? I brought the wagon to take you home."

Lukia snorted. "I have none."

"You still have your land."

Relief washed over her, and Lukia blinked away tears. "That's good to hear. I was afraid we'd lost it, too."

"You'll come to our place and stay as long as you need to rest up. Once you're rested, you can start again."

Lukia shook her head. "When I think of . . ." She trailed off as she watched other families disembark from the train. Most seemed disoriented as they struggled with their possessions and looked for some way to get home. "How did you know I was coming today?"

"Gregory wrote."

Lukia's heart skipped a beat. "He's alive?"

Irina nodded. "At least the mail works. Better than our armies. When he got word you were being sent home, he had his sergeant post a letter for him." Irina grabbed Lukia's hands and squeezed. "He also mentioned they'd be sending him home soon."

Lukia crossed herself. "Thank God." She felt like crying with joy but held back. When she could hold him in her arms, then she'd know for sure. "Have you had word from anyone else in the family?"

Irina's face fell.

"What is it?" Lukia asked, with panic rising in her throat.

"Your sister, Panashka, passed away from typhus."

"What?" Feeling suddenly faint, Lukia looked around for a place to sit down. "When?"

"Four months ago. I wanted to write you but the authorities told me you'd be home soon. If I'd known it would take this long, I would have sent word."

Lukia's eyes misted over as she rocked her head from side to side, trying to digest what she'd heard. She could only guess how her mother was faring. To lose a child was the worst loss imaginable.

Irina put her arm around Lukia. "You don't look well."

"Of course. It's a shock. How she must've suffered. She didn't have a good life. You know her husband beat her. My Panashka didn't have a chance." Lukia swallowed her tears. "What about her daughter? Where's Tania now?"

"With her father."

"A man who made her mother's life a living hell."

"That's how it goes." Irina wrinkled her brow and regarded Lukia closely. "Are you sure nothing hurts? You know typhus is going around."

"I'd know if I had it. I only have a headache and a few other aches. It's to be expected. We're not getting any younger."

"It's true what you say." Irina picked up one of the lighter sacks. "Let's go. Dmitro is waiting with the wagon."

Irina and Lukia sat up front with Dmitro, a short, stocky man with a pleasant face and brown whiskers. The children hopped in the back. During the ride, they took turns holding their goods, which slid and shifted as their uncle did his best to avoid the ruts on the roads. It wasn't easy; other carts jockeyed for position on the main avenue. Some carried wounded soldiers to the hospital. Lukia moaned more than once when she looked at the men packed tightly in the wagons, their heads and limbs bandaged, their eyes dull, their minds most likely deadened by what they'd seen.

As for the city of Lutsk, it wasn't as badly damaged as she'd imagined. The synagogue had been heavily shelled, as had the Lutheran church, but to her relief, the Holy Trinity Cathedral and Monastery stood unharmed. The Catholic church was also intact, but a red poster advertising the glory of the Bolsheviks hung on its façade, underlining the ongoing struggle between the God-fearing and the godless.

"The Bolsheviks threw out chalices, ripped icons from their frames, and stomped on the priest's vestments," said Irina. Even on the Blessed Virgin's face."

"Oy," said Lukia, her face pleated with sorrow. "To turn your back on God is to court the devil."

"The rich didn't escape either," said Dmitro. "The hooligans broke into their manors, stole anything of value, and broke or smashed the rest. Then they burned the buildings and slaughtered their animals. I think there's only one manor left."

Just ahead, several young men pelted the windows of a fine coach with clods of earth. "Rich bastards!" they yelled. "Get out, bourgeoisie!" Their angry faces mirrored the hell still going on.

Irina patted Lukia's knee. "We've traded one enemy for another."

Lukia glanced back at her children, whose eyes were fixed on the angry youth. She had hoped their return would be to a calmer place, but the rebellious street scene suggested otherwise.

Though Lukia had been anxious to return, the news of her sister's death made it difficult to find any pleasure in seeing familiar surroundings again. If not for the news that Gregory was still alive, Lukia would've sunk into a depression. She'd realized some time ago that some women just had bad luck, whether it was in choosing men or avoiding sickness. Her sister had been one of them, unlucky in both. And now she was gone. Lukia would have to find out where Panashka was buried and pay her respects.

As they drove away from the chaos of the city and down the familiar road to Kivertsi, Lukia noticed the bushes and trees had grown but otherwise the farmlands looked the same. Though Irina had warned her their church had burned down, the sight of the charred remains caught Lukia off guard. She froze at the sight. A black area, the size of the former church, marked the destruction. All their family records, kept in the building's office, were now lost forever.

She groaned. "Why? What did it hurt?"

"We have to meet in each other's homes now," Irina said.

"Did the Bolsheviks do this?"

"No one knows."

Riding through the village, Lukia noticed that in Kivertsi, too, the police had been replaced by the militia and the Tsar's portrait had been removed from public buildings. "I don't remember the village being so tidy."

"You can thank the Germans for that," said Irina. "They forced the rabbis and the shopkeepers to sweep away the mud and cart off their garbage. If they refused, they had to pay a fine."

"And do you see any pigs?" said Dmitro. "They're now hidden away. The Germans told the owners to keep them in their yards. If not, they'd be taken."

When Dmitro turned down the dirt road leading to her farm, Lukia gasped. She and her children stared at the spectacle of their torched house surrounded by fallow land. What hadn't been incinerated had crumpled to the ground. Only their blackened brick and clay pich stood waiting for a rescue.

Lukia sank in her seat. There was so much work ahead. With her energy depleted, she couldn't fathom starting again. They had the land but no house, no animals, and no crops. And yet, despite feeling overwhelmed, she felt blessed to be back in Kivertsi with her children.

At least, we have our land, she thought. And with any luck, her husband would be home soon.

On the main road, heading to Irina and Dmitro's farm, a group of soldiers on horseback rode toward them. "Those are our Ukrainian troops," said Dmitro.

When the soldiers got closer, Lukia noticed the lion insignia on their grey uniforms. The Bolsheviks had a red star on theirs. Dmitro slowed down and Lukia shouted to the officer leading the men, "How is our army doing?"

"Not well," said the officer, a hefty man with a grizzled beard in need of a trim. "Kiev has changed hands five times already." Kiev was their capital, four hundred kilometers away. It stood to reason that whoever won that city would rule Ukraine.

"Are we safe here?"

The officer shrugged. "Nobody knows. The major conflict is far from here, for now."

His words were discouraging. The family rode in silence the rest of the way, consumed by thoughts of what would happen if war came to their doorstep again.

Irina and her husband lived in a beautiful house with a wood floor and thatched roof in Zhabka, a village west of Kivertsi. Their home had survived the war. Lukia guessed it hadn't been on any military route. The Savitskys made space in the main room for Lukia and her children by shoving aside their dining table and chairs and putting perinas over beds of straw they'd brought in from the barn.

"I'm sorry we have to put you out like this," Lukia said to her sister-in-law.

"It's nothing," said Irina. "We know you would do the same for us."

Dmitro put most of their goods in the barn. As the spring weather was still damp and chilly, Lukia and the children held on to their felt-lined boots.

No sooner had they rested from their long train ride than all Lukia's children, with the exception of Egnat, fell ill with typhus. Lukia boiled their clothes and soothed their hot foreheads with cold wet cloths. Fearing the worst, she was soon on her knees praying.

Dmitro had left early in the morning to buy some lye soap and romyanyk from the village; he returned, hours later with the soap but none of the chamomile herb Lukia had requested. Others had likely discovered its curative properties and depleted the supplies. He also brought back news—people were dying by the thousands. Doctors and nurses couldn't keep up and a few of them had fallen ill as well.

Lukia held her head and rocked it. "What will become of all of us?"

"What can we do?" Dmitro said. "We have to believe we'll survive."

Though exhausted from caring for her young, Lukia helped Irina peel potatoes for supper. While doing so, she heard through the open window a horse galloping toward the house. She peered out and saw Bohdan arrive on horseback. She quickly wiped her hands on her apron and rushed to the door. Opening it, she saw the young man tie his horse to a post and then bend down to wipe some dust from his wool trousers. She stepped outside and closed the door. "Good day, Bohdan. What are you doing here?"

A broad smile lit up his face. "Good day, Panye Mazurets." He pushed a blond curl off his forehead. "You know, our family lives in Zhabka."

"Of course. How's your mother?"

"She's doing the best she can."

Lukia nodded. Marusha would also be waiting for her husband to return.

"When I heard your family was here, I had to come see Hania."

"I'm sorry you can't. She's sick with typhus."

Bohdan's smile disappeared as fast as it had come. "I can't leave without seeing her."

Lukia folded her arms. "I'm sorry you came all this way, but you understand how serious this is."

He shuffled his feet and strained his neck toward the windows as if stretching and staring would give him the power to see through the curtain-covered glass.

"Bohdan, listen. Even if she were well, it's not good for you to see one another. It's a sin. You're both godparents."

"Please," said Bohdan. "You know I love her."

Lukia stiffened. "Love. What's love? Bohdan, you're still young. You have lots of time. There are many girls out there." Lukia believed what she was saying, but the way he'd pleaded made her heart stop. She understood he loved her daughter, but what good was that, if they couldn't marry in church? Without the priest's blessing, they wouldn't have a happy marriage.

"I don't want many girls. I want Hania."

Shaking her head, she said, "You'd better go now. Give my best to your mother."

Bohdan stared at Lukia in disbelief and then at the house. Lukia turned to look as well, needing assurance the windows were still covered. She and Irina kept the rooms dark to help the children rest.

"You tell Hania I was here," said Bohdan loudly. He turned to go but then ran up to a window and yelled, "I love you, Hania!"

"Oy," said Lukia, "you'll wake the children." Though touched by his passion, her throat constricted and she said firmly, "Go already."

Bohdan scowled, then untied his horse, leaped onto it, and galloped away.

While watching him ride off, Lukia realized she'd been so busy that day tending to her children she'd forgotten to wash her face and hands. She went over to the basin on a stump and poured some water into it from a pitcher nearby. Suddenly, she felt unbalanced and unwell. Her forehead burned, her head hurt, and her body ached and shook with chills.

Irina, who had just come outside, took one look at her and said, "Are you sick?"

"I think I have typhus."

"My God. Not you, too."

Lukia staggered back to the house and steadied herself by placing a hand on the outer wall. She started unbuttoning her dress. "Wait," said Irina. "I'll help you take off your clothes, but first I have to get gloves."

"May God bless you, Irina."

By the time Irina had returned—wearing gloves and carrying one of her own dresses—Lukia was half undressed. "Look," said Lukia, holding out her arms. They were covered with a rash, as was her torso. The spots looked like flea bites, only a deeper red. Terrified, Lukia changed into her sister-in-law's dress and went inside to lie down.

As the day turned into evening, her symptoms worsened. Her rash grew darker and she began to cough. She couldn't believe this was happening to her. It was as if she'd been cursed—no matter how much she overcame, and how much she prayed, there would be no letup. Was God still testing her will to survive?

Dmitro took Lukia to the hospital in Lutsk, where—with no beds available—she was put on the cold hard floor of the crowded corridor. She lay next to a young man in his twenties, suffering from the same disease. Doctors and nurses walked by as if she and the young man were nothing more than pieces of furniture.

Weak, her mind wrestled with fears of death, which she tried to push out. She couldn't afford to die. She had too many depending on her. Time stretched seemingly for hours. Gregory moved in and out of her vision and for brief moments, she was convinced he'd come to see her. Upon discovering her imaginings were nothing more than that, she sunk into a deeper depression. She didn't know how long she'd been lying on the floor when she heard a recognizable voice somewhere behind her head.

"What is the meaning of this?" her brother Petro bellowed. "How can you leave my sister like this? I'll sue you if you don't get her a bed immediately." Lukia loved this trait of her brother's. His bluster often got results.

Lukia heard footsteps scurrying away, and soon a nurse came back with a bed on wheels. Two men picked her up and laid her on a sheet-covered mattress. Petro, younger than her by three years, stood above her smiling. He'd been a sergeant in the Tsar's army, but they'd lost touch since the war began. He was wearing a smart three-piece suit and looked surprisingly robust given what he must've gone through. Tall, with a ruddy complexion and a well-groomed beard, he commanded attention wherever he went.

"How did you—?"

"Shhh," he said, cutting her off. "We'll talk later. You rest now."

Comforted by his presence, she drifted off. Later, she learned the medical staff had mistaken him for a prominent criminal lawyer in Lutsk. Though inaccurate, it was a logical assumption because Petro was well-dressed and had a similar face and bearing to the well-known barrister. Much as she found her brother annoying, especially when he threw his wealth around—the wealth he'd gained by marrying well—she was grateful he'd come along. If it weren't for him, she would've perished like the young man with whom she'd shared the cold floor in the corridor. He'd died within days of his arrival. Now, thanks to her brother, she was bathed and her hospital gowns were changed frequently.

But in spite of the good care, her chills continued and her fever ran high. She slipped in and out of consciousness. She found it difficult to open her eyes, seemingly shut tight by the disease.

At one point she assumed she was dead, as she found herself on a staircase at the top of which was God, surrounded by angels. Alarmed, she blurted out, "I can't die. I have six children who depend on me. Isn't it enough what you've put me through? I can't leave them now." She saw Him gaze upon her and consider her plight.

Then God said, "You can live."

Relieved, she let out a long breath and dozed off once more. When she was awakened by faint female conversation, she had the sense she'd slept for quite a while.

As if through gauze, she saw a nurse standing by her bed. She held up a mirror to Lukia's nose. "Look," said the other voice. "She steamed it up with her breath. She's alive."

Lukia dozed off again, thankful she would see another day.

As days went by, she stayed in quarantine. Then one afternoon, Hania came to see her. At first, Lukia didn't recognize her. Her daughter was dressed as a nurse.

"Mama," said Hania tenderly.

Lukia's eyes widened, and she grinned. "Hania, is that you?"

"Yes, Mama. I had to sneak in dressed like this, otherwise they wouldn't have let me see you. It's a miracle you've come through."

"I dreamt you had married Bohdan. I told you not to."

Hania clasped her own hands. "How could I marry without your permission? I would never marry anyone while you're sick."

Reassured, Lukia smiled and fell into a deep sleep. Soon after, her fever broke.

Lukia decided to go to Mass in Lutsk the first Sunday she was back at Irina's. She hadn't attended since she'd left Kivertsi as a refugee. The children weren't enthusiastic because the service was three hours long and, with no pews in the nave, they'd have to stand the whole time.

After listening to Egnat argue and Michalko whine, Lukia said in a stern voice, "Listen to me. Aunt Irina's neighbour not only lost his wife to this typhus, but also his mother, two sons, and a pig. We have to be thankful we're still together." The boys grumbled but agreed.

Near the cathedral, the Mazurets family were slowed by a funeral procession. It wasn't anyone Lukia knew, but one of the mourners said to her, "Our countrymen are dropping like flies."

Lukia turned to her children before they entered the church. "We need to thank the Lord. He spared us."

For once, the children behaved and there was little fidgeting during the service. At the end of the mass, the congregation sang the national anthem, Ukraine Hasn't Died Yet. Their voices—particularly heartfelt after what they'd gone through—rang with conviction as they sung the lyrics: "Ukraine hasn't died yet, nor her glory, nor her freedom; upon us fellow Ukrainians, fate shall smile once more. Our enemies will vanish like dew in the sun, and we too shall rule, brothers, in a free land of our own."

Shivers went up Lukia's back as the anthem reverberated through the nave. She looked at all the holy images on the iconostasis and asked God to be merciful to her and her family. There wasn't much more she could take.

STARTING OVER

A
FTER ANOTHER WEEK passed with no sign of Gregory, Lukia decided it was time to leave her sister-in-law's home and start building. She and her children needed shelter for the winter ahead. She asked Dmitro to take her and Egnat scavenging in the countryside for farm implements and a large tarpaulin—one the family could live under while they built a new home.

They visited a number of farms before they found what they were looking for. One of the farmers had taken advantage of the abandoned wagons at the train station years before and gave Lukia one for nothing. Though thankful, she missed her wagon; it was sturdier and didn't have rickety wheels. The same farmer also gave them a tarpaulin that the Russian army had left behind.

Dmitro and Irina had two horses and loaned one to Lukia for the time being. After the wagon had been packed with the Mazuretses' belongings and enough ingredients to set up a kitchen, Irina handed Lukia three sealers of cabbage soup, a covered container of potato-and-cheese varenyky, a ring of homemade blood sausage, and two loaves of rye bread.

"Go with God," said Irina, kissing her sister-in-law.

"I can't thank you enough," said Lukia, overcome with emotion. She held Irina's hands and kissed her again.

"It's nothing," said Irina, her warm eyes underscoring her sentiment.

Lukia shook her head in wonder at her sister-in-law's generosity. "What do you mean 'it's nothing'? You gave us food you need yourself."

"Ach, you flatter me too much," said Irina, smiling. She waved as Lukia and her children—anxious to get started—almost danced to the wagon.

Egnat drove to the accompaniment of joking and laughter as they passed one field after another. Their joy didn't subside until they spotted the ruins of what had been their home.

Lukia's heart lurched once more at the sight of the scorched land. She turned to her children. "We'll be all right. We'll make ourselves a nice home again."

While they were setting up, their neighbour, Ihor Striluchky, drove his wagon up their farm road and stopped near their tent site. "Good day, Lukia. I'm glad you've all arrived safely. I came to warn you not to use the water in the well. It's poisoned. The Bolsheviks threw a cat down there."

Her brow furrowed. "What?"

"You can use the water from my well. I brought you some for now." He got down from the wagon and, with Egnat's help, lifted the jugs of water in the back.

Egnat laid one jug by their tent. "Don't worry, Mama. We'll dig a new one."

Her son's willingness to help eased the burden, but it was still another cross to bear. Lukia turned to Ihor. "We'll try not to take too much. How are Nina and your son?"

Ihor took his hat off, revealing hair that had thinned considerably since she'd last seen him. "You didn't hear?"

"No, what?"

"Victor died at the beginning of the war. I told him he was too young to go, but he didn't listen." Ihor's eyes were pools of sadness.

"Oy, don't tell me." Lukia blinked away tears. "So young. That's terrible, terrible news. Please give my love to Nina. May God take care of your Victor now." She put a hand on Ihor's arm. "Children, children. What can you do with them? You try and tell them, but they won't listen. How are you both managing?"

"We get up in the morning, get dressed and do what needs to be done. Vodka helps. You know how it is."

"Irina gave me some nice cabbage soup. Can I give you some to take home?"

"No, thank you. You keep it for yourself. You're going to need it."

With her sons busy getting wood for kindling and picking stones out of the field, Lukia decided she'd unpacked and arranged as much as she could. It was time to make some bread. Luckily, their clay oven had survived the fire. She gave it a loving pat as if it, too, had overcome unimaginable misery and was now on the mend.

While she kneaded dough on a tea towel-covered crate, she listened to Hania sing to Eudokia, who was having her bath outside the tent in a tin tub, one of the abandoned items they'd found on their property. Her daughter's voice was so sweet, that for a short time, Lukia forgot about the challenges ahead. She was about to form the loaves for rising when she heard a horse galloping hard up the road. She stuck her head out from under the tarpaulin and saw Bohdan. He was carrying a shotgun; his jaw was set and his eyes were dark with determination.

Lukia briefly considered exposing herself but decided against it. The look in his eyes had given her pause. There was a hint of madness there. She quickly withdrew and hid in a corner of the tent, far from the opening. Soon after, she heard Bohdan's horse stop near her daughters.

"Bohdan," said Hania, "what are you doing here?"

"I've come to kill your mother."

"What?" Hania's voice had risen a notch. "Are you crazy?"

Alarmed, Lukia looked around for something with which to defend herself. There was a knife on the table, but she couldn't move without making a sound.

Eudokia started to cry. "Mama!"

"Shhh," said Hania. "No one is going kill our mother."

Lukia peeked through a hole in the canvas. Bohdan's face was flushed, and his hands shook. He pointed his weapon at the tarpaulin. Had he been drinking? Egnat had taken their rifle into the forest in hopes of shooting a deer or a rabbit. Now she wished he hadn't gone.

Hania wiped her wet hands on her apron and faced Bohdan. "How can you say something like that?" she said, her voice tremulous. "Do you think I would marry you if you did away with my mother?"

"What else are we supposed to do?"

"Maybe things will change. Maybe the priest will make an exception. We can't give up." She hesitated then said, "I won't."

He regarded her for a moment and lowered his gun. Eudokia whimpered.

"Shhh," said Hania, putting a hand on her sister's shoulder. "Bohdan's not going to hurt anybody."

Bohdan stared at the tarpaulin. Lukia swallowed hard and wondered if he could see her through the hole. He then turned back to Hania and tucked the gun into the holster at the side of his saddle.

Hania shifted, seemingly relieved. "You'd better go before my mama finds you here," she said, her eyes pleading.

Bohdan got off his horse. Startled, Hania stepped back. But then, he pulled her to him. Hugging her tightly, he buried his face in her hair, and she trembled with passion. Lukia couldn't help but feel a deep sorrow for the two young lovers, who were being held back by the church's laws. After a few moments, he let go reluctantly, kissed her, and climbed back on his horse. Taking the reins, he said, "Don't find anyone else. We'll be lovers forever." He turned his horse around and galloped off.

"See," said Hania to Eudokia. "You didn't have to be afraid. He just loves me too much, that's all." She began to shake.

"Are you cold?" Eudokia asked.

Lukia herself felt unsteady.

"Mama," said Hania, entering the tent.

Lukia shook her head. "This is why godparents can't marry one another. Nothing good can come from such a union."

"How can you say that? Keeping us apart is driving him crazy."

"Enough!" said Lukia, her voice rising. "He wanted to kill me! You want someone like that?"

"No. Of course not. He wasn't thinking."

"I don't want to hear any more about it. Go! Take care of your sister."

After Hania left—her face full of anguish—Lukia crossed herself and slumped down on a stool by the table. It was a good thing Gregory wasn't home. He would've grabbed his rifle and either chased Bohdan off or shot him. But what if the young man, in his rage, had killed her husband? How could any of them have lived after that? Yes, it was a good thing Gregory hadn't returned yet. It would've been a wound in the heart from which none of them could've recovered.

The Old Man on the Road

A WEEK LATER, LUKIA saw an old man limping down their farm road. He was carrying a dusty duffle bag and his long army coat hung on his narrow shoulders as though it were meant for a man twice his size. His hair was long and scraggly, his moustache a sorry mess. He walked with his head down as if each step could result in unexpected injury. It was only when he got close that she noticed his gait—though slow, it was familiar. She raised her hand to shield her eyes from the sun emerging from behind a cloud and squinted at the man walking toward her. His face crinkled like her husband's when he had something serious on his mind.

Her heart skipped. *Gregory.*

Picking up her skirt, she ran to him, her heart pounding. She couldn't get there fast enough and she stumbled on the road's stones, almost falling. He raised his arms to hug her and she leaned into his chest, feeling the roughness of his jacket as she put her arms around his waist. He shook as he held her. She held on even tighter. It had been raining and his collar was still damp. He smelled like a wet dog that had been around men smoking.

"Gregory, my Gregory. You've come back to us." Laughter and sobs mingled in her throat.

He held her at arm's length. "My dear wife." His brown eyes were hollow. Whatever he'd seen was buried deep. Seeing him broken, Lukia winced as if she'd been struck. She hugged him again, and even though she could feel his ribs, a sign of how much weight he'd lost, she relished the feeling of his body pressed against hers.

She pulled back and tried to put aside her grief over how he looked, but the ache in her chest told her it was impossible. Fighting back tears, she said, "I saw you limping. Did you get shot?"

"No, I was lucky," he said through yellow teeth that belonged to a much older man. "Just bad boots. My feet have suffered the most."

She grabbed his arm to help him continue down the road. "Thanks to God it wasn't worse.

Hania and Egnat came running, sending dust into the air. "Tato!" they shouted. Ivan, Michalko, Havrylo, and Eudokia were right behind, like excited geese. They quickly encircled their parents and embraced as one. Eudokia—the shyest and the one who didn't know her father—hugged Lukia's legs and peered at her father from behind her mother's knees.

Egnat beamed and straightened up to appear taller. "Tato, I've taken care of things while you were gone."

Gregory's eyes watered as he grabbed his eldest son's shoulders and kissed him. He then examined each child. Only Eudokia held back until her sister picked her up. "This is your tato," Hania said.

Gregory took his youngest in his arms. Delighting in her chubbiness, he stroked her plump legs. And then, pretending it took some effort to hold her, he said to Lukia, "What have you been feeding this one? I thought there was a food shortage." He laughed as he put her down. "She's going to be strong."

"Tato," said Egnat, "our house got burned. We have to build a new one."

"I can see that," said Gregory, as he scanned what they owned. Lukia followed his gaze. The makeshift tent flapped in the wind next to the burned remainders of their home.

Ivan tugged his father's coat. "I helped Egnat put up the tarpaulin."

Gregory stroked the top of Ivan's head. "Look how big you've grown." He turned to his wife. "They left us an oven. I suppose we have to celebrate that at least."

"Celebrate?" Lukia spat on the ground. "There's nothing to celebrate. We now have the godless Bolsheviks running around, shooting and beating up people. I'll celebrate your return, that's all."

"Wife," he grinned, "you haven't changed."

"What did you expect?" she said in a playful tone.

Havrylo grabbed his father's leg. Gregory tousled his son's hair. "Little Havrylo. How old are you now?"

Havrylo held up six fingers.

Michalko pushed Havrylo aside. "I'm nine." Havrylo pushed back, and Michalko shoved his younger brother again.

"Boys, enough," said Lukia quietly. Though her sons quickly settled, they glared at one another.

Gregory smiled. "Almost a man," he said to Michalko. "Come here." Michalko stepped forward and his father embraced him.

Egnat pressed his right hip and shoulder against his father's side and stretched upwards as far as he could without standing on his toes. "Tato, you've shrunk."

"No, son," Gregory said, laughing. "You've grown." They were now around the same height, both short for men. Egnat had the same sturdy body his father once had.

Lukia caught her husband's eye and then tilted her head in Hania's direction. She wanted him to acknowledge their oldest daughter, who was now taller than her mother.

Gregory stretched out his arms. "Come here, daughter."

Hania approached her father with a wide smile and embraced him.

"You were still a girl when I left. Look at you now. A young woman."

"It's been three years," said Lukia. "A lot has happened."

He stared into the distance and nodded slowly, as if he hadn't realized it had been that long. Or maybe he'd thought it had been longer.

Lukia exchanged a look with Hania and shook her head. She hoped her daughter understood this wasn't the time to say anything about Bohdan and her heartache.

"C'mon, Ivan. Let's race," said Michalko, obviously wanting to show off for his father.

Egnat brightened. "You think you can beat your older brothers?" He pulled up his pant legs and got in a ready position, body bent forward, his left leg back. All the boys lined up, copying Egnat's stance, even Havrylo, who had no hope of winning.

"I'll give the signal, okay?" said Hania.

Egnat nodded. He looked over his shoulder to see if his father was paying attention.

Gregory watched with pride.

"Ready, set, go!" shouted Hania.

With their children running ahead, Lukia regarded her husband. Though he appeared broken, she was thankful he was in one piece, that he'd come back alive. As they stood together on the road and watched their children race, she felt some of the torment of being apart for years slip away like water off an oilskin.

Egnat won, to no one's surprise. Havrylo brought up the rear, huffing and puffing, his round face flushed.

"Well done," shouted Gregory.

As he and Lukia walked slowly up the road toward their children and their temporary home, she looked tenderly at him. "I was so afraid you wouldn't come back to us."

"I know." His eyes glazed over and she guessed he was back on the battlefield or trying to make sense of the years he'd lost with his family. He'd fought to keep their land, a farm that had been ruined while he was away. He'd been through hell, not knowing if he would ever return home.

After several moments of silence, Lukia said, "Our country is still a mess."

"Of course," he said, sighing. "You can't escape it. So much waste. So many deaths, and for what? So many soldiers deserted after they heard about the revolution. They were worried the land would be divided up before they got back. They were afraid they'd end up with nothing."

She groaned. "The Bolsheviks are turning people's heads. They're saying we should get some of the gentry's lands. Now the people are arguing about how the land should be distributed. They're asking why the landless should get some—they didn't work for it. Others think that those with many sons should get more."

Gregory stopped walking and gazed at his farm, seemingly transfixed. "Can you blame them for getting their heads turned? We all need good earth to survive, and the gentry have always had more than they needed."

She put her arm through his. "I can't imagine any good will come from all of this."

He nodded and his body slackened.

"You need to rest now," she said and guided him to their dwelling.

Egnat got his father a crate to sit on and helped him take off the boots which were worn through in several spots. Ivan lit a fire in the pich so his mother could heat some water on the stove. Afterwards, she poured hot water into a basin and took off her husband's holey and dirt-crusted wool socks. His feet were raw where the leather had rubbed his skin away. His soles were covered in red, puffy blisters, and his toenails were ragged and filthy. She got a brush and some soap to wash his feet, but first she gave him a shot of rye whisky, which he downed like water.

He smacked his lips. "I missed this." After relishing the foot bath for a few minutes, he regarded her. "You've aged."

She chuckled. "As if you haven't, you old fart."

He grinned. "Ho ho ho, this is how you talk. You think you can push me around now that you've been running things on your own for so long."

She locked her gaze with his. "No, Gregory. You're still the master of the house, but you need to know you weren't the only one fighting. I didn't pick up a gun, but I fought to keep our children alive. I fought hard to keep myself alive, too."

His weathered face creased with concern. "What are you telling me? Did any men try anything with you?"

She shook her head. "No, nothing like that. Worse. We all got typhus, except for Egnat. I almost died. If it weren't for Petro coming to the hospital . . ." She swallowed her tears.

Gregory's face crumpled. "Shhh, my dear one." Seemingly on the verge of crying, he turned away and looked over at his children playing tag.

Lukia got down on her knees and gently washed the dirt from his bruised and battered feet. "I'm going to get you something to eat. After supper, you can lie down. And in a few days, when you have your strength back, we'll begin rebuilding our home."

Lukia had thought that once Gregory was caught up on his sleep, he would talk to her about what he'd endured. Instead, she found him tight-lipped and tense, as if still preparing for battle. He did nothing to help around the farm, and on occasion, she found him staring off into space.

Pushing her unease aside, she carried on with her chores, acknowledging his presence but letting him be. She continued to go into the woods to gather nuts and berries with the children. Hania helped her in the kitchen, and the boys went fishing and even managed to kill a couple of rabbits.

When a week had gone by with little change, Lukia could take it no longer. She was worried about her husband and wondered what demons he was still fighting. She wanted him back the way he'd been before the damn war started. She waited until the children were occupied with their chores before asking Gregory to go for a walk.

It was a crisp evening with little wind. The bright moon and star-lit sky illuminated the road as they walked past their unplowed fields with only a nightingale's song to interrupt their thoughts. Though the scene was peaceful, she felt her husband's uneasiness. His steps were heavy and he avoided looking at her. They hadn't gone far when she grabbed his arm, forcing him to stop.

His brow wrinkled in annoyance. "What is it?"

"Gregory, I don't know the horrors you've seen, but I want you to come back to me."

He lowered his head as if to hide his pain.

"We have a beautiful family. We've waited for years for your return and God has answered our prayers." He didn't respond. "What can I do to help you?" she asked, her voice cracking,

"Oy, wife," he said, so quietly she barely heard him. He then took her hand off his arm and strode back to their campsite. His head was bowed, his back hunched, his footsteps heavy.

"Gregory, wait!" she called, but to no avail. He marched on. She had no choice but to follow him. He didn't look back once, and she felt the marital cord connecting them growing thinner.

That night, troubled by Gregory's relentless thrashing, she stayed awake for hours, thinking once again that her family had been cursed. She was fortunate to have her husband back in one piece, but was it good luck if he was now only a shell of a man? Drifting in and out of sleep, she stewed about the men who orchestrated wars, never thinking of the damage they wrought, only about their own pride and greed.

In the morning, she was surprised to find Gregory gone from their bed. She later discovered he'd risen early and gone into the forest with Egnat and Ivan to chop down a few trees. His return to work gave her hope. Perhaps he was beginning to mend.

That evening, while Lukia was throwing the dirty dishwater behind the tarpaulin, a Cossack's wife galloped up their road on a black steed. She was striking for an older woman, her dark hair mostly hidden under a flowered babushka and her black eyes rimmed with charcoal. Over her beige smock and matching pants, she wore a royal blue beshmet— a caftan-like garment—and on her feet, red leather boots.

Curious and a little apprehensive, Lukia put the basin down and greeted the woman as she got off her horse. "Good evening."

"Good evening, Panye Mazurets," the woman said, bowing her head. "Is your husband home?"

"Yes." Lukia glanced in the direction of the forest, on the other side of the field. Gregory was just coming out. He'd gone to relieve himself. "Who's asking?"

"Panye Lubchenko. I met your husband through mine. They were together in the same campaign." While they waited for Gregory to join them, they talked about the war and what a disaster it had been for Russia.

When Gregory walked up, the Cossack's wife wasted no time telling him what she wanted. "My husband told me you fought well for the Tsar. He'd like you to join his army to fight the Bolsheviks."

Gregory's face went pale. "I've had enough of war," he said. "There is no honour in what is going on right now."

"Please," said Panye Lubchenko. "Our Ukraine will be lost. Already the Bolsheviks have taken over Kiev. They could be marching here as we speak." She lowered her voice. "They even killed a priest. Hacked him to death. With his head half off, he prayed to the end, kneeling in the snow."

"Oy," said Lukia, crossing herself. "What's happened to people's brains?"

Gregory raised his chin. "If they come, I will defend myself and my family as best I can, but asking me to return to battle is too much."

"What are you saying?" She turned to Lukia. "Surely, Panye Mazurets, you would want your husband to fight for Ukraine."

Lukia drew closer to her husband. "It's not my blood he'd be spilling. He can make his own decision. He always has."

"Gregory," Panye Lubchenko pleaded, "you must go and save your country."

He snorted. "I did go, and I couldn't save it."

The Cossack's wife looked over at Egnat and Ivan, wrestling in the long grasses not far from their campsite, and Hania, seated on a crate under a crab-apple tree, telling the younger ones a story. The wind whistled plaintively across the empty fields, an echo of the mood brought on by the stranger's visit.

"It's a pity what's happened here," said Panye Lubchenko. "Listen, Gregory. I know you only have five deshyatin."

"It's all anyone has." He met her gaze with his jaw tight and fists clenched.

"Would you like something to eat?" Lukia said, to break the tension.

"Thank you, but no. I have to get back before it's too dark to travel."

"Yes," said Gregory, crossing his arms. "It's too dangerous to be out at night alone."

Panye Lubchenko clasped her hands. "I beg you to reconsider. If you join the Cossack's army, you'll get twenty-five deshyatin in the Caucasus for each of your four sons. Think hard on it. It won't be long before your sons will need land to raise a family."

The Caucasus was beautiful with its mountainous backdrop, but its soil wasn't as fertile as the land in Volhynia. Even so, Lukia was surprised her husband was hesitating. He'd rushed into battle for the honour of serving the Tsar, and yet here, the Cossacks were offering him land five times the size of what they could ever hope to have. Lukia glanced from one to the other but said nothing for fear he'd misinterpret her words. There was no way she wanted him to go. If he went to fight, he might not be so lucky this time.

Gregory shook his head. "There's no point in war. Innocent men are killed and maimed. Women are raped. Children are left without parents. All for a cause that only seems to benefit the rich and the powerful."

"I agree," said the woman with fervour. "This time you would do it for our Ukraine. For our independence."

"If that could be true, that would be something," said Gregory, sounding weary. "But you know that's only a dream. No sooner do we get our country back than some other tyrants rush in and steal it again. It doesn't stop."

Panye Lubchenko nodded. "I know it's been hard. Things can't be solved quickly, you understand."

Gregory cleared his throat. "You tell your husband I wish him well."

"He'll be disappointed." She studied him for a moment, as if she still expected him to change his mind. When he didn't, she climbed on her horse, looked back once, and galloped away.

Gregory sat down on the stump near the tarpaulin and put his head between his knees.

Lukia sat beside him on another stump. "My old Gregory would've taken that offer."

He raised his head, met her gaze briefly and then closed his eyes. "I'm sick of fighting and being afraid of not seeing my family again." He opened his eyes and his face twisted with some dark memory. "You learn to be savage and ruthless in the trenches. There's an animal in every man when he's cornered."

Lukia had no words to relieve his pain. Only someone who'd experienced what he had would fully understand. They sat there, watching their boys throw stones at an old scarecrow lying on the ground, seeing who could hit it the most times. Beyond them, Hania was running, trying to catch Eudokia, who'd run off giggling toward the forest. Her pudgy legs couldn't out-run her older sister, who scooped up the toddler and swung her through the air. It was good the children were lost in their own play, oblivious to the larger drama taking place around them.

Gregory was right not to go. She didn't want land that came with the heavy price of more killings.

A DIVIDED COUNTRY

HEAVY RAIN HAD delayed planting, but now that the ground was dry enough to till, Lukia asked Egnat to dig up the ceramic container she'd buried at the back of their home before they left for the Caucasus. In it were seeds for hay, wheat, barley, and corn—seeds that were like gold to any farmer. She stood back while Egnat stuck a spade into the earth.

"Be careful," she said. "I don't want you to break the pot."

"I'm careful, I'm careful," said Egnat, annoyed. He was at the age where boys showed their dislike of orders of any kind. She'd seen it often enough when she was young and her older brother was her son's age. At the time, her wise mother had picked only the fights she could win.

When Egnat finished digging, he took the burlap bag from inside the crock and handed it to his mother.

"We'll seed tomorrow," she said. "It's late to do it, but maybe we'll be rewarded with a longer growing season."

Egnat picked up the spade. "I'll go feed the horse."

Pleased with the bag of seeds in her hand, she didn't notice her husband come up behind her until he'd wrapped his arms around her. "Gregory!" she said, jumping. "What are you doing, scaring me like that?"

He laughed and gave one of her breasts a squeeze.

"What?" she said teasingly. "You can't wait?"

"How can you say that? You know how long I've waited."

"I know." With all the adjustments and fatigue, their lovemaking had suffered.

He pointed to her burlap bag. "What are you holding?"

She took several cloth packets out. "Our precious seeds."

He grinned. "I sometimes forget what a smart woman you are. With all you had to do, you thought about saving these as well."

She shrugged but could feel herself puffing up with pride. "Of course. I had to do something when you ran off."

"Do you have to go on about it?" he asked sharply. "I don't want to hear about this until my dying day."

She was about to say he didn't have to be cross with her when Ivan came running from the far side of the field waving an old tiller. "Tato! Mama! Look what I found!"

"Wonderful, son," said Gregory, taking it from him. He examined the implement, turning it over in his hand. "It's definitely ours. Maybe one of the locals borrowed it and then left it."

"We lost a lot," she said, "but little by little we'll get it back." As the words left her mouth, she realized she was beginning to believe it.

"Yes," said Gregory. "Little by little." He turned around to see Havrylo and Michalko play-fighting. Eudokia circled her brothers with a cloth doll in her hands. "Where's Hania?"

"At Irina's." Lukia put the seeds in her apron pocket. "She went to Zhabka to return her sealers and dishes. She also took her some bread I baked. I don't know what we would've done without your sister's help."

Gregory raised his hand and shielded his face from the sun. "How did Hania get there?"

"Ihor offered her a lift. He was going there to sell some cream and eggs." Lukia wasn't sure it had been a good idea to let Hania go. She had seemed too eager to do the errand. Knowing the fire burning inside her daughter, Lukia suspected she might try to see Bohdan while she was in the village.

Gregory looked at Lukia. "What are you thinking? I rarely see you standing still doing nothing."

"If I want to stand here for a few moments and do nothing, what's wrong with that?" When he didn't answer, she said, "You don't like me standing here, I'll go back to the tarpaulin." She picked up the crock and stormed off.

He'd been startled by her outburst, but what could she do? She wasn't about to trouble him with her fears. He'd find out soon enough. Let him enjoy a period of calm first. Like her, he would find comfort through working the soil and breathing in the fragrant air of the woods nearby. She couldn't tell him about Bohdan. Not yet.

Lukia had just finished putting Eudokia down for a nap when she heard voices down the road. Stepping outside, she saw Ihor dropping Hania off at the junction. As Hania got closer to home, Lukia noticed her daughter's distraught face and wondered if it had anything to do with Irina and her family. "What happened?"

Tears rained down Hania's face. "Oy Mama, Bohdan has typhus."

"How do you know?" Lukia tensed, fearing what her daughter was about to say.

Hania's face fell even more. "I went to see him."

"Oy." Though sympathetic, Lukia was disappointed her daughter had disobeyed her.

"I'm sorry, but I couldn't stay away." Hania rubbed her arms. "I was walking past his place with Pan Striluchky, and Bohdan saw me through his window. He beckoned me to come in, so I told Pan Striluchky to go ahead and I'd meet him later for the ride home." Hania bit her bottom lip. "Mama, he's so sick. He told me he'd been out in the field days before and saw wild cats running at him. He was so shocked and afraid it was real that he took to his bed."

Lukia rocked her head from side to side and groaned. "You went inside."

"He wanted me to try some plum compote that he'd cooked. He kept saying, 'Taste it, taste it. It's made from plums. It's delicious.' I took a spoonful."

Lukia wanted to yell at her daughter and tell her again that no good could come from this relationship and that she had put herself at risk. Instead, she moaned and said softly, "You foolish girl. You can get sick yourself. Why did you do such a stupid thing?"

Hania glared at her. "He's my boyfriend—why not?"

"You've lost your mind!" said Lukia loudly, no longer able to hide her true feelings. "You better pray you don't come down with that hellish disease again. Foolish, foolish young love!"

"If he dies, I'll die, too. I won't want to live anymore." Hania ran off to the forest crying.

Lukia wondered what she'd done wrong in raising her daughter. This wasn't what she'd wanted for her. She'd tried to explain the importance of a blessed union, but her daughter was so besotted that she'd not only turned against her own mother, but also against the church's teachings.

Later, when Lukia caught Hania standing in the field—her eyes directed toward Zhabka—she shuddered to think of where this love was heading. Had her daughter already sampled sex with Bohdan? Was that why he had such a hold on her? As far as Lukia knew, Hania still had her monthly. She'd seen her scrubbing her panties, her blood staining the water in the basin pink.

Days went by, and there was nothing Lukia could do to lift the pall hanging over Hania. Her daughter did her chores, but the spark that had lit her from within was gone.

With one sunny day after the other bringing calmness to the land, the family planted their grain. It was a before-the-storm kind of calmness. Egnat tilled each row marked off with string. Lukia and Hania followed, throwing barley down from bags slung on their shoulders.

One afternoon, when Lukia stopped to take a rest, she heard the familiar sharp twang of an axe hitting wood in the forest bordering their fields. Gregory, his brother Vasil, Dmitro, and Ihor had gone into the woods to cut trees for their new home.

Even Levko, one of Hania's friends, had come over to help. Lukia suspected it was because he was sweet on their daughter. A slim and serious young man, Levko took every opportunity to be near her when he wasn't in the woods with the men. He and Hania talked easily with one another, kibitzing and laughing like two girlfriends. Lukia could see he was a wonderful catch; he was good to his mother and unafraid of hard work. Playing matchmaker, she invited him to stay for supper and made sure Levko and Hania sat next to each other at the table. During the meal, Lukia kept glancing over, hoping to see some evidence of an attraction.

After Levko had gone home, Lukia pointed out his qualities as she and Hania did the dishes. Encouraged that her daughter seemed to be listening, she added, "He'll make someone a good husband."

Hania said, as she was drying a dish, "He's nice, but not for me."

Scrubbing a bowl hard, Lukia said, "You don't know what's good for you."

"I do know but you won't accept it."

Lukia said nothing more but scrubbed each dish as if it had an inch of scum on it. They worked in silence until a burst of laughter caused Lukia to look behind her. Michalko, Havrylo and Eudokia were playing catch with a cloth ball their mother had made a few days before. So far, no one was quarrelling.

Lukia washed the last plate. If only her countrymen could stop fighting. And what if the ongoing battles reached Kivertsi? She couldn't erase from her mind the image of the man shooting his brother. Before he died, the young man's face had twisted in disbelief, and when he fell, his brother froze, as if shocked to discover he'd been the executioner. What horrors had Gregory seen? His constant writhing beside her at night made for a restless sleep. He'd scream at some unseen enemy and wake up in a sweat. She feared his nightmares would last forever.

Whenever she asked him what had awakened him, he'd mumble, "It's nothing. Go back to sleep."

As if she could. It seemed as if there were another person in bed with them—a person with no face and no heart.

With each night a turbulent one, Lukia dragged herself through the day, one foot in front of the other, going through the motions in a dreamlike stupor. If only she could rest, but there was no time, not with seeding underway.

One morning, Lukia's work was interrupted by Eudokia's crying. She called out to her older daughter, who was a row over. "Hania! Go see what's happening with Dunya."

Throwing down more barley seeds, Lukia smiled as she recalled how Eudokia had gotten her nickname. During one family get-together, Egnat and Michalko had sung a folk song about a young girl named Dunya, who went into the woods to gather nuts. When they sang, "Hey Dunya, Dunya ya," Eudokia laughed and repeated the words. Her brothers had called her Dunya ever since. Now, the whole family did.

Lukia's thoughts jumped to Hania's brooding. Her daughter continued to mope because she couldn't visit Bohdan, not with all the work on the farm. Lukia had tried to reassure Hania by reminding her that the whole family had been infected with typhus and recovered. But this reassurance hadn't helped to change her daughter's mood.

Lukia was disturbed again, this time by her husband's shouting from the edge of the forest. "Michalko! Come here!" She turned to see her son running to help the men drag a large pine tree out of the woods. It was hard work for a boy not yet a man, and hard work for a man beaten down in war. Each cut pine tree would be trimmed of its branches, brought back to their encampment, and sawed into logs. The bones of their house were finally coming together.

As Lukia threw more seeds into rows, she revelled in the fact that despite their losses, they still had their skills. She was in demand as a seamstress and also good at bartering for what the family needed. They had already managed to get some chickens, and a farmer near Lutsk had promised them a cow, paid for by some of Gregory's paltry army earnings. The boys, in turn, proved adept at helping fill the food coffers through fishing and hunting. The stream running by their farm contained a bounty of perch and pickerel, easily caught with a makeshift fishing rod. As for meat, Egnat had become a good shot and could be counted on for the occasional rabbit or deer. However, his trips into the bush were few and far between. No farmer, young or old, had the time to sit in wait for a skittish animal.

After several days of sowing seeds, Lukia and Hania planted a vegetable garden and sunflowers. The latter they did before sunrise, as folklore suggested this would improve the yield. It was also when the birds were less likely to pick the seeds. In a matter of months, the flowers' sunny faces would not only provide tasty bites between meals—they would also lift the family's spirits.

Though her body ached, Lukia had no time to massage her sore back and legs. Meals had to be prepared for not only her family but also for the men who'd been up since dawn working on their home. They'd come faithfully every day for the past two weeks. The only one not staying for supper was Levko, who had to rush home to do his chores.

At least now they had a dining table, which Gregory had improvised out of a couple of sawhorses and planks of wood he'd found in a deserted army tent not far from their property. Around the makeshift table covered by a yellow oilcloth, old log stumps and wooden crates served as chairs.

The men took their places and Lukia couldn't help smiling when she saw how quickly the food disappeared after it was set on the table. "You must have holes in your legs," she said teasingly. "I can't keep up with all of you."

"Your food is too good," Dmitro said, before wolfing down a hunk of rye bread that had been dipped in a mushroom sauce.

"Yeah, yeah," she said, laughing. "Flatter me, flatter me."

After the meal and several drinks of whisky and kvass, a fermented grain drink, the men talked politics. Fortunately, Gregory and the others agreed when it came to their views—politics and drinking could be a volatile combination. Lukia remembered family events where the mood hadn't been so genial and fights had erupted.

Seeing the men defer to her husband, Lukia wondered if it was because he was the one who'd seen the most conflict. Perhaps he understood more than the others what was at stake.

Gregory leaned back from the table and wiped his mouth with his hand. "They're all fools. Petliura is trying, but what can he do when they're all fighting each other?"

Petliura was the head of the Ukrainian National Republic. He had led Ukraine's struggle for independence.

Ihor raised his glass and took another drink. "Yes, what can he do?"

Gregory nodded. "There are seven armies battling in Ukraine."

"Seven? How do you get seven?"

"I'll tell you," said Gregory, as he poured himself another shot of whisky.

Concerned he might become quarrelsome, Lukia said to her husband, "Maybe you've had enough."

He glowered and told her to be quiet before turning back to the men. "Wives think they have all the answers."

Lukia felt her cheeks flush with anger. She stood abruptly and began clearing the dishes from the table.

Gregory—seemingly oblivious to his wife's irritation—turned back to Ihor. "I'll tell you how I get seven. There's the Ukrainian Galician Army, the Bolsheviks, the White Army, the Poles, the Romanians, and the anarchists. That's six. And then you have the Entente—the British, the French, and the Americans. They can't keep their hands off our country."

"Can you blame them?" said Dmitro, wiping the last bit of food from his brown whiskers. "You can't find better farmland anywhere in Europe."

"The Entente is especially worried the Bolsheviks will win," said Gregory. "The threat of communism is too great."

"Maybe with Petliura, we'll win."

Gregory scoffed. "Win what? Do you remember what happened when we turned in our Russian rubles for Ukrainian *hryvnia*? They gave us receipts. What good was that? Did you get any money for them? They were worthless!" He spat the last word out.

Ihor nodded gravely. "Afterwards, a woman in the village hung herself."

That poor woman, thought Lukia. She was sure many others had contemplated doing the same. She wanted to ask if the woman had children. Lukia couldn't imagine leaving her children to fend for themselves. It was why she had fought so hard to get over typhus.

Gregory stared at his empty glass and poured himself another stiff drink. "Then there's all the Bolshevik propaganda. Petliura had airplanes drop papers everywhere claiming that what they were saying in the news was false. That he wasn't guilty of committing pogroms against the Jews."

"Do you think the people believed him?" asked Dmitro.

"Who knows."

"Many can't read what was written," said Ihor.

Lukia finished gathering the dishes on the table. She wasn't interested in politics—what had it ever given her? Each government seemed to be as bad as the last. Not one of them had succeeded in reassuring her of the future, one where there'd be enough land to support a growing family. Now with the different armies fighting for control over their country, it was a stew with unknown ingredients and too many cooks. Nothing good could come of it.

Like the poor woman who hung herself. Did she just want enough farmland to feed her family? That wasn't so much to ask for, and yet, with the threat of Bolshevism, what was to become of them all?

The sky lit up and thunder crashed as if to emphasize the gravity of the situation. Ihor looked at the darkening clouds. "Time to get home before it's too late."

"Wait a little," said Gregory. "One more for the road. A little lubrication will help you repel the rain."

Dmitro guffawed.

Having had enough of the men's talk, Lukia stacked the dishes on the counter and leaned against it. Pain shot up her legs, and it felt as if she'd walked miles without boots on. How could her husband toss all night, work all day, and then drink till he could hardly stand? She wished his brother hadn't brought over the homebrew. Gregory had drunk heavily before the war, but now it seemed he had no bottom.

Thankful to finally have a chance to rest, she went behind the curtain marking off their sleeping quarters. Hania and Ivan could take care of cleaning up. Gentle and considerate, Ivan was the best of her sons. She only hoped he'd find a woman who wouldn't push him around. He had the kind of spirit that could be broken by the wrong woman.

While undressing, Lukia heard snippets of the men's discussion.

"So many regions are cut off by so many fronts," said Dmitro. "The cities, too. They can't send letters anywhere. The politicians don't know what to do."

"People are starving," said Vasil. "Bread is scarcer than money."

Ihor groaned loudly. "They're desperate. I heard one village barricaded itself against intruders and strangers."

Another thunderclap—louder than the last one—suggested rain was close at hand. One of the men must've stood up, as she heard a crate scrape against a sawhorse leg. "Stay, neighbour," said Gregory. "One more drink."

Lukia said her prayers and climbed into her bed, which was nothing more than a mattress on straw. Lying there, she recalled how Gregory had reprimanded her in front of the other men. If they hadn't been there, she would've given her husband a piece of her mind. He'd suffered, yes, but so had she. What's more, he hadn't even noticed her leaving the room.

If Not for the Cows

LUKIA AND HANIA left the younger children sleeping and went to the creek to wash clothes. Mist covered the rippling water; the dew on the banks glistened in the rising sun's glow. Lukia put the wicker basket full of laundry down by a large rock at the water's edge and savoured the fresh morning air. She looked over at Hania, who hadn't said a word since she got up.

"Are you still mad at me?" said Lukia, as she sat down on a rock.

"I don't want to talk about it." Hania picked up a small stump and moved it closer to the creek.

"Don't be like that." Lukia sighed and dunked one of Gregory's shirts in the water. Her heart ached. She missed the easy banter she and her daughter usually had when they did their chores.

Lukia scrubbed the shirt with a bar of soap and tried again. "My child, I want what's best for you. Listen—"

"Mama, there's nothing you can say. I wish I could marry him. At least if I could be with him, I could help him get better."

Lukia stopped her scrubbing. "You know nothing good could come of it. Even if I let you, the priest wouldn't allow it."

"Stupid religion."

Lukia sucked in a breath. "Hania! Don't say that! Cross yourself and ask God to forgive you."

Pouting, Hania refused to cross herself and rubbed an undershirt on a soaped-up washboard.

Lukia regarded her daughter's back. "I'm sorry it's not to be. If only you liked Levko."

"Why do you bring him up?" Hania said crossly.

"He follows you like a dog waiting to be petted. He would make some girl a fine husband."

"I'm sure he would."

"Hania—"

Her daughter scrunched up her face in frustration and put her hands over her ears.

Lukia groaned as another strained silence took over. While she wrung her husband's shirt in the stream, she remembered how Bohdan had visited her in the hospital when she was suffering from typhus—he'd pleaded for Hania's hand in marriage. Her heart had felt heavy at the time, knowing it was impossible. She wondered why God had cursed her like this. And why had He cursed her daughter? She wished she'd never let Hania become godmother to Stepan. If she'd known they'd fall in love, she would've said no.

While Hania went to check on the children, Lukia hung the clothes on the line that Gregory had strung up between two poplar trees near their tent. Then she looked over at the men building the walls of their new home. They had arrived before the rooster crowed.

Half the logs were already in place. With the days getting shorter, the men were pushing themselves to get the house finished. It took three men to lay the logs horizontally on top of the rock foundation—one log on top of the other to form the walls. Then the logs were joined at the corners by saddle-notching or dovetailing. It would be the same type of home as they'd had before, a two-room cottage, but considerably longer than the one they had. As was the custom, the men left openings for a door facing south and three windows along the front. Lukia hoped they would have time to add covered stalls for their livestock. So far, they had only one horse and one cow, but with any luck, they'd get a few more cows to milk, another horse for chores, and a few pigs for meat.

She couldn't wait to be rid of the crowded conditions. It was impossible to keep their belongings clean. A dirt floor exposed to the open air meant dust came in on the children's boots and stayed.

Back under the tarpaulin, she gazed again at the building site. Soon the thatched roof would be added, thanks to Ihor, who had an abundance of rye straw they could use. Once the structure was completed, she and Hania would be called upon to help Gregory plaster the exterior with clay. They couldn't keep relying on the other men for help, as their own farms needed tending. As it was, the Mazurets family had leaned on their kindness for too long—a kindness they hoped to repay in time.

Why just yesterday, when Dmitro arrived, he'd mentioned that one of his cows had gone astray. Since Irina wasn't feeling well, he'd asked if Ivan wouldn't mind going into the bush to find her. Lukia was glad to oblige, as her in-laws had been so generous. Besides, Ivan was old enough to take on more responsibilities and loved being out on his own. He'd stayed at his aunt and uncle's house overnight and was to return home this morning, but Dmitro had arrived without him, reporting the cow was still missing. Ivan had gone out again to look for the wayward animal.

Lukia looked up at the sky. Dark clouds were moving in. She scanned the horizon in the direction of Zhabka. It was dark over there as well. Perhaps raining. She wondered if Ivan had found the cow and was waiting for a ride back.

It wasn't long before the rain began pouring down in sheets and the men had to abandon their work for the day. Not wanting to trouble Dmitro more, she asked Gregory to ride over to his sister's place and bring Ivan home. If their son hadn't found the cow by now, there was no point in searching any longer, not with this foul weather.

Gregory delayed leaving, hoping the rain would let up so that driving in the open wagon wouldn't be so uncomfortable. The skies gave no sign of letting up. Pools of water formed on their fields and roads. Their tarpaulin sagged with the weight of the water that had gathered on top and they had to use a broomstick to raise the roof and release some of the load. She didn't mind the torrent. The young barley and wheat shoots were strong enough to withstand the pounding, so long as it stopped soon.

Gregory set out in his wagon when the setting sun emerged from behind a cloud, signalling the end of the downpour. While she cleaned up the supper dishes, she wondered if Ivan would be hungry when he returned. Likely Irina would've fed him. However, Lukia knew her son. He had a healthy appetite but was usually too polite to ask for seconds, especially at his aunt's table. And Irina wasn't the type to coax her guests by suggesting they have another serving. With that in mind, Lukia put aside some leftovers that could be warmed up when he arrived.

The sun had set by the time Gregory returned with Ivan in the wagon. In the low light, Lukia could see the water splashing as the wagon wheels hit the puddles on the uneven road. Ivan sat beside his father, his body bundled in a perina that partly covered his face. Sensing something was wrong, she rushed out to greet them.

"What's the matter?" she asked, her voice cracking with concern.

"He got chilled," said Gregory. "He kept looking for that dumb cow even though it was raining. He didn't want to come back without her."

She felt Ivan's forehead. It was hot. "Oy, Ivanshoo." She helped Gregory carry their son inside and put him on top of the pich; the oven was still warm from supper. "What were you thinking, my silly boy?" she asked, shaking her head.

"Mama," said Ivan, shivering. "I'm sorry. I wasn't thinking. I know how much the cow meant to Auntie and Uncle."

"What's a cow? We can replace a cow." She said it even though, given the hardship that had come over their people, a cow wasn't easy to replace.

After exchanging Irina's damp perina for a dry one to cover Ivan, Lukia soaked a clean cloth in cold water, wrung it out well, and placed it on her son's forehead. Then on top of the cold compress she placed a dry wool babushka that had been folded a few times lengthwise.

Ivan breathed heavily and put his hand on his chest. "Mama, my chest hurts."

"I know," she said, stroking the top of his head. "You rest. I'll make you some hot milk with butter and garlic."

Ivan's condition worsened during the night. His lips turned blue, as did his fingernails. He complained of pains in his side and began to cough up a pinkish sputum. Lukia reapplied cold wet cloths and the dry wool overlay on his forehead. She also gave him clear broth to drink and more of the garlic-infused milk. All the while, she prayed and told herself she'd rescued one son from death, she could rescue another. But there was a part of her that doubted. This wasn't typhus. Pneumonia was a determined killer.

Another twenty-four hours passed with no improvement. With her stomach in knots, she could stand it no longer. She asked Hania to keep watch while she went to find Gregory. He and the other men had completed the walls and were getting ready to work on the roof. She ran to him and grabbed his arm just as he was about to climb the ladder. Breathing hard, she said, "Ivan's not good. I think you should get Mama. She might know what to do."

Lukia knew some herbal remedies, but it was her mother, who was regarded as the expert in the field.

Gregory's forehead pleated. "We don't even know if she's still living with your brother. Besides, you know how far the Carpathian Mountains are. It would take days to get there and back."

"Gregory," she said, tears welling in her eyes. "We can't lose him."

"What about the doctor?"

She shook in frustration. "He knows nothing and he's a drunk. When he's sober, he's at the hospital." Blinking back tears, she added, "I know you don't believe in prayers, but please pray for Ivan. Pray for him to get better."

Gregory nodded solemnly. All they could do was wait and pray. At the hospital in Lutsk, people died all the time from pneumonia. There was no point taking him to a place where he could end up dying on a cold concrete floor.

Ivan's fever raged through the next day. None of her folk remedies had helped. She'd even massaged her son's chest with garlic to no avail. She slept only when Hania or Egnat offered to stay beside Ivan and give him sips of vegetable broth.

When his sputum turned brown and his body was sheathed in sweat, Lukia sent Hania to get her father.

Gregory came running.

"He's so young," said Lukia, choking on her sobs as they stood over Ivan, watching him sleep. His skin was ashen, his cheeks hollow, his body restless. Gregory said nothing, but his silence and hand tremors communicated his agony. His mouth twitched but no words came. The other children had also gathered around, worry painted on their faces. Lukia turned to Egnat and told him to fetch the priest. Egnat hesitated, looking over his mother's shoulder at his brother.

"You have to go," she said but held onto Egnat's shirt, as if afraid to let him out of her sight. "There's nothing more we can do." Her body went numb. She couldn't believe what was happening. She wanted to scream at God, ask him why He had let her down. Why He had let her son down.

"Mama," said Egnat, his voice breaking. "Let go my shirt."

Shocked by his words, she released her grip. Soon after, she heard Egnat galloping away on horseback.

With a heavy heart, she bit her lip and stroked her son's brow. "Poor, poor Ivan."

Ivan's eyes flickered open. He looked delirious. "Mama, am I getting better?" His voice trembled.

"Son, don't be afraid," she said, holding back her tears. "Pray to your angel. This will pass soon."

She couldn't believe how quickly their fortunes had turned once again. Her precious Ivan, so good, so kind. This was the third child she would lose. This was why women had so many children. In life, you never knew when one could be taken away.

The priest arrived too late to see Ivan alive. He performed the last rites anyway while Lukia continued to pray for a miracle.

When the priest had finished praying, she threw herself on her son, sobbing. "Ivan, wake up. Wake up." She kissed him on the lips, hoping to breathe some life into him, but he was already cold. She looked at the icon in the tent. "Please, help us. Don't take him yet." Gregory gently peeled her off their son as her body heaved with sorrow.

As the priest drove away, Lukia fell into Gregory's arms. She tried to catch her breath. The sounds she made were like those of an animal she'd never heard before. It was as if her lungs had been pierced along with her heart. Why had she let Ivan go to search for that damn cow? She should've sent Gregory as soon as she noticed the turbulent sky. Now her beautiful boy was gone. Why hadn't God taken her instead?

DEATH IS NO STRANGER

IN SEPTEMBER, WITH the civil war raging only a few hours' ride away, Dmitro and Ihor finished helping Gregory and Egnat build a new dwelling, complete with a komorra to store preserves and root vegetables. They also added a chicken coop and covered stalls for the animals: one for the horse, one for cows, and one for pigs. And with the older boys' help, Lukia and Hania plastered and white-washed the walls well ahead of the heavy fall rains.

Though it felt good to finally have a home again, Lukia found her work interrupted by visions of Ivan's gentle face. He was in the kitchen standing by the pich or in the main room lying on one of the beds. Haunted by memories of her son, she would sometimes stop her work and check to see what the other children were doing, just to assure herself they were still there, that God hadn't taken another when she wasn't looking.

When Havrylo first took the spot Ivan had once filled at the supper table, she opened her mouth to say something but then stopped herself. It was enough that she had trouble letting go— she didn't have to make the children feel guilty. Her customary shot of alcohol with the meal did nothing to dull her pain.

She knew Gregory was also stuck in a downward spiral of mourning—his son's death layered with those of his fellow soldiers. He drank enough whisky or vodka to knock himself out before bedtime. Once, she found him slumped over in a chair. She'd tried to rouse him but that had only enraged him. After that, she let him find his own way to bed. Sometimes she heard him in the middle of the night, bumping into the table when he got up to pee and then staggering to bed.

This went on for weeks until she could stand it no longer. Though tired and drained with all that had gone on, she stayed awake in bed, hours it seemed, until he joined her.

"Gregory," she said, "you can't keep doing this. You'll ruin your stomach and your liver. What good will you be then?"

He lay on his back and stared at the ceiling. "What good am I now? Nothing is as it was."

"How can it be, with everyone fighting everyone else."

"The Ukrainian Galician Army has been decimated. The men who weren't killed by the Poles or the Bolsheviks fell from the plague—typhus has killed tens of thousands."

"I know. Come here." She opened her arms and he rested his head on her bosom, the smell of whisky strong on his breath. They fell asleep to the sounds of a wolf howling. Perhaps he, too, was awash in grief.

The following day, when Lukia was collecting eggs, she heard a wagon approaching. It couldn't be Gregory back so soon. He'd gone to drop the older children off at the village school and would then go with Eudokia to see a farmer about a sleigh for sale. Lukia put her basket of eggs on the ledge inside the chicken coop and stuck her head out the door. Hania was already at the wagon to greet Ihor. He'd taken his hat off and was saying something Lukia couldn't hear.

Hania fell to the ground before Ihor could catch her.

Rushing outside, Lukia nearly tripped on the rough ground. "What happened?"

"Bohdan Pilutik passed away last night."

Lukia quickly bent over Hania and felt her forehead. "Her temperature is good. Help me get her in the house." Together, they carried Hania inside, where they laid her on the bed and covered her with a perina.

Ihor fingered the rim of his hat. "I was in Zhabka and heard the news. Complications after the typhus. It weakened his heart, brain, and kidneys."

Lukia held her head in her hands and rocked it. "Tragedy. You know, their love was cursed. That's how it is." She said it matter-of-factly, but her stomach was churning. Had she done the right thing by standing in their way?

As if sensing her mother's thoughts, Hania opened her eyes. Lukia stroked her daughter's forehead then went to the kitchen to get a cup of cool water. After Hania had taken a few sips, she buried her head in her mother's chest. Her body heaved.

Lukia felt her daughter's sobs course through her veins.

When Gregory came home, Hania got up from her bed, her face swollen and blotched from crying. She put a hand on her father's chest. "Tato, would you take me to Bohdan?"

His brow furrowing, he regarded Hania. "You can't help him now. Wait for the funeral. We'll all go together then."

"No, I have to go now. Please. Please take me."

Lukia wrung her hands. "Hania, listen to your tato. There's nothing you can do. He's with God now."

"If Tato doesn't take me, I'll walk." She waited for only a moment and then put on her felt boots.

"I'll take you, I'll take you," said Gregory, already getting his coat.

"What good will it do for you to go?" Lukia said pleadingly. "Bohdan had typhus. Who knows what else he caught. God forbid you get sick."

"Mama," Hania said through tears, "I have to see for myself. I promise you I'll be careful."

"It would kill me if anything happened to you."

"I know, but I have to go."

Resigned, Lukia said, "Well, if you must, take some borscht for Bohdan's parents." She went to the stove and poured some freshly made soup into a sealer. She then put the glass jar of soup in a flour bag for Hania to carry. "Let his parents know we're sorry and that we'll pray for Bohdan's soul."

Lukia had just finished covering several rows of boiled varenyky with tea towels to keep the dough from drying when Hania returned with her father. Lukia greeted them at the door. "Did you see him?"

"Yes," said Hania. She walked inside and sat down on a stool.

"How is his mother taking it?"

"Not good. She said to thank you for letting me come, and for the borscht." Hania lowered her eyes. "I don't understand. How can I believe in a god who takes away those I love?"

"It's not for us to question. We have to believe. Someday you'll see Bohdan. Believe that. You'll be together."

"What good will that be then?"

Lukia had no answer. A mother's job was to comfort her children but there were times when no comfort could be given.

THE ACCIDENT

THOUGH THE BITTER December cold stilled most farm activity, trouble in the country showed no signs of abating. Given the recent news that the Polish army had conquered the Ukrainian forces, Lukia wasn't surprised to find two Polish policemen at her door one afternoon.

"Panye," said the burly one with the greying beard, "we're looking for a criminal who's escaped."

"There's no criminal here," she said, folding her arms across her chest.

"How many live here?"

She wanted to tell him it was none of his business, but if she did that, he'd probably slap her face or knock her over as he forced his way in. She swallowed hard. "Seven. My husband, myself, and five children."

His eyes strayed, and a look of lust crossed his face as he leaned sideways to get a better look inside. Lukia turned to see Hania bending over to put away pots on the cupboard's lower shelf, her curvaceous backside on display. Lukia muttered, "pig" under her breath.

"What did you say?"

"Nothing. Something's caught in my throat." She coughed to emphasize the point.

The other officer, a weaselly-looking man with a pencil moustache, said, "We need to look around."

Before Lukia could protest, the officer wiped his boots on the outside rug and barged in. She wished Gregory were home. The other children were in school, so she and Hania were alone. Fear of what these men could do kept her from challenging them further.

The burly one studied Lukia's face and glanced from time to time at Hania as his partner went through the house, lifting up perinas, looking under the bed, and peering in the komorra. Lukia saw him check behind the barrels of sour cabbage and cucumbers. She ground her teeth in frustration.

"Nothing here," said the weaselly one. "I'm going to look at the outbuildings."

After they departed, Lukia stared out her window at the snow-covered fields. Unspoiled and peaceful—a stark contrast to the turmoil she felt inside. Was it always going to be like this? Living under the rule of one autocrat after another?

The next morning, Lukia woke up unwillingly to the sun streaming through the frosted bedroom window. A disturbing dream had made for a rough night. Gregory was already out getting wood for the fire. When she heard stomping outside the front door, she threw on a sweater over her nightgown and went into the kitchen.

"You're finally up," said Gregory, coming in and wiping the ice off his moustache.

Annoyed by his comment, she grumbled, "Don't say anything. You know it's not like me to sleep late." The day before had taxed her. It had been December 19, Saint Nicholas Day, and the saint had left the children a treat in their shoes—a piece of dried fruit. Times were lean, but fortunately, she'd been able to help the saint by finding sweet treats in the village. Trudging there through the deep snow on top of her other chores had tired her more than usual.

"I had a bad dream, Gregory." He was putting wood into the stove, his back turned. "Are you listening?"

"Yes, but I have lots to do."

"This won't take long. Sit."

He reluctantly sat down beside her at the table.

"I dreamt about a big cow with swollen teats. She came to the house, and try as I might, no matter how much I drank, I couldn't drain her milk. It kept flowing and flowing." She shook her head. "It's not a good dream."

He snorted. "Maybe it means we'll be so well off we won't be able to spend what we have."

"Don't make fun of me. You know dreams aren't that simple. It's usually the opposite of what they say."

"So, we'll be poor. We've been poor before. If we're poor again, we'll manage."

She was about to argue, but a knock on their front door interrupted their conversation. While she got dressed, Gregory went to see who it was. She heard him greeting Vasil and quickly pulled her hair back into a bun.

"Vasil," she said, coming out of the bedroom. "What brings you here so early?"

"Good day. Your neighbour, Ihor Striluchky, was arrested yesterday. The Polish police found a rifle in his house."

Her stomach sank. "They arrested Ihor? What's wrong with having a rifle? We all have them for hunting."

"It was one like the Ukrainian army uses. They think he was plotting against them."

"That's crazy," she said.

"I'll go see his wife, see what she knows," said Gregory. "I'm about to have breakfast. Will you join us?"

"No, thank you. I've already eaten." Vasil remained standing at the door, his cap in his hand. "I hope this doesn't mean these raids are going to be common. They've already imprisoned thousands of our best people. I doubt they'll give Ihor counsel."

She groaned. "Poor Ihor. The Poles are squeezing us every chance they get. Isn't it enough they make our children sing the Polish anthem at school? Soon, they'll forget their own language."

"What can we do?" said Vasil, putting his cap back on.

When Michalko had come home from school singing the anthem, she had yelled at him, "What are you singing? That's not ours." Her outburst had surprised her son, and she had to calm herself before saying she wasn't blaming him. It was the damn Polish government. She also had to admit the anthem's chorus was catchy: "March march Dabrowski." But she told Michalko to never ever forget his own anthem. Too much blood had been spilled fighting for an independent Ukraine.

Vasil was right. What could farmers do? Naturally, they wanted an independent Ukraine. Some Ukrainians had even elicited help from the Germans, but that had turned out to be a problem because they were outsiders, like the Russian Bolsheviks. Both groups were intent on imposing their ideas. Already, the Bolsheviks had taken over farms in the east and turned them into collectives. There was no easy solution.

After Vasil left, and Gregory and Egnat were eating their breakfast of potatoes and eggs, there was another knock on the door. It was Taras Ewanciw, their neighbour from down the road. His face was red as a beet from the harsh wind.

"Come in, Taras," said Gregory.

"Would you like something to eat?" asked Lukia.

"That would be wonderful." Taras took off his sheepskin coat and Cossack fur hat and hung them on a hook by the door. "I was hoping you'd help me. I need to go to the bush and get a big load of wood."

"Of course," said Gregory. "I was going to see Nina Striluchky, but maybe Lukia can go in my place. You heard her husband was arrested?"

"Yes, I met Vasil on my way here and he told me." Taras sat down on a stool and took off his leather boots.

"I don't see how they can keep Ihor in jail," said Gregory. "But who knows what they have up their sleeve."

Lukia cooked a few more eggs and heated some potatoes. After serving Taras, she sat down at the table. As she watched her husband eat, a feeling of dread swept over her. "Gregory, I don't think it's a good idea for you to go to the bush today."

"Why not?"

"Something could happen to you. We've had a heavy snowfall and you'll have to go by the tracks. You could get hit by a train."

He laughed. "I'll stay away from the tracks."

"That's not my only concern. You could get hit by a falling tree in the bush. It's not a good time of year."

Gregory looked at Taras and winked. "Women. They're always worried about something."

Taras nodded. "My wife's the same."

"I have to go anyway. We're low on wood. Between the two of us, we can cut enough for both our homes. And whatever extra we cut, we can sell."

"I'll help, too," said Egnat.

Her throat tightened. "Listen to me. This was not a good dream."

"I hear you, but if I have to stay indoors every time you have a bad dream, what's to become of us? We'll freeze to death."

She moaned. How easily he dismissed her fears. When the men were leaving, she said to her husband, "At least cross yourself."

Gregory looked at her in disbelief. "Don't be foolish. Leave it already."

"It wouldn't hurt you to cross yourself."

He ignored her and raised the door's latch.

"Gregory, cross yourself!" she said angrily.

He turned to Taras and Egnat. "Let's go." He then faced Lukia. "Tell Nina they won't be able to keep Ihor long in jail. They have no cause."

She clicked her tongue. "I'll tell her."

Standing at the door, Lukia crossed herself three times and watched the men and Egnat plod through the deep snow toward the bush. Their footsteps created dark holes in the blinding-white landscape. She watched until the bitter cold pushed her back inside.

"Mama," said Hania, putting an arm around her mother's waist. "Why are you so worried?"

After Lukia told her about her dream, she said, "It means I'll be crying a long time. As if I haven't cried enough."

"It doesn't mean anything will happen to Tato. Didn't you tell me about the gypsy fortune-teller who said Tato would die before he was forty?"

"Yes."

"Did he die?"

Lukia made a face. "It's true what you say. He's strong as an ox and he's forty-five."

"See. No one can predict anything. So why believe a dream?"

Lukia studied her hands, grown rough with age and hard work. "Pray anyway. It won't hurt."

"Mama, Tato went through four years of war. Over eight million soldiers in the Tsar's army were wounded, died or ended up in prison, and yet Tato came home in one piece. Even the hellish typhus didn't get him. You worry too much."

Lukia stroked her daughter's soft cheek. "Since when did you become so smart?"

Though obviously pleased, Hania shrugged.

"I have to go visit Nina," said Lukia taking off her apron and hanging it over a spindle chair's back. "I won't be long." She wrapped her feet in onoochky—long strips of linen cloth for extra warmth—before putting on her felt boots. She then dressed herself in her *bikasha*, a long quilted-cotton coat she'd made and lined with cotton and wool batting. Lastly, she put on her sheepskin hat. If Nina hadn't been Hania's godmother, she wouldn't have considered going out in this frigid weather, but Nina would do the same for her if her husband had been arrested and put in jail.

The snow in the fields was mid-calf deep, so Lukia didn't bother with the shortcut and stuck to the road to avoid getting snow in her boots. All the way to Nina's, she ruminated on her bad dream. She was also frustrated that Gregory had turned away from God. No good could come of it, she was sure.

Nina opened the door before Lukia knocked and welcomed her with a kiss. "Thank you for coming."

"It's nothing," said Lukia, banging the snow off her boots before entering.

"Horrible times. I'll put the kettle on for tea."

Lukia had taken off her hat and bikasha and was sitting down when she heard crying outside the door. Nina opened it to find Michalko, red-faced and out of breath.

"Mama," he sputtered, "a tree fell on Tato."

Lukia's body went rigid as if she'd been hit by lightning. "What are you saying?"

"Uncle Taras and Egnat brought him home."

Lukia immediately stepped out into the cold but stopped when Nina put a hand on her shoulder. "You'll kill yourself if you walk out like that. Dress yourself first."

Lukia stumbled back into the house and put her outer garments back on. "I'm sorry I can't stay."

"Of course not," said Nina.

"I told him not to go," said Lukia, moaning. "You have your

troubles, I have mine."

Nina hugged Lukia. "Think for the best."

Lukia trudged as fast as she could through the snowy terrain after Michalko, who bounded ahead on the shortcut. The snow was high and uneven, and her effort, along with her panic, made each step a heavy and precarious one. She fell once, and Michalko had to turn back and help her up. They walked without talking. All Lukia could think of was her dream and how her husband had tempted fate.

When Lukia and Michalko reached their cottage, it was already full of people—family and neighbours who'd heard of the accident. Gregory, covered by a perina, was lying in the main room on the narrow bed Lukia's mother used when she came to visit. Around him stood Taras and her children, who seemed to be waiting for their mother to join them. Lukia exchanged glances with Taras. Her heart stopped. The look on his face said the end was near.

She quickly took off her coat and boots and rushed to Gregory's side. Her usually strong husband lay listless and pale; his breathing, shallow. Beside him, Egnat stood as if on guard. His face indicated he also expected the worst. Noticing Havrylo standing to the side, Lukia brought him forward to join his sisters and brothers around the bed.

Lukia knelt by Gregory and said to the children, "Pray God will give you your tato back."

While they said the Lord's Prayer, Michalko stopped several times to cry. His sobs were so loud they drowned out the mumbled words of his brothers and sisters.

After she'd finished praying, Lukia squeezed her husband's little finger, hoping to get some reaction. "Gregory, tell me, what am I supposed to do with our small children?"

He opened his right eye, and a tear, the size of a pea, trickled down his cheek. When he shut it, he drew his last breath.

"Stay with me," said Lukia, shaking him. Behind her, the children wept. She clutched his shirt, willing him to come back to life. Already, his warmth was seeping away. He'd laughed with her just that morning. Had teased her. He'd been unwilling to give in to her fears. Why hadn't he listened? Why did he have to be so stubborn?

She should've yelled at him, clung to his jacket, threatened to leave him if he didn't listen. Would he have heeded her then? She wanted to sleep and wake up to find this was just another bad dream.

Master of the House

IN THE MORNING, Lukia asked Egnat to drive her to Fedor's house. She hoped to get a shirt in which to dress her husband for the funeral. Gregory's brother wasn't home but Katerina, his wife, was.

"I can't give you one," she said, and pressed her thin lips together. "I'm afraid if I give you one of his shirts, my husband might die, too."

"Fedor has tuberculosis," said Lukia. "I should be the one worried. I could get infected just being here." When Katerina shrugged, Lukia added, "His sickness won't get worse because of Gregory. He had no disease. A tree fell on him."

"I'm sorry. I can't."

Though Katerina seemed distraught, Lukia took her sister-in-law's refusal as a major slight. She mumbled a goodbye and left quickly with Egnat.

As they drove away, Lukia fumed in silence. She couldn't remember doing anything that would've brought on such coldness. She thought she'd been sympathetic during Katerina's depression in the refugee camp. As she ruminated further, she recalled that Katerina had once loved Gregory and had wanted to marry him herself. Spurned, she'd married his brother instead. Perhaps that explained why her brother-in-law was unhappy in his marriage. Who would want to be second choice? Maybe that also explained why Fedor had wandering hands.

Early in her marriage, when Lukia and Gregory were living with his parents, Fedor had dropped by to visit. Lukia had been alone in the house, mashing potatoes at the stove. They exchanged greetings, and then he came up behind her and grabbed her breasts. Startled, she turned and kicked him hard in the stomach. Soon after, her mother-in-law returned from the barn and found Fedor holding his stomach and groaning. There was no hiding what had taken place. Her mother-in-law had said to her son, "Are you crazy? Do you want your brother to kill you?"

Now Lukia's mind churned. Had Katerina found out about that incident? Was that what this was about? Maybe that was why Katerina hadn't been generous. She was either still jealous of Lukia or angry with Gregory for not choosing her. Regardless, they were family. Sisters-in-law were supposed to support one another, especially in grief.

Next, she and Egnat drove to see their neighbour Nina, who upon hearing Lukia's request instantly opened up a trunk in her home, revealing a few crisply ironed shirts. "Take what you want," she said.

Though relieved, Lukia said, "Won't Ihor mind?"

"No. He'd be honoured." Nina's eyes were sympathetic. "You'd do the same for me."

"Thank you," said Lukia, choking up. She picked out a beige linen shirt. "I'll never forget this."

"It's nothing. Gregory was a good man."

Back at home, Egnat and a carpenter from the village set about building a coffin with four boards while Lukia and Hania prepared the funeral lunch. Lukia worked as if in a fog. Nothing was recognizable. She kept hoping Gregory would surprise her by walking out of the bush or come driving down the road and waving. Her heart broke further when she went to the chicken coop to get some eggs and saw Egnat in the yard, hunched over, his body trembling as the burial box took shape. There was nothing she could do to ease his mind or hers. Death was not a friendly visitor. Only after they had wrung themselves dry, could they get on with living.

With the help of Dmitro and Vasil, Egnat laid his father to rest on the satin-covered straw that Lukia had placed inside the coffin.

That evening, mourners came to pay their respects. They stopped at the open coffin in the main room before offering their condolences to the family. Lukia was oblivious to all except Ihor, who had just gotten out of jail—a Polish bureaucrat had provided proof he wasn't a member of any enemy army. After paying his respects, he sat down beside the coffin and read the Bible aloud until daybreak. The front door's opening and closing would muffle his voice as people arrived and departed. At those times, the cold winter air rushed in as if it too wanted to have its last say.

After Mass in the Lutsk cathedral the next day, the coffin was closed. The pall-bearers placed three embroidered towels under the box and carried it out to Ihor's wagon, parked in front of Petro's covered carriage, which would carry Lukia and her children. Fedor was the only one of Gregory's brothers who did little to help, which was understandable given his weak condition. At the house the evening before, he'd stayed by the door with a handkerchief over his mouth to cover his occasional coughing. Lukia had given him a stool to sit on.

At the graveside, the priest chanted while swinging his censer on a chain, tracing the sign of the cross over the crowd, coffin, and grave. The Cantor sang "Forever Memory," and the mourners joined in, their voices mingling with the wind that rustled in the nearby poplar trees. As the coffin was lowered into the ground, Lukia, who'd hardly slept, felt her knees buckling. If it weren't for

Hania and her sister-in-law bolstering her, she would have fallen to the earth herself.

Her husband was buried next to Ivan and the two babies they'd lost.

The funeral luncheon was held in the Marzuretses' home. After the priest had blessed the food, Egnat offered each mourner a shot of vodka from the bottle he carried. Each person drank from the same glass. With space at a premium, only the adults sat on chairs, stools and crates. The young ones filled their plates and stood wherever there was room.

Lukia downed the vodka in one gulp, its warmth jolting her. How was she going to manage alone on a farm with five children in a country continually beset by wars? She sat for some time with her hands in her lap, until finally Irina came up to her and said, "Lukia, you have to eat something. You need your strength now."

She ate half her meal, though nothing tasted right. Friends and neighbours expressed their sorrow, but after they left, she couldn't remember who had come and who hadn't.

Within a week of Gregory's passing, Lukia's mother Fedoshya arrived. It had taken a while for the news to reach her and then several days before she could get to Kivertsi from the Carpathian Mountains. She was the type of woman who showed up at her children's homes only when there was a need for her help. Otherwise, she was out travelling to various villages curing the sick with her herbal remedies.

With Christmas around the corner, Fedoshya rolled up her sleeves and helped Lukia and Hania with the cooking and baking. While they worked, she told them stories of miraculous cures she'd seen and heard about.

More than a few times, the children's laughter caused Lukia to look up from the dough she was rolling. Her young ones were decorating a small fir tree, which Egnat had hung from the ceiling, with apples, cookies, and nuts. Egnat, who'd been so solemn, cracked a smile when he saw Eudokia sneak a bite of a cookie before she hung it on the tree. Their preparations weren't much, but they were enough to lift some of the pall that had settled over all of them.

On the morning of Christmas Eve, the family went to the cathedral. The church was already packed as they walked up to the front of the nave, where a *vertep,* a replica manger, had been adorned with hand-carved wooden figures of Joseph, Mary, the three kings, a few shepherds and Baby Jesus. Candles on polished brass stands flanked the shrine, shining a light on the Holy Family. The Mazurets family bowed and crossed themselves at the nativity scene before leaving to stand in one of the rows. Thankfully, the service was short, allowing much-needed time to prepare for the traditional holy supper.

As was the custom, no one had eaten all day. They had to wait until the first star came out.

Back at home, everyone scurried to get the supper ready. Michalko and Havrylo scattered hay on the kitchen table, a reminder of Christ's birth in a manger. They also put a clove of garlic at each corner of the table to ward off evil spirits. Over the hay and garlic, Lukia laid her best embroidered tablecloth. Then she set a plate for Gregory.

"I miss Tato," said Hania, placing a *kolach,* a round braided loaf of bread, in the middle of the table.

"I know," said Lukia, inserting a beeswax candle into the bread. "Maybe his spirit will join us." She stared out the window at the darkening sky and wondered if he could see what she was doing. Did he know what she was thinking, and how much she still loved him? He had died still a young man, with many good years left—gone because he wouldn't heed her warning.

Eudokia's excited voice broke her mother's reverie. "I'm watching for it."

Lukia turned to see her youngest standing at the other window, her nose pressed to the glass. "Good," she said. "You keep looking."

It wasn't long before Eudokia shouted, "I see it! I see the first star."

Lukia gathered with the others to see a lone white star twinkling. The moment of peace and awe was soon exchanged for the bustle of getting food on the table.

Fedoshya, Lukia, and Hania had prepared twelve meatless and dairy-free dishes, symbolic of the twelve apostles and the Virgin Mary's hardship on her road to Bethlehem. The candle in the kolach was lit, as well as a candle on the window shelf to show any homeless person who might be passing that they were welcome to come and eat with them.

Fedoshya placed a sheaf of wheat in the corner of the room and said, "Thanks be to God for his help."

The family was barely seated when Eudokia grabbed the bowl of potatoes. "First prayers and *kutya*," said Lukia, placing a hand on her youngest daughter's. "Then you can eat."

Eudokia put the big spoon down and pouted. "Why do we have to eat kutya first?"

"Because it stands for family," said Hania, seated across from her. "All those grains of cooked wheat stand for those who are here and for those who've passed away."

Sheepishly, Eudokia bowed her head.

After prayers, Fedoshya took a spoonful of kutya—a mixture of cooked wheat, poppy seeds, and honey—from the bowl and raised it in the air, saying, "Christ is born."

The others replied, "Let us glorify him."

Then the bowl of kutya was passed around the table for each to take a spoonful on their plate. Eudokia took more than a few.

"Eudokia," said Hania. "I thought you didn't like it."

"I love kutya. I just didn't want to wait to eat the other food."

Lukia clicked her tongue and raised her glass of whisky. "*Daye Bozhe.*"

The rest of the family repeated the toast—"God willing"—and clinked their glasses. Dish after dish was passed around the table, and for dessert, a honey cake and a dried-fruit compote.

Though Lukia found solace in the holiday meal, she kept glancing at the empty plate at the head of the table as if Gregory might miraculously appear.

The next day, Lukia was up earlier than usual. Since her husband's death, she'd tossed in her sleep nightly and would wake up at times to think about her family's future. Egnat, at sixteen, was certainly capable of hard work but he was still a boy. He'd been thrown into a man's job during their years in camp but now, with a farm to run, he would have even greater responsibility. Would they be able to make it on their own, without a man as the head of their family?

She threw on a sweater and went into the main room, where she found Egnat already dressed and putting on his boots.

"Where are you going?"

"I have to feed the animals and get the sleigh ready for church."

"What a good son," she said. Here he was, once more taking charge.

He only grunted in her direction. Lukia wished he'd talk more. He hadn't said much since his father passed away. He'd crumpled with grief while he was building his father's coffin. She hadn't realized until days later that Gregory had died on Egnat's sixteenth birthday. In her sorrow, she'd forgotten to acknowledge her son's special day—not that any of her children expected anything on their birthdays. Because they had little means, the family acknowledged birthdays but never celebrated them.

She peered out the window and watched him hitching the horses, stopping on occasion to lovingly pat them. She knew she expected a lot from him. She hoped in time he wouldn't rebel under the weight of being the eldest son in a house without a father.

It was still dark when Fedoshya and the Mazurets family set out for Lutsk. Lukia sat with Egnat in the front of the sleigh, while the children snuggled next to their *baba* under heavy perinas in the back, their warm breath playing with the frosty air. Lukia marvelled at how blue the snow-blanketed fields looked under the navy sky. The quiet was only broken by the pounding of the horse's hooves and the sound of metal runners on the icy road.

The church was crowded but Fedoshya and the children found places at the end of one row. Lukia continued to walk up the centre aisle to the table in front of the iconostasis. She stooped down and kissed the gilt-framed icon on the table before going to the brass stand on the right to light candles for the deceased— Gregory, her three children, and her father.

Despite the uplifting service, the children fidgeted. Lukia couldn't blame them. Mass was long enough, but today, with the inclusion of Christmas carols, the priest's long holiday sermon, and the announcements, it stretched beyond the usual three hours. Uncomfortable, Lukia shifted her weight from one foot to the other before looking down the row to see Egnat sneak out with two other boys, probably for a smoke.

She was tempted to leave the mass and bring him back but she didn't want to provoke an argument. Not on Christmas Day. Lukia glanced at her mother, whose eyes were closed in prayer. She wished she could pray with her mother's fervour, but her once strong faith had been shaken. She'd always believed that if she lived a good Christian life, she would be rewarded on earth as well as in heaven. But now, with the agony of losing both Ivan and Gregory, life was hard to bear. She wondered if she could rely on

God in the future. She recalled her time in the hospital and how she'd died briefly and met God on the staircase to heaven. She'd begged Him to let her stay on earth and He had let her return to her children. Maybe it had all been part of His plan. She looked at the icon of Mary with Christ and asked God to forgive her for her questioning.

Christmas supper had all the offerings of the holy evening before, but it also included borscht with sour cream, *studenetz*, and *kishka*. Lukia and her family were still eating when they heard carollers singing outside their home, their raised voices a welcome interruption.

Egnat opened the door to a group of young men and women with winter-bitten noses and rosy cheeks. Levko was among them holding a large silver star on a long stick. The group began to sing, "Good evening, master of the house . . ."

Lukia saw Egnat frown. Was he thinking about his father's death and how it had made him master of the house before he was ready? The carollers likely knew about the Mazurets family's loss, but they always sang this traditional song on Christmas Eve.

"Please," said Lukia, joining her son at the door. "Come in."

The carollers continued to sing while stamping the snow off their feet and entering. They gathered in a semicircle, facing the family. When the singing was finished, Lukia turned to Egnat and said, smiling, "Get the whisky. They need a warm-up."

The young men took off their Cossack fur hats and grinned while Egnat poured whisky into a shot glass. Levko kept glancing at Hania affectionately, but she didn't seem to notice. Frustrated that her daughter was ignoring such a fine young man, Lukia shook her head. A few of the young women giggled as they unbuttoned their coats and took off their fur hats and heavy babushkas. After one singer drained the glass of whisky, Egnat refilled it and did the same with the next.

Refreshed, the young people sang a few more carols, including "God Eternal" and "In Bethlehem." With alcohol fuelling their spirits, the choir sang with even more animation. The Mazurets family joined in. Egnat's voice, which now had rich timbre, was a pleasant addition to the travelling songsters. Afterward, a tall caroller said to him, "Get your coat and join us."

"How about you, Hania?" asked Levko. "We could use your beautiful voice." One of the young men jabbed another with his elbow and whispered in his ear. It appeared they were aware of Levko's infatuation.

"Thank you, Levko," said Hania, warmly. "Maybe next year."

Levko's face fell. "Good," he said, unconvincingly.

Lukia could see by Egnat's expression that he wanted to go. He loved carolling, the joking that came with the visits to each home, and, of course, the whisky provided to cheer and warm the carollers. She hesitated—she wanted her family to stay together on this holy evening. They had enough emptiness to deal with without his leaving. She was about to say he couldn't go, when Egnat said to the tall caroller, "Thank you, but maybe next year."

Lukia looked at her son and nodded gratefully as the carollers buttoned up their coats and said their goodbyes.

A Crack of Hope

WITH EACH DAY blurring into the next, Lukia went through the motions of mothering, housekeeping, and farming. Waking up groggily, she would forget her husband was gone and listen for his footsteps, expecting him to come in from the cold, his whiskers covered with snow, ready to tease her. She couldn't bear to part with any of his things. His clothes were still draped over the spindle chair in their bedroom. At times, she'd pick up his shirt and bury her nose in the flannel to inhale the lingering scent of tobacco and dried sweat.

On occasion, her children shared memories of their father. One time, Lukia found Hania weeping in front of Gregory's jacket, which was hanging on the hook by the front door. Another time, she found Egnat outside gawking at the forest, as if he expected his father to walk out of it.

After the snow had melted, Egnat erected an oak cross on his father's grave. The cemetery wasn't a long walk and was on the road to Kivertsi, which meant Lukia could visit the family graves whenever she went to the village. It was a place where she could think out loud in private.

On one of these visits, she put her hand on the cross bearing his name and said, "Gregory, nothing much has changed. Everyone is still fighting over the region." She half-expected him to answer, and when he didn't, she sighed. "You know how small our farm is. Right now, the children are young and we can manage somehow, but someday it won't be enough. We're still under Poland's thumb, but the Bolsheviks are threatening. I tell you, if the Bolsheviks come for our farm, they'll have to drag me off of it. I won't let them take it. I won't."

Just then, the wind picked up and a few loose hairs flew across her face. She tucked them into her babushka and said, "Oy, why have you left me with such small children?"

"Why are you crying?" a voice asked. Then Lukia felt someone shake her shoulders.

She turned but there was no one there. Only the wind blowing across the graves. She shuddered and fled from the cemetery, almost tripping on another grave's low marker. After that, she stayed away but vowed to return after Easter for the priest's annual blessing of the graves. There would be no worries then about a disembodied voice talking to her. Not with a cemetery full of families praying for their loved ones.

In the spring, when the *kalyna* trees began to bud along the edges of her fields, Lukia felt a glimmer of hope she hadn't felt for some time. She took a bag of potatoes outside and sat on the bench by the door. As she watched the peels fly into the pail at her feet, she took stock of her life. She was a forty-five-year-old widow with five children. The oldest was eighteen, and the youngest five. Though she wasn't happy with the current government, her farm was her own and most things were available in Kivertsi. The village had grown to include a school, a store, a chemist's shop, a blacksmith, a tailor, a shoemaker, an oil press, a mill, a surgical and obstetrical station, a post office, a telegraph office, a Roman Catholic church, and two cemeteries, all of which served forty-nine homesteads with over five hundred inhabitants. It wasn't a large community, but Lutsk was only sixteen kilometers away, where you really could get anything, as long as you had money.

Their farm had also improved with the addition of an outhouse. A Polish government agent had visited recently and said it was against the law not to have one. Lukia had no problem with his demand, as Egnat had already mentioned he wanted to build one from scraps of lumber he had amassed on their property.

As for a social life, now that she was unattached, she was bothered by the occasional suitor. Though the Great War had taken its toll on the men, there was the odd bachelor sniffing around, as well as a widower whose wife had died in childbirth. These men might've had something to offer, but Lukia had no interest in nor patience for anyone courting. Nor was she interested in taking care of another woman's offspring. She had enough of her own. Besides, it was too early to consider another marriage. It hadn't even been a year since Gregory passed.

Lukia and her children got their crops planted early, but there was no rain. A nation-wide drought followed. The ground became parched, and any seedlings that had emerged struggled to survive.

As bad as it was in their oblast of Volhynia, it was worse in the east, under Russian rule. Lukia's neighbours told her that those who'd been forced to collectivize their farms weren't able to satisfy the impossible quotas, nor pay the excessive taxes levied. Farmers had to sell their remaining machinery or seed more grain just to stay on their land. With famine widespread in these regions, desperate men were taking desperate measures. Already, groups of bandits and various armies had commandeered or stolen most of the livestock. Buildings and businesses had been destroyed and land confiscated.

Given the stories of unrest in the east, Lukia resigned herself to living under Polish rule for the time being. Many of her countrymen were still dreaming of an independent Ukraine, but Lukia dreamt only of pulling her family through the drought and having a property big enough to support them. She was thankful the war years, with all their turmoil and upheaval, had taught her how to survive.

In the fall, rain brought hope the following year would be better. There was always hope.

An Unexpected Courtship

OVER THE WINTER, Lukia's sister-in-law came down with a chest infection that mushroomed into pneumonia. Even Fedoshya's herbal remedies did nothing to ease Irina's discomfort and pain. Her quick passing wasn't a surprise. There had been too many tragedies in the past few years—death was no longer a shock. But it was a surprise how quickly Dmitro came calling. His poor wife had been dead barely a month.

At first, Lukia—grieving the loss of her wonderful sister-in-law—felt sorry for Dmitro and invited him to share a family meal once a week. He never arrived empty-handed. One time, he brought a rabbit he'd shot, some fruit preserves Irina had canned, and a bottle of store-bought whisky. When he started bringing her children candy and chocolates, Lukia realized he was looking for more than a home-cooked meal. The problem was she wasn't ready to have a suitor. She still sensed Gregory's spirit near her, so the idea of sharing her bed with another man—even though it had been well over a year since her husband passed—was unthinkable. She would feel unfaithful. It was with this in mind that she kept all of their conversations light and hosted him only in the presence of her family.

After one supper though, Lukia found herself alone with Dmitro at the kitchen table. Fedoshya had gone to visit her son, Egnat had taken Hania and her friend to Lutsk to hear a Cossack choir and the younger children were outside playing. It was getting dark, and Dmitro showed no signs of leaving. Instead, he poured himself another shot of whisky. His head was bowed, and Lukia got the impression he was ruminating about something serious.

After a minute or so, he raised his head. "Lukia, you know I love you. We could have a good life together."

"Dmitro," she said, "don't say anything. Irina's still warm in the ground and Gregory's shadow hangs over this house."

He raised one eyebrow. "What are you saying? Even the church says a year is enough."

She leaned back. "Where does it say that?"

"I don't know. It says it somewhere." He took another drink. "A beautiful woman like you shouldn't be alone."

"I'm not alone. I have my children."

"You know what I'm talking about." He paused and looked at her so directly she became uncomfortable and lowered her head as if there was a spot on her skirt that needed attention. "Besides, marrying me would help your children. You have only five deshatin for the whole family. When your sons get married and have babies, it won't be enough. Marry me and what I have will be yours."

She anxiously rubbed her hands. It was a generous offer. Marrying Dmitro would solve a lot of problems, for he was a wealthy man. She wouldn't have to worry about her livelihood or her children's futures. So, she didn't love him, but what was love? It didn't put food on the table. But then she saw his head wobble from too much drink. He was rich now but could she count on him to stay that way down the road? A man who loved the bottle couldn't be trusted to keep what he had. She'd had plenty of worries with Gregory. She'd worried he'd turn out like his father, a lumber contractor who'd lost his good fortune due to his drinking binges and generosity.

Dmitro leaned forward. "Why are you so silent? I'm asking you to be my wife. Maybe not right away, but soon."

"How can you ask? People will talk. You have to wait at least a year."

"So, let them talk." When she made a face, he said, "Okay, I'll wait a year."

She shook her head. "I don't know."

At that moment, Michalko stomped through the front door, his face flushed.

Startled, she said, "Son, why are you so red?"

"We were playing tag." He looked at Dmitro and frowned.

She gave Michalko a disapproving look. "Why are you frowning at Uncle like that? What is the matter with you?"

"Nothing." His demeanour didn't change. He remained by the door, eyeing Dmitro and then his mother. "Is everything good, Mama?"

"Of course." She wondered if Michalko also thought it was too soon to have another man courting her.

"Michalko," said Dmitro gruffly. "You're almost as tall as Egnat. How old are you?"

"Thirteen."

"You must be a big help to your mother. It's not easy for her to manage this farm alone."

She straightened her apron on her lap. "Uncle Dmitro thinks it's too much for me without a husband. He thinks I should marry again."

Michalko's eyes darkened. "Mama has her children to help her. She doesn't need anyone else."

Dmitro groaned and turned to her. "You're letting a boy, still wet behind the ears, run your life? In a few more years, he'll get married and you'll be sitting here alone."

Michalko began to shake. His voice rose as he said, "I'm not getting married for a long time. I'll be here to help Mama."

"Don't scare my children," she said to Dmitro. She could see her son wasn't going to calm down anytime soon. "You'd better go." She stood and began clearing the dishes. "Dmitro, you're a good man, but I'm not ready. Thank you for the whisky you brought."

Dmitro grunted then downed the rest of his drink. He wiped his mouth with his sleeve. "You know where I live if you change your mind. Thank you for the supper."

"Nothing to thank me for."

She stood in the doorway watching him ride off and wondering if the cold reception he'd received meant the end of further courting.

As she cleared the table, she glanced over at Michalko, who continued to pout while he polished his boots. Annoyed, she said, "Why did you talk like that to Uncle? He was concerned about me, that's all."

Michalko's lips tightened. "I don't want a different father." He mumbled something and went out the door.

That night, she lay in bed reviewing Dmitro's visit. Had she been too quick in rejecting his offer of marriage? Her mother certainly had that opinion.

When Fedoshya had returned that evening from treating an ill child and heard about the marriage proposal, she said, "Why are you listening to Michalko? He doesn't know what you need. Your children won't always be with you. They'll find partners of their own and you'll have no one."

She knew her mother was right in one way. But what would be the good of marrying Dmitro if he disturbed her child? She didn't think Egnat would mind. He was more practical than Michalko, who was her most sensitive son. There was no way he'd let another man replace his father.

Lukia wasn't the only one in the family being romanced. Hania had a constant suitor, too. Given her daughter's long grieving over Bohdan's death, Lukia knew she should've been thrilled, but Hania's new love was a hoodlum. It was well known in the village that Damien Sabiuk, though dashing in his army uniform, was a rascal, a young man who shied away from work and had an eye for the ladies.

The first few times he'd come courting, Lukia had offered him whisky and something to eat. But then she'd noticed how unwilling he was to give a hand. He never offered to help Egnat laboring in the fields. Instead, he'd pace or stand by the house smoking, impatiently waiting for Hania to finish her chores so they could go riding or for a walk in the woods.

Now when Damien visited, Lukia fussed less, sometimes even ignored him and continued with her household chores. It didn't seem to faze him one bit—as long as Hania continued to fawn over him. Why was her daughter drawn to such a cavalier man? Did he sweet-talk her in private? Perhaps his false promises of undying love had swayed her daughter.

Lukia had never been one to let anger get the best of her, but one day, during one of Damien's visits, she lost her composure. She'd taken two loaves of bread out of the pich and placed them on some tea towels to cool. Turning, she saw Damien enter the house quietly and sneak up behind Hania, who was busy at the stove seasoning the borscht.

When he grabbed Hania by the waist, she jumped. "Damien," her daughter said, sounding annoyed. "What are you doing here so early?"

He laughed. "It's not early. The sun's been up for hours."

Lukia's mouth twisted. "Damien, you're here almost every day. Doesn't the army need you? Don't you have work at home?"

"I'm on leave from the army," he said. "As for work at home, it'll always be there. I wanted to come and see your beautiful

Hania. Maybe she'd like to go for a ride with me on such a lovely day." He flashed Hania a wicked grin, plunked himself on a stool, and stretched his legs out.

Lukia couldn't help but notice his crisply ironed uniform and polished brown boots. She figured his good looks and well-dressed figure were part of his appeal. He obviously cared about his grooming, if nothing else.

Lukia's face tightened. "Are there many of you at home? Who does the work when you're not there?"

"Who? My parents and a hired hand."

As Hania continued to season the borscht and move around the kitchen, Damien unashamedly savoured the view.

Lukia harrumphed. "There's always lots to do on a farm. Work doesn't wait because it's a beautiful day."

Hania turned to Damien. "Can I get you some tea?"

"Please. And make it as sweet as you," he said, winking.

Unable to handle any more of his talk, Lukia took her sweater from the back of her chair and said in a pinched tone, "I'm going to prepare the soil in the garden. After you pour Damien his tea, I'd like some help."

"Yes, Mama," said Hania, her voice carrying a hint of disappointment.

Lukia put on her sweater, and without glancing back, left the two of them sitting in the kitchen.

After grabbing the hoe by the front door, she walked briskly to the vegetable patch. There, she tackled the weeds ferociously, as if each hack would bring her closer to cutting Damien out of her daughter's life. It wasn't only his laziness that bothered Lukia—it was also his unpredictability. His blue eyes danced when he was flirting, but when provoked, they flashed with anger and turned a steely grey. Lukia had seen evidence of his quick temper when he'd last visited. He wanted to have another drink, but Hania told him he'd had enough. In response, he gave her such a fierce look that she immediately backed down. Lukia wished Hania could see what she saw: a man more in love with himself than with the girl he was courting.

Late in the afternoon, after Hania had returned from a wagon ride with Damien, Lukia summoned her daughter. "Come with me. I need to talk to you."

"Mama, if this is about Damien, I'm not interested."

Lukia gave Hania a cross look. "I'm still your mother. You're not out of the house yet." Hania reluctantly followed her mother outside. They walked through the farmyard and down the road in silence. Lukia breathed in the soothing smell of rich, freshly-turned soil as she considered how to broach the subject. At times, she glanced at Hania, who walked straight ahead, with her head lowered, as if she were a little girl going to the woodshed for a spanking.

When they were far enough from the house and the prying eyes of her other children, Lukia turned to her daughter. "Nu, what do you see in him?"

"Mama! What kind of a question is that? I love him. He's good to me."

Lukia pursed her lips then sighed heavily. "What does he do for you? I don't see him doing anything. He comes over and sees Egnat working hard in the fields and doesn't even offer to help. Damien knows you've lost your father and yet he sits there like he's got nothing to do."

"He has his own work at home. He helps his mother and father."

"Have you seen him help?"

"No," said Hania sourly. "He told me he does."

Lukia studied her daughter's face. How had she raised a woman who could be seduced so easily? She'd be Damien's servant, catering to his whims.

"Listen," said Lukia. "Do you understand what trouble you'll be getting into? If he won't lift a hand now, what will he do when he's married?"

"If you have nothing good to say about Damien, there's no point talking." With that, Hania turned and headed back to the house.

Lukia followed Hania's retreating shape—so young and beautiful, her strides long and purposeful. Her daughter could have anyone in the village, and yet she'd picked a scoundrel.

Several evenings later, when Lukia was sitting on a bench outside darning socks, Hania came out of the house and sat down beside her. She picked up a pair of socks from the basket on the ground and a threaded needle from her mother's pincushion. They darned in silence for a few moments; only the howl of a wolf somewhere in the forest broke the quiet.

After darning one sock, Hania put it down in her lap. "I know you don't like Damien."

"It's not that I don't like him, I don't know him." She met her daughter's eyes. "I don't know if he'll be good for you."

Hania hesitated, and then said, "He's asked me to marry him and I said yes."

Lukia's mouth fell open. "Oy. What are you thinking? He's no worker."

"Is that all you can say?"

Lukia grabbed her daughter's hand. "Listen, you're not thinking ahead. If you marry him, I won't be able to help you when you have children. You'll be too far away." After marrying, girls lived with their in-laws to begin with, and Damien's parents' farm was a long day's ride from Kivertsi.

Hania said nothing.

"Did you hear me?"

"Yes," said her daughter, her nostrils flaring. "I heard all I want to hear." She stood up.

"Hania, I'm only thinking of you."

"You're not thinking of me," said Hania, spitting the words out. "If you stand in my way, you're going to have a sick girl on your hands." She stormed off down their farm road.

"Oy, child," said Lukia, holding her head. Stopping a stubborn horse from leaving the farmyard would've been easier.

Hoping to find out more about what was in store for her daughter, Lukia invited Damien's parents over for lunch. She wanted some assurance that they knew what a prize they were getting. She also wanted to find out how much they supported their son's lackadaisical behaviour.

Mr. and Mrs. Sabiuk, who were shorter and stockier than their son, brought a bottle of vodka. During the meal, they praised their hostess's cooking. Damien and Hania said little, perhaps taking note of what their respective parents were saying. Lukia waited until they'd all finished eating and her younger children had left the table before addressing her concerns.

She cleared her throat. "Hania and Damien are still getting to know one another. And since there's no rush, I think it would be good if they waited another year before marrying."

Hania's face fell. Damien took her hand and said, "What's the point of waiting? Look around us. War is constant. I could go into battle at any time. I wouldn't want to go without knowing Hania's my wife." Hania gave him a grateful look.

"Mr. Sabiuk," said Lukia. "I know Damien's been busy on the farm, so I—"

"There's no problem with the farm," Damien said firmly.

Lukia raised her eyebrows and looked at his parents, expecting them to say something about his rudeness, but they avoided her questioning eyes. "That's good to hear," she said reluctantly. Not ready to give up, she then turned to Mrs. Sabiuk. "What do you think? You have only one son. They're both so young. They have lots of time to get married."

Mrs. Sabiuk shrugged. "They have their own minds." Hania smiled at Damien, seemingly pleased to have gotten her future mother-in-law's support.

Lukia groaned. Times had changed. A young couple didn't need a mother's approval anymore, but she had hoped for some support from the Sabiuks, some appreciation of their son's unreadiness for marriage. Couldn't they see he wasn't the responsible type? She wished Gregory were still alive. He would've known what to do. Maybe he would've known how to stop his daughter from marrying a lout. The Sabiuks seemed nice enough, but what did anyone know after one visit?

Before Lukia fell asleep that night, she found herself talking to her late husband. Her head rested on her pillow as she gazed at his shirt on the chair, the one item she couldn't part with. It still had his smell. She told him how she felt about Damien and what she was afraid of. She imagined Gregory deep in thought, smoking a handmade cigarette as he listened to her. She could almost hear him say, "Wife, why worry? What will be will be."

"I know," Lukia muttered. "Remember how headstrong she was over Bohdan? That was a sin, and yet she couldn't be talked out of it. She said she loves Damien. Love! Why can't she see she's marrying the wrong man?"

Lukia could almost hear him laughing at her question; his deep crusty laugh had always put a smile on her face. "She's a grown woman," she heard him say. "Do you think anyone would've talked you out of marrying me? You remember what your mother said?"

"I remember," said Lukia, addressing Gregory's shirt in the dark. "She told me you were a drunk." She snorted. "You were, too, but you were also a hard worker. You'll be pleased to know Egnat has taken after you. Both the drinking and the hard working."

She moaned as she thought of how Gregory would've taken all this in stride. He didn't fret about the things he couldn't control. Then again, he was a man.

THE WEDDING

DESPITE HER RESERVATIONS, Lukia went along with Hania's plans. She told herself to be thankful her daughter and Damien were getting married after harvest time and that he'd followed tradition by showing up a month earlier with two *starosty*—elders—to ask for Hania's hand in marriage. The older married men from his village had brought a fine bottle of vodka, and Damien had presented Lukia with a round decorated loaf of bread sprinkled with salt and wrapped in an embroidered rushnyk.

"From my mother," he said. In return, Hania gave Damien a baked loaf of bread for his mother, also covered with a decorated towel.

Lukia couldn't help but wonder what Damien would've done if Hania had given him a pumpkin instead. It wasn't that long ago a bride's gift of a pumpkin would've meant rejection. Now many traditions were being lost. Young people no longer used the services of matchmakers, nor did they pay any attention to their parents' wishes.

As part of the wedding preparations, she spent one afternoon rolling out pastry for *hrystyki*, a fried sweet treat laced with honey. While she rolled, she thought of her sisters. Usually, a woman could count on them for help. Though Lukia had four, none was able to do anything for the celebration. Two had died—Tekla as a baby, and Panashka, from typhus at the end of the Great War. The oldest living one, Nastia, had moved to the Caucasus, too far to be of any help. And Onishka? Well, the family had lost track of her. As for Lukia's mother, if she wasn't praying, she was out tending the sick and dying. Thankfully, a couple of neighbours had offered to make desserts. But not Katerina. Lukia heaved a deep sigh as she remembered how afraid Fedor had been to approach Gregory's coffin. A lot of good his caution had done him. He'd still died from tuberculosis not long after. If it's meant to be, it's meant to be, she thought, and pushed the rolling pin harder.

With the wedding only a few days away, Lukia sat on her bed embroidering red, green, and blue flowers on Hania's linen bridal shirt. She lamented she hadn't been able to stop the marriage from going forward, but Hania was stubborn like her father. Lukia's bottom lip quivered as an image of Gregory filled her mind. What she wouldn't do to feel his warm lips on hers once more. "Oy, Gregory," she said. "You won't be here to give your daughter away."

Her heart ached even more as she ruminated about her daughter and how close they'd been. Now she acted like a different person. Then Lukia remembered she'd been no different. She'd insisted on marrying Gregory even though her mother hadn't approved. Fedoshya had worried about his drinking but her biggest complaint had been about his faith, or lack of it. Sure, he'd gone to church with Lukia, but he'd never stayed for the whole service. He'd leave early to have a smoke on the grounds with the other men. Just like Egnat did now with his friends.

Lukia sighed again. Would she be able to hold up during the wedding? She couldn't pretend to be happy about Hania's marriage. What mother could be happy knowing her daughter was marrying a man with one eye on the ladies and the other eye on the bottle?

Lukia hadn't seen Damien flirting with other women, but there'd been talk. If there was talk, there was truth to it. His being in the army didn't help. The way the soldiers caroused, it was almost expected. Infidelity was one thing she'd never worried about with Gregory. He was a loyal husband.

She completed the last rose on the shirt before fastening the threads with a few back stitches on the underside. After laying the finished garment on the bed, she admired her handiwork. One thing she could count on—Hania would be a beautiful bride, the talk of the village for months to come.

On the big day, Lukia woke everyone early to do their chores and get ready for church. After ensuring the children were dressing, she went into her bedroom to tend to herself. She was doing up the covered buttons on her beige rayon crepe dress when she heard a wagon approach. She peered out the window to see two wagons arriving: Damien's and his parents'. The groom's wagon was decorated with ribbons and flowers; his horse was festooned with garlands of primroses. Putting her doubts aside, Lukia admired Damien in his embroidered white shirt and royal-blue satin pants, accented by a red braided sash at his waist. He brought the wagon to a stop by the house and pulled out a pocket mirror, which he used to groom his hair.

"Mama," called Hania excitedly from the main room. "Damien's here."

"Good!"

Fedoshya's voice rung out as well. "Lukia, are you ready?"

"Of course," said Lukia, with some irritation. She was as ready as she'd ever be for a wedding that had bad luck written all over it. She took one last look in the mirror and left her bedroom.

The children were dressed in their Sunday best—dark pants and white shirts for the boys, and a new velvet dress with a smocked bodice for Eudokia. Her hazel eyes sparkled and her long dark braids, tied with white satin ribbons, danced as she twirled in the dress her mother had sewn for her.

"Very pretty," said Lukia. She glanced at Hania, pacing in front of the door. Along with the wedding shirt Lukia had embroidered, her daughter wore a long linen skirt, around her neck three strands of amber beads borrowed from Petro's wife and, on her head, a wreath of myrtle. She was a beautiful bride, but one look at Hania's gentle face was enough to stir Lukia's uneasiness again.

"You're jumping around more than the chickens," Lukia said.

"I know." Her daughter's cheeks were flushed. "What's taking him so long?"

Lukia couldn't help smiling. "His parents aren't that young. It's not easy for them to get down from the wagon. He'll be in soon enough." Hearing Damien's voice by the door, Lukia said, "See."

Upon entering, Damien took one look at Hania and beamed. "I'm the luckiest man in Volhynia."

"Only Volhynia?" asked Hania teasingly. They stood close together, their arms around each other's waist, while they waited for both families to gather inside.

Once everyone was assembled, Lukia said, "I was hoping to wait for Hania's godparents, but they live in the Carpathian Mountains and their train has probably been delayed."

"They'll have to get to church on their own," Fedoshya said. "We should leave soon. It wouldn't be nice if the bride and groom were late."

Lukia placed an embroidered rushnyk on the floor and asked the young couple to kneel on it. Then, holding a decorated loaf of bread and a framed icon of the Virgin Mary, she said, "This bread is life itself. It stands for abundance, which I wish for you. Your tato would've wished the same." She handed the bread to Damien, who bowed his head and held the loaf with both hands. She then moved the framed icon through the air in the shape of a cross. "As these two children stand before their own mother and their parents, we know there were times they did not listen, but I ask You now to forgive them and bless them."

"May Holy God forgive and bless you," said Damien's parents to the bride and groom. They repeated it twice more.

Lukia then gave Hania the icon. "May God bless you with a prosperous and happy life together."

"Thank you, Mama, for your blessing." Concluding the small ceremony, Hania and Damien bowed and then kissed their parents' faces.

Turning to Damien, Lukia wanted to say she'd choke him if he didn't take care of Hania. Instead, she looked deeply into his dark eyes and said, "I'm giving you my blessing, but you have to be good to my daughter."

He cocked his head. "Panye Mazurets, I know you're not sure about me. We plan to live with my parents, this is true, but in a few years, we hope to get a farm of our own. I'll take care of Hania."

Lukia raised her eyebrows. "I hope you're saying the truth."

"Mama," said Hania. "Don't start anything."

"I'm not starting anything." She glanced at his mother. Her lips were tight—too tight, as far as Lukia could see. As if she wanted to say something but was holding back. Maybe she'd heard such promises from her son before, ones that had turned out to be empty. Or maybe, Damien was sincere and his mother wasn't happy about the prospect of sharing his love with another woman. With a wife, there would be new demands. They were getting older and would need more help on the farm, not less. Then again, had he been much help to begin with?

While Damien's parents prepared to leave, Lukia beckoned Hania into her bedroom and closed the door. "Hania," she said quietly, "when you're in church, and the priest asks you both to kneel down, make sure your leg is on top of Damien's pants."

"What?" asked Hania, her eyes widening.

"You heard me. If you do this, your husband will listen to you."

"That's nonsense! That would be a terrible thing to do."

"Don't be so surprised. What I'm saying is true."

Hania grew serious. "Did you do this with Tato? Did it help?"

"Of course," said Lukia with conviction but the truth was Gregory had been a stubborn husband. When Hania shook her head, Lukia realized she was wasting her time trying to convince her of anything. She'd stopped listening when Damien came into her life.

Lukia, her children, and the Sabiuks watched Damien carry Hania from her doorstep to the wedding wagon and then join her on the front seat. While Hania's brothers joked around with the groom, Eudokia circled the wagon, leaping up and down in excitement. Lukia blessed the couple further by throwing raw wheat at them.

Egnat was about to help his mother climb into her own wagon seat when Mrs. Sabiuk came up to Lukia and touched her arm. "Don't worry. My son won't shirk his responsibilities."

"I hope you're right," said Lukia.

Mr. Sabiuk smiled. "We are joining together as families."

Lukia blinked. We'll see, she thought. She took Egnat's hand and grabbed the corner of the wagon seat to pull herself up.

The priest greeted Damien and Hania at the church's entrance. He wore a gold brocade vestment over his black frock for the special occasion. After the bride's and groom's families had taken their places at the front of the nave, the priest took the couple's hands and wrapped them together with an embroidered rushnyk. Holding the free end of the towel, he guided them, followed by their attendants, down the centre aisle past family and friends, all standing in the pewless interior. Lukia watched with a lump in her throat.

For part of the long ceremony, sung by the priest and deacon, the bridesmaids held gold crowns on the couple's heads as they walked around the altar three times. On either side of the altar, all the candles were lit on the polished brass candle stands. Lukia could see the maid of honour making sure Hania's dress didn't come too close to the candles' flames. If it caught fire during the service, it would mean bad luck for the bride on her wedding day and would also be a bad omen for her marriage. The bridal party managed the circuit without mishap. Shortly after, the couple knelt before the priest and Lukia noticed that Hania did so without touching Damien's pants.

Lukia's frown remained until the end of the service.

The reception was held at Lukia's brother's farm. Petro was the only one in the family with a barn big enough to hold the hundred or so invited guests. He and a few of his neighbours had spent days clearing the floor of hay and dung, and through his connections, he'd also arranged for a band to play at the feast. The rousing notes of the violin, tsymbaly, sopilka, and drums had many feet tapping before supper was even served. It seemed everyone who'd been invited from the village and the neighbouring farms had shown up.

Long banquet tables, fashioned from large plywood boards over sawhorses, had been set up on the floor and covered with embroidered tablecloths, which had been borrowed from family and friends. The dishes and cutlery had also come from different homes for the occasion. Despite Lukia's earlier worries, there was no shortage of food. In the end, neighbours and family members had helped to prepare the feast that belied the fact they were all living through hard times. There was roast pork, chicken, kybassa, kishka, varenyky with various fillings, *holupchi*, piroshky, studenetz, and freshly cooked vegetables. In the centre of the main banquet table Lukia had placed a *korovai*, a large decorated wedding bread, to be torn to pieces and distributed later. For dessert, there was cheesecake, honey cake, and pastries.

With more vodka available than usual, Lukia had to worry not only about Egnat but also about Michalko, who had developed an appetite for alcohol. After a few drinks, the brothers tended to argue. As it turned out, the one she should've been worrying about was Damien. He got drunk early. Lukia hoped for Hania's sake that Damien wouldn't make a fool of himself.

Once the wedding guests had filled their bellies and quenched their thirst, the tables were cleared and dismantled to make room for dancing. The guests took to the floor, kicking up their heels to the band's polkas and kolomeykas. A large number of men and women formed a circle and clapped as the younger guests took turns dancing in the middle, showing off their twirls, jumps, and flying kicks. Egnat and Michalko competed with a few other young men to see who could jump and kick the highest.

Havrylo stayed on the sidelines. Lukia wished he'd participate but knew it was hard for him to shine alongside his boisterous brothers. His confidence had been shaken by all the teasing he'd endured both at home and at school. When he spoke, he drew out some of his letters—saying "pay" instead of "p." for example—a speech problem she expected he'd grow out of in time. Her scolding had stopped his older brothers from mocking, but the damage had been done.

She turned her attention back to the dancers. For one wedding custom, Damien was shut out of a circle dance. His goal was to get under the dancers' arms to claim Hania. Drunk, he stumbled around the outside of the group and missed several opportunities to get inside the circle. Other guests crowded around the dancers to witness the fun. They laughed each time he was kept out and teased him all the more. Hania was also teased by their friends as to whether he'd be able to perform later in bed.

Lukia had to admit she was enjoying herself. When Petro came up to her and bowed, she laughed at his formality and said, "You'd think you were the one getting married, all gussied up." He was dressed in a fine grey suit and his thick moustache was waxed to perfection. Raising her eyebrows, she added, "I'm surprised you're asking me to dance." Secretly, she was pleased he was being so considerate.

"I want the men to see you're available."

She pushed his chest with the palm of her hand. "Don't be crazy. I don't want another man."

"Ho, ho, ho," he said, twisting his moustache. "My sister is so high and mighty; no man is good enough for her."

"You don't know, so don't say."

"Do what you want," he said, "but you're still an attractive woman."

She shrugged. "Enough talking. Let's dance."

He put his arm around her waist and spun her around the floor. Her brother was an excellent dancer and dancing the polka with him made her feel young again. They danced only once, because Petro was also a good drinker and went off to get another shot of vodka. This was fine with Lukia, as a number of other men stepped in to take her brother's place.

First, there was Dmitro, who continued to hound her about marrying him. The others, lesser known to her, showed their interest by asking if they could come to her place for a visit. She couldn't take any of them seriously, not after seeing the effect such an idea had had on Michalko.

As for sex, she wasn't interested. It had been all right with Gregory. Even when he drank too much or was too rough, he stopped his advances when she pushed him away or wasn't in the mood, which was much of the time. Eight children in fifteen years was more than enough for any woman. Of course, their sex life had changed after the war. By then, she was that much older and he, having been beaten down by the horrors of what he'd been through, was no longer aggressive or demanding. If he'd lived, she was sure there would've been at least one more baby to care for.

The band had taken a rest and was now playing a few bars to get the crowd's attention. It was time for Hania to throw her bouquet of sunflowers. Standing on a chair, Hania smiled broadly as she surveyed the young women who had crowded around, yelling for her to throw it their way. Lukia smiled when she spotted Eudokia squeeze through the group to get a better view. With her back to the crowd, Hania threw her bouquet over her shoulder. A young woman from the village leaped up and caught it, squealing as she did.

Then it was time for Hania to take off her wreath of myrtle and replace it with a babushka, signifying she was now a married woman. Lukia and all the other women made a circle around Hania and clapped as the band played a folk song celebrating her new status.

In the midst of the clapping, Lukia happened to glance over at the open barn door. Levko stood alone, watching Hania with a reddened face. At first, Lukia thought he'd drunk too much, but then she realized he'd been crying. When he caught her eye, he turned abruptly and left. She understood that unrequited love could break a heart, but there was nothing she could do about his sorrow. If only a mother could choose.

After the midnight buffet—a snack of various cold meats, pickles, rye bread, and sweets laid out one long table—Lukia met Hania and Damien on the dance floor to wish them on their way.

As was the tradition, the young couple would spend their first night at the groom's parents' home. In their komorra, the Sabiuks had prepared a marital bed of straw covered by a large sheepskin coat. It was the one room in the house where a couple could be guaranteed some privacy.

When Lukia hugged Damien, she noticed he reeked of alcohol. Since her daughter seemed happy, Lukia said nothing about his drunkenness and once again pushed aside her fears.

As other guests rushed to bid farewell to the bride and groom, Lukia remembered her wedding night with Gregory and how afraid she'd been of her first sexual experience. Though she'd heard it was painful, what had frightened her the most was the aftermath. The need to show the community she was a virgin. Now it was Hania's turn.

Lukia needn't have worried. She didn't see for herself, but when the couple returned to her home in the morning to continue their festivities, Hania said that all had gone well; she'd left blood on the white sheet. Her daughter had saved herself for her husband and had brought no shame to her family.

TRULY ALONE

LUKIA SHOOK THE braided entrance rug outside, scaring the chickens that pecked on the ground. She waited for the dust to settle before taking a deep breath of crisp spring air. The day smelled freshly washed after the long winter. The trees were budding, the snow in the fields was almost gone, and the last of the icicles was dripping from the roof, making a puddle near the house.

It had been an especially harsh winter, but then, each winter seemed colder than the last. Her body ached more, a sign of rheumatism. At forty-eight, she was long past being a young woman.

She shivered once and closed the door. She thought again of Hania. After her daughter's wedding, Lukia hadn't been able to shake the sadness that had enveloped her. It seemed as if Hania had died, instead of just marrying and moving to Lokacz. Even replaying scenes of her daughter—braiding her hair by the pich, comforting Eudokia in bed after a frightening dream, or peeling beets for a pot of borscht—gave her little comfort.

Hania's absence added one more layer of emptiness to the others Lukia carried in her waking hours. She still saw her sweet Ivan's skinny legs running out the door, or his daydreaming face as he herded the cows to pasture. She also saw her obstinate husband seated at the table, throwing back another shot of whisky and giving her a "you can't stop me" look. What she wouldn't give now to be able to scold him again and then later, feel his hands on her breasts, and hear his teasing about what was to follow.

Too much heartache in life. Her mother was right. Best to keep busy. When Lukia was busy, she had no time to feel sorry for herself.

But in the midst of her longing for what was gone, she suddenly smiled, recalling the news of a joy to come. Hania and Damien had announced in February they were expecting. The baby would arrive at the end of summer. Perhaps then, Lukia would see more of her daughter. Hania would need help with the infant, as her mother-in-law wasn't the nurturing type. Besides, with Damien still in the army, her daughter would be on her own for long periods and would need her mother's support.

One day in late spring, her neighbour Ihor asked Lukia if he could use the bricks from her useless and contaminated well to build an oven. He also asked if she wouldn't mind climbing down to the bottom to fill a pail with those bricks. She couldn't refuse—he'd helped her out with water after the war.

Hania, who'd dropped by for a visit, came with her to the well site. "I'm sorry Mama," she said. "I should be the one going down."

"Don't be foolish. You're expecting a child."

While Ihor and Hania watched, Lukia lowered herself into the dark well. It wasn't easy finding footholds to climb down the mud walls, but moving slowly, she managed. She slipped only once, and caught herself by clinging to a strong tree root that had penetrated the interior. It wasn't until she was at the bottom looking up, that she realized the danger she'd put herself in. Some dirt she'd loosened in her descent tumbled down the inner wall.

Chunks of dirt fell on her face and arms, and she trembled with fear. At any moment the walls could collapse and crush her. She was thinking less about her safety and more about the fact her children would be left orphans.

Wiping the grit from her mouth, she quickly filled the pail with bricks and cried out, "Ihor, throw me a rope! The walls are crumbling! They're about to cave in!"

"Pan Striluchky, please hurry!" said Hania.

"Don't be nervous," yelled Lukia. She didn't want this crisis to affect her daughter's unborn child.

When he threw the rope down, she grabbed it tightly. The cord's rough threads bit into her palms. Her arms strained as she was lifted. It took both Ihor's and Hania's hands to pull her up along with the full pail. She was barely out of the well when it collapsed. The sound of the bricks and chunks of packed mud falling caused her to tremble. Seeing the debris fill the hole where she'd stood, she shook with the realization of how close she'd come to being buried alive. Leaning on Hania, she crossed herself and mumbled some prayers.

"Oy, Mama," said Hania. "You could've died."

Ihor took Lukia's other arm. "Are you all right?" She was still shaking as they guided her to a log nearby.

Sitting down, she said through chattering teeth, "What was I thinking to even go down there?" She looked at Ihor. "You should've gone yourself."

He frowned. "I didn't know if you'd have the strength to pull the bricks up."

"I could've called Egnat."

Ihor nodded. "You're right, Egnat could've gone down."

"And what? Lose my son?" she said harshly. No sooner were the words out of her mouth than she realized she'd been thoughtless. She took a deep breath and looked at Ihor's stricken face. He'd meant no harm. What was she doing, arguing with such a good neighbour, one whose heart ached from losing his son in the war?

"Ihor, don't pay attention to me. I'm complaining because I scared myself half to death."

"I understand," he said kindly. "I never would've asked you if I'd known the danger."

With her hand over her pounding heart, she said, "I know, Ihor, I know."

The well incident had been one kind of danger. It had brought into question Lukia's ability to make wise decisions on her own. Yet another threatening situation soon after made her question her place in the village and, subsequently, her family's security.

Lukia had assumed she was well respected. She had never quarrelled with the merchants, always offered a fair price for any goods she bought or sold, and minded her own business. The week before, everything had seemed fine. She'd sold a chicken to a local woman and used the money to buy some fabric and a fancy blue button in Kivertsi. Once home, she'd sewn a purse for herself with thread she'd spun, and used the button as a fastener for the opening. It was a fine purse, a perfect copy of one she'd seen on the arm of another villager. It was what she prided herself on—her ability to sew any design without a pattern.

When she returned to the village the following week to sell a few dozen eggs at the general store, the tailor's wife, who was a customer there, pointed to Lukia's purse. "That's the one I thought I lost," she said. "You stole it and all my money. Give it back to me!"

"What are you talking about?" said Lukia, jerking her arm away from the woman's grasp. "How dare you call me a thief! I made this myself." She could feel her face redden as a few shoppers gave her disapproving looks. One of them was Katerina, Fedor's wife. Her sister-in-law wouldn't meet her eye and hurriedly left the shop. A few others also knew her, but not one of them vouched for her.

"That's my blue button!" shouted the woman. "My husband is a tailor and he's the only one who has buttons like that. He made me a purse just like the one you're holding."

"I know he sells buttons like this. I bought it from him. I'm not the one who stole your purse. If you think I'm guilty, let's go see the gendarme now."

Startled by Lukia's offer, the woman calmed down and agreed to have an officer settle the dispute. While they walked to the gendarme's office, Lukia tried to figure out how much money she had left. It was hard to concentrate, since she was still smarting from the public accusation. Why had Katerina left the shop so quickly? They'd never been close, but still, family was family, and Katerina should've come to her defence.

After the officer heard the details of the dispute, he asked the tailor's wife how many zlotys she had in the purse that was missing. He then asked Lukia how much she had in her possession. Handing him her purse, Lukia recounted aloud how much she'd had when she left home, how much she'd spent, the amount she'd made in sales, and what she had left. While the officer counted out the cash, Lukia avoided any eye contact with the woman. Though seething as a result of being publicly humiliated, she also felt vulnerable. Would the policeman choose not to support her, even if the evidence supported her story? Being a widow with a farm to run, Lukia had been too busy to develop any meaningful relationships in the village. The tailor's wife was better known. Would the policeman be swayed by her and charge Lukia with theft?

Turning away from the woman's dagger-like looks, Lukia stiffened her back and raised her chin in defiance. After the gendarme had finished counting the money, he looked at them both for a few moments without saying anything. Lukia's heart pounded. Finally, he said to Lukia, "You've told the truth. Since this woman has sullied your reputation, you can take her to court."

"Ha," said Lukia, scowling. "I have no time or interest to take her to court. Let her sit in her lies." She spat at the tailor's wife and left.

On her walk home, Lukia reviewed the row. Though stunned by the woman's outlandish accusation, what was truly upsetting was how she'd been treated by Katerina and the other villagers. She'd always been an honest woman, and yet no one had come to her aid. She wondered whether this had something to do with the changes in her country. Or had it always been like this and she hadn't noticed? Were people so afraid to get involved they'd rather turn the other way or walk by as if nothing out of the ordinary had happened? Maybe she was being too harsh. Her life hadn't been at risk. It didn't need saving like all those innocents who'd gone to war. This wasn't a high crime. It was only a matter of a purse. However, the more she reflected on what had taken place, the sadder she felt. It was more than a purse; it was her honour. She decided that from now on, she'd have to be careful with her trust. She kicked at the stones as she walked down the familiar road leading from the village, past familiar farms and manors with cows grazing in the pasture. The quiet and beauty of the countryside had always comforted her, but today it was different. Today, she felt truly alone.

AN UNFAIR TRADE

IT HAD BEEN over a week since Lukia received word that Hania had given birth to a son—Kolya. She would've left sooner for Lokacz, but she wanted to prepare some dishes for her children and mother in case her visit took longer than expected. Fedoshya was capable of managing the kitchen on her own, but with all the requests for her cures, she might get too busy to make a proper soup or varenyky.

The Sabiuks' farm was two hours away by horse and wagon over dirt roads and cobblestone ones built by the Romans. This time, though, she'd have to go by train; Egnat had enough to do on the farm without having to drive her as well.

She was in the midst of packing her nightgown, a change of dress, and underwear when she heard a wagon drive up. Glancing out her window, she saw it was Ihor. She opened the door before he had a chance to knock.

"Good day, Ihor. What brings you here?"

"Lukia," he said, his face grim. "I've just come from Lutsk. By chance, I visited my uncle in the hospital and saw Hania lying in a bed in the next room. She's very ill. She asked for you."

"What are you saying?" She stumbled, and Ihor grabbed her arm to steady her. "She's in Lutsk? I have to go see her." What was her daughter doing in Lutsk? There had to be a hospital closer to where she lived. And Ihor had said she was very sick. With what? Had her labour been difficult?

"Where's Egnat?" said Ihor. "I didn't see your wagon."

Startled out of her thoughts, she looked at him wide-eyed. "Egnat?" She hesitated then said, "He went to the market to sell some eggs and cheese."

"Don't worry. I'll take you."

"Thank you." She turned around a few times as if lost in a forest and trying to decide which trail to take. Ihor waited by the door. "You're a good neighbour," she said, and then went to wrap four freshly made buns with stewed prune fillings in wax paper. They were Hania's favourite. As she was putting on her bikasha and babushka, Fedoshya came into the house.

"Oy, Mama," said Lukia, "Hania's in the hospital."

"What happened?"

"I don't know. Please take care of the children while I'm gone."

"Go with God," said Fedoshya, giving her daughter a hug.

Lukia grabbed her parcel of buns while Ihor donned his hat. He said to Fedoshya, "Until I see you again, Panye Korneluk."

At the door, Lukia looked back to see her mother cross herself three times. The sight filled her with such a sense of foreboding. "Please God," she mumbled, as she went out the door. "I don't ask for much myself. Please watch over Hania."

As Lukia rushed down the hospital corridor, she was struck by its cold white walls and the strong smell of ammonia. A patient could easily lose her grip on life in such ugly surroundings. She hesitated before entering the room containing eight beds, each one occupied by someone groaning or sleeping fitfully. Hania was in the far one, by the wall.

"Oy, Mama," said Hania. "It's my misfortune. I did a stupid thing."

"What did you do?" asked Lukia, taking one of her daughter's hands.

Hania moaned. "After Kolya was born, I felt strong enough so I cooked a chicken and some piroshky for Damien to take on his next posting. I took the food to his station, and when I got home, I was so cold from the long walk that I warmed myself by sitting on the pich. I didn't think. It must've been too hot for me because I hemorrhaged. There was blood everywhere. Damien's mother tried to help, but . . ." She started to cry. "I got infected. I made such a big mistake."

"Shhh. You didn't know." Lukia recalled how she'd done much the same. Too soon after giving birth, she'd taken a heavy basket of food to Gregory while he was waiting to go to the front. Had she planted in her daughter's mind that this was the right thing to do? What had she been thinking? How foolish a woman's love is.

Tears slid down Hania's cheeks. "I didn't want to die in Lokacz. I want to be buried next to Tato and Ivan in Kivertsi."

"Oy, daughter, don't talk about dying," said Lukia. Fear gripped Lukia's heart. Had Hania had a premonition? She held her daughter's hand tightly, needing to keep her in the land of the living.

"I dragged myself and Kolya to the train station. At first, they wouldn't let me board. The conductor saw how weak I was. I was almost crawling. He was afraid, but I begged and begged, and he let us come on board."

"What about Damien's mother? She let you go like that?"

"She didn't know I was leaving. I waited until she went to the village store. I didn't want her to hold me back or keep Kolya from coming with me."

"Where is Kolya now?"

Hania raised herself a little and looked toward the door. "The nurses have him."

Lukia surmised that her daughter must've been delusional

when she left her home. Why else would she have travelled so far, being so sick, with a child? But this wasn't the time to question her. There'd be time for that when she recovered.

Beads of sweat lined Hania's brow. Lukia took a handkerchief from her purse and wiped her daughter's forehead. She was about to reach for a glass of water on the side table to give Hania a few sips when a baby's cries caused her to turn her head. A nurse, holding a bawling Kolya, came into the room. Hania opened up her gown to feed him, exposing her swollen breasts. The nurse laid Kolya on Hania's chest and as the weeping child found his mother's nipple, he stopped sniffling and sucked greedily.

The sight of her sick daughter with her new grandson was too much to bear—joyfulness and sadness mushed together in one ungodly mess. In the midst of her mixed emotions, Lukia wondered if Kolya was getting enough milk. Surely Hania's sickness would affect her flow, but it was likely better for both that Hania go on as if there were nothing out of the ordinary. Mother and child were a comfort to one another. Lukia touched her grandson's little foot and marvelled at the softness of his skin. Love for this baby rushed in to squash some of the sadness that was threatening to overwhelm Lukia's heart.

"Please," said the nurse, tapping Lukia on the shoulder.

Lukia turned to see the chair the nurse had brought over. "Thank you," Lukia said as she sat down beside the bed.

"Mama, they're going to operate tomorrow. The doctor is going to open my stomach to find the cause of my bleeding."

Lukia bit her lip to keep from crying out loud. The sight of her daughter's wan face cut her heart like so many knives.

Hania looked at her baby. "Kolya, Kolya, my dear child, I won't be with you long."

"Hania," said Lukia sharply, "don't talk like that! You have to pray."

"I know how this is. Damien's mother has already offered to

take care of my son if I should die. I know you would've helped, but you have enough children to care for. Besides, Damien would never allow it."

"Hania, you'll see. You'll come out of this." Lukia said it as convincingly as she could, even though she had doubts.

Hania gazed at Kolya as if it would be her last time.

The hospital's waiting room was no haven. With Kolya asleep in her arms, Lukia kept looking at the nursing station for signs of Hania's doctor. Patients came and went, some with pneumonia, others with flu, and a few with injuries from accidents on the farm or on the road. A few times she got up from her seat and asked one of the nurses if her daughter's operation was over yet. Each time, she was told that as soon as the doctor came out of surgery, he'd be notified that she was waiting to hear how it had gone.

Though Lukia was anxious, her grandson calmed her nerves. His tiny warm body curved toward hers as if she, too, could nourish him. She must've dozed a bit, as a while later, she heard a voice that sounded muffled. "Panye Mazurets?"

Startled, she awoke and saw a doctor removing his rubber gloves. "Yes," she said.

"Your daughter's resting. Unfortunately, I couldn't get all the poison out, so I had to leave the incisions open. Maybe the poison will drain, maybe not."

He'd given her the outcome in such a matter-of-fact way that it took a few moments for Lukia to realize what she'd just heard. She stared at the doctor, her mind whirling. "What does this mean?"

His voice softened. "It doesn't look good, but we can hope."

"Can I see her?"

"She's still unconscious. You can see her in an hour when she wakes up."

Kolya had awakened and was beginning to fuss. "I don't know

if this child can wait."

"You can tell the nurse. They have some milk to help out for now."

With the doctor's retreating footsteps, Lukia felt her helplessness grow like a bad weed.

When Hania finally came out of her anesthetic stupor—looking pale and drained, her hair matted against her skull—Lukia took her hand. "How are you feeling?"

"My mouth is dry. I'd love an orange."

"My darling child, I'd get you one, but the stores are already closed. I'll bring you an orange tomorrow." Though Lukia had promised, she didn't know where she could get an orange. She hadn't seen any for sale lately, but she couldn't tell her daughter that.

Hania nodded and closed her eyes again.

The following morning, Lukia went to the store in Kivertsi and four in Lutsk, looking for oranges, but it was harvesting time—not the season for the sweet fruit. Desperate, she settled on a lemon and thought Hania might have it with tea. But her daughter rejected the lemon, saying it was too sour.

For the rest of the week, Lukia trudged every day to the hospital. Often, farmers going to the city would stop and offer her a lift. Egnat couldn't drive her as the wagon was needed for harvesting.

Damien visited one time when Lukia was still by Hania's bed. His head was bowed when he entered, and his eyes darted from his mother-in-law to his sleeping wife.

"It's good you came," Lukia said. "She's been asking about you."

Hania's eyes flickered open, and a smile curled her lips. "Damien," she said softly. Lukia got up to let Damien sit in the chair. She stood at the end of the bed and watched him lift Hania's hand and kiss it. Lukia hoped this wasn't a show for his mother-in-law's benefit.

Damien fixed the pillow under his wife's head and lovingly stroked her cheek.

"Did you see our son?" said Hania.

"Yes, he's getting big so fast. He's thriving on your milk."

Lukia wondered if he believed that or if he knew, as she did, that the nurses were supplementing the little that Hania was able to give. If he knew and was lying to his wife, Lukia was grateful, at least for this.

Though frail, Hania understood it was harvesting time and asked Damien to help Egnat on the farm when he wasn't occupied with the army. Lukia thought her son-in-law should stay by his wife, but on the other hand, she understood men didn't know how to be around sick women. Damien could be of more use driving horses or stooking hay bales on the farm.

When Hania closed her eyes again, Lukia said to Damien, "Let her know I'll return tomorrow." He nodded, and it was then that she saw a tear pooling below one eye. Lukia crept out of the room thinking her son-in-law was more caring than she'd given him credit for.

Despite the nurses' help, Hania grew weaker. Fedoshya visited several times but found there was no herbal cure she could offer to stem the toxins preying on Hania. Her skin greyed and her voice grew quieter. By the end of the week, she could barely speak above a whisper. With Hania weakening, Kolya ended up back in Lokacz with Damien's mother, who'd found a wet nurse to feed the child.

Lukia wished there was something she could do to lessen Hania's suffering. It was heartbreaking to see her daughter pick at her hospital food. Lukia had planned on bringing some borscht or varenyky from home, but even Hania's favourite buns had been left untouched. They sat dried up on the table beside her bed.

One evening—a week after Hania had been admitted—Lukia was at home straining sour milk into a bowl to make cottage cheese and noticed Damien, Egnat, Michalko, and Havrylo kibitzing around the pich. She hadn't heard what they'd said, but it must've been funny, as the four of them couldn't stop laughing.

"Boys, don't laugh so hard!" she yelled. "While you're laughing, Hania could be giving up her spirit." What was on her mind had spilled out like a pail of warm milk accidentally knocked over. The four quietened down so quickly that she regretted she'd spoken so harshly. While she considered what she might say to lift the mood, Damien and Egnat went outside for a smoke. Michalko and Havrylo followed shortly after, their heads lowered as they walked past their mother.

Lukia's scolding turned out to be prophetic. Hania's godmother arrived at the house early the next day carrying her godchild's pillow. She handed it to Lukia and said, "Hania is no more."

Dazed, Lukia sat down so abruptly on the stool that she almost toppled over. She caught herself and moaned. "Oy, oy, oy! That's how it is." And yet, was it true? Or would she wake up and discover it was all a bad dream? She closed her eyes and prayed for a miracle.

After a few moments, Hania's godmother said, "So young. Twenty-one years old and a new mother."

Lukia looked at the floorboards. It wasn't a dream. There was no way to change the news. She said to Hania's godmother, "God took four from me and left four behind. Was anybody with her when she died?"

"No. She died alone, but the nurse told me Levko kept vigil all night praying for her soul."

"What a nice young man." Lukia's eyes watered again. "Thanks be to God he was there." She'd have to thank him for his thoughtfulness. Damien should've been the one with Hania at the end.

Lukia's body suddenly felt heavy, as if there were someone standing over her, pressing down on her, keeping her from rising. She forced herself to stand on her leaden feet and go outside to find Damien and Egnat. When she called them, her voice didn't sound like her own. It belonged to someone screeching, someone in dire pain. When they came running, she fell into Egnat's arms. "Hania's gone." She shook, wracked with sobs, and Michalko ran over to comfort her.

"Mama . . .," said Michalko, holding her tightly as he cried as well.

Damien fell to the ground in front of her. He had loved Hania after all.

Their emotions still raw, Lukia, Damien, and Egnat drove to the hospital to get Hania. Amid more tears, they wrapped her in a sheet, carried her out of the hospital, and gently laid her in the wagon. When they got to the farm, they placed her on the dining table in front of the pich. Then the men left the house, taking the younger children with them, so Lukia and Fedoshya could prepare Hania's body for the funeral.

Removing the sheet off to wash her daughter, Lukia was shocked to see all the incisions—ten holes across her abdomen. She fainted. Fedoshya's screams for Egnat sounded like faraway echoes.

Lukia awoke to find her mother reviving her with cold cloths to her face and neck. Egnat had helped her onto a chair. Lukia looked over at Hania's body and remembered the work that needed to be done. She made a move to stand but felt her mother's firm hand on her shoulder. "No, daughter. You have to get your strength back."

"Mama," said Lukia, meeting her mother's gaze, "this is my work, my daughter. You can help me, but don't ask me to sit. I can't sit." Then Lukia fainted again. She found out later that it was a good thing Egnat had remained close by, as she was to faint once more.

After she'd been revived for the third time, Lukia asked Egnat to build a pine box for his sister. His face turned pale, and she recalled what he'd done for his father's burial three years ago. She wanted to tell him she knew how much he was suffering, but did she really? A mother's pain was different from a brother's. She tried to hold herself together. She had to, for the family's sake.

Lukia and Fedoshya laid straw inside the coffin and covered the bottom with white satin. Then, after laying Hania to rest in the coffin, they placed three small icons backed with cheesecloth on her body—one on her forehead, one on her chest, and one on her feet. Lukia gazed at her daughter's sweet face. Hania looked as if she were only asleep, not gone forever. Lukia's throat knotted and she began to cry. Her tears flowed like a waterfall, constant, with no beginning and no end.

The house was so full of family and friends the priest had difficulty moving around the coffin. He thrust out his incense burner, almost hitting a few of those gathered, as he chanted and prayed for Hania's soul. The sweet and woodsy smell filled the air. Fedoshya held Lukia on one side and Egnat held her on the other. Only Eudokia covered her nose when the smouldering incense came her way—Michalko smiled and patted his sister's head with affection.

After the sorrowful "Vichnaya Pamyat" ("Eternal Memory") was sung, the mourners lined up to say their goodbyes. They crossed themselves before kissing an icon on Hania's body. Some lingered longer than others, staring at her face. Damien, carrying Kolya in his arms, wept when he bent down to give her a final kiss on her lips.

When Damien hugged Lukia soon after, she smelled alcohol on his breath. For once, she didn't disapprove. She understood his need to escape misery however he could. She waited until the very end of the service to kiss Hania, and fell apart when she felt her daughter's cold, hard cheek. Sobbing uncontrollably, she rooted herself beside her daughter's pine box, and Egnat and Fedoshya had to pull her away.

Following the church service, six men, including Egnat, Michalko, and Damien, grabbed hold of the three long decorated towels under the coffin to carry it out to the wagon. Egnat drove with the priest sitting next to him while the family and other mourners walked behind the funeral wagon to the cemetery.

Hania was buried alongside her father and Ivan, just as she'd wanted. Lukia gazed at the earth, wishing it would swallow her up. She must've jerked forward, threatening to fall, because suddenly, she felt someone grab her. She turned from one side to the other and saw Egnat and Michalko holding her tightly. What good was she? She hadn't been able to keep her loved ones from dying. It was only Havrylo's and Eudokia's sad faces that kept her from jumping into the open grave.

STILL LOOKING FOR A MIRACLE

O N THE ANNIVERSARY of Hania's death, Lukia woke up realizing she'd passed the year mostly in a stupor, unable to recall much. Her mirror showed a haggard face and lustreless long brown hair, marked with grey. Most days, she didn't care how she looked, but today, she'd washed her hair and pulled it back in a bun while it was still wet.

As she put on her navy crepe dress, she remembered how the priest had tried to console her at Hania's funeral. He emphasized that her daughter's life on earth had been only temporary. He explained that martyred saints were commemorated on the day they died—the day their true life began. Although Hania wasn't a saint, he said, her life had been a preparation for her true life in heaven with Christ. Lukia had listened to his words but she found no solace there, nothing to close the wound in her heart. No matter how much she prayed, she couldn't understand why God had taken away such good people and let the criminally guilty live. She expected He would explain when she joined her husband and children in the afterlife.

Her mother had tried to console her as well. After one of her visits to the cemetery, Lukia found her mother sitting on the bench outside the house shelling peas.

Eyeing the pot beside her mother's legs, Lukia said, "You've done a lot. You should've waited for me."

"It's nothing."

"Oy, Mama," said Lukia, sitting down beside her. "The flowers I planted on Hania's grave died. I should've stopped by earlier and watered them."

Her mother stopped shelling. "How long are you going to walk around like you have iron in your shoes? You have four children left. Be thankful God spared you those."

Lukia gazed off into the woods across the field and questioned how she could be thankful when she'd lost her husband and four children. Her pain was still as fresh as ever.

She buttoned up her dress and went into the main room to set the table for the luncheon following special prayers for Hania. This time, Lukia hoped to pay more attention to her children. At the funeral, she'd neglected to talk to them about their sister's passing. She couldn't recall how they'd grieved.

She looked out the window and saw Michalko and Havrylo talking in the yard, but there was no sign of Egnat. She suspected he was fussing with the horses—now that they had two again—brushing their coats, untangling their manes, and cleaning their hooves. It was his way of standing out in the village, where he'd already caught the eye of quite a few girls. Lukia had to admit he looked handsome in the long coat she'd sewn to keep him warm while he ran errands for the Jewish merchants and their families. The young men had teased him about his clothing, but Egnat had laughed it off. He told his mother they were just jealous.

He'd become engaged in the past year to Elena Kotyza, a girl whose father was Polish and whose mother was Czechoslovakian. Lukia had some reservations about the match, as the Ukrainians and Poles acted like natural enemies, especially now that the Polish government ruled the country. It was too bad, as the people in both countries were more alike than different.

Also, Elena's parents were much better off. They had a large garden and a house twice the size of Lukia's, four rooms compared to two. It seemed to her that marriages worked better if it was the man's family that had the greater wealth.

Though Lukia would've been happier if Egnat had picked a nice Orthodox girl, Elena was a hard worker and not a woman to put on airs. She'd even gone a few times to pick *hmeel* with her future mother-in-law and Eudokia. With the money they'd made selling the hops for beer, Lukia was finally able to buy a Singer treadle sewing machine—the machine she'd dreamt about getting even before the war. With its shiny black head designed with painted-on gold swirls, it was a source of pride in the corner of her bedroom. It was also a reminder of Elena's help. Egnat had chosen well. The problem was her parents didn't think Elena had.

Close family and friends gathered in church to commemorate Hania. Lukia stood holding a long candlestick and listening to the priest read name after name from the Book of the Deceased—a small book with a Greek Orthodox cross embossed in gold on the maroon cover. It contained the names of every family member and intimate friend who had passed away in her mother's lifetime. As there were many, he read them quickly. Lukia swallowed hard when she heard Hania's name at the end.

Following the brief service, the parishioners sang the mournful "Vichnaya Pamyat," which brought tears to many eyes. They were also remembering the loved ones they had lost. When Lukia saw Damien's face, wet from crying, she forgave him for being self-centred in the past.

Back at the house, Damien, his parents, and Kolya were among the last to arrive for the memorial luncheon. Wiping her hands on her apron, Lukia greeted them at the door. "Kolya, come to Baba." She stretched out her arms, and he wriggled out of his father's grasp and into hers.

Kolya snuggled into her neck and when he pulled his head back, Lukia admired his cherubic face. His rosy cheeks were so plump that they looked as if they were stuffed with food. With Damien's posting in Lutsk, Lukia had been fortunate to see Kolya many times over the past year. As a result, they'd grown close.

After the food had been placed on the table, drinks were poured, and prayers were said. Lukia sat down beside Petro and raised her glass. "Daye Bozhe." Everyone at the table clinked their glasses and echoed the toast.

Downing her whisky in one gulp, Lukia relished the sudden warmth in her stomach. The alcohol stimulated her appetite. Perhaps too much, she thought. She'd noticed her girth broadening. Surprisingly, her added weight hadn't kept suitors away. Dmitro, who was sitting at the end of the table, kept glancing over as if she were the meal he'd rather have. She wished he'd give up and look for some other woman.

While the various dishes were being passed around the table, she said to the priest, "Have you been to Pochaev lately? Mama went last month for her annual pilgrimage."

"I was there a month ago," said the priest.

"What's Pochaev?" asked Eudokia, from across the table.

Startled by the child's voice, the priest looked blankly at Lukia's youngest.

Petro wiped his moustache. "That's the monastery where they have the golden icon of the Virgin Mary and the miraculous footprint. Hundreds go hoping for a miracle."

"A man's blindness was cured there," said the priest.

Eudokia's eyes grew wider.

Lukia turned to the priest. "I want to take Eudokia there. Her ears have been bothering her since she was two. I rub the insides of them with a piece of soft twisted rag, but she doesn't like it. She tells me to stop."

"It hurts," said Eudokia.

"Even a rag filled with cooked onions placed over her ears doesn't help," added Fedoshya.

"Maybe she can experience a miracle, like the blind man," said Lukia.

The priest nodded. "Maybe. I don't think you'd have any trouble there."

Lukia's brow furrowed. "What do you mean, 'trouble'?"

"Just this past year, the Polish Orthodox Church took it over."

"Pochaev? Don't say," said Lukia, alarmed.

"Yes," said the priest, wiping his mouth with his hand. "The monks have had their trials. First, the Austrians looted the cathedrals, then the Bolsheviks, and now, who knows what the Poles are doing."

"It's a tragedy," said Fedoshya.

The priest groaned. "Yes, it is, but they can't stop the pilgrims from coming. No matter who's running it, it's still God's place."

Lukia found the priest's revelations discouraging, but she believed, as he did, that no matter who was in charge, they couldn't stop the faithful from following their beliefs.

The priest took another helping of almost everything on the table.

Seeing the priest's plate heaped twice as high as everyone else's, Petro winked at his sister.

Lukia grunted and avoided any direct response that could prove embarrassing. Instead, she looked down the table and saw Dmitro—his face already ruddy from too much alcohol—pour himself another shot of whisky. She felt relieved she'd rejected his proposal. Gregory drank, too, but at least she'd loved him. Even if she'd wanted another man, it seemed the only ones eligible needed more care than they could give her. They were either disabled from the war, hobbled with rheumatism, or drunks. It was tiring taking care of her family on her own, but not so tiring she'd choose a man who would give her nothing but misery.

One morning, three weeks later, Lukia, Eudokia, and Egnat left for the monastery before dawn. Eudokia was still sleepy and snuggled against her mother for warmth. Pochaev Lavra was eight hours south, and the road was potholed in places. Egnat drove slowly over those rough sections and managed to steer the wagon around the deep ruts. A broken axle or an unexpected spill had to be avoided—they had no money for accommodations.

Just approaching Pochaev gave Lukia goosebumps. The immense complex of three cathedrals on a high hill overlooking a small village and a green wooded area—now glorious with autumn shades of red and gold—was awe-inspiring, even at a distance. The Dormition Cathedral, with its impressive baroque structure, golden cupolas, and a towering bell tower, promised peace and hope to the hundreds of pilgrims walking and riding the way lined with pyramidal cedars. Since two main pilgrimages had occurred a few months back, Lukia had hoped to avoid a mob, but now it looked as if she'd have to jostle others to get to the blessed icon.

After Egnat parked their wagon at the base of the cathedral, the family climbed hundreds of steps to the front door of the church. Around the doorway was a gold-bordered mural, depicting a scene of Christ's sermon on the mount. Like the other women who had entered the cathedral, Lukia and Eudokia wore babushkas and long skirts, as dictated by the church's teachings.

Once inside, they stood in a long line with the other faithful to see the footprint of the Virgin Mary, which had been left when a vision came to a monk in the fourteenth century. He had ascended Mount Pochaev to pray when suddenly he witnessed a column of fire burning in the forest. Standing on a rock, surrounded by flames, was the Mother of God. When she finally vanished, she left her footprint embedded in the rock. Because of this miracle, the monks had built a monastery on the site.

Lukia looked around the cavernous interior: the walls were decorated from floor to ceiling with icons in intricately carved gold frames, and in the dome and vaults were painted frescoes and tall windows. The main aisle was lit by massive crystal chandeliers, and on each side of the elaborate iconostasis—covered with images of Christ and his disciples—stood side tables holding large vases of flowers and stands with hundreds of candles. The bishops and priests were dressed in ornate gold brocade vestments, and each wore an embroidered and jewelled crown with a cross on top.

As Lukia listened to the liturgy, Gregory's words about the ostentatiousness of the clergy seeped into her thoughts. Her husband couldn't understand why the priests, bishops and metropolitan had to wear such opulent clothing. "They dress and act like emperors," he'd said. She smiled, for that was one matter they agreed on. Yet, she reasoned, the clergy represented God, and that was why they wore such regal garments. They had to impress the people with the importance of their positions. However, she believed, as Gregory did, that a go-between was unnecessary. Why pray directly to God then if you needed someone to forgive your sins and interpret your gratitude, hopes, and dreams?

She breathed deeply then gazed at the ornate golden icon of the Blessed Virgin suspended from the ceiling in the middle of the nave. The sun streaming through the windows bounced off the icon's gold frame, creating a dazzling light display on the walls. Egnat read that the icon had been donated to the monks in the sixteenth century by the noblewoman whose brother had been cured of blindness after praying to the Virgin. Viewing the glorious icon, the three of them prayed for a cure.

They left the cathedral in the midafternoon hoping Eudokia's painful ear problem would soon go away, but a half-year later, Lukia was still waiting for a miracle. Though she continued to believe in God, she began to believe his miracles were intended for other people.

BETWEEN LENIN AND THE POLES

USUALLY EGNAT TOOK the children to school in their horse-driven sleigh on his own, but one January morning in 1925, Lukia decided to go along for the ride. She wanted to go to the village to sell some eggs and use the money to buy some kerosene and oil. She was also anxious to get out among other people; she'd been in the house for too many days. She enjoyed browsing in the household goods store and seeing what the other women were wearing. The one shop she avoided was the tailor's. She refused to give him any more of her business and made a point of telling her neighbours about how she'd been wronged. She now bought her fabric and sewing supplies in Lutsk.

As it was bitterly cold, Lukia and Egnat put on fur Cossack hats, sheepskin coats, and felt-lined boots. They sat up front on the wooden bench while the children huddled under an old perina in the back. Their breath produced clouds of fog in the frigid air, and it wasn't long before their cheeks were stung red by the north wind. Other than the swooshing sounds of the sleigh's runners over the snow-covered road, all was quiet, making the ride a peaceful experience, despite the cold.

Egnat dropped the children off at the village school, and Lukia watched them clomp through ankle-deep snow with Eudokia leading the way. Because they'd missed several days, due to bad weather and family chores, they were far behind. Lukia hadn't gone to school herself but knew her numbers and could calculate whether she was getting a good deal or not. As for legal matters, she relied on Egnat, who could read well enough to understand basic contracts. So far, there hadn't been any dispute over her property. She hoped the day would never come, as she didn't trust any government, especially one that kept changing.

Lukia had heard that some of the Ukrainian intelligentsia were planning on setting up private schools in their mother tongue. It was a good idea, but she wondered how it would work. Her children couldn't go to one school during the day and another one after that. Who would do their farm chores? And if there was a cost, how could she afford it?

She brushed those questions aside as Egnat pulled up the horse and sleigh to a hitching post by the blacksmith's shop. While he went inside to replace their shovel, which had rusted over the years, she went to the general store to sell her eggs, and then to the butcher's shop. There, she ran into her neighbour, Nina Striluchky, who was just coming out the door carrying a parcel of meat.

"Ah, Lukia," said Nina, her forehead ridged with concern. "How have you been feeling?"

"You know, it's been hard."

Nodding, Nina said, "Of course. There isn't a day that goes by when I don't think of my son. But you've lost four children and a husband. I don't know how you manage."

"I have to."

Nina nodded again. "Have you heard about Lenin?"

"No. What do I care about him."

"He died a few days ago."

"What are you saying? He's not that old."

"Fifty-four. I'm actually surprised he lived so long. You know," Nina said, arching her eyebrows, "his enemies tried to kill him a few times. Then he had a few strokes. Now, some are saying it was syphilis that took him."

Lukia harrumphed. "Good riddance. He brought nothing but grief. What kind of a man turns his back on God? But what do I know? I thought when Poland won we'd be better off under the Poles than the Bolsheviks."

"I thought the same."

"We're still suffering. The Poles say they're Christian, but they don't want us to attend mass in our own churches. I have to hide in a crowd of Jews when I walk to the cathedral in Lutsk, so the Poles won't pester me." Lukia shivered. "It's too cold standing here. Come over for tea soon."

"Maybe next week. Till we see each other," said Nina, walking off.

While Lukia finished her shopping, she reflected on her conversation with Nina. Lenin's death could set the country on fire again. His followers would likely be challenged, and if that happened, any unrest could quickly turn violent. With Ukraine's borders made for trampling, it was anybody's guess how long the current government could hold on. Worry filled Lukia as she considered what lay ahead for her sons. Egnat was twenty and Michalko, though only fifteen, was a scrappy one. If the Polish forces needed more men, would they draft the young ones and force them to fight? And what if she and her family had to flee? She shuddered. She did not want to become a refugee again.

On the ride home, they passed the scorched site of their church, now covered with snow. "I wonder if it will ever be rebuilt," said Lukia.

Egnat frowned. "Not if the Polish government has any say."

Her son was right. Given the political climate, the Orthodox congregation would find it hard to get a permit. The thugs who had burned down their church had gone unpunished because no one could say who was responsible.

Between the Bolsheviks and the Poles, her faith was being challenged on all sides. Even one of her nephews had fallen in with some atheists and was going around the countryside burning icons and bibles. When she'd seen him igniting a pile of religious artifacts, she yelled first and then scolded him. He paid no attention, just looked the other way. In the end, she was relieved to have rescued a few icons before they were too badly burned.

Maybe Gregory was better off where he was. He no longer had to deal with the suffering in his country.

BECAUSE OF A HORSE

THE PASSING OF another winter brought little change to Volhynia. Various conflicts continued, especially among the youth, who naturally rebelled when they got to be a certain age. With one faction fighting another, the hope for an independent Ukraine dimmed with each passing day. Thankfully, her sons had avoided those skirmishes. Perhaps being fatherless and having to work hard to keep the farm running kept them out of trouble.

With her mind at ease, Lukia was glad to be out in the warmer weather hoeing the weeds among her sprouting vegetables. After working steadily for half an hour, she heard a dog's excited yips and raised her head. In the pasture near the field, Eudokia was herding the cows with the help of a stray dog that had latched on to their family in the fall. She was scolding the confused animal, who kept circling the cows. Lukia laughed. He wasn't much of a herder, but he was a good companion for her daughter. Now that she was ten, Eudokia was a big help. She had even helped herd her neighbour's cows, and as a reward, she'd been given bread baked with both rye and white flour and smeared with butter. Bread with any white flour was a luxury.

Lukia looked beyond her daughter at nature's awakening: the wild grasses, the elderberries, the ash berries, and the forest of alders, birch, and willow—all in bud. By the house was the cherry tree; its pink blossoms made every heart sing. Along with good crops, the Mazurets family now had four cows, two more than last year, and therefore more dairy products to sell. This year looked promising indeed.

But as Lukia thought more about the land that supported them, her brow creased. Already, Egnat was planning a marriage. His wife would move in, and then children would follow. The farm could possibly provide for one or two more but not many beyond that. When it was Michalko's turn to get married and then Havrylo's, what would they do? There was no way the farm could support all the extra mouths. The Polish government had limits on land expansion. Lukia could see nothing but anguish ahead. If her sons left to seek their fortune elsewhere, could she manage without them? She couldn't bear to think of her family splintering.

Shaking her head, she picked up the hoe again and went down the rows of cabbage, cucumber, and potatoes, turning over the weeds. She'd been working for a while when she heard Egnat yelling at Michalko to hitch the plow to the horse. She was thankful she had two strong sons to help her, but she knew it was Egnat who kept Michalko at his chores. Though sixteen, Michalko was still a daydreamer. When he wasn't at home, he was out looking for a party. It worried Lukia. He liked liquor, not unusual for her countrymen, but he wasn't a pleasant drunk. Being sensitive, he was apt to take some comment the wrong way and then raise his fists. He'd already come home once with a black eye after some stupid argument.

She was nearly finished hoeing when she heard their dog barking as if there was an intruder at the door. She looked over to see him snapping at their horse. The horse reared up and tried to back away but tripped on the plow and fell to the ground. Egnat, who was just coming out of the outhouse, ran toward the stricken animal. Ashen, Michalko also rushed to the horse's side. Lukia dropped her hoe and crossed the field quickly to join them. She saw that the animal had been gored by the plow. He raised his head, whinnying and snorting. He tried to move his crumpled legs into a better position, but he was too weak and fell back on his side. His belly, stained dark red, shone mercilessly in the late-afternoon light.

Lukia reached Michalko before Egnat did. "My God, how did this happen?" She moaned as she held her head in her hands and rocked it from side to side.

"Mama, I'm sorry. I,..." Tears rained down Michalko's cheeks.

Egnat rushed in, took one look at the scene, and faced his brother. His eyes bulged. "What the hell were you thinking? You put the plow upside down in the field, you idiot! Can't you see what you've done? It should be you lying there."

Lukia put her hand on Egnat's shoulder. "Oy, don't say. God will punish you."

"Let him punish me," said Egnat, jerking away. "You don't think this is punishment enough?"

Michalko said nothing to defend himself. What could he say? What his older brother had said was true. He'd been careless.

Egnat muttered an obscenity under his breath and pulled a handkerchief from his pocket. Kneeling by the horse, he pressed his hankie on the wound. Blood soaked the cotton cloth within seconds and spilled over Egnat's fingers and on to the ground. The horse brayed—a mournful sound—and looked at Egnat as if Michalko's mistake could somehow be remedied.

Egnat lay his head on the horse's mane. "It's too late."

"Oy, what are we going to do?" said Lukia. Their horse was more than a worker; he was Egnat's best friend. He was also an animal the family couldn't afford to lose.

"Michalko," said Egnat, "stay with him. Comfort him as best you can." He took off running to the house.

While Michalko stroked the horse's neck and mane, he whispered "I'm so sorry" over and over in the animal's ear. Lukia couldn't believe how irresponsible her son had been. Why didn't he think more before he acted? If his mind had been on his work, this accident wouldn't have happened. She wanted to berate her son for his stupidity but knew doing so would only serve to heighten his guilt. It wouldn't bring the horse back. How quickly their luck had changed, once again.

"No!" said Michalko, half moaning, half shouting, when he saw Egnat running back with a rifle in his hand. He began to wail. "I'm no good. I'm no good."

"Don't say," said Lukia, helping her son rise from the ground.

Standing behind the horse's head, Egnat aimed his rifle at the animal's right temple and pulled the trigger. Michalko flinched. The gunshot sent a flock of starlings into the air.

"Mama," cried Eudokia, from far off in the pasture.

"No, no. Stay there," Lukia shouted back. "It's all right." She waved her arms, indicating Eudokia should stay with the cows.

Egnat and Michalko froze, each wary of the other. Lukia was sure if she hadn't been standing there, Egnat would've punched his younger brother for what he'd done. When Egnat stormed off down the road moments later, Lukia didn't try to stop him.

She walked back to the house to tend to her chores. Michalko was left to deal with his despair alone. If they were lucky, Havrylo would soon be home with some fish he'd caught. They were down to one horse again, but at least there would be food on the table.

It wasn't long after that Lukia noticed Egnat brooding. She was in the main room mending a hole in Havrylo's pants when Egnat came into the house with his shoulders stooped, walking like an older man. He took his tin of tobacco and cigarette papers off a high shelf and sat down on a stool beside her. He pinched some tobacco from the tin, dropped it on the paper square, and then rolled it to make a cigarette. He looked up at her. "What kind of a catch am I now?"

"What? Is there some kind of trouble?"

"Mama, I didn't tell you because I didn't want you to get upset."

"Well now that you've opened your mouth, tell me," she said, putting her mending down.

Egnat's forehead creased. "Elena's parents have been trying to convince her for months to not marry me. They say I'm too poor. And now that we only have one horse—"

"What do you mean not marry you?" She couldn't imagine anyone turning up their nose at her son. He was short but handsome with his brown hair, moustache, and manly physique. And though he'd left school early to help her on the farm, he was nobody's fool.

He stopped rolling his cigarette but avoided looking at her. "Elena's father thinks it's bad luck for her to marry the son of a widow."

"What are you saying?" she said, accidentally pricking her finger with the needle. "Such nonsense. May the devil get him!"

"Don't get so mad. That's why I didn't tell you."

"What can I do?" She sucked her finger to stop the bleeding. "Is it my fault my husband died? Is it yours?" She paused then said, "I'll speak to him."

"No, Mama, don't."

"Why not?" asked Lukia, her face flushing.

"What good would it do? You'll only make it worse."

"He's such a big shot. Just because he has a big garden and four rooms, he thinks you're not good enough for his daughter. He should be so lucky to have a son-in-law like you. You're a hard worker. The Polish people, they always think they're better."

Egnat sighed. "If you must talk to him, at least wait until after we've bought another horse."

She raised her eyebrows. They could be waiting forever. Maybe her brother could lend her the money to buy another animal. He was well off. He could afford to be kind.

Lukia rolled one ball after the other into flat rounds for varenyky. Her hands moved erratically as if she wasn't sure whether to roll the dough or throw it against the wall.

She was furious with her brother. It was a good thing he wasn't at her home right now or she might've hit him with her rolling pin. He'd given her a loan for another horse, but not without grumbling. She didn't know why Petro was so full of himself. He hadn't struggled to get to where he was on his own. It was his wife's money, everybody knew that. She was the wealthy one. Lukia sometimes thought that was the only reason he'd married her, as he still had his eyes on other women, especially young ones. She'd even seen him eye Eudokia, who was already developing little bumps. Imagine, his own niece! The old fart. All men liked to chase skirts, but her brother went beyond just looking. He'd grab at breasts whenever he could, even if it meant getting his hand slapped.

She placed the flat rounds under a damp tea towel to keep them from drying out. On and on she rolled, pressing the rolling pin down hard as she ruminated about Petro.

Gregory had been different—he'd been respectful of women. He'd never forced himself on her. Nonetheless, she knew her duties as a wife; she'd birthed eight children.

As images of the children she'd lost filled her mind, sorrow rose in her like an incoming tide. She sat down on a spindle chair and, using her apron, wiped the flour from her arms and hands. As she did, she became aware of the veins that had grown more prominent with age. Nothing she could do about that. If God let her, she would live long enough to ensure her family had enough land to support them in life. How she would do that was still unclear. For now, she would continue to work hard, and if there was any money left over, she'd save it to buy another parcel of land—that is, if the Polish government ever decided to relax its property laws. There was also the possibility Ukraine would win its independence again. If that happened, life would be easier for farmers. There were a lot of ifs.

She stood and placed a large spoonful of the potato mixture on a flat circle of dough, folded it over, and pressed the edges together. Her thoughts turned to Elena, her soon-to-be daughter-in-law. She must love Egnat a great deal to defy her parents. Lukia had heard from Egnat that Elena's father was still trying to dissuade his daughter from marrying him, but Elena had cried and cried, saying it didn't matter he was poor. She was just like Hania. Letting love dictate her life. At least Elena was getting a hard worker.

When Fedoshya arrived home after visiting a sick child, she rolled up her sleeves and began helping her daughter with the varenyky. "Have they decided where they're going to get married?" she asked.

Lukia shook her head. "First, he was going to get married in the Polish church, and now, I don't know."

"With the Catholics?" asked Fedoshya, her nose wrinkling in disgust.

"Yes, but the priest said Egnat had to learn the Lord's Prayer in Polish. He doesn't have time with all his work here and delivering goods for the Jews. He doesn't even have time to wipe his backside." She scraped the last bit of potato filling out of the bowl. "He shouldn't have these problems. He's such a good son. He always gives me some of the money he earns."

"Every bit helps."

"Yes," said Lukia, making the last varenyka. "After Egnat and Elena saw the Polish priest, they went to the Orthodox one. He said as long as Elena knows Our Father, even if it's in Polish, that would do. But you know what else he said?"

"What?" asked Fedoshya, sitting down on a stool at the table.

"He asked Egnat why he couldn't find a nice Ukrainian girl."

"Naturally."

"When Elena's mother found out what the priest had said, she told Elena it was an insult and she shouldn't marry Egnat if she had any pride. Elena cried and cried again, so what are you going to do. It's love."

Fedoshya nodded. "It's true what you say."

Lukia put on some water for tea. "I don't know how it's going to be. Her father said, 'Go, Elena. Go, child, marry Egnat, but if his mother says you're not a good daughter-in-law, I don't even want to know you.'"

"That's how it is," said Fedoshya.

Despite their displeasure with the match, Elena's parents said they would buy two cows for the wedding—an expensive gift. Lukia's wedding gift was going to be a soft perina filled with goose feathers, which she'd almost finished sewing. The Kotyzas, with their larger house, agreed to host the supper and dance. Of course, Lukia and her family said they would help out with food and drink. That was to be expected.

ALL THE ZLOTY IN HIS POCKET

THE DAY BEFORE Egnat's wedding, while Lukia was preparing holupchi for the wedding feast, Eudokia returned from visiting Lukia's godson with her face red and blotched.

"What happened?" asked Lukia.

Eudokia turned, hiding her face.

"Child, there's no point in hiding," said Lukia, putting down the knife she was using to cut the ribs off the cabbage leaves. "Tell me. Did you see my godson? Did you invite him to the wedding?"

"I wish I'd never gone. I was coming out of the toilet, and Ivash grabbed me. He said, 'Goonya, give me a little.' I didn't know what he wanted. Then he pointed to my breasts." Eudokia scowled. "He couldn't even say my name right. Called me Goonya. He knows my name is Dunya."

"He's a pig," said Lukia, disgusted. If he'd been in front of her, she would've smacked him. He was thirteen, old enough to know better. It was too bad her daughter was developing so quickly. "You'll have to stay out of his way," said Lukia to her daughter. "If it happens again, give him a good swift kick between his legs. That will teach him a lesson."

It was what Lukia had learned to do to her brother Petro when they were young. He never touched her again.

On the morning of the wedding, Lukia watched Egnat pace in front of the house, smoking one cigarette after the other. She understood his anxiety. He'd been the best man for many in the village and now it was his turn. Being a great joke teller, he had also acted as marshal—master of ceremony—at wedding celebrations. He was probably realizing that with marriage came responsibilities. He wouldn't be able to come and go as he pleased. He'd have a wife to answer to.

The day before, Egnat and Elena—carrying a ceremonial cone-shaped loaf of bread—had walked down the main street of the village to invite all to their wedding. Egnat had shouted, "My mother, Panye Mazurets, and Elena's parents, Pan and Panye Kotyza, would love your presence at the marriage of their children." He said they'd been warmly received and everyone who could, would turn out to celebrate their union.

As Lukia sat on the bed to tie up her black oxfords, she recalled Hania's wedding day. It was around the same time of year: the maple leaves were starting to fall.

"Gregory," she said, "your son is getting married today. I think we're getting a good daughter-in-law. Whether this business about their different religions will get in the way, I don't know. I know if you were here, you'd tell me not to worry."

Fedoshya came into the bedroom. "Are you talking to your husband again?"

"You have good hearing." Her mother was wearing a maroon rayon dress with matching covered buttons and an ivory lace collar. Her thinning grey hair had been pulled back in a bun.

"It's been six years now. Time to let him go."

"I know, but it gives me comfort."

Fedoshya said gently, "God has to give you the comfort now."

Lukia didn't say anything. Since the deaths in her family—Ivan's, Gregory's and Hania's—she'd found little solace in prayer. She couldn't fathom a time when she would stop thinking about her husband. He'd left her when he was still in the prime of his life. Her mother meant well and she'd managed to move on when her own husband died, but Lukia wasn't her mother.

"Are you ready?" said Fedoshya. "Petro is already here."

"Wait a minute." Lukia went to her bureau and from a wooden box on top took a brown beaded necklace. With her mother's help, she fastened it around her neck.

Following Fedoshya out the bedroom door, Lukia noticed how trim her mother looked. From the back, her body was that of a woman three decades younger than her eighty-five years. Perhaps her healing work kept her young, or maybe it was her temperament. Fedoshya didn't dwell on what couldn't be changed. Lukia looked down at her belly and realized she'd never have her mother's figure—or her nature. She was too much of a worrier.

Egnat was already waiting outside with Michalko beside the wedding wagon, which was festooned with ribbons, bells, and evergreen branches. Lined up behind it was Petro's new carriage and horse with a leather harness, as well as a couple of other wagons to make up the wedding train.

Petro stood beside his carriage, erect and proud in his white embroidered shirt and tailored grey suit. He held a hand mirror and admired his greying whiskers, groomed and waxed to perfection. Lukia sighed at the sight. The least he could've done was let Egnat use his carriage for the wedding. But then, he wouldn't have been the rooster with the finest feathers.

Fedoshya approached Petro. "Son, give me a hand."

He took her by the arm and helped her onto the front seat. His wife, Anna, and their two-year-old daughter, Rita, were already in the back.

Lukia walked over to Egnat and threw a handful of grain at him. "May good fortune follow you."

"Thank you, Mama," said Egnat, kissing his mother. She leaned on his shoulder and then climbed into Petro's covered wagon to join her sister-in-law and niece.

In front of them, Egnat urged his horse forward. His siblings rode with him in the wedding cart. The rest of the wagons followed behind.

The village was small, so it didn't take long to get to the Kotyza family's home. Lukia could see it up ahead, its gate decorated with flowers and evergreen boughs. But in the middle of the road and blocking the way was a square table covered with an embroidered cloth. Behind the table, which held a plate of sandwiches and a half dozen empty shot glasses stood Elena's father and two male cousins, dressed in their Sunday best.

When Egnat stopped his wagon several yards back from the table, one of Elena's cousins shouted, "What do you want here?"

"I've come for my bride, Elena."

"You think it's that easy," said the other cousin, a tall man with a wispy mustache and a smirk on his face.

Egnat reached under his seat and pulled out a bottle of vodka before stepping down from the wagon. Michalko and Petro stepped onto the road as well, to give the groom support. Egnat put his liquor on the table. "I thought you might be thirsty," he said to Elena's tall cousin.

"Ho, ho, ho," said the squat cousin. "You thought right." He took the top off the bottle and poured a drink for six. Petro leaned forward and quickly took a glass off the table before anyone else could claim one.

Elena's tall cousin then said to Egnat, "You must be hungry. You've come a long way. Have a bite to eat and let us drink and get to know one another."

Egnat clinked glasses with him, said a toast, and then they both took a swig of the vodka.

Wiping his lips with his hand, the tall cousin said, "Good vodka, but do you think that's enough to let you pass? You think that's all Elena's worth?"

Lukia liked this teasing, a custom that had been around for generations, but what she didn't like was Elena's father's giving Egnat the once-over as if her son wasn't good enough.

Egnat didn't seem to notice his prospective father-in-law's scrutiny and looked instead at Elena's house. It was hard to see anyone inside, due to the bright sun and the reflection on the main window, but Lukia suspected Elena and her mother were watching, so she smiled.

Egnat pulled some zloty from the right-side pocket of his pants. When he put the coins on the table, the tall man said, "You must be joking. That's not even enough to buy a good chicken."

Michalko guffawed as he saw his brother dig deeper in his pockets.

"A chicken, you say. Here." Egnat threw more zloty down. "That should buy a few, maybe even a rooster."

Laughing, Anna said to Lukia, "Egnat sure knows how to joke around."

The tall cousin shrugged. "I can see you're not serious. You may as well turn around and go home."

Shaking his head, Egnat emptied both pockets and then turned them inside out. "This is everything I have," he said, throwing more zloty on the table. "You can buy a brood of hens with that."

At that, Elena's father nodded his approval. The men then moved the table aside and allowed the groom and his party to pass.

Egnat was near the gate when Elena came running out of the house in a long white dress. She wore a myrtle wreath on her brown hair, swept up for the occasion, and her bouquet of sunflowers carried a promise of fertility and unity. Egnat's grin was as wide as the palm of his hand. He embraced her to the whoops of those gathered and carried her to his wagon.

After the church service and wedding feast at the Kotyza home—where it seemed all the dishes people knew how to cook were offered—dancing began outdoors. With daylight fading, Elena's tall cousin lit the kerosene lamps hanging in the trees near the plywood dance platform in the yard. The odd moo from the family's cows and the gobbles from their turkeys were drowned out by the musicians—accordionist, sopilka player, bandurist and violinist—who played kolomaykas, polkas, and the odd waltz.

The familiar smell of freshly mown hay wafted in and out of the crowd of guests, who were lubricated by booze and bent on kicking up their heels. Eudokia and the other children jumped around even when the band took a break.

Lukia gazed longingly at the diamond-like stars in the darkening sky and wondered if the ones she'd lost were watching the celebration.

Early in the evening, Michalko had asked his mother to do the kolomayka with him and she found herself spinning like a young woman again. Catching the glances of a couple of admiring widowers, she couldn't help but blush.

Later, she joined a group of dancers in a circle and clapped her hands, while the younger ones took turns in the middle doing their kicks and leaps. All the hooting and hollering from the crowd urged the young men to even greater heights.

Then Michalko, as best man, danced a flirtatious dance, and a crowd gathered to appreciate the sport of it. He put a piece of the wedding bread on a dish and then balanced it on his head while dancing in front of a popular girl from the village. She responded with a song that stated she wasn't home because she was out herding the cows and that he should keep dancing anyway. So Michalko danced some more, and again she said she wasn't home as she was out milking the cows but to please dance some more. He continued to dance and asked for the third time if she was home. She replied she was out herding the geese but told him to keep dancing. Getting tired of the runaround, Michalko, who was quite inebriated, stopped dancing and instead sang that she wasn't out feeding or herding but out working as a whore.

Seeing more than a few shocked faces, Lukia tightened her lips. Her son was making a fool of himself.

The young girl's face turned red with anger, as did her father's. They stormed off, leaving the crowd to gossip about the incident. Lukia immediately went up to Michalko and bawled him out for being rude, but it did no good. Being drunk, he wasn't in a mood to listen. He turned and headed for the drinks table. She shook her head. Her advice always seeped through his head like water through a holey bucket. She feared the road ahead for her son was going to be a rocky one.

The crowd's buzzing eventually waned and dancing resumed. The music didn't stop until midnight, when more food was put out on long tables.

After the late-night snacks, Elena and Egnat went to Lukia's home to spend their first night in the komorra. Lukia and Eudokia had made a bed of hay for them in the storeroom and covered it with sheets and the perina Lukia had sewn as a wedding gift. She'd also made two soft pillows stuffed with feathers. Tired from all the work and the dancing, Lukia slept soundly and didn't hear the couple making love in the komorra.

The next day, Lukia told Egnat and Elena they could have her bedroom and that she'd share the bed in the main room with her mother. The sharing would be short-term, as Fedoshya would soon return to the Carpathian Mountains, where she had many customers. Lukia would miss her mother's support.

While making her bed, Lukia wondered how long it would be before her daughter-in-law became pregnant. And then what? Lukia saw no possibility of getting more land to feed a growing family. She might be forced to marry, an idea that made her cringe, especially if that marriage had no love in it. With no acceptable prospects, she began to pray fervently for her country. She tried to hold on to the hope that Ukraine would rise again, even though history had proven that hope was like a soap bubble, there, but nothing you could hold on to.

Taking Charge

THE FALL OF 1926 proved to be a hot one. Lukia and Elena donned light linen shirts, long cotton skirts, and babushkas to protect their skin from sunburn and sun stroke, but there was no escaping the heat. Sweat layered their skin and stayed there until the sun dropped in the sky. Their hems gathered dirt and fragments of stalk as they worked the rows. It was back-breaking work and hard on their lungs—dust and pollen swirled over their heads with each whack of their scythes. They took turns leaving the field whenever they started coughing. They would run to the house to inhale fresh air and a drink of water. It was either that or risk having a coughing spell that went on and on for months.

It took several days to cut the tall stalks and remove their seeds. Next, Lukia and Elena had to soak the stalks in water for weeks before tying them together in stooks to dry in the sun. Once the hemp was dry, they had to beat the stalks with sticks and bands of leather to strip the tough outer bark and loosen the long threads that could be spun into rough yarns to make mattress covers and shirts.

Though the work was arduous, Lukia was thrilled with her crop. Even short bits of stalk or waste could be used as food for their pigs. As for the hemp seeds, some were saved for replanting, some compressed for oil to be used for the lamps, and the remainder roasted or left raw for nibbling between meals.

Now that Lukia had Elena's help, Eudokia returned to school. She'd taken off much of the previous year but she wasn't behind other farmers' children. They'd also taken breaks to help out at home. It was the way it was. First came work to help with food and shelter, then learning.

But it wasn't all joy with Elena's joining the household. Egnat was no longer as willing to follow his mother's orders. He'd grumble and stall when she insisted he do something. It all came to a boil at the end of harvest time.

She remembered saying, "Egnat, come here." Maybe it was the way she'd said it, but she'd always been direct, so she couldn't understand his explosion.

With eyes blazing, he'd jumped up from his stool and yelled, "I'm not a dog! If I start barking, then you can treat me like a dog."

"Egnat!" she sputtered, "Why are you yelling? Have you gone mad?"

"Mama—"

"Has the devil got you?"

"I have a wife now. You can't boss me around anymore."

"So that's how it is," said Lukia, pouting. "You're under my roof and this is how you treat me?" Anguished, she turned her back.

"Mama, you have to understand, I'm married now. I'm not a little boy you can push around."

She shook her head in disapproval. How could he turn on her this way? And then she wondered what Gregory would think. He probably would've whipped off his belt and gone after Egnat. But then she remembered that Egnat was only sixteen when his father died, and how pale his face had been when he'd built his father's coffin, and how he hadn't complained when asked to take his father's place. In fact, he'd done more than she'd asked him to do.

He'd maintained the farm as if his father had never passed away. And he'd acted more like a parent to his siblings than a brother. He had served her well. Until now.

She must've sat there for at least a quarter of an hour, speechless after her initial outburst of anger. Reflecting on how much he'd helped in the past pacified her a little. The fire was out, but the embers continued to smoulder. She turned to him. He was still standing nearby, his head bent, his face unreadable.

"Egnat," she said, letting out a huge sigh. "You're right. Your first duty now is to your wife."

His body relaxed, and he sat down again.

"But never," she said, shaking her finger at him, "never yell at me like that again, or you can find the door. This is still my house!" Her voice and body shook with the last proclamation.

"Are you finished?" he said, unmoved.

She blinked. "Yes."

Later, as she was undressing for bed, she ruminated on Egnat's outburst. Hadn't she noticed him pacing in front of the house, tense before the wedding? Hadn't she realized he now had a wife to answer to? Well, he had a wife, but he had a mother first.

How could she have forgotten he had a temper? He never sat back and ignored a slight. She recalled how he'd dealt with their neighbour, Halyk, who had used their pasture to feed his cows. After Halyk ignored a number of warnings, Egnat went over and hit him across the back with his rifle butt. Halyk was so scared he shit himself. She smiled at that.

It wasn't just Halyk's sneaky use of their pasture that had riled Egnat. Five years ago, during the drought, Halyk's son had stolen a deer right from Eudokia's arms. Lukia's youngest had gone wild-strawberry picking with a few of the villagers. Any money she got from selling fruit was used to buy bread, as they hadn't had enough wheat from their farm to bake their own. While Eudokia was picking strawberries, she saw a small deer running through the patch. She caught it and began to carry it home wrapped in her sweater. She was passing Halyk's field, when his fifteen-year-old son, Meetka, stopped her and told her the deer was too small and wouldn't be any good to eat. Hearing that, she let it go. She later learned he'd caught it and taken it home for his mother to butcher and cook for their table.

It was a tough lesson for Eudokia but a necessary one, as far as Lukia was concerned. Her daughter was learning she couldn't always trust what someone said. She would need to use her brain if she wanted to get by in this world.

When Egnat learned about the deer, he went to see Meetka's father, who said, "What can I do? It was Eudokia's choice to let it go. She didn't have to." Egnat then told his mother old-man Halyk had stood there with a sneer on his face. Lukia had never seen Egnat so angry. She couldn't blame him. She was angry, too. Meat was a treat. They rarely had it. The episode followed by the pasture problem had tipped it for Egnat. He wasn't a big man, but when he was enraged, his face was enough to throw fear into any man. Lukia thought again about Halyk losing control of his bowels. Served him right.

The fact that Egnat could be so ferocious was something she'd always admired. He was nobody's fool, but she lamented he was no longer her man of the house. He'd made that clear. And he hadn't apologized. This was a quarrel she wouldn't forget easily. It wasn't until winter set in that son and mother were able to talk to one another without strain and the thorny matter became a distant memory.

Though winter brought some rest for Lukia and her family, it also brought new challenges. Handwork was becoming a luxury as thread was suddenly in short supply. With the economy in tatters due to the wars, manufacturing had suffered, and shops were unable to get what they'd ordered. Lukia had barely enough for darning. To get more thread for mending the pants the boys were forever ripping, she unravelled old stockings and wound the thread carefully around a piece of cardboard.

Soap was also hard to find. With beef or sheep tallow, they could make their own, but even that was difficult to get. Lukia and Elena used the little soap they had to scrub the sheets, towels, and clothes in a washtub of hot water in the house, and then load the wet pile on a sled which they dragged to the icy creek to rinse. When the ice was too thick, Egnat or Michalko would cut a hole in it so they could plunge their washing in.

One morning, when Lukia and Elena were hanging up the laundry, they heard a rider and horse approaching. Lukia turned to see Damien pull up. He looked upset, and his shoulders stayed hunched even when he got off his horse and tied it to the post. He wiped the ice off his moustache with one of his gloved hands. "Mama, do you have time to talk to me?"

"Why not?" said Lukia. She was about to ask Elena if she wouldn't mind hanging up the rest, when her daughter-in-law said, "You go ahead. There isn't much left"

As Lukia walked to the house with Damien, she wondered what had distressed him so much that he'd ridden over to see her. Was it something to do with Kolya? His father had only visited a few times since Hania had died but Lukia figured it was because he had a new wife. He'd remarried less than a year after Hania's death. The suddenness of his decision had astounded Lukia, even though she knew he'd been looking for someone to mother Kolya. Raising a child was woman's work and Damien was hardly cut out for it, but why couldn't he have waited? It was much too soon, especially for Kolya. At least, her grandson continued to visit with the same frequency. Damien's parents dropped him off on their way to Lutsk and picked him up when they were finished with their shopping and appointments.

Damien scraped the snow off his boots and followed Lukia into the house. While she took off her babushka and sheepskin covering, he took off his tall fur hat and coat and hung them on an empty hook by the door.

"It won't take me long to boil water for tea," she said.

"Have you nothing stronger?"

Lukia laughed. "You know I have." She went to the cupboard and pulled the curtain covering the shelves aside. She took out a three-quarters-full bottle of vodka from the lower shelf and poured Damien a shot.

He toasted her, and then Lukia put the bottle on the table and sat down. "Sit," she said. "Tell me what brought you here."

Clearly agitated, Damien remained standing. "I have a big problem."

"What kind of problem?"

"I made a big mistake. I never should've married her."

"What are you saying? Isn't she a good wife?" Lukia wondered if he'd discussed this with his mother.

"Not a good wife, not a good mother." His face bore a sadness she'd never seen before. "She's more interested in my money than me and my son."

Taken aback, Lukia wanted to say she'd warned him about rushing into another relationship. Hania had been a wonderful wife, impossible to replace so easily. Instead, she said, "Is that true?"

He gazed out the window as if he needed to collect his thoughts. Then he sat down across from her. "I don't know where to begin." He sighed. "Soon after we were married, I came home to find she'd boiled some milk on the stove and had poured it into a glass for Kolya to drink. There was something about the way she was moving, the way she looked. I became suspicious. I went to taste the milk, fearing she'd poisoned it, but she knocked the glass over. Spilled it on the counter. I wanted to save some of it for testing, but she quickly wiped it up."

"Oy, my God!" said Lukia, a heavy feeling settling in her stomach. "What did you do then?"

"Nothing. What could I do? She became nicer and I began to think my suspicions were all in my head, that she now realized she'd been a bad mother and needed to make amends. That didn't last. She soon became distant again." He looked at the bottle on the table. "Do you mind if I have another drink?"

"Help yourself."

Damien poured himself another shot, this one almost overflowing. He took a drink, savouring what he'd swallowed. "One time I came home and found Kolya crying, dirty and unfed. It was awful. He didn't smell good. He'd wet himself. I suspected the worst again. But still, I didn't know what to do."

"What about your parents? What do they say about all this?"

He lowered his head. "I haven't told them yet. They warned me not to marry her. They didn't like her from the start."

She shook her head. "What are—?"

"Wait," he said, interrupting. "There's more. A few days ago, we were going to visit her parents. Kolya was already over there. I didn't want to go but I went. Along the way, to test her, I pretended to pass out in the snow. Even though I didn't trust her, I was surprised she did nothing to help. I was lying on the cold ground. She didn't make a move toward me, at least not for a few minutes. It was so quiet, I wanted to open my eyes to see what she was doing, but before my curiosity got the best of me, I felt snow being heaped on my body and face."

Lukia's mouth fell open. "You were lying there and she threw snow on you?"

"She wanted to bury me alive. I stayed still. I could hardly breathe. I waited while she threw more and more at me. After a few minutes, she walked away. When I figured she was some distance away, I got up and shook the snow off. I followed her to her parents and eavesdropped outside their front window. You can imagine how cold I was, but I stood outside freezing, while she told them I didn't want to come with her, that I hadn't been feeling well. When I heard her lies, I decided to file for divorce."

Nodding, Lukia said, "You have grounds for it. You could also charge her with attempted murder."

Damien gave a sarcastic laugh. "I could, but it would be my word against hers."

"Well, the sooner you get divorced the better."

Damien drank the rest of his vodka. "That's the problem. She won't give me a divorce and I have no proof."

Lukia gripped her hands tightly in her lap. "Listen to me. You need to watch Kolya. I wouldn't leave him alone with her for one moment."

"I know. Mama and Tato are watching him right now. I know I have to tell them. I'm so ashamed."

Lukia looked at Damien. He'd softened with time. "Kolya can stay with me until you get this sorted out. Your wife won't care. She'd welcome not having him."

He shook his head. "Thank you, but I would miss him. I'm sorry you live so far from us. Her parents are good, but they don't know the devil they have for a daughter."

"You should consult a lawyer. He might know of some way for you to get out of the marriage. In the meantime, promise me you'll talk to your parents about caring for Kolya." She reached across the table and grabbed his hand. "If you don't do that, I'll tell them myself."

"I promise," he said, locking his gaze with hers.

Elena came in from the cold, rubbing her hands. Lukia stood up and put the kettle on for tea.

"I'd better go," Damien said. "Pray for me, Mama."

"I always do. May God help you with your troubles."

"I'll come up with something," he said, and donned his coat.

"Just don't do anything foolish," she said, handing him his hat. "Kolya's lost a mother. He doesn't need to lose a father, too."

"Don't worry." Damien buttoned up his coat and said to Elena, "I'm not lucky in love like Egnat, but that's life."

Watching him leave, Lukia worried that Damien with his quick temper and drinking habits would do something rash like murder his wife in her sleep. Men who were desperate did bad things. And why didn't Damien's new wife like Kolya? He was such a sweet little boy. Would she really have poisoned him? It was hard to believe. Yet, she'd left her husband in the snow. He could've died. It was as if Satan had gotten hold of her.

Something had to be done. Lukia knew she wouldn't be able to rest until she could see for herself what was going on. Maybe Damien would change his mind and Kolya could come and stay with her. Tomorrow, she'd ask Egnat or Michalko to take her to Damien's house.

LITTLE CLENCHED FISTS

LUKIA LAY AWAKE for most of the night fretting about Kolya. It didn't help that a storm was brewing outside. A bitter northeasterly wind howled around the corners of the house and shook it with such force that she got up to look out the window. The white of the blizzard coated the glass and blurred the landscape. Shivering, she climbed back into bed, covered herself with her perina, and managed to doze for a few hours before sunup.

She woke up to see her farm blanketed with heavy snow. She had to ask Egnat to help her open the front door—snow covered half a meter of its base. It took Egnat and Michalko over three hours just to clear the roof and the paths to the stable, chicken coop, and outhouse.

By the time Egnat was ready to drive his mother over to Damien's, more than half the day was gone and the wind was picking up again. With the temperature well below freezing, Lukia wasn't sure if it was wise to drive in these conditions, but she couldn't let the matter of her grandson's welfare wait. She peered out the window and saw that Egnat had already harnessed their two draft horses to the sledge, and Michalko had thrown two shovels into the back of it. With the blowing snow and icy roads, they weren't taking any chances.

Lukia packed a basket with a few sealers of borscht and some honey cake that Kolya loved. "I hope to be back before nightfall," she said to Elena, who was eating breakfast with Havrylo and Eudokia.

Elena swallowed her porridge. "Do you want us to save supper for you?"

"Maybe." From what Damien had told her, Lukia couldn't count on being fed in his home.

She bundled herself in her sheepskin coat, fur hat, and felt-lined boots, grabbed the basket, kissed her children goodbye, and trudged through the deep and blowing snow to the sledge, where Egnat and Michalko were waiting.

She was about to climb on the sled when Michalko said, "Mama, I think you should stay home. It could be rough going. You know it's a long way to Lokacz."

"I know, but I want to go."

"Michalko's right," said Egnat. "We may be forced to stay overnight there."

She frowned. "What if Kolya needs our help?"

Egnat's face was grave. "If he does, I'll bring him here in the morning. I wouldn't want to take a chance with a child in this kind of weather."

"Good." She gazed upwards. The sky was darker than usual. Though she badly wanted to go, she knew she could be a hindrance if they ran into any trouble on the road.

She handed Michalko the basket of food. "Make sure you give it to Damien and Kolya. And be careful."

Though Michalko nodded, Lukia wasn't reassured. She watched the sledge go down the road, occasionally leaning to one side as it glided over uneven patches of snow. She hoped she hadn't made a mistake by not going with them.

For the rest of the afternoon, her mind wandered. In one moment, she worried that Damien might do something foolish;

in another, she worried about her sons, especially Michalko. A few drinks and he was ready to fight. The more she worried about it, the more she scolded herself for staying back.

Lukia rose early and was relieved to see a calm sunny day. The sound of horses' hooves sent her rushing to the door. Egnat and Michalko, both bleary-eyed—likely from too much booze and not enough sleep—had returned. Kolya wasn't with them.

"What happened? How's Kolya?" said Lukia, her breath turning into frosty waves in the open doorway.

"Kolya's fine, Mama," said Egnat. "He's with Damien's parents." He walked unsteadily to the door. Michalko followed in a similar fashion.

"He's staying with the Sabiuks?" she said, raising her eyebrows.

"For now." Egnat stomped the snow off his boots before entering. Michalko did the same while grinning sheepishly at his mother. Lukia assumed he expected a scolding for drinking too much, but for once, she had more important questions to ask.

Closing the door, she said to Egnat, "Did you see him?"

"Yes. He was happy."

"And Damien's wife. How was she? Did you see anything strange?"

"Damien told us she's moody," said Egnat, hanging his coat on the hook. "She's seeing a local doctor, who's giving her some herbs. He's hoping medicine will make the difference. Then Kolya could come back to live with them."

"Moody? When does a woman have time to be moody?" Lukia shook her head. "She's lucky she has her parents to help out. You're sure Kolya's alright?"

"He's good. His face lit up when he saw the honey cake."

"Thank God," Lukia said, as she watched her sons warming their hands over the pich. "Have you eaten?"

"Yes," said Michalko.

"Damien's wife fed you?"

"No, she was in bed. Damien gave us eggs and rye toast."

"A lazy woman." Lukia harrumphed. "I didn't know Damien could cook."

"With a wife like his, he has to," said Egnat.

"Poor Damien. I'll make Kolya some plum buns. He likes those too. Maybe in a week or two, I can go see him."

Lukia never got around to making the plum buns because Kolya and his father arrived in a week's time, surprising her.

Kolya threw off his hat, jacket, and boots and ran to her. "Baba!" he shouted, hugging her legs. Delighted by his spirited hug, Lukia took him on her lap. At three, his feet could almost touch the floor.

"You're such a big boy now," she said, tucking a curl behind his ear. Looking closely, she noticed dark circles under his eyes and when she took him by the hand to give him a pastry, his little hand was a clenched fist tucked in hers. My God, she thought. What this poor child must be going through.

She gave him another hug and sent him to play with Eudokia, who was sitting by the pich, cross-stitching a border on a towel with threads her aunt Anna had given her.

"Kolya," said Eudokia, putting the cloth down, "let me show you something." From the sewing basket, she took an empty spool that had strings through its centre hole. Holding the ends of the strings, one in each hand, she pulled and made the handmade toy whistle.

Kolya's squeals of delight made Lukia smile. She turned to Damien. "Nu, how are things now?"

"I'll tell you," said Damien, sitting down and taking off his leather boots. He exhaled sharply as if he'd run all the way over.

As usual, she had to wait until he'd had a drink to find out more. This time, she brought out the bottle before he even asked.

Smacking his lips after a stiff drink, he said, "Everything is fine now. You don't have to worry about my wife anymore." He said it with such solemnity that Lukia's heart stopped. She feared the worst.

He grinned when he saw her face. "Don't be afraid. I didn't hurt her." He laughed out loud. "She's my wife no longer. She moved out."

"What? How? You said she wouldn't give you a divorce."

"I went to Warsaw and had papers drawn up. I brought them back, and said I needed her signature for a property disposition. She can't read Polish." He threw his head back and laughed. "The bitch signed it. It was a divorce agreement."

"What about Kolya?"

"My parents will help out until I can find somebody in my village."

"Thank God," she said, meeting his gaze. "You know, Kolya could always stay here until you're settled."

"I know. If only you were closer."

Damien and Kolya stayed for supper. Lukia's heart sank further when her grandson left with his fists still clenched.

Big Children, Big Troubles

AMIEN'S DIVORCE WENT through in March, and Lukia's worries about Kolya subsided. She no longer spent her waking hours worrying about her grandson. Unfortunately, doubts crept in once again a few months later when she learned Damien had found another woman to love. Someone from Kiev.

Damien broke the news in late spring. He rode over to tell Lukia and waited until he'd had a few drinks before he announced, "I want to marry her."

Lukia frowned. "How do you know she'll be any better than the last one?"

"Don't worry, I haven't asked her to be my bride yet. I'm taking my time."

Taking his time, ha! How some people could bounce from one to the other was something she couldn't fathom. Maybe they were in love with love, not realizing that the passion of a new love carried them only so far. She still hadn't found anyone to replace Gregory, not that she tried. She would've loved companionship, but the more she thought about having a man inside her again, the more she realized it wasn't what she wanted. Not that she was worried about getting pregnant. That was no longer a concern since she'd passed menopause. It was more because of the stories she'd heard of the roughness of some men, and without love, who needed sex? Besides, she could still pleasure herself, lonely as that was.

Before long, new sorrows crossed Lukia's threshold—concerning Havrylo. As he was her quiet one, she'd expected to have any difficulties with him. He'd stopped school the year before and was working on the farm, as well as in the village. He loved tinkering and had convinced the locksmith he could fix clocks and locks. He seemed content.

She wasn't prepared for the shock of Egnat rushing through the door one late afternoon shouting, "Havrylo's in jail!"

"What?" She turned around so quickly she almost knocked over the cabbage soup on the stove. "Why?"

"He shot a boy in the head."

"No! Havrylo? Did he kill him?"

Egnat shook his head. "He injured him, but I don't know how badly."

She held on to a chair as her mind whirled with the news. "How did it happen?"

"The boy was riding his bicycle," said Egnat, waving his arms. "The one who teases him all the time. Havrylo shot him in the head."

"What boy? What kind of teasing?"

"You know how Havrylo talks."

"Oy, oy, oy." Her breath came fast and her heart pumped wildly. "We have to go," she said, rushing to get her coat. "We have to pray it's not serious. When did this happen?"

"A few hours ago."

She put her hand to her face. "My God, what was he thinking? Did you see him?"

"No. I came straight home to tell you."

She turned back to the stove. "Look what I've done!" The cabbage soup was boiling over, spilling onto the hot metal plate and the floor. Using a tea towel, she picked up the pot by the handles and placed it on the small table by the pich.

While she hurriedly put on her boots, Egnat tended the fire to let the flames die down.

"Oy, Elena," she said, as her daughter-in-law walked into the house carrying a basket of fresh eggs. "Havrylo's in trouble. Egnat and I are going to the jail to see him. I don't know how long we'll be. I was so upset I left a mess."

"Don't worry, Mama. I'll clean it up."

"Thank you. When you see Michalko, tell him to stay home. Egnat and I will deal with this." She never knew whether Michalko would come home sober. Sober, he could be helpful, but if he was drunk, there was no telling what he'd say to the authorities.

"My stupid brother shot someone," said Egnat.

Elena muttered, "That doesn't sound like Havrylo."

"Let's not stand here talking," said Lukia, motioning Egnat with her hand. "Let's go."

She mumbled prayers for her son and the boy he'd shot almost the entire way to the jailhouse in Kivertsi.

When she entered the jail, the sheriff, a portly man with brown whiskers, asked for her identification papers. After she'd shown them, she said, "Why are you holding him?"

"For reckless endangerment."

"I understand," she said, "but he's a child."

The sheriff pointed his finger at her. "He's fourteen. He should know better. Fortunately, the boy has only a superficial wound. The bullet grazed his forehead. His father hasn't pressed charges yet."

Relieved, she exhaled deeply. "Thank God he'll be okay. I was fearing the worst. Who's the father, please?"

After Lukia got the man's name and found out where he lived, she and Egnat visited Havrylo. He jumped up from his bench as soon as he saw his mother.

"Son, son," she said in a gentle but scolding tone as she walked into his cell and sat down beside him. Havrylo shook as he hugged his mother. His skin was pale with fright. Shooting someone even by accident was a serious offence.

"Mama, I just wanted to scare him. I wanted him to leave me alone. I never meant to hurt him."

"What do you mean you never meant it? You had a gun in your hands. If you didn't mean it, you shouldn't have picked up a gun. Where did you get it from?"

He turned red. "I asked the locksmith for it, and he gave it to me."

"What have I taught you? You know the Ten Commandments. What were you thinking? You could've killed him! Then where would you be?"

"I'm sorry, Mama. I got so mad." She stroked his back as he cried on her shoulder. "He kept teasing me and teasing me. He said I talked stupid. I'm not stupid."

"It's true," said Egnat. "I heard him myself."

"That's no excuse," she said, looking at both boys. "I'll go see the father. See what he plans to do. I'm going to talk to the locksmith, too. He had no business giving you a gun.

Havrylo sniffled. "Don't blame him. I don't think he knew what I wanted it for."

Shaking her head, she looked into Havrylo's bloodshot eyes. "You better pray the courts go easy on you." She feared her son could be charged with aggravated assault, even attempted murder. The courts might be lenient because of his youth, but if the father pressed charges, Havrylo could end up spending years in jail with hardened criminals.

The boy's father's house wasn't far from the jail. The structure was poorly built and in need of repair. When the man opened his door partway, Lukia could see the inside wasn't much better. There was no evidence of a woman's touch anywhere. In one corner of the main room, the boy was lying on a dirty bed, his scalp covered by a white bandage marked with blood.

When the father heard that his son had been bullying Havrylo, he turned to him and bellowed, "You didn't tell me you had anything to do with this! See what your words got you? See how you pushed Havrylo? You should be ashamed of yourself."

"My son should be ashamed, too."

"That goes without saying," said the father tersely. His son shrivelled in his bed and faced the wall. The father turned back to Lukia. "Panye Mazurets, thank you for coming. I hope this is the last we hear of any trouble between them."

"Thank you for being so understanding. I'm sorry your son was hurt." Lukia paused. She didn't want to push things, but she had to know. Her stomach was tied in knots, as she said, "You're not going to press charges?" She held her breath waiting for his answer.

He looked again at his son, whose back was the only thing showing. "No, I'm not going to press charges."

Her legs shook, and she steadied herself by grabbing the doorframe. She'd expected the worst and hadn't realized how much fear she'd been holding. She swallowed. "So be it. I hope our boys have learned a valuable lesson."

The father glanced back at his son. "Words can cut like knives, too."

She thanked him again and left feeling there were good people in her village. It was heartening after her experience with the tailor's wife and her sister-in-law, who would take an incident like this and blame her for being negligent somehow.

Thinking of Katerina didn't help her mood as she marched over to the locksmith's shop. He turned white when he heard about the shooting.

"Panye Mazurets, I didn't think . . ."

She felt her head throb. "You have to think. What possessed you to give him a gun?"

"When Havrylo asked if he could take it home with him overnight, I assumed it was for target practice," he stammered. "I never dreamt he had this in mind. Havrylo's a good boy. I've never seen him angry, but you know what they say—it's the quiet ones we need to watch."

She took a deep breath. There was no point in arguing with this man. It wouldn't change what had happened. She leaned over the counter. "It's true what you say and yet you gave him a gun." When the locksmith didn't reply but looked contrite, she went on. "He's never given me cause to worry before. You know his father is no longer with us. If you could also talk to him, explain how close he came to disaster, that would help me, too."

The locksmith agreed. Satisfied, Lukia and Egnat went back to the jail to get Havrylo.

It wasn't long after the shooting incident that Lukia learned Havrylo wasn't the only one in the family being bullied. She'd just poured boiling water over the tea leaves when Eudokia came home from school complaining she was dizzy. Putting her books on a kitchen chair, she said, "I don't want to go anymore. School is giving me headaches."

Frowning, Lukia put the kettle down. "You're too young to have headaches." She felt Eudokia's forehead. There was no fever. She looked into her daughter's eyes; they seemed clear.

"The teacher's not good to me."

"Why isn't he good to you?" asked Lukia. "You're a good student."

"The teacher left Hanyuta and me alone in the classroom with three boys. They started acting silly. One of them came and touched my breasts, so I slapped him. He was surprised that I did that and left me alone and then he and the other two started chasing Hanyuta." Lukia had heard in the village that the girl was a wild thing, known to steal from others. Her parents had lots of problems with her.

"Where was the teacher?" asked Lukia.

"He went outside to the garden to see what the workers were doing. The boys were all laughing and teasing Hanyuta. She seemed to like it, but then they grabbed her and pinned her to the floor. One boy spread her legs and the second one held them and the third raped her.

"What? My God!"

She was screaming, 'Help! Help!' I couldn't help. I was too scared to do anything. I was scared they would start bothering me too, so I ran away."

"That's good you ran away, but why didn't you tell the teacher?"

"I was afraid the boys would hurt me later if I told him."

"This is bad," said Lukia, her forehead creasing. "What kind of teacher is this? Are you sure they raped her?"

"Yes," said Eudokia, sobbing.

Lukia hugged her daughter. "Poor Hanyuta. I'll talk to the teacher. If he won't do anything, I'll go higher up."

"I don't want to go back," said Eudokia, blowing her nose.

Lukia pursed her lips. "We'll see."

The sound of a wagon pulling up interrupted their talk. They looked out the window and saw it was Hanyuta's mother.

Lukia opened the door. "Good day, Alisa." The woman's pinched face spoke of her suffering. "Please come in. I just made some tea."

Alisa wiped her boots on the bristle mat before entering. She took off her babushka and sat down at the table while Eudokia hovered nearby, looking anxious. "You heard what happened to my daughter?"

"Yes," said Lukia. "Eudokia told me."

"Ah, Eudokia," said Alisa. "Come here, child." Eudokia reluctantly approached Hanyuta's mother. "What did you see?"

Eudokia twisted her lips. "One of the boys tried to touch me but I hit him across the face and he ran off. Hanyuta was giggling and running with them as if she liked them touching her."

The glum expression on Alisa's face was that of a mother who didn't know what to do with a wayward child. She ran her finger back and forth across a small printed rose on the table's oilcloth. "I'm thinking of taking the boys to court. Will you testify?"

Trembling, Eudokia looked at her mother.

"Don't be afraid," said Lukia, as she poured two cups of tea.

Eudokia swallowed. "I'm sorry. I have to say what's right. Hanyuta's always teasing the boys. Before this happened, I saw her take a boy to the outhouse. She lifted her skirt and showed her *junyou*."

"You saw this?" said Alisa.

"They had the door open. Other boys saw, too."

Momentarily shocked, the two women exchanged concerned glances. Lukia then clucked her tongue and said, "Even if she'd been walking naked in the classroom, it's still wrong what those boys did."

Eudokia nodded with a grave expression on her face.

Alisa groaned. "I don't know what I'm going to do with her. I don't know who she takes after."

"I'm afraid of what they'll do to me if I say anything in court," said Eudokia. "Even the teacher." She paused. "He takes the boys' side all the time."

"Not good," said Lukia. She took a sip of tea and considered what had be done. "I'll talk to him."

That seemed to satisfy Alisa. She rose quickly, grumbled something about her daughter and left without touching her tea.

Lukia put the cup in front of Eudokia. "You may as well drink it."

Sitting down, Eudokia said, "Something is wrong with Hanyuta, the way she acts with boys."

"Dunya, you have to be careful. Boys know a good girl when they see one. They won't bother a good girl. They may want to fool around with the other kind, but they won't want to marry her."

Wasting no time, Lukia saw the teacher the next day, and when she returned home, she told Eudokia, "The teacher says you have nothing to worry about. He talked to the boys and nothing like that will ever happen again. He gave them a good strap for what they did."

"I don't care," whimpered Eudokia. "I don't want to go back."

"You have to go." Lukia studied her daughter's stubborn face. "Look how much school you've missed already. Do you want to be like me, not be able to read and write? I know you're a girl, but who knows what kind of husband you'll get. You may need to read documents. Look what happened to Damien's wife. She couldn't read, and she signed a divorce agreement without knowing it."

"What good is it, learning Polish? It's not even our language."

"I know but learning anything makes you smarter."

"What about Hanyuta? What will happen to her?"

Lukia shrugged. "I stopped at her house on the way home and learned her mother isn't pressing charges. She doesn't want her daughter to be humiliated in court. She's worried Hanyuta will look like she was the one who'd done something wrong."

Eudokia's forehead wrinkled. "That's awful."

"Yes," said Lukia. "I don't think Hanyuta's going back to school. See how important it is for you to be a good girl?"

Eudokia returned to school but continued to complain about her head spinning. After a week of hearing her daughter grumble, Lukia took her to the village doctor. After examining her heart, mouth and ears, he declared her healthy.

His diagnosis did nothing to change Eudokia's complaints. The day after the doctor's appointment, she said her head and right ear were still hurting. To ease her daughter's suffering, Lukia placed a small cheesecloth bag filled with cooked onion slices over her ear. "Are you telling me everything?" she asked.

Eudokia blinked back tears. "Mama, it wasn't my fault. The boys put a thumbtack on the teacher's seat. When the teacher asked who did it, the boys said 'Eudokia Mazurets.'"

"What did you say?"

"I said I didn't do it. The teacher didn't believe me. He said, 'Donkey, go stand in the corner.' The boys laughed, and after classes they followed me. They called me donkey until I was halfway home."

When Lukia heard this, she realized that going to school was torture for Eudokia. She stroked her daughter's hair and said, "You can stay home and herd the cows. There's enough for you to do here. Maybe if Egnat has time, he can teach you to read."

All of Lukia' children had quit school once they'd learned how to read and write. To supplement what they could get from their crops, Havrylo continued to work for the locksmith, Egnat made deliveries for the Jewish merchants—and even chauffeured them around on occasion—and Michalko, well, he tried his hand at everything. Mostly, he found horseshoes on the road and sold them at the market. With the children's help, Lukia managed to feed them all, but for how long? She'd always believed that where there was a will, there was a way. She'd have to keep her eyes and ears wide open for one that was more promising.

ONE THREAT TOO MANY

B Y JULY 1928, after fourteen years of conflict—the Great War, the Russian Civil War, and the Polish-Bolshevik contest that had ended with Poland conquering Volhynia—all joy had seeped out of Lukia's and her countrymen's lives. How could it not, with all of them so poor? So many had lost sons, husbands, homes, and a place to practice their faith. Even the land showed its weariness. Along the rivers that flowed through the countryside, more than half of the structures, including many manors, had been ruined—if not by war, by vandalism.

Lukia couldn't walk down one street in Lutsk without seeing a destroyed building. Though left unharmed, the cathedral was still closed. After the Poles had taken power, they'd slowly shut down all the Orthodox churches. They seemed to be afraid of what the religion had to say.

All of the waste and change played on Lukia's mind, but she couldn't afford to dwell on it. She'd left for the city early that morning to buy some material to make a dress for Eudokia. The one her daughter had was straining across her chest. Barely thirteen, Eudokia had developed quickly.

The merchant, a robust man with spectacles, was a hard man to bargain with, but after they settled on a price, which included some extra fabric for growth, he took out his measuring tape and marked off the amount she'd requested. As he cut the material, he said, "I don't know what's to become of our oblast. Did you vote?"

"Of course," said Lukia. "Even if I was sick, I'd vote."

He nodded. "Me, too. Did you hear the Polish authorities discounted the election? They say there were too many irregularities."

"Oy, why do we even bother? We trade one devil for another. They're all the same."

"Yes, yes, so they are, but we have to try to unseat them," he said, wrapping the fabric in brown paper.

Walking home, she recalled her conversation with the merchant. Was there going to be another round of voting? She was getting to the point where she didn't care one way or the other. She was growing numb to the forces at play. Each new enemy brought its own version of trouble. Promises were made; promises were broken. People scratched their heads trying to figure out who to vote for.

She turned the corner and began to walk down her farm road. Ahead, she could see the cows at pasture and one of her two horses tied up against the fence. The grain stood tall, but with the dry summer, her fields showed signs that rain was sorely needed for a good harvest. To make matters worse, agricultural prices were collapsing. Given the low yield and prices, many of her countrymen wondered if farming was worth the effort. Lukia had to grow enough for the table, but she also needed good grain sales to survive.

She tried to dismiss her fears, but the news was depressing. The Communist Party was still trying to get a foothold in Volhynia. They promised equality for all, but how could they make it happen? Not everyone was a worker. She could see it in her own family. Egnat was a worker, but Michalko wasn't. His late-night carousing got in his way. Why should anyone be forced to share what they produced with those who drank until all hours and slept in late? She was sure Petro would be against it as well. If the Communists got elected, his wealth would be re-distributed, and then what would he do?

Entering the house, Lukia found Elena shaping bread loaves into greased pans. Thankful to have her help, she said, "You've been working hard." It couldn't make up for losing Hania, but her daughter-in-law's loving support had lessened her sadness.

"It's nothing. When you were out, Damien stopped by. He has news."

Lukia's brow creased. Elena's tone suggested the news wasn't good. "What kind of news?"

"He's getting married."

"At least he waited a while," said Lukia, pouring a ladle of water from the pail into a glass.

"That's not all," said Elena. "He's thinking of moving to Argentina with her and Kolya."

"Argentina? Oy! Too far away." It was where many Ukrainians had emigrated because farm land was affordable.

After putting the bread pans in the pich, Elena said, "I'm going to feed the chickens." She turned. "Do you want me to make you a cup of tea?"

"No thank you," Lukia said morosely. "Go feed the chickens."

Lukia's mind spun as she prepared supper. Kolya was the last reminder of Hania. If he moved to Argentina, it would be like losing Hania all over again. Some villagers' sons had left over a year ago and hadn't been heard from since. But how could she stop Damien from doing what he wanted? Well, he wasn't married yet. Maybe this young woman, whoever she was, would change her mind, but the more Lukia thought about it, the more she realized it was wishful thinking. Damien had a charm that drew women to him like moths to a light. Her Hania had fallen for him, despite the warnings. There had been no persuading her otherwise.

Lukia considered telling Damien to give his homeland more time, that opportunities would soon emerge, but she'd be lying. There wasn't much going on in Volhynia to attract young people anymore. If the land couldn't sustain them, what was the point of staying?

Perhaps fearing a mass emigration or a revolt, the Polish government had begun loosening some rules. Some Ukrainian teachers had been hired and a few Ukrainian schools had been established. But it wasn't enough to pacify the locals, not when securing more land was every farmer's dream.

The young could leave but how could she? She couldn't imagine going to some strange country to start over again. She'd lived in Volhynia her whole life and had travelled only as far as the monastery in Pochaev. She wasn't counting her arduous trip to the Caucasus.

She also figured the government's drive to expand the Polish army could have something to do with Damien's decision. With the continuing threat of a possible Bolshevik assault or revolt by the natives, the Polish government was on the lookout for strong and hearty men between the ages of eighteen and twenty-eight to serve as reservists for twelve months. Perhaps this was the main reason behind Damien's wish to escape. A year back, Egnat had avoided conscription only because Lukia, being a widow, had convinced the authorities she needed her eldest son at home.

Just thinking about that close call reawakened her fears. Michalko had turned eighteen the year before and the pressure to join the Polish forces was growing. With word that a secret Ukrainian army had been formed, Lukia feared Michalko could end up fighting his own people if war broke out again between Polish and Ukrainian soldiers.

When Lukia mentioned the likelihood of conscription to Michalko, he told her he could always go to Argentina with a friend who'd told him life was much better there. It was the last thing she'd wanted to hear. Now that Damien was thinking of going, Michalko might argue the point even more. The year ahead was looking grim indeed.

A few weeks later, on her way to the market in Lutsk, Lukia walked behind two Czech men who were talking about going overseas. Their tailored clothes and immaculate grooming suggested they were rich, and yet they wanted to leave. The one with pockmarks on his face said he had an orchard and could have one in America, too. Then he said it was too bad that immigration was no longer being encouraged, especially from Eastern and Southern Europe.

The other man, whose baby face looked odd with its wispy mustache, said, "How unfortunate. I heard America's streets are made of gold."

"That's what they say," said his companion. "America might be closed, but Canada is looking for farmers. There's farmland for the taking. Their government wants farmers to come and till the land. Can you imagine a country so large they still have uncultivated land?"

Wanting to hear the rest of their conversation, Lukia followed them for a few blocks.

"I farm millet. I wonder if I could do it there," said the man with the baby face. "How much are they offering?"

"One hundred and sixty acres."

"For one family?"

"Whether it's for one family or for one man, it's all the same."

"What kind of land?"

"Land with good black soil for grain. All the Canadian government expects is for the farmer to come, pay the administration fee, and clear the land."

"Goodness! How much is the fee?"

"Ten dollars."

"And anyone can go?"

"Any male farmer, twenty-one years or older. He also has to promise to cultivate at least forty acres of that land and build a house on it."

Her head swam with the information. She had ten morgens—about thirteen acres—for a family of five. The idea of having one hundred and sixty was unbelievable. Why, each of her sons would have plenty for themselves, plus enough to support a growing family. She didn't know much about Canada except it had mountains like the Caucasus. Could there be this bountiful and beautiful land that would welcome her and her children?

But how could she leave her homeland and everyone she knew behind? Especially her mother, who was currently living with Pavlo in the Carpathian region. Though her mother was still travelling to cure the ill, she was too old to make the trip to Canada. It would be an impossible voyage for a woman in her nineties, and immigration officials likely wouldn't allow her to go.

Lukia agonized about her age and the challenges of moving to a foreign land. She'd turned fifty-three in the spring. It would be monumental moving to a country on the other side of the world. She wondered what language they spoke in Canada. She didn't know anyone who had moved there. Applying for exit papers would be difficult, and she'd also have to sell the house she'd dreamt of fixing up. It still had a mud floor. The government had provided wood for flooring, and Egnat had bought materials for a new roof, which they planned to install before the snows came. Perhaps if she sold the farm, she'd have enough money to get her family to Canada, enough to start a new life. But what if life over there was more expensive than in Volhynia?

Then there were the graves. Who would tend them if she left? She and Eudokia went regularly to weed the plots and plant the flowers, and Egnat made sure Gregory's, Hania's and Ivan's crosses stood straight at the heads of their graves.

The challenges of emigrating seemed so overwhelming that by the time she reached the market in Lutsk, she'd decided to put the idea aside.

At the end of November, some unexpected news changed Lukia's mind. She was sitting with Elena in the main room mending clothes by the oil lamp. Her daughter-in-law had been quieter than usual. She seemed to be preoccupied as she secured a button on one of Egnat's shirts. The only sound was the wind howling outside and the odd creak of a chair when one of them shifted in their seat.

Lukia finished taking down the hem of Michalko's pants and said, "You're quiet this evening."

"Just a little tired."

"Go lie down. This work can wait."

Elena continued with the mending.

"I saw you vomiting out back this morning. You don't have the flu, do you?"

Elena shook her head and looked up. "Mama, I've missed my monthly. I'm pregnant."

Lukia smiled. "Such good news." She chortled. "Why didn't you say something earlier?"

"I wanted to be sure."

Lukia got up and hugged her daughter-in-law. "My son is going to be a father."

While she wished her daughter-in-law well, Lukia felt some qualms. Not about the risk of childbirth, because Elena was a healthy woman, but about what another addition to the family would mean.

It wasn't long after that Lukia shared her concerns with Egnat. Her other children had gone into Lutsk to see a play and Elena was visiting her parents. Egnat had just finished rolling a few cigarettes and was lighting one at the kitchen table when she took a seat beside him. "What are we going to do? You know how hard it's been this year. If Michalko leaves for Argentina, we'll be short a pair of hands. With no money, we can't afford to hire anyone to replace him. You know Havrylo doesn't have an appetite for the farm. He'd rather fix watches and locks."

Egnat's forehead pleated as he puffed hard on his cigarette.

Lukia leaned forward. "I told you what people are saying about farmland in Canada. Their politicians are begging people to come and farm. Maybe this is a gift from God."

He snorted. "God has nothing to do with it."

She looked at him intently. "Look how many years we've struggled on this land. You're going to be a father. Maybe you'll be blessed with more than one. And it won't be long before your brothers find themselves brides too, and then, more babies will come. I know it would be hard to leave here, but together, maybe we can make something better for ourselves."

"Is this what you want?"

"I don't know but it has to be better than this." She looked at him steadily, as she waited for his answer.

"I'll ask around tomorrow how we can go about it," he said finally.

Though he'd said the words she wanted to hear, a sadness enveloped her. Just thinking about her native land affected her breathing and she felt her heart race. It took her several minutes to breathe normally again.

ARE YOU STILL GOING?

WHEN EGNAT RETURNED from seeing an agent in Lutsk, he confirmed what Lukia had heard. The administration fee was only ten dollars but in addition, each family had to have five hundred dollars—the cost of travel and a start in Canada. It was a lot but not impossible to raise if they could sell their farm.

The news that Egnat was inquiring about emigration spread like wildfire. Neighbours and people Lukia hardly knew came knocking on her door, asking what she'd found out. She told them what she'd told everyone, that she was considering going because her family was expanding and the future in Volhynia looked grim.

By the end of the following week, there were at least five other heads of families thinking about emigrating—Petro, one of Gregory's brothers, a nephew, her godchild, and a neighbour. While she appreciated the company, she worried what this would mean when it came time to sell her farm. Who would buy it if there were others for sale? If she could sell it, would she get the five hundred dollars she needed to go to Canada?

Brushing her fears aside, she decided it would be best to sell her farm in the summer, when her crops showed the most promise. She and her sons were known for their ability to get the most out of their soil. Surely, any prospective buyer would see the potential and give her a good price. She also knew they would have to leave no later than the end of July, as she'd heard it would take a month to get to Canada. First was the wagon ride to the railway station in Kivertsi, and then a series of trains to Gdansk. From there, they'd board a ship to the port of Rotterdam, where they'd find the ocean liner destined for Canada. She wasn't sure of the climate overseas, but she'd heard winters were long with temperatures below freezing. They would need to get settled before the snows came.

Lukia spent the next several months ruminating about leaving her beloved Volhynia. Everything she knew was here. March winds had brought no change to the land or her troubled thoughts. Competing with them was the whirr of her sewing machine as she pumped the treadle and guided the navy serge fabric under the needle. Normally she loved seeing her ideas take form. She loved figuring out how to construct a garment—how much material to give for the arms, the legs, and the neckline. But today, she sewed with little enjoyment. She was making a sailor suit for Kolya, who'd be leaving soon for Argentina with his father and new stepmother.

Wiping her eyes, she recalled how he lit up each time he saw her, how he ran to her on his sturdy legs, wanting to be held. She'd cuddle him on her lap and he'd find delight jiggling the loose flesh on her upper arms. He'd started to talk, and his words tumbled out like apples from a barrel. When he mispronounced words, it was hard not to chuckle. The notion of him leaving lodged in her heart like a lump of coal. She couldn't imagine never seeing him again.

Yet, she couldn't blame Damien for wanting to escape, not when she and other farmers were thinking about doing the same thing. Hope for a better life in their own country was in short supply.

With each succeeding thought about moving, her anxiety escalated. She couldn't look at her fields or walk down the road to the village without getting a sinking feeling. At these times, she'd stop and take deep, long breaths. Shortness of breath had been foreign to her, despite all the stresses she'd experienced in her life. But the idea of leaving the only homeland she knew—where the ground was so familiar she could walk it blindfolded—was frightening. Her heartbeat quickened and her palms grew clammy as she considered travelling to a country on the other side of the world. She couldn't fathom such a journey.

She was surprised to learn from Egnat—who'd talked to the agent again—that many Ukrainians had already emigrated to Canada decades before. That was good to hear, but since it was a big country, there was no guarantee she'd find land near others who spoke her mother tongue. She could end up farming far away from people of her own kind, and she'd have difficulty figuring out how things worked if she couldn't understand what people were saying. Would she be trading one set of problems for another?

After days of worrying, she walked to the cemetery to visit the family graves—almost in hopes that her dead husband would answer her questions.

All was still in the graveyard except for the long grasses swaying in the breeze and the crickets sounding like a badly played violin. Groaning, she stroked the top of Gregory's cross and said, "It seems I have to go. Michalko could end up in the Polish army or go to Argentina. If something happened to one more of ours, that would be the end of me. I don't want to leave you or the children's graves, or my mother or my country, but I don't know what else to do."

She stood there for a long time, hoping the answer would come if she waited a bit longer.

On her walk home, she mused on the two young men she'd heard talking on the street in Lutsk. Their excitement had been contagious. To stay in her homeland was to entertain the prospect of famine. She'd prayed for some other solution, but nothing had materialized except this offer from Canada. She needed to be brave for her children. She needed to lead them there, even though she'd be leaving behind everything she knew. Even her mother, who'd been strangely quiet about her daughter's musings.

Fedoshya had stopped by the week before. It was a sunny day with no wind, so they had taken their tea outside on the bench by the front door. Fedoshya listened to Lukia's plans, and when her daughter had finished, she sat silent for several moments. Then she turned to her. "I will pray all goes well."

"Thank you, Mama." She patted her mother's knee with the realization she was beginning to loosen the strings between them. The thought of never seeing or hearing her mother again was too much to bear, and she had to swallow her tears several times to avoid crying out loud. She'd always been a good daughter, but what good daughter left her mother at the last stage of her life? They both stared into the distance, past the fields, as if they were both trying to see what lay ahead.

A few days later—when Lukia and Elena were cleaning up after supper and Egnat was about to go and tend to some work in the stable—Lukia's other godchild Timofiy Krupsky arrived with a bottle of homebrew. He said he'd been passing by and decided to drop in. Egnat, always happy to have company for a drink, told him to sit down and went to the cupboard to get some shot glasses.

Timofiy looked at Elena's growing girth and said, "Maybe you'll get a son to help out."

"Maybe," said Elena, caressing her belly.

He nodded then looked over at Eudokia who was sitting near the pich, cross-stitching a colorful border of flowers on a white cotton tablecloth. When Egnat brought the glasses to the table, Timofiy asked, "Where's Michalko and Havrylo?"

"You know Michalko," said Egnat. "He's probably out with his friends drinking. And Havrylo's at the locksmith's working late."

Timofiy poured them all a stiff drink. They clinked glasses and said, "Daye Bozhe."

"That's good horilka," said Egnat, smacking his lips.

Timofiy's face grew serious. "I came to tell you, I won't be going with you to Canada."

Lukia put down her glass. "What are you saying? Did you hear something bad that changed your mind?"

"No, nothing like that."

"Then what? You put your farm up for sale."

Timofiy's face fell further. "I was all set to go with my mother and sister."

"I know. At first, I was surprised you even wanted to. You have such good land, a barn and a house with real flooring, not like ours."

"Yes," said Timofiy, "I have it good here, compared to most. But who can resist such an offer of large acreage in Canada. Oy, what's the use. I can't go." He poured himself another strong drink.

"Why can't you go?"

"You know, the business with my father."

"Surely people have forgotten. That was some time ago."

"Yes, but the fact he did it in the barn means no one is interested in buying our property. You know our people. They're superstitious. It's as if there's a curse on the land."

Lukia shook her head. It was true. She'd been so busy thinking of how she could move that she hadn't stopped to think about Timofiy's prospects. Of course, his farm would be hard to sell. A year ago, his father had been charged with aggravated assault. He'd come to Timofiy's rescue by pummelling his attacker, a local brute who was known for being mixed-up in the head. No one had blamed old man Krupsky. Everyone agreed the bully had it coming. Unfortunately, Timofiy's father had concluded that the outcome of the legal case would go against him and committed suicide.

Timofiy swirled the drink in his glass. "Mother wanted the priest to bless the house, but the priest said there was nothing he could do. He said it was a sin for my father to have killed himself, so God's now punishing his family."

Lukia nodded. "It's how it is." God was merciful like any good father but also harsh when his laws were broken. She felt sorry for Timofiy. It was unfair that he was being punished. But who was she to judge what God had in store for all of them. She finished her vodka and licked her lips.

Egnat lit a cigarette. "Timofiy, you're not the only one who's run into problems."

"I heard," said Timofiy, wiping his mouth. "Your father's brother can't go, either."

"Trachoma. It's hit the whole family." Egnat exhaled a large plume of smoke.

Lukia waved the smoke away. "My brother-in-law even took his family by train to Lviv to see a specialist, but the doctor wouldn't give them clearance. Told them the eye infection was too contagious."

Eudokia looked up from her embroidery. "What about cousin Ihor? Is he still going?

"No," said Lukia. "Even though Ihor is the head of his family, the emigration authority said he's too young. He has to be twenty-one."

"How old is he?" asked Elena.

"Fourteen. Such a good boy, dependable, but the agent didn't look at that. Ihor was just a baby when his father died. He had to grow up fast." Lukia snorted. "In this country, everyone has to grow up fast." She glanced at Eudokia. "No time to be children."

Once the bottle was empty, Timofiy staggered out. Lukia left Egnat to extinguish the oil lamp and went to her room. Uneasy after their discussion, Lukia took her time taking the pins out of her bun. She found several grey hairs sticking to the teeth of her comb. What if she was too old to go? The agent Egnat had talked to hadn't mentioned any age restrictions, but there might be. She'd have to find out. There was no sense in planning if she wouldn't be allowed to go.

As Lukia made her way to Kivertsi to sell some cheese, she brooded over Timofiy. He'd said his farm was cursed. But maybe it was the whole land that was cursed and the people in it.

That possibility was underlined when she ran into her neighbour Volodymyr Sawchuk in the village. "Panye Mazurets," he said, tipping his cap and bowing slightly. "Are you still going?"

"I hope so," she said, "but I have to sell the farm first. What about you? How are you doing?"

His mouth twisted into a frown. "You know my situation. It's my wife's mother who owns our farm. She won't sign the papers to sell it."

Lukia cocked her head to one side in sympathy.

He turned his pockets inside out. "You see, I have nothing."

"Maybe she'll change her mind."

"You don't know her. She doesn't want to go, and nothing will make her. Because of that, she won't let us go, either."

"I'm sorry to hear about your troubles. Pray—maybe God will help you." A blank expression crossed his face, as if God was a stranger and the idea of praying hadn't occurred to him. Maybe the Bolsheviks had got to him. She cleared her throat. "Please give my best to your wife."

A month or so ago, there were five families going. Now there were only two. Hers and her brother Petro's. Would the curse find them as well?

Lukia went about her business in the village, trading her cheese for some yeast and flour from the grocer, but her mind was elsewhere. Egnat had left that morning for Lutsk to see the agent and inquire about age restrictions. She was afraid to ask the authorities herself for fear of bringing attention to her age. She would be fifty-four soon. If she wasn't allowed to leave because she was too old, any hope of escaping a dismal future would be shattered.

For the rest of the day, Lukia fussed and worried like a hen whose chick had died. When she wasn't cooking or in the garden weeding, she rubbed her finger against her thumb endlessly, a habit she'd developed in recent years. She tried not to think about the worst outcome, but having heard of others' plight, she was no longer hopeful.

When Egnat returned, Lukia and Elena were in the stable milking cows. The fresh smell of milk hitting the metal pails filled the air.

"Nu," said Lukia, trying to stay calm. "Did you find anything out?"

"Yes," he said, frowning. "Bad news. The agent said fifty years old is the cut-off."

"Oy, that's terrible." Lukia squeezed the cow's teat so hard that the cow backed up and swung her tail in protest. "Are you sure?" Was God playing one more trick on all of them, holding a carrot out only to snatch it away at the last moment?

"Yes. Fifty years old."

"Did you mention how old I was?"

"No."

"Good" Lukia exhaled sharply and massaged a sharp pain in her chest.

"How is that good? We can't go." Egnat dug into his pants pocket and pulled out a hand-rolled cigarette. After lighting it with a match, he went outside.

Lukia's mind raced as she continued to milk, at times too hard. The cow objected by trying to move away and she patted its rump, letting her know she understood. She returned to her usual rhythm of milking.

Egnat returned minutes later.

Looking up, she said, "Son, our documents were burned in the church. The authorities have no way of knowing how old I am. I'll tell them I just turned fifty."

Egnat's jaw dropped. "You would do that?"

"Why not." The idea of lying bothered her—she'd always been an honest woman, but under these circumstances, she felt she had no choice. "I'll have to talk to Petro. I don't want him to say anything and give me away." She looked down at her milk pail. It was only half-full. She suspected her anxiety and the way she'd pulled on the cow's teats had affected the animal's supply. Shrugging, she stood and took the pail with her. She glanced back at the two cows. If she and her family emigrated, they wouldn't be able to take their animals with them. Out in the moonlight, she prayed that if all went well, they'd find cows as good in Canada.

Once the chores were done, Lukia and Egnat paid Petro and his wife a visit. Petro looked surprised to see them. Lukia understood why—she wasn't in the habit of visiting much. Being a widow, she had little time for small talk.

While Lukia waited for Anna to brew some tea, she and Egnat sat down at the mahogany dining table, which was covered with a fine lace tablecloth. Her brother poured himself and Egnat shots of brandy from a crystal decanter.

After Lukia told her brother her plan, he said with a twinkle in his eye, "I won't tell anyone, but you must know, you look like an old babcha. Let's hope they believe you."

Lukia disliked his kind of teasing but couldn't afford to antagonize him with a harsh retort. "If you don't say anything, they'll believe me," she said assuredly. She turned to Anna, who was placing a plate of sweets on the table. "What about you, Anna? Are you getting ready to go?"

"Not so easy, Lukia. Petro doesn't know what to do with our rental property."

"What do you mean?"

"I don't want to sell it," said Petro. With that, he raised his glass and downed the amber alcohol.

"Why not?"

"It's been a good investment." Petro leaned back in his chair. "We get good rent. Ten apartments."

"Petro, you know how the Bolsheviks are always stirring up trouble. War could explode at any moment. They could defeat the Poles, and then poof," Lukia said, snapping her fingers, "your investment would be gone. They'd take over and give it to their comrades."

She could see by his face that he knew she was right. The Bolsheviks said they rejected any kind of wealth, but their actions said something different. What they rejected was the existing wealthy. They took over properties belonging to the rich, citing Lenin's propaganda that everything should be shared because everyone was equal. What a laugh! Their leaders moved into the properties themselves or sold them and kept the monies.

"I'll see what I can do." Petro twirled his waxed moustache. "My problem is finding an agent who can send me the rents, someone I can trust. One who won't rob me blind." He poured himself and Egnat another brandy each. "Don't fret," he said, shaking a finger at her. "Let me know what you need." Her brother wasn't generous by nature but he had come through in the past when matters were urgent and for that she was grateful.

With Petro's promise to keep her age a secret and loan her funds if necessary, Lukia walked out her brother's door feeling some hope.

She and Egnat rode home in silence. She gazed at the glorious fields, at the black soil that grew the best grain in Europe. All would have to go—her fields, garden, animals, implements, and home. There was only so much they could take with them, and yet, they'd have to take the tools necessary to build a house and cultivate the fields, as they had no idea what they could get in Canada.

Another pain shot through her chest. It felt as though her heart was attached to the land; any thought of severing that attachment caused an unbearable tug. She massaged her chest until the pain subsided. She hoped this wasn't a sign there was something wrong with her heart. This was no time to have any kind of ailment.

More Than Gossip

H ER LIFE, AS she knew it, was being upended. Damien had brought Kolya over to say goodbye. They were set to leave for Argentina the following week. Shortly after these tearful farewells, Elena gave birth to a daughter—Genya. God was sending one grandchild far away but blessing Lukia with another at home.

Lukia had no time to question her maker, as new troubles arose. She and her children had placed signs advertising their farm for sale, on fence posts along the road to Lutsk and in a few shop windows in Kivertsi. Soon, Lukia noticed her neighbours and the town folk whispering among themselves whenever she passed. It wasn't until later in the week, when her brother-in-law dropped by, that she learned what the gossip was all about.

"Come in, Dmitro," said Lukia. "Sit down. Can I make you something to eat?"

"No, thank you. I'm not staying long. I have too much to do at home." He took off his tweed cap and sat down by the table. He looked over at Elena, who was ironing by the pich. "Elena, you're looking well. I hear you just had a beautiful girl. Where is she?"

"Resting in the other room."

"How is she at night?"

Elena put down her iron and smiled. "Sleeps well. Like an angel. Can I get you some tea?"

"A little would be nice."

While Elena poured the tea, Lukia studied Dmitro. The years had not been kind to him. His face was heavily lined, and his hair had thinned so much half his crown was showing. He also sat with the rounded back of a much older man. It was a fate she saw in many of her countrymen. To live under occupied conditions made men and women age before their time.

He took a sip of tea. "I only stopped by to tell you what I heard in the village."

She rolled her eyes. "What are the hens gossiping about now?"

"You're not going to like it."

"What else is new?" She sat down beside him. "Tell me already."

Dmitro played with the rim of his cap. "I won't tell you who said what, but a number of the women are suspicious. They think you're planning to drown your children on the way to Canada, so you can keep the proceeds of your farm sale to yourself."

Lukia's mouth fell open. "That's ridiculous! You're lying. Why would anyone say such crazy things? You just don't want me to go."

"I'm not lying!" he said vehemently. "I swear on a Bible. You know our people. They get jealous. They say lots of things. I told them it was dumb to think that. They said you wait and see." He looked down at his cap. "I'm sorry I had to tell you."

"I bet it was Katerina who spread those lies."

The look on Dmitro's face confirmed her suspicion.

"I thought so," she said, harrumphing. "She's never forgiven me for marrying Gregory."

Lukia's anger quickly faded. She agreed with Dmitro. The gossips were just jealous. They were also ignorant and not worthy of her attention. Since they couldn't emigrate or had no desire to do so, they couldn't accept anyone else leaving.

Lukia thanked Dmitro for coming and accompanied him to his wagon. The light was fading and already the early summer day was turning. Feeling chilled, she hugged her body. "Dmitro, you're a good brother-in-law."

He scratched his jaw. "Good you think so. I wish you thought I was good enough to marry. You still could, you know. Together we would have a comfortable life."

She regarded him once more. Such a decent man and with a disposition to match. He could make her life easier but at what price? "Oy, Dmitro, it's too late, now. If I stay, I could lose another son. You know how it is."

He left with his mouth downturned and his body slumped as if he were carrying a heavy sack of grain on his back. How she hated to see him beaten like that, but she knew in her heart there was no future for herself and her family in Volhynia. They would always be at the mercy of some occupying force.

When Egnat and Michalko returned from a trip to Kivertsi, Lukia wasted no time in telling them about Dmitro's visit. They weren't surprised as they'd already heard what people were saying.

"What's more," said Egnat, pulling off his worn leather boots by the door, "the elders want to hold a vote to stop the sale of our farm. They think it's the way to stop you from taking away our inheritance rights."

"What foolishness! Can they do that?" asked Lukia, wringing her hands. She couldn't believe how quickly the rumours had spread, like untended weeds by the roadside. Of course, people were envious. Though her farm of ten morgens wasn't a large one, it was still substantial compared to many of her friends' and neighbours'. It stood to reason that the rumour-mongers believed she was going to be rich. What she hoped to realize from the sale might be a lot to them—as it would be to her if she were staying—but it wasn't really. She'd be lucky to end up with enough money to cover the cost of immigration and settlement in Canada. If only they could see that.

With all the ill will in her village, Lukia went to bed thinking her fate was sealed. She and her family were destined to stay in Volhynia.

The next morning, while Lukia cooked porridge for breakfast, she agonized over the upcoming town referendum on her right to sell. The more she thought about it, the angrier she got. Though cooking oats was a simple task, she nearly burned them. Swearing to herself, she scraped the sticky oats from the bottom of the pot and stirred them into the rest of the cereal. Soon her children would be coming in for breakfast. She bent down to get some bowls for the table and spotted the half-empty bottle of vodka on the shelf. Annoyed it'd been put in the wrong place, she took it out, and as she was returning it to the cupboard on the other side of the pich, she got an idea. She whooped and, in her excitement, almost dropped the bottle. She ran to the door and opened it. Egnat was pacing outside, his cigarette smoke rising and scattering in the air.

"Egnat!" she yelled. "Come here."

He jumped. "What's the matter? You scared me."

As he approached, she said, "I know what we can do. You can tell the young voters I'll buy whisky for them if they'll vote in our favour."

"You think that'll work?" he asked.

"Of course. Whisky softens many minds."

With Michalko's help, Egnat solicited the votes of the eligible young people. It took a few days to connect with each one and there were tense moments, when he didn't know if he had convinced enough to vote in their family's favour, but in the end, his mother was right. The bribe worked. The motion to stop her from selling was defeated.

Relieved, she thanked God for the whisky that influenced the referendum and given her the right to sell. And sell she did—the farm and the tin roofing—at a price that matched what it had cost her in the first place. The lumber donated by the government was also sold at a fair price. Egnat even found old scraps of iron lying around and got six zlotys for them. Anything of value went: their wagon, their plow, their animals. As most items were bought by relatives or close friends and neighbours, there were no complaints about her hanging on to some things—like the wagon, some implements and the stock—until it was time to leave for good.

With each sale, Lukia tried not to think about what she was giving up. In total, she made the equivalent of over a thousand dollars. Though she figured her money would be enough, as a precaution, she took advantage of Petro's generosity and borrowed another hundred.

With a month to go, Egnat arranged for the family to get their pictures taken for their passports. Lukia worried again about her age. She figured if she was going to fool the authorities, nature needed a little help. She surprised her family by buying hair dye to turn her greying head into that of a brunette. According to the store clerk, it was the colour now favoured in Europe.

Back home, she picked a spot in her farmyard, wrapped her shoulders with an old cloth and—much to her son's amusement—asked Eudokia and Elena to pour the dark brown liquid over her scalp. She used a mixture of baking soda and soap to remove the dye colouring her skin near the hairline, a remedy recommended by the clerk.

Once her hair was dry, she examined it in her hand mirror. Was it enough to fool the authorities? Would her passport photo show a woman who lied? Whatever the future held, there was no turning back now, not with all the sales. If she weren't allowed to emigrate, her family would have to go on without her. She could end up standing at the station waving goodbye as they boarded the train out of Kivertsi.

Dressed in their Sunday best, the Mazurets family sat in a line on benches at the passport office in Lutsk. Anxious, Lukia tightly held a packet containing the family's passport photos taken five days ago. She hoped their application wouldn't take too long, as her granddaughter had been fussing ever since they left home. It was only a matter of time before she started bawling. Lukia was sorry they hadn't remembered to bring a soother. A clean cloth dipped in sweetened whisky would've quietened her down.

Elena rocked Genya in her arms and said quietly to Lukia, "I don't think it's her stomach that's bothering her. My right breast has hardened. She doesn't want to suck there."

"It happens like that sometimes. As long as she's getting enough milk from the other side, you don't have to worry. In time, it'll soften. Until then, massage it. It'll ease the discomfort." She whispered, "Maybe Egnat can suck it."

Elena gasped. "What are you saying?"

Lukia laughed. "Suit yourself, but if it helps, what does it matter?" She sighed, thinking of the times Gregory had relieved the pain of her distended breasts. She wasn't sure if he'd liked sucking her nipples and now it was too late to ask.

"Next!" the agent barked.

Lukia and her family rose from the bench and approached the agent's desk. He squinted his eyes under his gold-framed glasses and looked at Lukia questioningly. She felt his scrutiny and wondered if he'd noticed she'd dyed her hair. That alone could arouse suspicion. Why hadn't she thought of that? Since she could do nothing about it now, she stood as straight as she could and returned an unflinching gaze. She hoped her demeanour and lack of grey hairs made her look four years younger.

He looked at Lukia's passport photo once more then returned his gaze to their application and began filling it out as they provided information about where they lived, where they were going and why they were going. When he'd finished his questioning, he looked at each family member gravely and then placed their completed form on a pile of others.

"Next," he said.

Lukia kept her glee to herself as she strode away.

Don't Forget Us

OUT OF ALL those from Kivertsi who'd shown interest in emigrating to Canada, Lukia and her family were the only ones who'd managed to get this far; they'd sold their farm and obtained passports. Nonetheless, Lukia fretted. There were still too many unknowns ahead.

Pushing her qualms aside, she concentrated on what needed to be packed for their new life. She'd kept some implements, such as the two large saws with a handle on each end. Egnat and Michalko sandwiched them between two heavy boards and then secured the package with a strong hemp rope. While her sons were wrapping the saws, Lukia asked Elena to help her bundle up the household goods; among them was the large steel basin they used for bathing Genya or mixing bread.

Lukia also insisted on bringing her heavy Singer sewing machine head. When Egnat complained about the weight, she said, "I know you think I can buy one when we get there, but this one came from America. I might not be able to buy one as good in Canada."

Egnat walked away with a disgruntled look on his face. Lukia understood that it wasn't only her sewing machine upsetting her son. He'd moped for days after she sold the animals, especially the horses—his pride and joy. Knowing there was little she could say to lift his spirits, she left him alone.

As for bedding and clothing, Lukia and Elena packed feather perinas, the family's sheepskin coats, fur hats and felt boots in their blue steel trunk. The agent had warned them about Canadian winters.

Little by little, their home took on a ghostly feeling. The walls were stripped bare of their icons; shelves full of dishes and condiments were emptied; braided rugs were removed from the floors and rolled.

The day before the family's departure, Lukia's mother and her brother Pavlo, as well as his wife Marusha and their two children, came to say goodbye. When Fedoshya walked in the door and saw the main room naked of holy pictures and personal belongings, she put her hands to her face and moaned. "Oy, where are you going, child?"

"I hope it'll be a better place." Lukia then looked at her brother and his family standing in the doorway like strangers, as if they were already practicing being less intimate.

"Where did you put the Virgin Mary?" her mother asked.

Lukia went into her bedroom and opened the blue trunk on the floor. Pulling out the icon, she handed it to her mother. Fedoshya propped it on a kitchen shelf. "Let us pray."

"Wait. I have to get the rest of the family."

After Lukia rounded up the others, they all got down on their knees, with the exception of Fedoshya, who found it too difficult at her age and bowed her head instead. In unison, they said "In the name of the Father, the Son, and the Holy Ghost" three times, crossing themselves with each repetition.

"God, help my children," Fedoshya said. "Grant them luck on their voyage across the sea and in their search for a new home in Canada. Keep them safe and healthy. Amen."

Rising from her knees, Lukia said to her mother, "Sit for a little. Have a drink. We don't know if we'll see each other again." Her heart broke as she said the words.

Fedoshya's sadness was evident. "Only God knows."

"I'm sorry we have to leave you. I thank God Pavlo will take care of you."

"Nu, that's how life goes. Old age isn't happiness; death isn't a wedding," said Fedoshya with a sigh.

Lukia kissed Fedoshya's hands. Gazing into her mother's eyes, Lukia realized she'd never looked at them so intently before. She didn't look long, as the sorrow there was too much to bear. It was the kind that could hold her back from going.

On her final day in Kivertsi, Lukia rose with the sun and walked to the cemetery to bid farewell to her family buried there. After praying at the graves and saying a few words to Hania and Ivan, she brushed some dirt off Gregory's cross and placed her hand on top of it. "I'm sorry I won't be visiting anymore. I wish I could take you with me, but I promise that wherever I go, I'll carry you in my heart until the day I die."

As she uttered her vow, the trees rustled their leaves and a bee buzzed and landed on one of the marigolds she'd planted at the beginning of the summer. Who would plant the flowers now? "I'm sorry," she said. "There may not be anyone to tend the graves. I hope a few relatives will visit you." Then she smiled. "Gregory, I dyed my hair. It's supposed to make me look younger, but . . ." She laughed. "You'd probably tease: 'Once an old hen, always an old hen.'" She kissed his cross, stroked the length of it, and walked away, looking back several times to lock the picture in her mind.

Everything had been packed. Lukia bustled from room to room as if searching for something she'd forgotten. She couldn't even stop to calm her nerves. She was too afraid that if she rested, she wouldn't be able to move again. When she finally slowed down enough to look out the window, she saw many familiar faces—Vasil, Dmitro, several cousins and their spouses and children, as well as Ihor and Nina Striluchky and other neighbours. Excited that one of their compatriots was leaving for a new land, they had arrived in droves to see them off. Lukia's sons, along with Elena and Eudokia, were in the yard organizing their belongings. Petro had also arrived with his wagon and two horses to take them to the train station.

Lukia exhaled deeply and continued her inspection. Though she knew the house was bare, she examined each shelf, hook, and wall to make sure nothing of value remained.

"Mama!" Egnat shouted from the doorway. "It's time to go."

Lukia looked around the two empty rooms. As she stared at the pich, her eyes welled up and her feet became rooted to the floor. "May God help us." She crossed herself and willed herself out the door.

She walked into the crowd of well-wishers and was immediately overwhelmed by all the attention. Arms came at her for their final hugs, little children jumped and darted between their mother's knees, and adults wrote down addresses on scraps of paper and begged her and her children to write. Egnat promised to send news as soon as they were settled.

She was surprised to see Katerina watching the activity. Lukia was tempted to say something to her sister-in-law, to let her know she knew about her mean gossip and outright lies but she said nothing. This was neither the time nor the place to make a scene. What was done was done.

While Lukia's sons loaded the wagon, Eudokia flitted from one person to the next, chattering away and giving last-minute hugs. She stopped to give her dog another pat. Nuzzling her face in its neck, she explained why he was being left behind. Ihor and Nina had gladly accepted the animal, even though the dog was no good at herding cows. They said he would give them some comfort.

Though Egnat and Michalko complained that the wagon was already piled high with their goods and clothing, room was made for the bags of food their relatives and neighbours had brought—hard-boiled eggs, kybassa, piroshky, and freshly baked bread. Elena, with Genya in her arms, was the first to climb into the wagon, followed by Michalko, Havrylo, and Eudokia.

Just as Lukia was about to board, Katerina approached and hugged her awkwardly. "I wish you well," she said." I'm amazed by how you've managed to make this move. You've surprised me."

Lukia managed a smile. "God's will is stronger than anyone else's," she said pointedly.

Katerina looked as if she wanted to say something but Lukia turned and, with her son's help, climbed into the back of the wagon. She sat beside Elena and faced her children, whose knees were hunched up because of all the goods piled in the centre.

Michalko and Havrylo fought back tears, unlike Eudokia, who remained dry-eyed. Ready for a new adventure, she looked modern in the outfit Lukia had sewn for her—a long-sleeved white percale blouse tucked into a black-and-white checkered knee-length skirt, gathered at the waist. Lukia noticed the glee Eudokia and Havrylo expressed when their generous aunt Anna gave them each five zlotys for the trip. Eudokia clutched hers, whereas her brother quickly hid his in his pocket.

Lukia smoothed out the wrinkles in her navy crepe dress and patted her bodice, under which she'd placed all her money for safekeeping. With watery eyes, she looked at her garden by the house—at the tall corn stalks, the depleted rows of root vegetables, and the stripped tomato plants. It had served her family well. She hoped the soil in Canada would be as generous.

Her brother slapped the reins on the horses' backs and the wagon lurched forward. Lukia admired, one more time, the yellow sunflowers by the house. They danced in the light breeze, unaware their owners were leaving them forever. She would have to plant some in the new land to remind her of home.

Family and friends ran after them waving and yelling, "Good fortune", "Go with God", and "Don't forget us." Lukia bit her lip to keep from sobbing as she recalled her mother standing by the farmhouse and their sorrowful farewell. She knew she'd never see her again.

Craning her neck, Lukia watched the dust fly off the back wheels as the wagon traversed the narrow road lined with poplars. On each side of the road, golden fields of grain promised a good harvest in a month's time. Her home receded in the distance, getting smaller and smaller with each turn of the wheel. And still, she kept looking back. She kept looking until a long row of tall bushes blocked her view.

AUTHOR'S NOTE

I've struggled with how to tell this story. It's one dear to my heart as it draws on the anecdotes my mother shared over the years.

My baba, Lukia Mazurets, came to live with us when I was still a baby, and she basically raised me, as my parents worked six days a week. We spoke very little. When she did talk, it was mainly to my mother over cigarettes they thought would help them lose weight.

I remember her as an overweight woman with long, thinning, white hair, which she pulled neatly back in a bun. She always wore a calf-length housedress with a wool cardigan over it, small gold hoop earrings, a strand of pearls, long beige cotton hose on her arthritic legs, and sturdy black oxfords. She worked hard around the house—making borscht, shelling peas from our garden, cleaning mushrooms that had been picked, or braiding rugs out of rags and old nylons.

Until I was fifteen, Baba and I shared a bedroom. She slept in one twin bed, and I slept in the other. One of the few bedtime conversations I recall took place just months before she died at the age of eighty-three. She asked me to teach her how to count to ten in English. She was still trying to learn what she needed in order to survive.

Looking at her, no one would ever have suspected that this woman had survived several wars in Eastern Europe and suffered unimaginable losses in her family. She knew only a few words in English and was illiterate in her own language, but she could communicate with those who spoke Ukrainian, Polish, Russian, or Czech. She even knew a few helpful phrases in Yiddish and German. Although uneducated, she was smart in the ways of the world.

My grandmother left much unsaid, but her daughter, Eudokia, was a born storyteller and made sure the family history was passed on. If it weren't for my mother's tales of what her family had endured, I might have given my grandmother short shrift. But now, having dug deep into her history, I feel I've touched her spirit.

Though my mother was a great storyteller, and many of the conversations between family members and others in this book really happened, there were others I had to imagine in order to bring my baba's story to life. As this period in history was tumultuous, and the land my baba lived in war-torn, I've relied heavily on history books, the Internet, and scholars to fill in the blanks.

ACKNOWLEGEMENTS

First and foremost, I'm indebted to my mother for the rich stories she passed on. I wish she were still alive to see how they ended up on the page.

To fill in the blanks of my mother's tales, I used countless resources found in the library and on the Internet. The following books were especially helpful: *A Whole Empire Walking: Refugees in Russia During World War I*, by Peter Gatrell; *Europe on the Move: Refugees in the Era of the Great War*, edited by Peter Gatrell and Llubov Zbavanko; *Sketches from a Secret War: A Polish Artist's Mission to Liberate Soviet Ukraine*, by Timothy Snyder; *The Blaze: Reminiscences of Volhynia 1917-1919*, by Sophia Kossak; *A Survey of Ukrainian History*, by Dmytro Doroshenko; *On the Russian Front in World War I: Memoirs of an American War Correspondent*, by Stanley Washburn; *Typhus Fever in Poland 1916-1919*, by E. W. Goodall in Sage Publications online; and *Russian Oppression in Ukraine*, by Ukrainian Publishers Ltd.

My editors, Eileen Cook and Rachel Small, combed my manuscript and found the sentences and scenes that needed attention. Janet Smith at JKS Editing proofread my manuscript. I'm so thankful for all their comments.

I'm also indebted to Dr. Oleh Gerus, Professor of Russian History at the University of Manitoba, who generously answered my questions.

The old folk saying about sunflowers at the beginning of my novel was found on proudofukraine.com. Sunflowers are the national flower of Ukraine.

Thanks to my writers' critique group: Kristin Butcher, Shari Green, Sheena Gnos, Jocelyn Reekie, Janet Smith, and Liezl Sullivan; they gave me great notes and encouragement.

My husband, Robert, read all the drafts of this novel; his patience and enthusiasm kept me going. My daughters, Karen and Robyn, were my first beta readers, and it was granddaughter Chloe who first lit the fire under my feet and told me I should write this story. And I would be remiss if I left out grandson Michael, granddaughter Mimi, and sons-in-law Diego and John who I know have been cheering in the background.

But in the end, it was Lukia, my wonderful baba, driving me every step of the way. Her photo on my desktop inspired me to dig deep into her past and discover the woman she was.

GLOSSARY (ALPHABETICAL)

Baba - grandmother

Babushka – headscarf

Bikasha – heavy coat made from cotton batting

Borscht – hearty soup made with beets, potatoes and cabbage.

Daye Bozhe – "God willing", the toast given when glasses are clinked before drinking

Deshyatin – sections of land; a deshyatin is equivalent to 2.5 acres.

Hmeel – hops for beer

Holupchi – cabbage rolls

Horilka – vodka

Hrystiki – twisted sweet dough which is fried and dipped in honey

Hryvnia – Ukrainian currency

Junyou - vagina

Kalyna tree – national tree of Ukraine; a high bush cranberry plant

Kasha - buckwheat

Kishka – blood sausage

Kolomeyka – rousing Ukrainian folk dance

Komorra – small cold storage room in cottages

Korovai - wedding bread

Kutya – dish of cooked wheat with honey and poppy seeds for Christmas Eve

Kvass – fermented beverage from rye bread

Kybassa – ring of garlic sausage

Oblast – region of the country, like a province or state.

Onoochky – strips of linen wrapped around the feet, as a liner for boots.

Pan/Panye – Mr./Mrs.

Paska – a sweet yeast bread made with saffron and raisins

Perina - comforter, filled with feathers or down

Perogies - dumplings filled with potato, cabbage, or fruit

Pich – clay oven with a brick shelf overhead that is used as a stove.

Piroshky – yeast dumplings filled with either fruit or vegetables.

Pysanky –finely decorated eggs using melted wax and various applied colours

Romyanyk – chamomile herb

Rushnyk – a tea towel, often made from white cloth and embroidered.

Smarkach – smarty-pants

Starosty – elders

Studenetz - jellied pigs' feet

Varenyky – filled dumplings that have been softly boiled.

Vertep – a manger scene, often displayed in churches on Christmas Eve.

Vichnaya pamyat –eternal memory

BOOK CLUB
DISCUSSION GUIDE

1. At the beginning of the novel, Lukia argues with her husband, Gregory, about his decision to volunteer for the Tsar's army. She believes his first loyalty should be to her, not to his country. Is she right?

2. When her eldest daughter falls in love with a young man deemed unsuitable because of a certain rule in their religion, Lukia is faced with a difficult decision—to support her daughter or side with the church. What are your thoughts on this?

3. Gregory returns from war a changed man. Back then, post-traumatic stress wasn't even considered by those who fought and those who ordered them into battle. Are there people in your family tree who suffered as a result of their time on the battlefield? How did it affect their lives?

4. Faith pulls Lukia through the harshest of times. With religion on the decline, what are people relying on today, if they don't have any faith? Is it enough?

5. Lukia and her children become refugees. Today, there is so much focus on refugee populations and people fleeing from conflict. Did this story change your views or did it confirm what you already believed about refugees?

6. The Romanovs were executed by the Bolsheviks. Many of their leaders became consumed by greed, the very thing they accused the royal family of. Some believe that power corrupts. What are your thoughts on this?

7. Lukia believes her dreams can forecast the future; therefore, she needs to pay attention to them. What are your thoughts on the power of dreams? Is there anything to them?

8. In this story, one battle after another affects those fighting and those fleeing. There are different reasons for the different wars. After reading about them, do you believe some wars are justified? Which disputes do you believe are worth the sacrifice?

9. Annual prayers for the dead are commonplace in Ukrainian culture. Other cultures have similar practices. Discuss the value for the living of remembering the deceased and what's missing without that remembrance.

10. Much of the history of life in Ukraine before World War II has been lost due to the many wars on her soil. Family records were often kept in churches, which were destroyed by different enemies. What is the value of carrying on traditions even when there is little family history?

ABOUT THE AUTHOR

Diana Stevan is the author of the well-received debut novel *A Cry From The Deep*, a time-slip romantic adventure; *The Rubber Fence*, women's fiction; and *Lilacs in the Dust Bowl*, the sequel to *Sunflowers Under Fire*. She is currently working on the third book of Lukia's Family Saga series, *Paper Roses on Stony Mountain*.

Her varied background includes work as a clinical social worker, teacher, professional actor, and freelance writer-broadcaster for *Sports Journal*, CBC Television. She's had poetry published in *DreamCatcher*, a United Kingdom publication, a short story in the anthology *Escape,* and articles in newspapers and an online magazine.

Diana lives with her husband, Robert, on Vancouver Island and in West Vancouver, British Columbia.

For more, visit her website: https://www.dianastevan.com

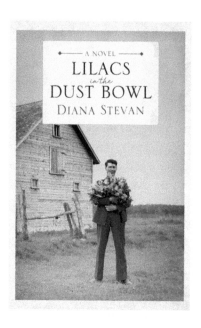

Hoping for a better life, Lukia Mazurets and her family leave war-torn Ukraine in 1929 and immigrate to Canada, but the land that was promised is nowhere to be seen. An inspirational family saga about love and heartache during the Great Depression.

Lilacs in the Dust Bowl, the sequel to the Award-winning *Sunflowers Under Fire* is now available at major booksellers everywhere.